Dear Reader,

One of life's biggest heartbreaks can be someone's inability to conceive a child. Doctors and researchers have worked tirelessly to change that painful situation, with increasing success. My hero, Ted Bonner, is such a doctor, a man on a mission to treat infertility. I imagine him to be like so many others in that field: dedicated, devoted and driven.

But Ted needs balance in his life, too. So along comes nurse Sara Beth O'Connell, a woman just as dedicated to her work, but one who also knows how to relax—and to love. She has a lot to teach Dr Bonner.

I had a great time playing in the same sandbox with the other terrific and talented authors in this series. I hope you enjoy the results of the fun we all had.

All my best,

Susan

THE DOCTOR'S PREGNANT BRIDE?

BY
SUSAN CROSBY

First published in Great Britain 2011
Harlequin Mills & Boon Limited,
Eton House, 18-24 Paradise Road, Richmond, Surrey TW9 1SR

© Harlequin Books S.A. 2010

Special thanks and acknowledgment to Susan Crosby for her contribution to
The Baby Chase miniseries.

ISBN: 978 0 263 88869 0

23-0311

Harlequin Mills & Boon policy is to use papers that are natural, renewable
and recyclable products and made from wood grown in sustainable forests.
The logging and manufacturing processes conform to the legal environmental
regulations of the country of origin.

Printed and bound in Spain
by Litografia Rosés S.A., Barcelona

Susan Crosby believes in the value of setting goals, but also in the magic of making wishes, which often do come true—as long as she works hard enough. Along life's journey she's done a lot of the usual things—married, had children, attended college a little later than the average co-ed and earned a BA in English. Then she dove off the deep end into a full-time writing career, a wish come true.

Susan enjoys writing about people who take a chance on love, sometimes against all odds. She loves warm, strong heroes and good-hearted, self-reliant heroines, and she will always believe in happily ever after.

More can be learned about her at www.susancrosby.com.

To Paul, aka "Fandango," fellow foodie, with great appreciation—for your indefatigable help with research, legal and otherwise, and for all the times you crack me up. Thank you.

Chapter One

Sara Beth O'Connell slowed her bike to a stop at a red light, her gaze fixed on it. Red, the color of hearts and roses—

A car honked, jolting her into action. She pedaled through the intersection, picking up the bike lane again on the other side. The air was unusually mild and the traffic Sunday-afternoon light in Cambridge, Massachusetts, giving her time to think, time to decide that she wasn't really bothered by not having a date on Valentine's Day. It was more about what being dateless implied—that there was no one special enough in her life to spend the romantic evening with.

So what, right? No big deal. Only the minute hand on her biological clock was ticking, not the hour hand.

And then there was the man in the grocery store earlier...

Sara Beth tossed her head, her bike helmet preventing her long hair from falling into her face as she rode into the employee parking lot of the Armstrong Fertility Institute, the understated but modern structure where she worked as head nurse. Eyeing Lisa Armstrong's car in the distance, she locked her bike to a rack, then moved to the employee entrance. She slid her ID card into the security reader and pressed her thumb against a pad until a buzzer went off, unlocking the door.

Once inside, her footsteps barely registered in the quiet building as she headed to Lisa's office, finding her door open. The head administrator of the institute, a research center and fertility clinic, sat in front of her computer, her slender frame hunched, her dark eyes focused on the screen.

Sara Beth drew a calming breath, not because she was annoyed that Lisa had called her into the office on a Sunday, but because of the memory of the man Sara Beth had seen that morning buying a stuffed teddy and gummy bears for his five-year-old daughter. *My Valentine,* he'd called her when the clerk commented on the items. Sara Beth hadn't been lucky enough to have a father do that for her. This morning's reminder of that loss curled painfully inside her.

Ignoring the flash of pain, she set her helmet on top of a file cabinet, unzipped her jacket then plopped into a chair on the other side of Lisa's desk. "What's so all-fired important that it couldn't wait until tomorrow? Or you couldn't tell me on the phone?"

Lisa blinked. "You have something better to do?"

"Just because you work 24/7 doesn't mean I have to, you know," Sara Beth said, not letting Lisa off easy. "It *is* Valentine's Day."

Lisa's smile was a little crooked. Her dark eyes shimmered knowingly. "You don't have a date."

"How do you know?"

"How long have we been best friends, Sara Beth?"

Sarah Beth pulled off her jacket, not wanting to make eye contact, not wanting Lisa to play the best-friends card for whatever it was she'd called Sara Beth in on a Sunday for. "Since before we spoke our first words."

"Twenty-eight years. If you had a date tonight, I would know." Lisa sat back, looking satisfied with herself. "You tell me everything."

"Not everything."

"Everything important."

Sara Beth sniffed. "A date on Valentine's Day isn't important."

Lisa laughed.

After a moment, Sara Beth smiled. "So, what's up? Why the command performance?"

Lisa lowered her voice. "Shut the door, please."

"Someone else is in the building?" Sara Beth asked, complying. "Someone else doesn't know that weekends are for relaxation?"

"As a matter of fact—Dr. Bonner."

Which meant he didn't have a date, either. If a man

like Ted Bonner didn't have a date, she couldn't feel sorry for herself. Except, he still could have dinner plans. It wasn't too late for that. She wouldn't have minded going out with him herself....

"This has something to do with Dr. Bonner?" Sara Beth asked.

"Everything to do with him. You know the investigation he's supposed to be running on the protocol errors he and Dr. Demetrios discovered right after we hired them a few months back?"

"Of course."

"They haven't come up with results yet. We've learned that some outsiders are starting to question our recent cluster of multiple births. Bad press will hurt us, especially our funding. We already narrowly escaped a disaster when that magazine article was published a while back about donor eggs being misused here. We can't afford another problem, or even a hint of one. We need answers, Sara Beth, before the press gets wind of this one."

"Not just answers but exoneration," Sara Beth said.

"Well, yes, of course, but first and foremost, we need to know whether information has been falsified or breached in the past—or whatever the truth is. And we need to know now."

"How does that affect me?"

Lisa leaned her elbows on her desk. "We want you to assist Drs. Bonner and Demetrios so that the project gets done. You will report to us if they're doing anything to stall the investigation."

She would be working directly for the man she'd had a serious lust for since she'd first laid eyes on him?

"Um, us?" she asked.

"Paul and me."

"Why would the doctors stall? They weren't part of the problem, if there is a problem. It happened before they were hired."

"Because even a whisper of scandal could affect donations and grant money, which will limit Dr. Bonner's and Dr. Demetrios's hope of success in their research— not to mention the institute's reputation and credibility. If something unethical has been going on, our funds could dry up and their jobs could be eliminated. Wouldn't you stall if that was about to happen to you?"

Sara Beth didn't believe she would, but that was her. "So you're asking me to spy on them?"

"I wouldn't call it that. We're just lighting a fire under the doctors to get action before we get burned on this. You love the institute, and my father. This has to be important to you."

"Absolutely." The institute, and especially its founder, Dr. Gerald Armstrong, had been very generous to Sara Beth's mother so that she could retire early and comfortably. He'd been good to Sara Beth, as well.

"You're loyal to me, too," Lisa said.

"It goes without saying. Not just you, but also your brother Paul as chief of staff. But you know how I feel about deceit." Most of her life Sara Beth had been haunted by not knowing who her father was, which felt like an enormous deceit to her. All she knew was he'd been a sperm donor here at the fertility institute founded by Lisa's father, whom Sara Beth affectionately called Dr. G.

Anonymous donors never brought teddy bears or candy on Valentine's Day. Or sent birthday cards. Or pretended to be Santa. Or tucked a tired little girl in bed at night. Only a father did that.

"I do know how you feel about deceit," Lisa said. "That's my point. You could be *uncovering* a lie. Isn't that reason enough?"

Sara Beth wandered to the window but didn't really take in the sights. Could she pull it off?

Lisa joined her. "You're the eyes and ears of the institute, because in your job capacity you bridge both aspects of what we do, the medical *and* the research programs. You haven't hesitated to tell me when you've noticed something needing looking into, so how is this any different? Except that this time you're being assigned to observe and report something specific. Otherwise it's business as usual."

Lisa had a point. "What if they don't want me on board?"

"They won't have a choice."

"But how effective can I be if they won't cooperate?"

"When did you become such a worrier?" Lisa cocked her head. "You've always been optimistic and adventurous. What's going on?"

Sara Beth couldn't share what was going on, not this time, because she wasn't sure herself, except that lately, and especially today, she'd been feeling a little lost. Left out.

Lonely. She was missing a father she'd never known, and wishing for a man in her life, as well, a man to love and cherish, and be a hands-on father to whatever children they were blessed with.

She loved her job, but she didn't want to end up like her mother, who'd never married, having been married to the institute. And yet Sara Beth could see that she was following in her mother's footsteps, even taking on the job of head nurse, like her mom. Where *had* Sara Beth's adventurousness gone?

Being asked to spy for the good of the institute would be an adventure of sorts, wouldn't it? More important, their work was critical to the many people whose deepest dreams they helped fulfill—having a child.

"All right. I'll do it."

"Thank you." Relief coated Lisa's quiet words. "Let's go talk to Dr. Bonner."

Sara Beth clamped her mouth against the "Now?" that threatened to come out. She wanted to face him in her official capacity, wearing her uniform, her scrubs. Instead she wore cycling pants, a Boston College T-shirt and her old, comfortable riding sneakers. She'd left her hair down instead of pulled away from her face as usual, out of her way, her helmet taking care of that problem.

It wasn't the best way to start their new association, not as far as she was concerned, not if she wanted to keep a professional relationship—which she did. Unfortunately.

Sara Beth walked silently beside Lisa as they made their way through the cavernous hallways of the building, past the administration section, past examination rooms and consultation areas. During the workweek the hallways were alive with people. It wasn't a boisterous place—the work they did was too important to be treated frivolously—but it was always pleasant, the employees chosen not only for their abilities but their personalities. No drama allowed.

Until now, she'd only seen Dr. Bonner in passing or through the windows of the lab where he did his research. His partner, Chance Demetrios, was much more social and talkative, plus he was also a practicing physician, not just a researcher. Sara Beth often assisted him in his ob-gyn practice, whereas Dr. Ted Bonner had apparently discovered that he was better suited to the lab than patients. His too-direct bedside manner evidently wasn't the best for inspiring confidence or easing anyone's fears.

At least, that was the rumor floating around about him. Since she'd rarely had a discussion with him longer than "Nice to meet you" or "Good morning," she couldn't verify anything else. She'd intentionally avoided conversations with him because her throat closed when she was around him, something that never happened with anyone else. She always wanted to comb his hair away from his forehead with her fingers, too.

When Sara Beth and Lisa reached the lab, they stood side by side peering through the glass at the man inside. Tall, dark and gorgeous was a cliché, but the description fit him, if in an intellectual way. His hair brushed his neck, but she figured he'd just forgotten to get a haircut lately. Every so often he got it cut, and when he did, it was very short, as if he couldn't be bothered with regular trims.

He truly fit the stereotype of the absentminded professor: black-framed glasses; long white lab coat, pocket protector and all, his personal uniform; along with a white or blue dress shirt and dark slacks.

She shouldn't find him sexy, but she did. She'd heard he often forgot to eat, which was probably why he was so lean and wiry, and which also made him look even taller than his well-over-six-foot frame.

Lisa knocked. He continued entering information into a computer, his fingers flying over the keyboard. She knocked again. Still no response. Sara Beth looked to see if he was wearing earbuds and listening to music. He was only thirty-two, of an age to blast tunes in his head and work at the same time. No earbuds were visible, no dangling cords, either.

"Let's just wait until tomorrow," Sara Beth said, tugging on Lisa's arm. "He's in some impenetrable zone, that's for sure."

"I wonder if a fire alarm would get his attention?"

Sara Beth stared at her friend. "You wouldn't—"

"Of course not." Lisa laughed. "I was thinking out loud. You know, what would happen if? Would he hear it in time to escape?"

"He can't be *that* bad. Come on. Let's just go. He's doing important work, and we shouldn't disturb—"

Lisa entered her security information, turned the doorknob and stepped inside. Sara Beth sighed and followed.

"Good afternoon, Dr. Bonner," Lisa said as she drew close.

He didn't startle, but Sara Beth saw awareness click in. For one thing, he blinked. He held up a hand briefly then continued to type.

Sara Beth glanced around the lab. The two waist-high lab tables were neat and orderly, even loaded with equipment as they were—microscopes with projection screens, computers, other high-tech pieces she couldn't identify. Then there was the low-tech, standard lab equipment—stainless-steel sinks, glass vessels and tubes. Everything seemed to have its place, all order, no chaos.

Why aren't you on a date tonight, Dr. Gorgeous? she wondered. He was young, handsome and gainfully employed. She'd always assumed he played the field as much as his inveterate-flirt research partner, Dr. Demetrios, did.

"Ms. Armstrong," he said finally, turning toward Lisa. "And Ms. O'Connell. What can I do for you?" His gaze zeroed in and held on Sara Beth in an unnerving way as he gave her the same kind of complete attention he had given the computer just moments ago.

Not a multitasker, she decided, fascinated, as he took off his glasses and set them on the tabletop then shoved his fingers through his rich brown hair. She itched to do the same.

"I know you've been frustrated, Dr. Bonner," Lisa said, "at being unable to find answers to the protocol problems."

"An understatement."

"Well, I've brought the cavalry." Lisa turned toward

Sara Beth. "We've decided to free up Sara Beth from some of her regular assignments and let her help you and Dr. Demetrios with your investigation."

For a few long moments he stayed silent, his expression giving away nothing, then he said, "Her help is gratefully accepted."

That was way too easy, Sara Beth thought. Which was a good thing, right? If they could work without dissension, they could cover a lot more ground more quickly. Maybe she wouldn't feel as if she was spying, either. And maybe her pulse would stop pounding so hard.

"On one condition," he added. "Call me Ted. You, too, Sara Beth."

Sara Beth waited for Lisa's reply. Lisa's father, the institute's founder, had always insisted on using titles. But then, not only was he retired, he was almost completely bedridden. He never came into the institute anymore.

Lisa's shoulders relaxed. "Except in front of patients or VIPs."

"Fair enough."

"Should I call Dr. Demetrios or would you like to tell him?"

Ted pulled a cell phone from his pocket and pushed one button, then waited. "I hope I'm not disturbing you, Chance." His brows went up at whatever Dr. Demetrios's response was. "I'll make it quick, then. I just wanted you to know that Ms. O'Connell will be assisting us for a while so that we can get to the bottom of the issues around here…. Yes, Sara Beth…. Yes, the one with the long, dark red hair. How many other Ms. O'Connells are there? You work with her every— Oh. A joke."

He tipped the phone down. "When are you starting?"

"Immediately," Lisa answered.

Pride made Sara Beth not want him to know she didn't have a date for Valentine's Day, so she started to say she would start the next day, but he spoke first.

"Is tomorrow okay?" he asked Sara Beth. "I have plans tonight."

So. He *did* have a date. "That'd be fine."

"Tomorrow," Dr. Bonner said into the phone. "Yes, I'll do that. Bye."

He slid his phone back into his pocket. "Chance extends his thanks."

"I'll leave you two to work out a schedule." Lisa headed toward the door. "Sara Beth, you can plan on giving ten to fifteen hours a week to the project."

Then she was gone, and Sara Beth was left with Dr. Bon—Ted. Without Lisa as a buffer, they would have to talk....

"I'm looking forward to working with you," she said, twining her fingers. "I hope I can help you find the answers you need."

"Me, too. It's been frustrating. I'm a scientist. Discovering the truth is what I do."

The way he said that made him seem like a superhero, a man whose ethical core was the heart and soul of him, as if truth mattered more than anything in the world.

"What can I do?" she asked.

"Nothing that you'll find exciting. In fact, it's tedious

and painstaking, but it's the only way to get the answers. We need to know if previous doctors implanted too many embryos or manipulated the statistics to boost the institute's success numbers and therefore increase funding. So far we've been working with our more recent computerized records, but in order to dispute some of the claims, you might spend time reading old files from the archives vault, cross-checking and rechecking test results from before the institute switched to the new computer system."

The archive vault? Whatever else he said was lost. The archive vault. *The* vault. She would have reason to go inside it.

Her heart thundered, a deafening pounding in her chest. What had been denied her all her life was within her reach—because in the vault was her mother's medical file, detailing her artificial insemination.

A hundred times Sara Beth had almost asked Lisa to help her find that file, and a hundred times she'd decided not to risk their friendship by asking. Lisa never could have allowed it, even for her very best friend.

And now, if Sara Beth was lucky, she could find a reference to the name of the man who'd donated the sperm that had given her life.

Forget paper hearts. This could be her red-letter day.

Chapter Two

Ted stopped talking when he saw Sara Beth tune out, something that usually only happened to him when he was explaining data or experiment results, which wasn't the case this time. He'd only been telling her what tasks in the investigation she could take on in order to speed things up.

She was looking straight at him, her dark brown eyes glazed over. Should he wait for her to refocus or try to snap her out of it?

He decided to give her a moment, noting that she looked different today. Younger...

Her hair was down and loose—that was it. She usually had it pulled back in a braid as no-nonsense as her personality. Not that she was cold, but professional. Always. At least with him. He'd perceived her as shy at first, then had seen her interact with others and was bewildered by how she always seemed to avoid him.

She'd caught his eye, of course, during the months he'd been working at the institute, but he'd seen what could happen when coworkers got involved romantically, so he'd avoided even engaging her in conversation, taking away any possibility of temptation at all.

When he and Chance had accepted the offer to come to Cambridge to continue their research, he'd vowed to himself that he would try to be more aware of the world around him, to be more social, but that plan had been foiled almost immediately. He'd questioned the institute's various protocols, finding some statistics that didn't seem feasible, exaggerating the institute's success rate. Although he and Chance hadn't been involved in or responsible for the questionable issues, it was up to them to find the answers.

For Ted, work was all consuming. His research to find a reliable way to treat male infertility took precedence, but clearing up the protocol issues came a close second. As for a personal life, he didn't have one, and couldn't figure out how Chance managed to have his practice, do research and still have time to date. Ted couldn't manage all that.

He finally waved a hand in front of Sara Beth's face.

She jerked back slightly, her cheeks brightening. "Oh, I'm so sorry. I don't know where I went. You were saying?"

"You wanted to know what your duties would entail. I spelled them out."

"Specifically what will I be looking for?"

He gestured her toward a tall lab chair, then sat in the one beside it. "Do you know what I found? What I'm trying to verify?"

"I'd like to hear your take on it."

He got distracted by her sneakers, which she propped on the bottom rung, their scuffed toes at odds with her usually impeccable appearance. "You graduated from BC?" he asked, glancing at her T-shirt imprinted with the Boston College's flying eagle mascot, Baldwin.

She frowned at the change of subject. "From the Connell School of Nursing, yes. The institute gave me a full scholarship."

"I would venture to say you *earned* a full scholarship."

She seemed to relax for the first time since she'd walked into the lab. "I always loved to study."

"Me, too. I still do."

She gave him a knowing smile, as if he'd stated the obvious, which he supposed he had. He much preferred the confines of his lab to dealing with patients on a daily basis. He hated imparting bad news. And in the infertility business, bad news came frequently. He was happier in the lab.

"So, you were going to tell me about what you found," Sara Beth prompted.

"Shortly after Chance and I came on board here, we discovered that some of the lab's protocols weren't measuring up. Data was incomplete or missing. Statistics weren't matching results. Just as we were digging into the problems, *Keeping Up with Medicine* ran that story alleging that donor eggs and sperm had been switched for some clients, which raised all sorts of ethical questions about how we do business."

"The article never named the source of the allegations."

"Nor confirmed them. Then they were proved unfounded and a retraction was made. But at the same time that we were working on that issue, we discovered an out-of-the-ordinary number of multiple births following in vitro over the past few years."

"Which means what?"

"Numbers that big could pad the institute's statistics, making the program seem more successful than it is. We have standards about how many embryos to implant. It looks like the standards might have been ignored. Because of the unusual success rate, the institute was able to obtain a lot more private donations and grant money than usual. Now the numbers are being challenged, and rightfully so."

What he wasn't telling her was that every step he'd taken to resolve the problems had been met with resistance by Derek Armstrong, Paul and Lisa's brother and the institute's CFO. Chance was the only person Ted had confided in about *that*—so far. He couldn't make accusations without proof, but Ted suspected Derek was involved somehow, whether as part of a cover-up or something even worse.

"So, first of all," Ted continued, "we need to prove or disprove the statistics. Then we need to create a best-practices manual of lab protocols, so if we're ever questioned again, the answers will be readily available and backed up. I can use all the help I can get. The institute's reputation is on the line, but so is my ability to continue my research."

She rubbed her hands together, as if anxious to get started right away. "I'll check the appointment schedule for the rest of the week and see what I can do to re-arrange things and free myself up. Would you prefer morning or afternoon?"

"First thing in the morning."

She climbed off the chair and stuck out her hand. "Then I'll see you tomorrow."

He stayed seated, keeping himself closer to eye level. Her hand felt small in his, and warm, but also firm and direct. One of the traits he valued most in people was competency. She hadn't been promoted to head nurse without proving her competency. "I'm looking forward to working with you, Sara Beth."

"Thank you. I feel the same."

He believed it. Her expression showed anticipa-tion, as if she really couldn't wait to get started. He'd tried to get across to her how tedious the work would be, especially if she had to work with the old files in the vault, poring over the folders. Well, she'd find out soon enough.

"Have a nice evening," he said.

"You, too." She headed toward the door, then turned around, walking backward. "Happy Valentine's Day."

Valentine's— Damn. "Oh, uh, same to you," he said, but the door had already closed behind her.

Damn. Once again he'd screwed up. He glanced at his watch. He'd intended to leave more than an hour ago to buy a gift. Aside from the traditional, uncreative grocery-store offerings, what could he buy? When he'd lived in San Francisco he'd gotten away with having something sent, but Boston was home. He didn't have that excuse anymore. He needed to take a personal gift this time, something thoughtful.

From the lab window he spotted Lisa outside standing next to Sara Beth, hugging her helmet and laughing, looking much more carefree than the Sara Beth who'd just left his lab.

He went still. Thoughts swirled. A plan formed. She might be of some help....

Ted locked his computer, tossed his lab coat toward a hook, then raced out of the building as Lisa drove off. He encountered Sara Beth as she was buckling her helmet. Her face registered surprise—and a little wariness—as he descended on her.

"I know we barely know each other," he said. "But hear me out, please."

"Okay." The word came out slowly, curiously.

"This is the first time I've been home for Valentine's Day since I graduated from high school."

"Boston is home?"

He just nodded. "I'm supposed to be at my parents' house in forty-five minutes for dinner. I need to take a gift."

"I'm sure you'll be able to find roses at almost any market."

"And my mother would say 'how lovely' and that would be that. I want to do better than that. I want *you* to be my parents' gift."

Her big brown eyes opened wide. "Excuse me?"

He was pretty sure if she hadn't been straddling her bike, she would've taken a few steps back, deciding he was a mad scientist.

"If they think I'm dating someone, it'll make them happier than anything I could buy." He stopped short of begging, but appealed to the female tendency to nurture. "I know I'm asking an enormous favor. I know there's no reason for you to say yes. You may—you probably *do* have a date already."

Of course she would have plans, an attractive woman like her. He felt ridiculous now for asking.

"There's not enough time," she said finally, gesturing to her bike. "I would have to ride home and get myself ready."

"We're not formal. I'm wearing what I have on, just adding a sport coat."

She gave him a skeptical look.

He nodded toward his car. "I've got a bike rack."

Fifteen minutes later he pulled up in front of her beautiful old Victorian house, said he'd find a place to park, then come back with her bike, giving her no more time to answer than he had in the parking lot, not allowing her any opportunity to say no.

He understood now the expression about someone having a deer-in-the-headlights look. She mumbled something about how to get to her second-floor apartment, then headed toward the house.

He got lucky, coming across a car leaving just a block away. He hauled her bike to her place, where the front door was ajar. He climbed the stairs inside to her unit, where her door hung open.

"Where do you want this?" he asked, rolling her bike inside.

She pointed to an empty spot in the living room. "I'll hurry."

She rushed into a room down the hallway, shutting the door behind her.

Ted glanced around her living room. The house was probably built around the turn of the twentieth century, but had been remodeled recently, although still using original-looking hardwood floors, and an up-to-date kitchen with stainless-steel appliances. And yet the combined living room/dining area/kitchen space was also feminine. Flowers and pottery and bright colors and…comfort. Her furniture was built for sinking into, and looked inviting.

One of these days he would get around to buying his own sofa.

She had a nice view of the street. Most of the houses were from the same era, some better taken care of than others. She lived only blocks from the Red Line. She could take the subway or a bus to work, the bus being more practical—

What if he factored in twice as much of the primary enzyme…?

Ted grabbed a piece of paper and pen from her kitchen counter, sat down and started making notes, getting lost in a possibility he hadn't considered before. Later—and he had no idea how much later—he felt a tap on his shoulder.

He lifted his head so sharply he knocked into her. She yelped, fell back, grabbed her chin. He caught her by the arm to keep her from falling, the back of his hand accidentally pressing into her breast, her firm breast, surprisingly full for such a petite woman.

He let go. She steadied herself, repeatedly rubbing her chin, her cheeks flushing a little, too.

"I apologize, Sara Beth." He gestured toward the three pieces of paper he'd been using to capture his thoughts. "I didn't hear you. Are you all right? May I take a look?"

"I'm sure I'll be fine."

"I am a doctor, you know."

"And I know nothing about medicine?"

He smiled at the teasing tone in her voice, ran his thumb over her chin. "Move your jaw." Her lemon-scented perfume made his nose twitch and drew him closer. "Everything feel normal?"

"I'm fine. Really." She stepped back, and he finally got a full picture of her. Basic black dress, with long sleeves, the neckline not too low or too high, a gold locket, her hair down and curled, high heels that gave her a few inches extra height, which was probably why he'd banged directly into her chin.

"You look nice," he said, an understatement.

"Thank you." She frowned slightly. "Are you sure we can pull this off? It's kind of hard to pretend we've been dating when we really don't know anything about each other."

"We can exchange bios during the drive. If we say

we've only recently started dating, they won't expect us to know everything about each other."

"Well, that much is the truth, anyway." She grabbed her evening bag and keys. "It should be an adventure."

"You think so?"

She nodded. "And *adventure* is my middle name."

He couldn't tell if she was serious or joking, then her eyes twinkled mischievously, and he found that appealing. He tended to date serious women—

Whoa. Wait. This wasn't a *date* date. This was a please-rescue-me date. No kiss good-night at the door. No how-long-should-I-wait-to-call-her? dilemma. He'd see her at work in the morning, thank her again for her favor, then it would be business as usual.

It was a good plan, a solid plan. He liked plans.

"When will we break up?" Sara Beth asked as they walked to his car.

"When you're fed up with my lack of attention." *As usual.* The most common complaint he heard from women as they exited his life was, "You forgot I existed."

He didn't mean to. It just happened. He put most of his energies into his research. He had a good reason to find a solution to male infertility issues soon. A very good reason.

Yes, he wanted to help mankind, but he particularly wanted to help one man. Until then, Ted had given up his goal to be more social for a personal vow instead, a promise to devote his time and energy to the cause, putting his personal life on hold until he'd accomplished his goal.

Even though he felt ready—more than ready—to

marry and have children, he would delay it. He couldn't give his time to anything else but his research, nor ask a woman to sacrifice time with him so that he could reach his personal goal.

As Ted navigated streets and bridges, he gave Sara Beth a summary of his life. "Only child. Raised by strict but kind parents. Too clumsy to play basketball, even though everyone expected me to because of my height. Total nerd. Or geek. Take your pick of insult. I participated in all the science fairs and academic decathlons."

"And did very well, I'm sure," Sara Beth said.

He shrugged. Bragging wasn't part of his makeup.

"I wanted to get away from home after high school graduation, so I went to Stanford. I met Chance there. We were opposites in most ways, but both of us were determined to make a difference. We teamed up at the Breyer Medical Center in San Francisco and made some progress, but we didn't have the freedom to work in the way we needed. When Paul Armstrong extended the offer to come here, we said yes." Immediately. No hesitation at all. "How about you?"

"I'm also an only child, and my mother was strict but kind, but I was a jock. Played soccer from age five through high school and loved it. I didn't have any interest in leaving home, which is why I went to BC, and because of the institute's scholarship. I'd been working there since I was sixteen, starting as a part-time file clerk. I've never worked anywhere else."

"So you work there because you feel obligated?"

She didn't say anything for a while, then, "In some

respects that's true, but I believe in what they do, and it's a comfortable place for me. Lisa and I have been best friends all our lives, and so I spent a lot of time at the Armstrong home. I know her sister and brothers. Her father was always very kind to me, and my mother loved working for him. In fact, she was his first employee, was even kind of a girl Friday as well as his nurse until they got so big they needed more help."

She sat up straighter and looked around as he turned onto his parents' street. "Um, where are we?"

"Mount Vernon Square."

"As in, Beacon Hill?" she asked, sounding slightly short of horrified.

"Yes."

"I see," she said tightly. "And where do you live?"

"Back Bay."

She closed her eyes for a moment, then glanced at her dress. "Are you sure I'm dressed up enough?"

"You look fine." He almost said *beautiful,* which was the truth, but caught himself in time figuring she wouldn't believe him.

She went silent. He continued to talk as if nothing had changed, offering more family information, asking more questions of her, getting subdued answers. But when they arrived, he felt prepared to answer the basic questions his parents might put forward.

Ted let himself and Sara Beth into the 150-year-old Victorian house where he'd grown up. Inside, he pressed a hand to the small of her back and urged her toward the sitting room, where he could hear voices. He was appreciating the curve of her spine when he felt her stiffen a little. "They don't eat guests for dinner," he said close to her ear.

She laughed quietly, shakily.

"They've found that guests make for a better dessert," he added just as they walked through the open door.

Conversation stopped. His gaze swept the room. His mother and father were side by side on a settee.

But they were not alone.

Chapter Three

Sara Beth wanted to jab Ted in the ribs. Hard. Obviously he hadn't warned his parents he was bringing her, because they quickly glanced at a woman about Ted's age seated in a high-back chair, wearing a Valentine-red, body-hugging dress. She was blond, curvy and regal-looking, the silver spoon in her mouth invisible but obvious in her demeanor.

"Darling," his mother said as his father stood and came toward Ted and Sara Beth. "You brought a guest. How lovely."

Sara Beth gave her credit. She sounded genuinely pleased.

Ted shook hands with his father. "I thought I'd surprise you. This is Sara Beth O'Connell. Sara Beth, these are my parents, Brant and Penny Bonner, and a family friend, Tricia Trahearn."

Sara Beth caught a cool, speculative look from Tricia as they shook hands.

"It's been a long time, Tricia. How are you?" Ted asked, clasping her hand for a moment too long, in Sara Beth's opinion. Or was *she* doing the holding?

"I'm well, thank you. You're looking wonderful."

"I can't complain." He let go, then bent to kiss his mother's cheek. "Happy anniversary."

Shock surged through Sara Beth, then annoyance. Oh, yeah, she was going to get him for this. It was bad enough she seemed like a party crasher, but he also hadn't bothered to tell her it was his parents' anniversary.

"Thank you, darling," Penny Bonner said, lifting her glass to her husband. "Thirty-four years. Time does fly."

The only available seating was a second settee, facing his parents. Ted led Sara Beth there. She thought she was doing an admirable job of keeping her expression neutral, while an internal volcano threatened to spew. She'd accepted his invitation because she'd wanted an adventure, to recapture that piece of herself. Instead she felt like an intruder.

Which was Dr. Ted Bonner's fault, big-time.

Hadn't her mother warned her forever about doctors, particularly about doctors, love and romance? Yes, yes, yes. Forever. From as far back as Sara Beth's memory reached. Doctors lived in a world of their own, her mother had said. It was one of the reasons Sara Beth had kept away from Ted, since she'd been dazzled by an instant attraction to him. Nothing serious could ever happen between them.

"Glenfiddich on the rocks for you, I imagine, son?" his father said, then looked at Sara Beth. "What would you like?"

To dump a whole bottle of that pricey whiskey over your son's head. "White wine would be wonderful, thank you."

Brant moved to a bar cart, then returned with their drinks. No one spoke. The awkwardness grew by the second. Sara Beth didn't hazard a glance toward the sexy Tricia Trahearn, but felt the woman's interest. Or maybe she'd zeroed in on Ted. Either way, she didn't look anywhere but in their direction.

Sara Beth also wondered how irritated his mother was. Not only would she have to add another place at the table, there would be an odd number instead of even.

Ted's mother ended the silence. "Tricia is visiting her parents for a month," Penny said.

Penny was short for Penelope, Sara Beth recalled from Ted's conversation in the car. His parents were old Boston. *Very* old Boston, as in James-Bonner-arrived-in-America-on-the-ship-*Truelove*-in-1623 old Boston. Penelope and Brantley were family names from a long and duly documented genealogy through the centuries. Ted was officially Theodore, so named after ancestors from the eighteenth and nineteenth centuries. "It could've been worse," he'd told her as he'd parked the car. "Several were named Percival."

"How are your parents?" Ted asked Tricia, swirling his drink then taking a sip.

"Disappointed in me, as always."

"Why's that?"

She recrossed her legs and bounced her foot. "I haven't married and procreated yet." She offered a small toast. "I'm sure you've heard the refrain."

Sara Beth didn't appreciate Tricia's lack of subtlety, nor the way she seemed so familiar with Ted.

Ted smiled, returning the gesture with his glass. "Tricia is a judge," he said to Sara Beth. "Youngest on the bench at the moment."

Of course she is. Probably everyone he knew held positions of power and influence. Sara Beth was proud of where she came from and what she'd accomplished, but this was a whole new world to her.

"*Appointed* judge. Not here, but in Vermont," Tricia said. "We'll see what happens come election time."

"It'll be a landslide," Penny said with assurance. "And for the record, we don't pester Ted about marrying and procreating, as you so bluntly put it, do we, darling?"

"I suppose one would have to define the word *pester,* Mother," Ted responded, but with a smile. His father laughed.

"So, where did you and Sara Beth meet?" Penny asked.

"She's the head nurse at the Armstrong Fertility Institute."

"You work together?"

"Not together, exactly. I'm research. She's medicine," Ted said.

Sara Beth was fine with the fact he was fudging the truth a little. They weren't a couple, after all, and they wouldn't officially be working together until tomorrow morning.

"Do you help deliver babies?" Tricia asked.

"We don't do deliveries at the institute. We use the hospital next door. A lot of specialized staff and equipment is necessary, since we often have multiple births. I do, however, attend some of the births. Some of our patients find it comforting to have a familiar face present," Sara Beth explained.

"You enjoy your work?" Penny asked.

"I— Yes, I do. I've known since I was a child that it was what I wanted. I'm sure the decision was influenced by my mother, who was head nurse at the institute since Dr. Armstrong started it. She retired recently."

"And your father?" Penny asked.

Sara Beth wondered if Ted knew her background. In the car she'd only mentioned her mother, and he hadn't questioned her about her father. "My father has never been part of my life." *But maybe he will be. Maybe I'll find him, after all. The vault could hold the answers....*

She realized how quiet the room had gotten. No one knew what to say. "My mother and I are very close, though. How did you two meet?" she asked, diverting the conversation to his parents.

Brant laid his hand over Penny's. Love and affection radiated from her face, and it made Sara Beth hunger for someone to look at her that way. She'd been in a position to observe a lot of couples through the years, couples who were usually under a lot of stress, either trying to get pregnant or waiting out a complicated pregnancy, so they didn't always glow. Still, it was wonderful to see a husband and wife so obviously in love after so many years.

"Our mothers were in Junior League together," Penny said. "Brant and I hated each other on sight."

"We were four years old," Brant said. "She was annoying."

"And he annoyed."

"When did it change?" Sara Beth asked.

"On my sixteenth birthday," Penny said. "His parents made him come to my party."

"I did my duty and asked her to dance, a fast dance where we wouldn't touch, but the song ended right away and a slow one started. I felt stuck."

"That was all it took," Penny said, her smile warm as their gazes met. "The moment we touched—"

"Pow." He stroked her hair. "I stole a kiss later, and that was it for me."

"Same here."

Sara Beth glanced at Ted. He was looking into the distance, probably devising some chemical formula in his head—or maybe planning when he would see Tricia again. Or maybe he'd just heard the story too many times for it to have impact. To Sara Beth it was incredibly romantic.

By the time the party moved into the dining room, another place setting had been added. They were served an incredible meal by a small, wiry, white-haired man named Louis, who looked to be in his eighties and who winked at Sara Beth when she'd momentarily been overwhelmed by the situation. She relaxed then and enjoyed the seared salmon with ginger-lime sauce, roasted asparagus and brown rice with scallions. Dessert was carrot cake, an anniversary tradition because it had been Brant and Penny's groom's cake.

Conversation happened around her. Questions asked and answered, memories shared. "Remember when?" became Tricia's catchphrase, grating in Sara Beth's ears after the third time. And since Sara Beth didn't know enough about Ted, nor did she have a history with him, she couldn't counter anything Tricia said with a memory of her own. Ted didn't seem to notice, just nodded and kept eating.

"Remember the time we sailed to Providence?" Tricia asked Ted as Louis cleared the dessert plates. "We capsized," she said to Sara Beth. "He saved my life. My hero."

"You know, I've think we've bored Sara Beth with history for long enough," Ted said. He set his hand on the back of Sara Beth's chair, gave her what seemed like a tender look, almost bringing tears to her eyes, even though she knew he was only putting on a show for his parents.

She stopped being mad at him.

"We should be going," he said.

"Me, too," Tricia said, patting her lips with her napkin.

Their farewells were brief. "I'm sorry you didn't know ahead of time that I was coming," Sara Beth said to Ted's parents.

"Please don't concern yourself," Penny said. "We were thrilled he brought you. Truly, Sara Beth, your presence was a lovely gift."

Ted and Sara Beth left the house with Tricia, after Ted helped the woman into her coat. Sara Beth had figured out they must have dated in high school, and had seen each other at some point since, but none of Tricia's remember-whens seemed recent.

"Maybe if we both get after him," Tricia said, looking over her shoulder at Sara Beth, "Ted will finally furnish his loft. Penny says it reminds her of a college student. Do you agree?"

Sara Beth debated whether to admit she hadn't seen his place. "He works a lot." She felt Ted's hand cup her shoulder and squeeze.

"I heard. Penny wanted me to volunteer to take on the job of decorating for him. I have a knack for that sort of thing."

"I'll get around to it," Ted said.

"You've apparently been saying that for months."

"And I've meant it for months. When things lighten up at work, I'll take care of it."

"I already promised to help him," Sara Beth said, fed up with how the woman kept pushing.

To his credit, Ted didn't blink an eye at the lie. He just lowered his arm to Sara Beth's waist. His hand felt hot through her coat, which was an impossibility, she knew. Still…

"Really?" Tricia's brows arched. She looked Sara Beth over again, as if examining her for some kind of decorator gene—and coming up empty. "Why didn't you just say so, Ted?"

"He's a man," Sara Beth explained. "He doesn't like to admit he can't do something, you know?" She felt him laugh beside her and felt warm despite the cold night.

"Well, here we are," Tricia said, stopping next to a silver BMW. "Maybe we could have lunch?" she asked Ted. "Catch up. For old time's sake. Just friends, you realize," she said to Sara Beth.

For old time's sake? Right. For *now*. Her interest in Ted was as obvious as the cut of her neckline—low and open for invitation.

"I don't have much free time," Ted said, squeezing Sara Beth's waist a little tighter.

She leaned into him and smiled at Tricia.

"I'm sure we can work something out," Tricia said. "Mother and Father would love to see you, too."

"We'll see."

"Ted and I met when we were children, too," she said to Sara Beth. "Just like his parents."

"Without the same results," Sara Beth said, fed up.

"Good night, Tricia," Ted said in a tone meant to shut down the conversation.

He maneuvered Sara Beth past her and headed for his car, his arm still around her waist, even though he no longer needed to put on a show. He'd touched her earlier, twice. First, he'd accidentally touched her breast, catching her off guard—and himself, she could tell. Then later, at his parents' house, he'd rested his hand lightly against her lower back. It had startled her, because it was deliberate. But looking back now, maybe that wasn't all. Maybe it was the touch itself, which had revved her up.

"Thanks for the save," Ted said as they drove off a minute later. "And for realizing I needed saving."

"You *were* looking a little desperate." She smiled. "I'm kidding. What is your home like?"

"It's the top floor of a converted warehouse with a rooftop garden. That I never use."

She sighed. "If I had a garden, I'd rarely be indoors."

"There's no garden in the backyard of your house?"

"There is, but I'm just the renter. It's owned by a horticulture researcher at Harvard. I'm not allowed to touch his garden. Everything's an experiment."

"How long have you lived there?"

"Three years."

"I was envying your sofa earlier. Reminded me I should order one myself."

"So your loft does looks like a college student's?"

"It's…minimalist."

She smiled at that.

"I don't even know what's kept me from getting it decorated. I could order furniture online, so it's not like I'd have to spend time going from store to store. I just haven't done it. Chance gets after me, too."

She hesitated a long time before she said, "I take it you don't entertain much." How personal was she allowed to get?

"I never entertain. I should be reciprocating invitations. My mother drilled that particular etiquette into my head. Until I furnish the place, I can't."

"What's your style?"

"It would still be minimalist, but also comfortable. I have art—paintings and other pieces that I've collected or been given. They're piled in a corner. I suppose it makes sense to decorate around them." He pulled up in front of her house. "Do you see parking anywhere?"

"You don't need to bother." She gathered her coat around her and opened the door. "I'll be fine."

He looked at her directly. "You've met my mother."

She laughed. "Well, she's not here to see your breach of etiquette. Really, Ted, you could end up driving around for fifteen minutes. I don't need to be walked to the door." This wasn't a real date, anyway, she reminded herself.

"Thank you for going with me tonight. You saved my hide." He reached over and pressed her shoulder, his fingertips grazing her neck.

Her breath caught. The air around her crackled. Neither of them moved. She wanted to kiss him, saw his gaze drop to her mouth and linger, his fingers twitching at the same time, then digging in a little. *Move,* she ordered herself. *Get out. Don't look back.*

She didn't budge. "So. I'll see you bright and early tomorrow," she said.

He pulled away his hand slowly, cold replacing the heat fast—too fast. She shivered.

"Until tomorrow, then," he said, smiling.

She climbed out of the car, leaning back in for just a moment. "Good night."

"I'll wait until you're inside."

She nodded, was aware of his gaze on her as she crossed between two parked cars, walked up the sidewalk, then climbed the front stairs. Should she turn around and wave? Of course. He was being a gentleman. She waved, although she couldn't see if he waved back.

When she got inside she leaned against the door, her legs wobbly. What had just happened? Was she caught up in Penny and Brant's story of love at first touch? She wanted the same fairy tale. The same happy ending. She'd wanted that for a long time.

But with Ted? A man who turned her on just looking at him? A man she worked with? A *doctor?*

She climbed the stairs, went into her dark, quiet apartment, then didn't bother turning on the lights, moonlight casting just enough illumination. She slipped off her shoes, hung up her coat and sat on her sofa, curling her legs under her. Her body felt alive. Needy. Aroused.

How could she work with someone whose smallest touch left her breathless?

Her phone rang. She picked it up from the coffee table, her hello sounding shaky, even to herself.

"It's Ted."

She gripped the receiver with both hands. Her heart began to pound, loud and fast. "Oh, hi."

"Listen, I—"

What? You felt it, too? You want me, too?

"Sorry. A car just cut me off. Um, I left some papers on your kitchen counter. Would you bring them with you tomorrow?"

She closed her eyes, more disappointed than she should let herself be. "Of course."

"Thanks. See you."

"Bye."

She'd seen him around the building for months and been able to control it. So why this reaction today? And then there was the fact he hadn't seemed to notice her at all until today. Or had he studiously been avoiding her, as she had been avoiding him?

All she knew for sure was that she needed to be very, very careful from here on. First and foremost, she wanted to get into the vault.

And she couldn't—wouldn't—let her attraction to Ted get in her way.

Chapter Four

In the lab early the next morning, Ted made room for Chance Demetrios to study his computer screen. Ted had arrived well before dawn, needing to get started on his lightbulb moment of the previous evening.

"You came up with this last night?" Chance asked.

"Yeah. A purely random thought."

"How did we miss it before?"

"Because it's been a process. We had to go through the previous steps to get to this point."

"I think you're onto something, Ted." Chance stepped back. "This could be the breakthrough."

"Maybe."

They'd worked together for so many years that they didn't need to say a lot, could interpret each other's expressions. Chance grinned; Ted just nodded, their reactions as opposite as everything else about them. Although they were about the same height, and had similar dark eyes and hair, Chance was powerfully built and social, and the black sheep of his dominant and wealthy family, whereas Ted rarely made waves. Opposite in many ways, but similar where it counted.

Because what they had in common was a need to find a viable treatment for male infertility, although neither had told the other why. And both were stubborn and independent, which made them a good team, each other's checks and balances.

"Has Derek Armstrong weighed in on having Sara Beth working with us?" Chance asked.

"He hasn't stopped by today. Maybe he doesn't know yet." Ted figured Derek would have an opinion, since he'd had an opinion on everything else that Ted and Chance were doing as they tried to protect the institute's name.

"Did you spend the night here again?" Chance asked, booting up his own computer.

"No." But that reminded Ted that he needed to order a bed frame, his box spring and mattress being too low to the ground for comfort getting in and out of bed. "I went to my parents' house for dinner. It was their anniversary. How about you? You sounded hopeful about your date on the phone yesterday."

"Here's a piece of advice, my friend. Never have a first date on Valentine's Day."

With a few keystrokes, Ted forwarded the new hypothesis to Chance's computer. "Okay. Why not?"

"Expectations are too high." Chance tapped a couple keys, then his screen matched Ted's.

"For what? Roses? Candy? Sex?"

"All three."

"Your expectations or hers?"

Chance laughed. "In this case, hers."

"And you turned her down?" Ted had observed Chance in action for years. He flirted in the same unconscious way that most people breathed. "Got a fever or something?"

"Or something."

Ted studied Chance, but didn't continue the conversation. They worked side by side, their shorthand of familiarity being enough to convey their thoughts. Suddenly, Ted smelled sweet lemons and discovered Sara Beth standing beside him, wearing tie-dyed scrubs in blues and greens.

Technically she'd been his Valentine's Day date, but without roses, candy or sex. Without any expectations at all. She'd been a good sport about it, too.

"Good morning, Doctors," she said, unobtrusively setting down an envelope with what he assumed were his papers from the night before.

He hadn't needed them—he had a near photographic memory—but he'd gotten worried when her lights hadn't come on in her apartment after he'd dropped her off. The only reasonable way he could make sure everything was okay was to call her, using the excuse of bringing his notes to work.

"Good morning, Sara Beth," Chance said. "Thanks for agreeing to work with us."

"It's my pleasure. I know how anxious you are to have the situation cleared up."

Ted didn't take his eyes off his monitor, but he said good morning.

"Your first appointment just arrived, Dr. Demetrios," Sara Beth said.

He saved his work and shut down the computer. "Did you have a nice Valentine's Day?"

Ted heard her hesitation and wondered if Chance did.

"Yes, I did, thank you. And you?"

"She didn't have a sense of humor."

"Ah. Too bad. That's a requirement of yours, I'm sure."

Ted looked at her in time to see her eyes sparkling.

Chance nodded solemnly. "Number one priority. That, and being a redhead."

"Uh-huh."

He raised a hand. "Honest."

She tapped her watch.

"I'm going, I'm going." He headed to the door. "See you later."

The obvious ease of their relationship irritated Ted. "I'll be right back," he said to Sara Beth then followed Chance out the door, stopping him.

"Sara Beth is going to be working with us every day. You need to treat her more professionally."

Chance's brows lifted. "I've worked closely with her for months, Ted. We joke around. You've heard of the concept, right?"

"Joking is fine. But not flirting." He was making an

ass of himself, and he knew it, yet couldn't stop it. "You got yourself in trouble for that before, remember?"

A deep frown settled on Chance's face. He leaned closer to Ted, keeping his voice low. "How could I forget? But I wasn't guilty then, and I'm not guilty now. So lay off." He walked away.

It wasn't the first argument they'd had, and undoubtedly wouldn't be the last, but their disagreements were usually about intellectual or scientific issues, which eventually were proved or disproved. Plus, they enjoyed challenging each other.

This was different. They never intruded on each other's personal lives. Never had any reason to.

Ted shoved his hands through his hair, taking a few seconds to vanquish the irrational thoughts, then determine the reason for them.

Simple. He was jealous of how easy it was for Chance to flirt and tease.

Ted could learn, though. Tricia's presence last night had reminded him how far he'd come. In high school they'd both been labeled nerds. She'd blossomed into a beautiful, poised woman to match the intelligence that had been there all along. And he looked a little more put together now, which got him dates without him trying much. Not that he held any woman's interest for very long—

"I'm on the clock here," Sara Beth said from the open doorway, apparently having waited as long as she could while he self-analyzed.

"Sorry." He returned to the lab, and went directly to

a corner desk. "I had boxes brought up from the vault." He pulled up a page on the computer screen. "All you need to do is enter the information from the files into this spreadsheet."

She stared at the image. He was distracted by her lemon scent again, realized it was her hair that smelled so good.

"This seems like a job that one of the data clerks could do," she said, hesitance in her voice.

"So it may seem, but it's much more than just entering data. Plus, we want to involve as few people as possible. You need to read the files, to understand the information that's there, not just statistics. We're looking for reasons why there have been so many more multiple births in the past few years than in previous ones. The institute's protocols are exact. We don't allow more than three implantations, yet we've had more twins and triplets born than makes scientific sense."

She looked up at him. He'd gotten so close, he could feel her body heat, but he didn't move away from it. Neither did she.

"And because we had a big turnover of personnel after Dr. Armstrong retired, the people involved are gone and you're left holding the bag?" she asked.

"Not exactly, since we haven't been here long enough to blame, but Chance and I came here because of the institute's great reputation and what seemed to be unlimited funding. A scandal, which this is brewing to be, could cause a huge loss of funding, which could mean the death of our research." He almost brushed back a wisp of Sara Beth's hair that had escaped her braid.

"Okay. What am I looking for?"

He pointed out the items she should review, flagging anything questionable. "If you come across something that doesn't make sense or falls outside the category parameters, just ask. I'll be working in the lab all day."

She nodded. "When I'm done with these, should I go into the vault for more? I mean, how far back are we checking?"

He finally stepped away slightly. "I don't know yet. We may end up entering everything, converting all of it into the new program, something that would've been done, except that Dr. Armstrong said it wasn't necessary. Lisa and Paul want to bring the institute into the twenty-first century."

"Sounds like a good idea."

Ted wondered about her mood. She'd gotten quiet and businesslike since Chance had left. "Thanks again for last night, Sara Beth. I think I'm off the hook with my parents for a while."

"It wasn't a hardship for me." She fidgeted. "You and Tricia go way back, I guess."

He adjusted his lab coat. "We dated in high school." He remembered their first kiss, glasses bumping glasses. He hadn't known where to put his hands, so he hadn't made any attempt. They'd just sort of leaned toward each other and touched lips. They'd gotten a little better at it through trial and error, but it wasn't until he'd dated an older woman as a sophomore in college that he'd learned what he'd been missing.

"You haven't seen each other all these years?"

"Once, right before I graduated from Stanford." They'd slept together. She'd come to town for the sole purpose of sleeping with him, she told him, as forthright as always. It had been physically satisfying but left him feeling hollow at the same time, as if they'd needed to do it in order to move on with their lives, to prove to each other how far they'd come. That she'd shown interest in him last night was both surprising and un-comfortable. "She could be elected president someday. Or at the very least, be a Supreme Court justice."

"You can say you knew her when. Reporters will track you down to interview. You'll have your high school yearbook photos splashed on the tabloids and across the Web."

"My fondest wish," he said dryly.

She laughed, a bubbly sound that infiltrated his body and danced inside him, making him feel...edgy. He remembered the firmness of her breast against his hand, the tempting curve of her lower back...

Tempting? There was no denying it. She tempted him, even with her hair in a tidy braid, her bright scrubs and practical shoes.

"Would you go shopping with me?" he asked.

"Pardon me?"

He liked the way her eyes widened when she was sur-prised, her lashes long and dark. "I thought I'd look at furniture this weekend. Would you turn your lie into a truth by helping me?"

A long pause ensued, then finally, "Do you think that's a good idea?"

"I wouldn't have asked you otherwise. Why? Do you think it isn't?" He hadn't thought it through. The idea had struck, and he'd asked.

"We work together."

Ted was unprepared for the blow of a rejection. He rarely asked anyone for help doing anything, but he also couldn't remember being turned down before, either. "If you don't want to, just say so. It's not like it's a date."

Her gaze drilled his. "I'm sure Tricia would be glad to have you change your mind and ask her. She seemed ready and able."

"If I'd wanted to ask her, I would have. It could be fun, Sara Beth. An adventure," he added, appealing to that side of her.

They stood staring at each other. He waited her out.

"Okay," she said. "I need to see your loft first or I won't be able to picture the furniture in your space. I'm not a pro, you understand."

"You have good taste. Actually, anyone probably has better taste than me, but your apartment is comfortable. I want comfortable."

"And a place you can invite people over."

"Yes."

"Even if you don't really want to," she added, her eyes dancing with laughter.

They barely knew each other, but she'd figured him out. And he'd asked her to help him with the furniture because he'd already relaxed with her. She was easy....

No. That was a complete lie.

She was trouble.

Chapter Five

Sara Beth let herself into her mother's house at six o'clock on Tuesday night. No scent of food greeted her, which meant they would be eating out. "I'm here!" she called, then shut the front door.

"Be out in a sec," came Grace O'Connell's reply from her bedroom at the back of the house.

In reverse of Sara Beth's housing situation, Grace owned her two-story Victorian, lived downstairs and rented out the second story to a Harvard law professor. It was the house where Sara Beth grew up.

"Cute blouse," Grace said. "You actually shopped."

"Guilty." Sara Beth hugged her mom, wondering as usual if Grace was ever going to age. Although sixty-two, she looked much younger, her hair long, straight and blond, her few wrinkles mostly laugh lines fanning from the corners of her crystal-blue eyes. She and Sara Beth could trade clothes, if they wanted, they were built so similarly.

Sara Beth adored her. She'd had a wonderful childhood, had never felt denied anything—except a father, or even a father figure. If her mother had dated, Sara Beth never knew about it.

"How come you didn't call me to shop with you?" Grace asked, stepping back to look at her daughter more closely. "I would've been happy to go along."

"I didn't plan it. I found myself in front of the Gap yesterday. Everything was on sale. I still spent way too much."

Grace cocked her head. "Who is he?"

It wouldn't do any good to hold back. Her mother could spot a lie every time. "It's not what you think."

"Anytime a woman who hates to shop goes shopping, and buys more than she thinks she needs, there's a man involved."

"You buy new clothes all the time. I've never seen evidence of a man."

"I *like* to shop." She slipped into her coat and stuffed her wallet into a pocket. "Did you buy new lingerie?"

Sara Beth almost choked. "No, Mother. I did not."

"You're blushing. Hmm. That's interesting. Tell me about him."

"We're just friends."

Grace rolled her eyes, hooked her arm in Sara Beth's and headed toward the door. "Which is the most pathetic lie in the lexicon of dating."

"It's the truth in this case. I did go to a family dinner with him last weekend, but he called it a rescue date. His parents get on him about still being single and I went as a decoy." And ended up being aroused by his touch. Not exactly within the definition of "friend."

Outside, Grace slid her key into the lock. "So, he used you? How charming."

"I said yes because it suited my purposes, Mom, not his. I've gotten in a bad habit of staying home, especially now that Lisa practically lives at the institute. I decided to shake up my routine." She smiled. "So, where are we going?"

"Don't change the subject, young lady."

"There's no subject to change. Nothing's going on." They turned right at the end of the walkway. Sara Beth guessed they were going to Santini's, a small family-style restaurant two blocks away.

"Are you going out with him again?"

Sara Beth managed not to sigh. "Not on a date. I'm going to help him shop for furniture for his place on Saturday."

"Why?"

"Because he asked." *And because I want to.*

"Why aren't you telling me who he is, Sara Beth? If it's no big deal—"

"It's Dr. Bonner, okay? Ted Bonner."

Grace's brows arched. "The new research doctor?"

"Yes. I'm on a special assignment to help him and Dr. Demetrios, at Lisa's request."

"Somehow I doubt that includes tending to their personal needs."

"Look, Mom. It's a change of pace, something new to do."

"And you bought new clothes."

Sara Beth threw up her hands. "Because you'd been after me for months to do so. Now that I have, you're making a federal case out of it."

"Not about the clothes, sweetheart, and you know it."

"I remember all your lessons, Mom. All of them. Don't date doctors and especially don't fall in love with them. I got it. I've heeded it. Is that a new hairstyle?" she asked lightly.

Her mother laughed. "All right. I'll lay off. For now."

"Forev—"

"It's a little shorter," Grace said, fluffing her hair. "And just a tad blonder."

While her mother relayed the latest gossip from her hairstylist, Sara Beth debated whether to bring up the subject of her father…donor. She really didn't want to resort to sneaking a look at her mother's file, breaking rules, risking the chance of getting caught, but she'd waited long enough. And the opportunity to learn about her father might never come her way again.

But just then they arrived at Santini's, and the moment passed, at least for now. It wasn't a subject she could bring up in a public venue, especially if her mother got as angry as she had the other times Sara Beth had asked.

So they settled into noncontroversial topics for the rest of the evening, then on the walk home, Grace said casually, "I won't be able to have dinner next Tuesday."

"How come?"

"I'm going to Cancún for a week. I leave on Saturday."

Is she blushing? Sara Beth wondered, eyeing her.

"Who're you going with?"

"No one. I just wanted a break from winter."

"You're going *alone?*" She and her mother had traveled together a lot through the years, but mostly driving trips to the shore.

"Would you like to come?"

"I can't. Not right now. But why didn't you ask earlier?"

"I decided this morning. I found an incredible deal for an all-inclusive resort. I've never done anything like this, and I'm excited about it."

Something wasn't ringing true, Sara Beth decided. On the surface, maybe her mother was being honest, but there was more to it.

"E-mail me your itinerary," Sara Beth said, giving her mother a hug. Maybe after the trip, she would open up. "And have fun. Remember your sunscreen. I do envy you a week of sunshine."

"And margaritas."

"That, too."

During the bus ride home, Sara Beth tried to examine her mother's announcement. She wasn't a spur-of-the-moment person. Like Sara Beth, her mother analyzed, planned, then finally executed, usually to unsurprising results. Taking off for Cancún on only a few days' notice was shocking enough, but to go alone?

Sara Beth's cell phone rang as she stepped off the bus at her stop.

"Hi, it's Ted. I hope I'm not disturbing you."

She knew his voice already, the deep, even tone that shot a thrill through her. The voice she hadn't dared to hope she would hear. "No. Actually you're keeping me company."

"In what way?"

"I just got off the bus and I'm walking home. What's up?"

"You know that stack of catalogs and magazines you gave me today?"

"Of course." She'd asked him to thumb through them and turn down the pages of what appealed to him, then she could figure out where they needed to shop.

"I'm not seeing anything I like."

"Nothing?" She'd given him everything from *Pottery Barn* and *Restoration Hardware* catalogs to *Architectural Digest* magazines.

"Does that mean it's hopeless?" he asked.

"I don't know what it means. Maybe I'll know more when I see the art you want to display." She was curious about his loft, too, was looking forward to seeing where he lived. "Or maybe what it means is you should take Tricia up on her offer to help. Or hire a real decorator."

He didn't respond immediately. "Let's see what we can do first. Where are you?"

"Not far from home. Why?"

"Can you see your house?"

"No, but I will in a few seconds. There. It's in view. Why?"

"Just trying to get a picture of how far you'd gotten." His tone was casual, but—

It hit her then. He was watching over her. He was keeping her on the phone until she was safely home. Maybe he gave his mother credit for drumming etiquette into him, but this wasn't etiquette. This was a character trait, one she valued, and probably deeply ingrained in him.

Sara Beth was raised to be independent, like her mother. They'd never had a man around to help. It was always just the two of them, or the handyman they hired occasionally when a job was beyond their skills.

"I'm turning up my walkway," she said, letting him know she knew what he was doing. "Climbing the first step. The second. Third. I've reached the landing."

She heard him laugh softly, so she put a little drama into her voice. "I'm inserting the key in my lock. Oh, look! It's turning. I'm opening the door. Now I'm shutting it—"

"And locking it."

She put her phone next to the bolt as it fell into place. Locked.

"Did you hear that?" she asked.

"You're making fun of me."

"No." And she wasn't. Warmth at his concern wove through her. She swallowed, not knowing what to tell him, so she just continued on with her running commentary. "I'm climbing the indoor stairs…unlocking my door…going inside…shutting and locking it. Done. Thank you. I couldn't have managed it without you."

He laughed.

"No, seriously, Ted, that was very thoughtful of you, walking me home."

"That's what friends are for."

Friends. She toed off her shoes and sank onto her sofa. "I was coming back from dinner with my mom. We generally get together on Tuesdays."

"That's…nice?"

She laughed at how he turned it into a question. "Unlike you, my mom doesn't pester me—that was the word, right? *Pester?* Anyway, she's not after me about getting married." But Sara Beth felt ready. She didn't want to wait—had no reason to wait, in fact. She had a good job and money in the bank, had dated enough to know what she was looking for and who not to waste her time on.

"Which is why you see your mother every week, and I don't do the same."

"For my mom and me, it's a routine," she said, considering it. "We started the Tuesday-night dinners when I moved out after graduation six years ago, so it's not just a routine but an ingrained habit now."

"Like me not having furniture. I'm almost used to it."

"We'll figure out something. Maybe you can show me what you don't like."

"I'd be dog-earing almost every page. Well, I just wanted to warn you that the job may be harder than you were planning on. Might take longer than you think. I mean, if you have a date on Saturday night, tell me what time you need to be home."

She hated admitting she didn't have a date. He already knew she hadn't had a date on Valentine's Day. "I don't have plans."

"I appreciate your help, Sara Beth. You've been a good sport. See you tomorrow."

She hung up the phone with a sigh. A good sport. He wasn't the first man to call her that. Men enjoyed her company, and usually wanted to stay friends so that they could continue to unburden their personal woes on good-sport Sara Beth, who was a good listener, non-judgmental and accommodating. And here she was, repeating the pattern.

Technically he's your boss. At least until this project was done. Which was an excellent reason for just being a good sport, she reminded herself, particularly since her body tingled around him.

She could always step back. If, after Saturday, she felt too drawn to him, too attracted, she could say no if he asked her to do anything outside of the institute.

But…would she?

The next morning Sara Beth felt her pulse rev and her face heat as she walked down the hall toward the lab. She bent over at a water fountain outside the room and took a long drink, stalling. The anticipation of seeing Ted had made falling asleep hard, then she'd found herself awake an hour before her alarm went off.

Straightening, she swallowed the cold water, then caught a glimpse of Ted through the window as she pressed the back of her hand to her mouth. He was wearing his glasses and lab coat, his hair tousled as if he'd plunged his hands into it more than once. From frustration? Impatience?

Then Derek Armstrong moved into view, coming up beside Ted to look at his computer screen. Sara Beth frowned. Why was he there? As CFO of the institute, Derek wouldn't normally drop in on the research doctors. There wouldn't seem to be a reason for him to do so.

Even though Sara Beth had spent a lot of time in the Armstrong home, Derek and his twin brother, Paul, were eight years older. She'd lost track of them until she'd come to work full-time at the institute. She did know that Derek and Paul were opposites in many ways, ways that made Paul a good chief of staff, respected and liked, and Derek more hard-nosed, since he was the money guy. But he hadn't endeared himself to the staff.

Or at least not lately. People hadn't whispered behind his back until recently. His expression was stern now as he talked with Ted.

Suddenly Ted looked toward the window. Sara Beth pulled back before he could see her watching. She didn't know why she was nervous about seeing him this morning, except that as she'd gotten to know him more each day, she'd found more to like each day, too. Her last boyfriend, a six-month relationship that had ended a couple months ago, would never have kept her on the phone until she was safely inside her house. He'd always "respected her independence," as he'd put it—perhaps because she'd made sure he knew her independence was something she prided herself on.

But after last night she'd altered her thinking a little. Being independent didn't mean she couldn't let a man be considerate.

Ted had made her feel special. With a simple gesture he made her previous boyfriends seem uncaring. And Ted wasn't even her boyfriend.

Derek came out of the lab, smiled slightly at her, then held the door for her to enter.

"Good morning," Ted said, his posture a little stiff.

"Hi," she said, going straight to her desk, upon which was the shopping bag full of catalogs and magazines she'd brought him the day before.

"I found a few possibilities online and printed them off," he said. "Some styles that appealed to me. They're on top."

"That's great." She pulled out the papers, glanced at them, then nodded. "It's you."

"I don't know what's me, exactly, but I liked it."

"Casual elegance, clean lines, masculine, not fussy. That's you." She set the bag on the floor. "I'll come up with a list of stores to check out."

"Thanks. I really appreciate it. Why don't I pick you up around nine on Saturday?"

She hadn't looked at him yet, but kept herself busy turning on the computer, taking off her jacket and hanging it up. She would finish up the first stack of files today. Would she get to go to the vault and grab new ones?

"It's an easy shot for me on the bus, Ted. There's no sense in driving to my house only to drive back to yours."

"I don't mind."

Out of the corner of her eye she saw him move toward her.

She finally looked at him. Big mistake. Even with his

nerd glasses and lab coat on, he looked sexy. Crazy sexy. Like she-wanted-to-kiss-him-for-hours sexy.

"Are you all right, Sara Beth?"

Desire and guilt battled for control in her head. She couldn't tell him how hot she found him, nor could she tell him that the moment she was allowed into the vault, she would do something completely unethical. For a woman who'd always prided herself on her integrity—

"Sara Beth?"

She sat. She didn't want to come across as rude, but she really needed him to go away. "I'm just anxious to get to work."

He didn't go away. In fact, he moved closer, into her personal space, stealing her oxygen. "Have you changed your mind? Would you prefer not to help me shop?"

She shook her head. Once she made a commitment to someone or something, she followed through. But this would be it, she decided. One time only. "I just don't think you need to pick me up on Saturday."

He stared at her. She stared back, trying to keep her expression bland.

"Good morning, all," Chance Demetrios said as he breezed through the door. He came to a quick stop and looked from Sara Beth to Ted. "Everything okay?"

"Apparently," Ted said, then walked back to his computer.

Chance lifted his brows at Sara Beth. She smiled. "Something I can help you with?"

"I just sent Mrs. Jordan next door to be prepped for a C-section. I thought you'd like to assist."

She hopped up. "Absolutely. If you don't mind, Ted?"

"Someone special?" Ted guessed.

"Candy Jordan was my first patient when I started working here full-time. She went through seven implantations before it finally took, and now she's pregnant with triplets. I've held her hand a lot."

Ted gestured toward the door. "By all means, go."

She hesitated, then looked at Chance. "See you in a few." He left.

She waited for the door to shut. "I'll come back later and work," she said to Ted.

"You can skip a day. It's fine."

She couldn't get a handle on his mood. Which was probably fair, since she hadn't let him get a handle on hers. She moved up beside him. "I don't want to skip a day. I'll work later on."

"Whatever works out."

He hadn't stopped staring at his screen. She wondered if she'd offended him. "Does it bother you that I turned down your offer in order to ride the bus to your home?"

He made eye contact. "You're doing me a favor, Sara Beth. A big favor. The least you can do is let me pick you up."

So he *was* upset about that. "You're right. Thank you. Yes, I'd appreciate that." She said goodbye then left.

So. They'd had their first fight. She smiled. She'd

thought Ted was extraordinarily patient, but even his patience could be tested when he wasn't getting his own way.

Frankly, she was glad to see this new side of him. And wanted to see a whole lot more.

Chapter Six

Ted considered patience his strongest asset, and his ability to concentrate a close second. He could spend hours doing one thing, and only one thing, not even taking time to eat. Patience intact, he got to Sara Beth's house a few minutes early, hoping that parking spaces would open up along the crowded street of homes on Saturday morning as people went off for the day.

He didn't have to wait at all, a car pulling out just as he got there. He parked but stayed in the car, knowing she would be watching for him, sure of that much about her.

He drummed his fingers on the steering wheel. She was surprisingly stubborn for someone known at the institute as a nurturer. He hadn't seen evidence of any nurturing toward himself....

Which was fine with him. He'd never liked women who hovered. Not only did Sara Beth not hover, she kept a good distance—except for that night at his parents' house, and technically, he'd closed that gap several times. Having her working in the lab had been fine, unless she came to him with a question, her lemony scent breaking his concentration even before she talked.

He wasn't used to having his concentration broken so easily. It should annoy him, he supposed, but instead he was comfortable. He'd felt comfortable with a number of women, but not ones he'd had interest in touching.

He wanted to touch Sara Beth.

The front door of her building opened. She came out wearing jeans and a beige jacket that came to midthigh. She was pulling on gloves. Her hair was down and tucked into her jacket. Her warm breath misted around her in the cold morning air. Something caught her attention overhead, and she stopped, shading her eyes, then smiled. A bird, probably.

He tried to remember the last time he had stopped to watch a bird.

All work and no play— Was he that dull?

He climbed out of his car, leaned on the top. "You're prompt."

"So are you."

"You say that as if it surprises you."

"I had a fleeting thought that you may get involved in something and forget me."

"Not a chance." *Not a chance in hell,* he thought, as she got into his car.

He climbed in, too, then held out a cup of coffee with cream, which he'd noticed was how she took it, and a chocolate doughnut with chocolate frosting. "Good morning," he said.

She yanked off her gloves, tucked them in her lap, then accepted his offering. She toasted him with the coffee cup. "It is now."

Her eyes sparkled above the rim. Something shifted inside him, not uncomfortably, exactly, although not completely identifiable.

Ted started the engine and pulled away, but caught her eyeing him. "What?"

"Do you even own a pair of jeans?"

"Of course I do. Why?"

"You're always so dressed up, that's all. This is Saturday. Play day."

"I play fine in these clothes." But it got him thinking. If clothes made the man, did that mean he never played? This would take some thought, he decided.

The trip to his loft didn't take long and was mostly silent as he spent the time wondering if she saw him as being uptight, while she enjoyed the coffee and doughnut during the drive. He ate when he was hungry, didn't much care what it was. It refueled him, which was the purpose of eating. But watching her savor the chocolate frosting by licking it off the doughnut—

He looked away and just drove. Hadn't he been the one to chastise Chance for his dalliances in the past? In the end, it didn't matter if you were innocent of making unwanted advances. If people perceived otherwise, you were dead in the water.

He pulled into his underground parking space, almost commenting about how quiet she'd been, then decided not to. She didn't seem bothered by their lack of conversation. Her smile was as bright as usual. There was no stiffness in her shoulders, if she was holding back anything.

"Nice to have permanent parking," she commented as he punched in the security code to his private elevator that would take them to the top floor of the converted warehouse. "My mom does, too. It's great having a car available at times. Makes it easy to take weekend getaways."

"Having lived in San Francisco for so long, easy access to parking was on my list of requirements."

"Along with what else?" Sara Beth asked.

"A view of the Charles. Although I don't know why, since I'm hardly here to enjoy it. Lots of open space. I don't like small rooms. They make me feel hemmed in."

"Are you claustrophobic?"

"I just don't like walls." The elevator stopped. The door opened to a large, although not massive space, with cherrywood floors, exposed ductwork, brick walls and floor-to-ceiling windows facing an amazing view of the Charles River.

"This is stunning," Sara Beth said, slipping off her shoes as he did, moving into the loft, shrugging off her jacket as she went. "I can see your dilemma about decorating it. You need to create rooms without using walls, so everything has to flow from one space to the next."

She eyed him. "Are you sure you don't want to use a professional? I don't know that I'm up to the challenge, given that my education in decorating comes from watching the Home and Garden channel."

"Let's give it a shot. If you still feel the same at the end of today, I'll do something else." The truth was, he wanted to spend the day with her. He hadn't spent a day with a woman since he'd moved back, and now he found himself relaxed, work not pounding his brain, a rare occurrence. He needed a little R & R, then could return to work refreshed.

"Okay," she said, wandering into the kitchen, a newly renovated contemporary space with dark wood-and-glass cabinets, glass-tile backsplashes, stainless-steel appliances and black, brown and gold granite countertops.

A folding camp chair sat in eerie loneliness by the front window, an upside down cardboard box placed next to it to use as an end table, along with one floor lamp. A flat-screen television was mounted above the fireplace.

"Spartan," she commented, flashing a quick grin.

"That's a nice way of putting it." He gestured toward the rear of the unit. "Bedroom and bath are down this way."

The bathroom was large, the shower walk-in, the floor porcelain tile and the counters the same granite as in the kitchen. The bedroom space could be closed off by pulling large planks of polished wood attached to an overhead rail, spanning from wall to wall.

She glanced into his huge walk-in closet, where long-sleeved dress shirts lined one side, in blue, white and cream. Slacks in black, brown and charcoal took up the rack below the shirts. A few suits. A tuxedo. Quite a few shoes. A couple of polo shirts. And one pair of jeans, never worn, tags attached.

"*How* long have you lived here?" Sara Beth asked as they returned to the living room.

"Don't start." After a week of her being mostly businesslike, he was enjoying her playfulness now. "Or no more doughnuts."

She laughed, the sound echoing in his almost-empty space. "You get what you pay for."

She pulled out a notepad and measuring tape from her purse, and they went to work drawing a floor plan to scale. Then he spread out his artwork along the living room wall.

"Eclectic," she said, tapping her pencil against her lips as she viewed the minigallery. "No wonder you can't settle on a style."

"If I have a gut reaction to a piece, I buy it, whether it costs fifty dollars or five thousand."

From her purse she pulled out a digital camera and took photos of each piece. He could see her mind whirling with possibilities. He wished he had that kind of spatial vision, to see what could be instead of what was. Chance frequently accused him of having tunnel vision. Ted had come to accept that about himself.

He also knew that same tunnel vision may very well be the reason he would someday find that rare treatment, something reliable, that had eluded researchers forever. A scientist had to be devoted and single-minded. He was both, and unapologetic about it.

Ted heard his name being called. Sara Beth stood in front of him, waving her hands and smiling.

"Where'd you go?" she asked.

"Sorry." His defenses went up. So many women had become frustrated with how often he ignored them while delving into his own thoughts.

"Saving the world?" she asked, her smile softening.

She didn't seem at all upset that he'd tuned her out. Maybe because they were friends, not dating?

"You don't do that when you drive, do you, Ted?"

"No tickets. No accidents."

"But how many did you cause?" She laughed as she scooped up her purse and dropped her camera in it. "I'll use your bathroom, then we can go, if you're ready."

"Sure."

She breezed past him, leaving her fresh scent in her wake. He watched her walk away, her stride purposeful, her shiny hair swinging between her shoulder blades. An image flashed of her naked, straddling him, and bending over, her hair brushing his chest, then his stomach…

His body clenched. He turned away and moved to the window. She hadn't had a date on Valentine's Day, nor tonight. So…maybe she wouldn't mind spending time with him, helping him take a break now and then from his cause. Someone to share dinner with, have a conversation.

Of course, in the meantime, he needed to do something about sex. Or the lack thereof, in this case. As in, not since he'd left San Francisco. He figured that was why he'd reacted so strongly to Sara Beth, the only woman he'd touched in months.

He studied a couple strolling along the river's edge, hand in hand. Tricia would be a safer bet, he thought. She was home for a month, dedicated to her career, wouldn't expect the long term from him. They had a history. No complications to speak of. Except…he felt proprietary about Sara Beth. Unreasonably so, probably, but true.

"Ready?"

He turned around. Sara Beth returned his look, a small smile stretching her lips, curiosity in her eyes. He wanted to back her up until her legs hit his bed and she tumbled onto it, and follow her down. He wondered what she tasted like. Did her bra and panties match the brightly colored scrubs she always wore, or was she a pristine-white or invisible-beige lingerie kind of woman? No hint of an answer came from her V-neck black sweater that plunged only far enough to have him wishing for more.

Sara Beth's smile faltered. "Are you upset about something?"

"No." He laid a hand on her shoulder, then let go immediately. "I apologize. I was deep in thought."

She cocked her head. "I wonder what it's like, living in your mind. It must be fascinating."

It was the wrong thing for her to say. No one had ever considered his tuning out to be anything but negative. To have her think otherwise made him want to get closer.

"You'd probably find a lot of twists and turns and dead ends," he said, encouraging her toward the elevator.

"Did anything come from the idea that struck you at my house last week?"

"Yes. Chance and I are working on it." In fact, he should be in the lab now, but was determined not to feel guilty about taking a day for himself. He wasn't sure how to find a balance between work and social life.

"What do you think of Derek Armstrong?" Ted asked when they were in the elevator.

"Because Lisa is my best friend, I've known him all my life, but we haven't spent time together in a very long time—he's so many years older than me. Why?"

They stepped out of the elevator and headed to the car a few feet away. "I'm just trying to get a handle on him. He drops in now and then, asks a few questions. But I report to Paul as chief of staff."

Ted unlocked the passenger door and opened it for her.

She paused before getting in. "Well, Derek and Paul are twins, but that's where the resemblance ends. I get the impression you don't trust Derek."

How much could he say? Derek seemed much more interested in how the research for the treatment was going than the investigation of what could cause the institute a lot of damage. It should've been the opposite at this point.

"I don't know him," Ted answered carefully.

"I watched you when Derek stopped by the other day. Your spine stiffened. You never took your eyes off him. And he didn't ask questions, he interrogated."

So, he hadn't been wrong about that. He wasn't just being defensive. Sara Beth saw it, too. "You didn't say anything."

"It wasn't my place."

"I value your opinions, Sara Beth."

"You and I have an unusual relationship," she said after he'd started the engine. "You're my boss for part of the day, my coworker most of the day and I guess we're also friends."

She'd summed it up perfectly. And she was right, it was unusual but also complicated. "You nailed it."

"Which means it's just as confusing to you?"

"I'm not losing sleep over it."

She laughed. "Okay, then." She pulled a small stack of papers from her seemingly bottomless purse. "I've got a list of furniture stores I think might be suitable."

"How long did you spend online doing that research?"

She shrugged. "I had fun. I hope your mother likes the results."

"It only matters what I think."

"I know, but…"

"No buts, Sara Beth. It's a fact."

"And facts matter most to you."

Yes, most of the time that was true. He liked facts. Good, solid, unchangeable facts made the world go around—his world, anyway.

But he was coming to like the mystery that was Sara Beth O'Connell, too, the woman he could already call a friend, but who also made him want.

Friends with benefits, perhaps?

Now, that was an idea worth getting lost in.

Chapter Seven

Sara Beth had occasionally wondered what it would be like to have a lot of money. Not that she felt she lacked anything, but how having a lot of money could affect someone's life.

Now she knew. Or to a degree, anyway.

Having money meant being allowed to buy floor models and have them delivered the same day instead of waiting weeks or months. It meant the owner waited on you personally. It also meant having a credit card with a large enough balance to charge just about anything, including a loft's worth of furniture.

Sara Beth had bought a piece at a time for her apartment over a couple of years, not wanting to get into debt, and often picking up secondhand pieces she

would refinish or repurpose in labor-intensive, satisfying projects.

"Have you ever painted a room?" she asked Ted as
they waited in the owner's office at Caro Miro's
Design Studio, a high-end, contemporary furniture
store—the sixth store they'd visited, and the most successful shopping they'd done. Caro was off arranging
the delivery of a sofa, two side chairs, a dining room
table and chairs, a sleek dresser to fit in his walk-in
closet and a king-size bed frame and headboard. There
was more to buy—tables, lamps, more chairs, a bedspread—but not today.

Ted stopped thumbing through a furniture catalog to
look at Sara Beth, her out-of-the-blue question getting
his full attention. "Painted a room? No. Why?"

"Just curious."

"Have *you*?"

"Lots. I don't like to paint walls or ceilings, but I
don't mind doing the trim. You probably wouldn't even
need a ladder." She sighed. Being tall had its advantages.
"I'm thinking you should repaint the bedroom part of
your loft a deep, warm brown. Are you up to it?"

"I believe in letting the experts do the jobs they've
trained for."

She grinned. "I'll bet your father said that to you
while you were growing up."

He cocked his head thoughtfully. "It does sound like
him."

"So, you'll give it a shot?"

"Would you ask a painter to dissect a frog?"

She laughed. "When's the last time you dissected a frog?"

"In high school biology class." His eyes lit with humor. "If you think the walls should be painted, I'll have it done. As long as you choose the color."

"What do I get in return? I mean, I'm suffering for my generosity already."

"In what way?"

"My feet hurt. My back aches. And I'm hungry!" Before he got all serious or feeling guilty on her, she added, "But today was a whole lot of fun. I wouldn't have missed it for anything."

"We didn't always agree."

"Isn't that great?"

"You're strange." He softened the statement with a crooked smile.

She felt highly complimented. All her life, she'd been the least strange person ever. People could count on her to be unbiased, easygoing, and noncombative. If Ted saw her as something more lively—like strange—she was glad. She really was having an adventure. "Thank you."

He looked doubtful but said nothing because the owner/designer returned to the office.

"You're all set," Caro Miro said. She was a tall woman in her late thirties, wearing a vibrant blue outfit that hugged well-toned curves. Her catlike eyes zeroed in on Ted. "You'll have delivery by six o'clock."

"I appreciate it."

Sara Beth watched the interaction between the two. She'd come to realize that Ted had no idea how attractive he was. He never noticed when women stared, or flirted, which this one was doing, and he was missing all the signals.

"I thought I'd come with the delivery people to see your loft," Caro said, handing a credit card receipt to him to sign. "Then I would be able to make recommendations for the other pieces you're looking for."

Ted looked at Sara Beth then. "That won't be necessary. We seem to make a good team. But I do appreciate all the time you gave us today, and the quick delivery."

Sara Beth's heart did a little leap first, then she tried hard not to smirk at the much-sexier woman. Caro might be a few years older than Ted, but Sara Beth didn't think that would've stopped him from responding to her obvious flirtation if he'd been interested.

Which he wasn't—because he and Sara Beth made a good team. It wasn't her imagination or wishful thinking. He'd said so.

He started to sign, then stopped. "There's an error."

Caro used the opportunity to bend close to him. "Where?"

"You undercharged me by six dollars."

She pressed a hand to her chest and smiled. "Oh, for goodness' sake. It's not worth running it again. Consider it a thank-you."

Ted signed the slip, pulled out his wallet, drew out six dollars and handed it to her as he stood. "There."

Caro looked surprised. Sara Beth wasn't the least bit.

"Do you like Thai food?" he asked Sara Beth as they left the shop.

"Love it."

He pushed a speed-dial button on his cell phone and called in an order, requesting several dishes. She wondered how often he ordered in.

"At least I can take care of your hunger problem," he said, ending the call.

"Thanks." Darn. No back rub or foot massage.

When they reached the loft, Sara Beth pulled her "Ted" folder from her purse and set it on his breakfast bar as he headed to his bedroom to check his answering machine. She would've gladly flopped onto a sofa, if he'd had one.

"If you need to put your feet up," he called from the bedroom area, "feel free to use my bed."

Sara Beth froze in place, tempted. Too tempted. "I'm okay, thanks," she called back before she changed her mind. "Do you have any soda?"

"Maybe. Check out the refrigerator. Make yourself at home."

His refrigerator held several containers of take-out cartons and boxes, some orange juice, assorted condiments, three Cokes and two dozen eggs. "You've got Cokes. Do you want one?" she called.

"Sure," he said from right behind her.

She jumped. He'd come up while she'd been bent over staring at the contents. He set his hands on her waist and held her so that she wouldn't crash into him, but in doing so, her rear pressed against his pelvis.

She laughed as she stepped away, the sound shaky, then passed him a can.

"Let's sit down," he said. "The delivery people won't be here for a while." He guided her toward the canvas camp chair with built-in cup holders by the front window, made her sit there, then he sat on the floor, setting his can on the upturned cardboard box. He reached for her feet.

"What are you doing?" she asked, although pretty sure what his answer would be.

"Taking care of your second problem."

She was glad she'd decided to wear cute socks, the ones with the dancing polar bears, but she couldn't relax. What if he intended to massage her back, too? She would have to turn him down. She didn't want to, but she definitely had to.

Oh, but his hands felt good, his fingers strong, his thumbs finding the sore spots and releasing them with pressure. At work she was on her feet all day, but she always wore comfortable, cushioned shoes, instead of hard-soled ankle boots.

Sara Beth shut her eyes and swallowed the groans that threatened to escape her throat. *Pretend he's a doctor performing a treatment....*

Nope. That didn't work. He wasn't *her* doctor.

She opened her eyes a tiny bit, saw a peaceful expression on his face, as if he was enjoying himself, too. She wanted to run her hands through his long, wavy, soft-looking hair, then when he looked up at her, kiss him....

Dr. Ted Bonner fascinated her. When he set his mind to do something, he did it all the way, giving his complete attention. In bed, would he—

A buzzer rang, disrupting her escalating fantasy.

"Too soon for the food. Must be the furniture delivery. They're early," he said, hesitating for a moment, then standing and moving to look at a closed-circuit screen. He stepped into the elevator. "I'm sorry to cut the foot rub short."

Me, too. More than you'll ever know. She grabbed her soda, trying to look casual. Which worked until Caro came out of the elevator with Ted, talking animatedly, flirting outrageously. The woman didn't even have the sense to dial down the flirt volume when she saw Sara Beth.

"I was just explaining to Ted," she said, as he sent the elevator back down, "that he might not be happy with the rug you chose for the living area, so I brought a few more to look at, just in case."

"How thoughtful," Sara Beth said, keeping the sarcasm to a minimum.

"What a great space," Caro exclaimed. "You're going to need a lot more furniture, though, don't you think?"

"For now I'm going to live with what I got today," Ted said, "then decide what else I need."

Sara Beth was trying to get a handle on whether Caro was more interested in making sales or making Ted.

"I think that's a great idea." Caro moved to the window. "You have a fabulous view."

Ted winked at Sara Beth. She decided he'd figured out Caro just fine, was not as oblivious as he seemed.

When the elevator door opened, two burly men emerged then unloaded six large area rugs. The next hour was spent laying out each rug, rearranging the furniture each time. Their Thai food was delivered, Sara Beth's stomach growling as it sat on the counter, calling her name.

Finally they settled on the rug they'd originally chosen, the furniture was put in place, and his bed set up. Caro lingered, offering advice on what else he should consider. Ted committed to nothing, and finally got her out the door.

"I don't suppose you have place mats," Sara Beth said as she began heating up the food in the microwave.

He gave her a you've-got-to-be-kidding look.

"Paper towels?"

"I'll get them. You must be starving."

"I could eat the paper towels, I think."

He laughed. "She's quite a pitch woman, isn't she?"

Sara Beth shrugged.

"I know you have an opinion," he said.

"She's good at her job."

"Not really." He grabbed two plates and some silver-ware and set everything on the new dining room table.

"You bought a whole lot of stuff from her."

"I would've bought more if she hadn't been so pushy. Which means," he added, catching Sara Beth's gaze, "more shopping at different places to finish up."

So, he wasn't a pushover, wasn't just making choices to get the decorating over with. Good. "I'm available next Saturday."

"Thanks." He laid a hand over hers as she set a carton on the dining room table. "For today. For helping at the institute. For bringing a little fun into my life."

She swallowed. "Ditto."

"Ditto," he repeated, grinning, shaking his head. "Okay. You're welcome."

By the time they were done eating, hung a few pieces of art and made a list of everything else they thought he might need to buy, Sara Beth almost fell asleep standing up next to his bed, which they'd just made up. It was finally off the floor.

"So, you're not hungry anymore, I imagine," he said.

"Definitely not."

"And your feet feel okay?"

Shc wriggled her toes. "Fine."

"Which leaves your aching back."

Panic had her pulse thrumming in a hurry. "I'm rested. I feel good."

"You just spent a couple of hours climbing up and down ladders, and holding large pieces of art over your head." His smile was a slow burn, as if he knew how attracted she was—and how scared to give in to it.

Unless she was truly under the power of wishful thinking, he'd been testing the waters with her all day, making flattering comments, giving her the eye, smiling in that way that showed interest beyond coworker or friend, no matter what they labeled their relationship.

She waited for him to make it clear what he was after, but he didn't say or do anything. She decided to retreat, to think the situation over. "I should get home," she said, sidling around him to return to the living room.

"So soon?"

Sara Beth laughed. They'd spent twelve hours together. She stuffed her notebook in her purse. He swiped his keys from the counter, then stopped and looked around at the partially furnished living/dining room. "Already a big improvement," he said, eyeing the dark brown leather sofa and side chairs, the modern dining table and sleek nickel-and-leather chairs, and the red-and-brown area rug.

She nodded. "I have to admit I was feeling pretty cocky when you decided you liked the rug we picked out at the store best, instead of any of the others that Caro brought."

"When I make up my mind, I rarely change it."

"Even about decorating your place, apparently, which was way out of your comfort zone."

"I had great help." He tossed his keys lightly. "I may not have vision, but I know what I like."

"What do you suppose your parents will think?"

"It will only matter that it's done. And that my grand-mother Holly's portrait of my mom as a little girl is up in a prominent place."

They took the elevator down and got in the car. "Want to stop someplace for dessert?" he asked, putting the car in gear.

"I couldn't eat another bite."

They drove in silence. She wished she knew if he was thinking about his new decor, her or his work. Most likely, work.

"Look at that," he said as they neared her house. "Parking right out front." He parallel parked, shut the engine off and opened his door.

By the time she got out, he was there, extending a hand, which she took reluctantly. "You don't have to walk me to my door. It's not like this was a date."

"Humor me." He let go of her hand.

They moved up the short walkway, climbed the stairs. She put her key in the door then turned to him. "I'll see you Monday morning."

He reached around her, turned the key and opened the door, then gestured for her to precede him up the second set of stairs to her apartment. She wouldn't invite him in. She absolutely would not, even though she had cookies and cocoa, the perfect ending to the day. She made herself stand in the open doorway.

"Good night, Ted."

She thought he was going to kiss her, but he wrapped his arms around her in an all-encompassing hug. She felt enveloped...and safe. His body felt familiar, when it shouldn't. She curved her arms up his back, pulling herself closer, feeling him from sturdy chest to hard thighs. He wrapped one arm around her midback, one a little lower, his fingertips resting on the upper curve of her rear. Her nipples hardened, wanting his touch, wishing he would pull her even closer. She barely resisted pressing her lips to his neck.

She was aware of everything about him—his strength, his heat, the promise of satisfaction for the building need inside her—but also that they worked together. That he was a doctor. That he came from old Boston money, had a place in a level of society she didn't know.

That a woman like Tricia Trahearn was much more suitable for him.

"Your friendship has come to mean a lot to me

already," he said, his breath disturbing her hair. He stepped back, his hands on her shoulders. "Thank you."

Friendship. The word righted her world again, put her in her place. She smiled brightly, probably too brightly. "You're welcome."

He went down the stairs and was gone, leaving her body aching and unsatisfied—and grateful. She was ready for marriage, a family.

She didn't need the complication of Dr. Ted Bonner.

Ted spotted Sara Beth standing in front window, watching him. He raised a hand toward her then got into his car without waiting for a return wave. He drove off in a burst of speed.

Why the hell had he hugged her like that? Let his hand drift down to the tempting curve of her rear? He'd been wanting to touch her since he'd come up to her bending in front of his refrigerator earlier, then later on when she'd helped him make his bed after the furniture men had left. She'd leaned over to smooth his sheets. He'd almost cupped that fine rear, had been stopped by her standing up, banging into him, a habit they'd gotten into, being clumsy around each other.

Friends with benefits. He'd been thinking about it all day, as she'd frequently gotten into his space, brushing against him to get a better look at something, smiling at him or pursing her lips as she studied a piece. She had a quick, easy laugh, light and joyful, and a slow, smoldering heat that appeared less often, but did appear, although he had to catch her off guard to see it.

And then there was the hug. He'd taken her into his arms without thinking, prepared to just give her a good-night hug, a thanks-for-everything short embrace. Then it had become something else. Even she had felt it. She'd moved closer to him instead of away. Her breath turned shaky. She'd gone up on tiptoe, which had aligned their hips. He'd pulled back before she could feel his reaction to her, had seen her nipples pressing against her T-shirt, an invitation he wished he could accept.

Friends with benefits. He needed to give that more thought. Sure, he wanted marriage—but not yet, not even anything close to it. If he took a break now and then from his work, it needed to be for fun, for pleasure, not with an eye toward the future, no matter how much he wanted otherwise.

For pleasure. The thought settled, a hazy fantasy that lingered as he parked and went up to his loft. He admired the newly decorated space for a minute, then decided to take a shower. His answering machine caught his eye, and he remembered the message from Tricia earlier, a call he'd ignored while Sara Beth was there.

Friends with benefits. Tricia would fit the bill, at least the benefits part, and without complications. She'd invited him to dinner next Sunday for his birthday. He had no doubt they'd end up in bed, if that was what he wanted.

And he wanted. But not Tricia.

He wanted Sara Beth O'Connell. Exclusively.

Chapter Eight

A few days later Sara Beth peered into Lisa's office. "You texted?"

Lisa gestured her in. "Shut the door, please."

She was looking more stressed each day, her mouth set, a furrow between her brows. It was hard for Sara Beth to see her this way.

"How about we go out tonight?" Sara Beth asked, sitting. "It's hump day. Half-price drinks at Shots. Free fries with the burgers." The always-crowded pub and grill was nestled in the center of the Cambridge medical community.

"I can't. I really wish I could." Wisps of Lisa's long hair had fallen around her face, a slight messiness that was rare for her, and it was only eight o'clock in the morning.

Sara Beth leaned toward her. "I miss you. And I'm worried about you. You've lost weight. You can't afford to lose weight."

"I'll be fine." She sat back, all business. "I need an update on your investigation, please."

Sara Beth frowned at the change of subject. "It's moving along. We've gone back five years so far. The statistics haven't been analyzed yet, and I think Ted wants to take it back further before we do. To uncover patterns, if there are any, before he comes to any conclusions. He wants a once-and-for-all conclusion. Don't you?"

"Of course. So, let's do this. I want you to free up more time, as much as you can manage. We need to get to the bottom of this *now.*" Her hands were clenched, her knuckles white.

Sara Beth studied her, the way she wouldn't make eye contact, the lack of a smile. "What's going on? There's more than just what Ted and I are trying to learn, which is bad, but not enough to stress you out to this degree."

"There are some money issues...." Lisa put her hands over her eyes and groaned. "Oh, God. I didn't mean to say that. Sara Beth, you can't say a word to anyone. No one."

"I won't. You know I won't." Fear whipped through her—about the institute, her job, her future. Everyone's future. They'd helped so many people to have babies. That couldn't end.

And then there was Ted, so close to making that dream a reality for even more people.

"Do you need me to tell Ted that I'm increasing your hours?" Lisa asked.

"I will. He'll be glad." She wished she could confide in her best friend, tell her about last Saturday and get her opinion. Tell her that Ted was on her mind all the time. All the time. Maybe the distraction would be good for Lisa, too. "Please come to Shots with me, Lisa. You need a break."

"Not tonight." Her phone rang, and Lisa picked it up, signaling the end of their conversation.

Sara Beth headed to the lab, urgency in her step, worried for Lisa, fearful for the institute…and anxious for the opportunity to get into the vault much sooner than she'd anticipated. Through the lab window she saw Ted and Chance in an intense discussion, not arguing, just extraordinarily serious. Chance didn't smile once.

She hesitated, then finally opened the door and stuck her head in. "Is this a bad time? Should I come back later?"

"That'd be good. Give us ten minutes, please," Chance said.

Ted turned and looked at her but didn't seem to register her.

She backed out, letting the door shut on its own, and leaned against the wall beside it. It seemed everyone was having some kind of crisis. And secrets.

Annoyed at being left out of the loop, she wandered away, deciding to get a cup of coffee from the break room. As soon as she'd poured a cup, she got a text message from her mother:

Hvng wndrful tme. Styng xtra wk. Love.

Which reminded Sara Beth that her mother had never sent an itinerary. She'd said that she wouldn't be out of cell-phone communication range, so what more did they need?

Which possibly meant her mother wasn't where she'd said she was going. Maybe she was with a man. More secrets.

She typed Have fun in the text box and sent it to her mother, not asking the questions she wanted to, not calling her, either, figuring it would go to voice mail.

Sara Beth sipped her coffee. Her life had gone from routine to unpredictable. She'd wanted to recapture some adventure, but the fun-and-games kind, not all this serious stuff.

After ten minutes, she returned to the lab, dumping her mostly full coffee cup, since food and drink weren't allowed. Ted and Chance were standing next to the centrifuge. Chance elbowed Ted, as if trying to get him to laugh, so Sara Beth felt free to go inside.

"Thanks for waiting," Chance said.

"No problem. Is everything okay?"

"Yes," Ted answered, still looking serious, but not grim—or somber, or whatever that was she'd seen on his face before. "Good morning, Sara Beth."

"Hi. I have good news." She didn't know what to do with her hands, so she slipped them into her pockets. "I've been cleared to give you a lot more time so that we can finish up as soon as possible."

"That's great," Ted said.

"I'm looking forward to getting back to normal

myself," Chance said. "Carrie's doing an admirable job of filling in for you, Sara Beth, but she's not you."

She smiled at the compliment. They did work well as a team. She respected him as a doctor. He was particularly good with the husbands, often counseling them separately through the in vitro process, knowing that most of the attention so often focused on the wives and their emotions. Sara Beth liked that he went the extra mile.

"So," she said, anticipation making her stomach do flip-flops. "I finished the latest box of files yesterday. Should I go to the vault and get more?"

"I already did," Ted said, pointing to the box next to her desk, which she hadn't paid attention to, thinking it was the old box. "I hadn't realized before, but I found out you're not authorized."

Not authorized? She could never go into the vault? Never find her mother's file? She grabbed her stomach, the pain so intense that nausea rose. She swallowed hard.

"Hey." Ted grabbed her as she swayed. "Sit down."

Chance rolled a chair behind her. She sank into it.

"What's wrong?" Ted asked, crouching in front of her, putting a hand on her forehead. "Are you sick?"

She waded through the agony in her mind to find an answer for him. "I…had cereal this morning. Maybe the milk was bad," she said, knowing it was lame, unable to think of anything else.

Chance had his fingers on her wrist. Ted was lifting her eyelids, checking each eye.

"Do you need to throw up?" he asked.

The absurdity of the situation struck her. Here she was being tended to by two doctors, all because she'd been denied access to information she had no legal right to have, anyway. How guilty would she have felt if she *had* gone into the vault and gotten that information? What would she have done with it? She couldn't contact the man after all these years, could she?

No, it was better this way.

And maybe at some point, she would actually believe that…

"I'm okay. Really." She gently pushed their hands away. "I don't know what happened, but I'm all right now and ready to get to work."

"Just sit there for a while," Ted said.

She would rather go somewhere and cry, get it out of her system, but she was sure they wouldn't let her out of their sight until they were satisfied she wasn't going to pass out. "Okay," she said.

The timer on the centrifuge went off. As Ted reluctantly left her, Chance whispered, "Are you pregnant?"

Shocked, she met his concerned gaze, her face heating up. "No!"

"Sure?"

"Yes. Positive."

He patted her shoulder, then joined Ted. Only a few words of their discussion reached her. *Experiment. Risk. Won't know until…*

Were they on the brink of success, then? Did they have something ready to try? Wouldn't there be all sorts of hoops to jump through for the government first?

She used her feet to push her chair to her desk and opened the box, pulling out a few folders, then turning on her computer, trying to accept defeat by reminding herself that when push came to shove, she may not even have followed through on her plan. She just wasn't sure she could live with doing something so unethical.

Sometime later Sara Beth felt herself in motion. Ted was pushing her chair to the lab door.

"What? Hey! What're you doing?" she asked, holding her feet up as they went.

"You're taking a break. You didn't hear me call your name five times. I think I've rubbed off on you."

Not yet, you haven't, but there's hope. The thought made her smile, as did his taking care of her, worrying about her.

"Go fuel yourself," he said as she stood. "I don't want to see you for at least a half hour."

"Breaks are fifteen minutes."

"Are you arguing with your boss?"

"No, sir. I just don't know how to take a half-hour break. I can do an hour for lunch, but a break? Can't."

He didn't roll his eyes, but he might as well have. "Whatever."

She laughed. "May I ask," she said, getting serious, "if you and Chance have discovered something new? Something exciting? I couldn't help but notice that you both seemed so intense."

"Maybe. That's all I can say at this point."

The look in his eyes gave a different answer. "You *did*." She squeezed his hand. "I won't say anything, I promise." Yet another secret to keep. She grinned at his caution-filled expression then she left the room, knowing he hadn't shut the door yet and was watching her.

Her heart was lighter. Even though she'd hoped so much to see her mother's folder, she knew it would have weighed on her, too.

It was better this way.

Ted waited until Sara Beth was out of sight then he grabbed his cell phone and made the call he'd wanted to make for years.

"Hey, Ted. How's it going?" came the voice on the other end.

Caller ID had taken the element of surprise from phone calls, Ted thought. "Good. They're going really good."

A few beats passed. "Are you saying—"

"Nothing definite, you understand. But more hopeful than ever. Want to meet and talk about it?"

"You have to ask?"

Ted kept his gaze on the door, in case Sara Beth—or Derek—approached. Derek would be the last one Ted and Chance would tell.

"How risky is it, Ted?"

"If nothing else, it might actually make you healthier."

A quick, deep laugh came across the phone. "Not a chance. I've been preparing for this, following every detail of the regimen you put me on months ago. Vitamins, lots of sleep, eating well, exercise, no hot tub. I'm so healthy I should be the poster boy for it. Hell, Ted, I'm even doing yoga."

"Good. All those things help. But I don't want you to worry about risk. The compound is all natural—vitamins, minerals, protein enzymes, amino acids."

"Seems too easy."

"I know. Guess we'll find out in a few months."

"Okay. Man. Okay. Thanks, Ted. You don't know—"

"I do. Want to meet for dinner?"

"Yeah. How about six o'clock at Shots?"

Ted frowned. "Why there?"

"Noisy, anonymous."

"We could meet at my place. I even have some furniture now."

"Humor me."

Ted was confused but agreed. He wouldn't mind going out for dinner instead of having takeout. And he'd heard that Shots was the place to go. "You got it. See you then."

He hung up then dialed Chance. "Six o'clock at Shots."

"I'd prefer the Coach House. It's much quieter."

"His choice. He *wants* noise."

Ted slid his cell phone into his pocket. Now that they'd come this far, he wanted instant results.

So much for patience being his strongest asset.

"This is good," Lisa yelled into Sara Beth's ear. "Thanks for dragging me away."

"Purely selfish of me," Sara Beth replied, a partial truth, since she really believed Lisa needed a break, but so had Sara Beth after the day she had. Shots was the answer.

They'd shouldered their way into the fray of happy customers, found a small table and landed there. Sara

Beth had ordered a margarita in honor of her mother. Lisa was nursing a peach mojito. Burgers and fries would be up soon.

Sara Beth leaned back and surveyed the room. She always changed into street clothes before she went home, but plenty of people were wearing scrubs or at least the comfortable shoes they all tended to wear.

"We got a lot of work done today," Sara Beth said, leaning close to her friend. "I can see an end to the investigation."

"That's great. I hope that'll be it, and Chance and Ted can relax." She hesitated. "Well. Look who just walked in."

Sara Beth followed Lisa's gaze, spotted Ted and Chance with a man she didn't recognize. "Who's that with them?"

"I don't know. Attractive, though."

Sara Beth studied the man. He was about the same age as Ted and Chance, not quite as tall, but *attractive* wasn't a word she would use to describe him. Powerful and intense, yes. Alpha, yes. But, simply attractive? "They all seem really out of place. Doctors don't tend to hang out here." In particular, Ted didn't fit, Sara Beth thought, wondering if he would notice her and what would happen because of it.

But the crowd was dense, and they found their own table as a couple got up to leave. The only one facing Lisa and Sara Beth was Attractive Guy, and he was only looking at Ted and Chance, at least until the waitress went up to take their order. Then he looked around, his gaze landing on her and Lisa and holding for a few long seconds, long enough to make Sara Beth squirm.

"Intense conversation going on there," Lisa said as their burgers and fries arrived. They each took a big bite, nodded their heads at how good and juicy the burgers were, then Lisa picked up the conversation.

"So, what's new with you?" she asked.

"I'm falling for Ted." She hadn't meant to say it like that. She'd meant to dance around the topic, get some general advice. But she and Lisa were best friends. There wasn't much they didn't share.

"Ted? Him, Ted?"

Sara Beth nodded and bit into a hot, salty French fry.

Lisa sat back, looking stunned, then she smiled. "Wow."

"I know."

"Have you been…dating?"

"Sort of." She gave her a rundown of their "dates," and said they were meeting this coming Saturday, too. "I don't know what to do. I thought I would help him the one time then back away. I thought I could do that. But I can't."

"Or rather, you don't *want* to."

"Right. I don't want to." She pushed a piece of lettuce more securely under the bun and stared at it. "I don't know what to do."

"You can't just have fun with it? With him? He won't be your direct supervisor for much longer."

Which stung, too, Sara Beth thought. "But he's a doctor. And he's stayed single all these years. And he's absentminded, you know, which apparently has caused many of his relationships in the past to end. Or so he said. I would just be another in a string of forgettable women."

"You don't know that."

"Are you encouraging me toward him?"

"I'm not discouraging you." She smiled and waved. "He just spotted us. He's coming this way." They watched him walk over. "Hi, Ted."

"Lisa. Sara Beth. You didn't mention you were coming here tonight."

"I didn't know until the last minute," Sara Beth said.

"Come here often?"

"My first time, actually. It's…loud."

She grinned. After all the quiet hours he spent in the lab, then in his otherwise empty loft, she could see why he would notice the noise even more than she did. "I recommend the burgers."

"Thanks."

"Who's the man with you?"

"An old friend, in town for the day. How're you, Lisa?"

Fascinating. Not only did he change the direction of the conversation, he didn't name his friend, nor bring him over for an introduction. Sara Beth wondered what Ted's well-mannered mother would think of that. Chance waved, but that was all.

"What is this? Institute night?" Lisa said, looking toward the front door. "Brother Derek just arrived."

Sara Beth couldn't imagine anyone more out of place, even more so than Ted. Derek had an air of entitlement about him. Fitting in wasn't something he did well.

He spotted them and headed toward them. Sara Beth

felt Lisa stiffen beside her. Considering how close Lisa had been to her big brother all her life, Sara Beth was surprised at how reluctant Lisa was to see him now. Because of the money problems Lisa had alluded to earlier? He was the CFO of the institute. He would know before anyone else if they were in trouble.

"Good evening, all," Derek said, and got lukewarm greetings in return. "I haven't seen you here before, Ted."

"My first time."

"Are you alone?"

Ted gestured toward where Chance and the other man sat. "I'm with friends."

Everyone looked that direction. Even from a distance, Sara Beth saw Ted's friend go rigid, his already intense expression turning icy. Derek's, too, Sara Beth noticed, then he pulled his cell phone out of his pocket and answered it. She hadn't heard it ring, but maybe it was on vibrate.

"My friend just canceled," he said, slipping his phone back in his pocket. "Good to see you, sister dear. We should have dinner sometime."

Lisa didn't say a word. He left, not stopping to say hello to Chance.

"That was strange," Sara Beth said.

Ted told them to enjoy their dinner and returned to his table. Sara Beth picked up her burger again then noticed that Lisa had shoved her plate away, her food not even half-eaten. She didn't usually waste food.

"I shouldn't have let you talk me into coming tonight, Sara Beth. I need to trust my instincts more."

"Who could've predicted that Derek would show up? And don't tell me this has nothing to do with him. You were fine until he came along." Her voice drifted off as Ted, Chance and the stranger got up from their table and went to the door. Ted lifted a hand toward her. "Getting even weirder," she said.

"I'd like to go, too."

Sara Beth wanted to talk more about Ted, about what she should do. If she could talk it through, she might get a better handle on her feelings before she and Ted spent another Saturday together. But even if she and Lisa stayed at the pub, Sara Beth probably couldn't get the help she needed. Not tonight, anyway. Lisa was too distracted.

"I'm sorry, Sara Beth. I'm not good company tonight. Oh, look. Carrie and Lorene just got here. They can take my place at the table."

"I don't want to stay without you. Just give me a couple of minutes to finish my dinner."

Carrie and Lorene, both institute employees, pulled up chairs and livened the conversation until Lisa and Sara Beth paid their bill, then Lisa drove Sara Beth home.

"Again, I apologize," Lisa said, double parking.

Sara Beth gave her a big hug. For a moment, Lisa leaned into it.

"Call me night or day," Sara Beth said. "We've been through a lot, you know?" Closer than sisters most of the time.

"I do know. Thanks. Keep me up-to-date about how it goes with Ted. You've been ready to settle down for a while now. Maybe he is, too."

"I think he's married to his work."

"I get the same impression. But that doesn't mean it's impossible."

"Maybe." Sara Beth opened the car door, then turned to look at her friend. "Night or day, Lisa."

She nodded.

Sara Beth spent what was left of the evening doing laundry, paying bills and making out a grocery list—mundane, mindless chores that allowed her thoughts to run freely, which only left her more confused. How could she fight her attraction to Ted? *Should* she? She admired so much about him. Respected his intelligence and dedication. And she'd spent a whole lot of time wondering what it would be like to kiss him, to touch him, to feel him touch her beyond the mostly accidental brushes so far.

As she was climbing into bed, her phone rang.

"I hope this isn't too late," Ted said.

"Not at all."

"I didn't want to bring up our personal lives at work."

"Okay." She prepared herself for the worst. He'd decided to keep his distance from her, keep their relationship business only. Or maybe Tricia had gotten to him. Or—

"I'd like to take you out to dinner on Saturday after we're done at the loft. As a thank-you. Would you like to go?"

"Yes." Maybe she should've hedged a little, but she was so relieved, the word just flew out.

"I could either take you home to change, or you could

bring clothes with you when I pick you up that morning. Whichever you're most comfortable with."

"Okay. Thanks."

A small pause, then, "You're probably wondering why we left Shots."

"A little."

"We decided it was too noisy."

"Really? I would've said it had to do with Derek."

Silence, then, "Yeah. I get tired of defending my research to him. I've said over and over that a practical treatment will take time. We're going to put a dent in it, I hope, then maybe another and another. One step at a time. Everyone needs to be realistic."

"You're right. Hopes are high."

"As are mine for that burger. I'll try another time, maybe, when there isn't a need for conversation."

"They make good fish and chips, too." She smoothed her blanket. "We left soon after you. It was a noisier-than-usual night."

A few beats passed. "I guess I'll see you in the morning, Sara Beth. Sleep well."

"Thanks. You, too." She pressed the off button then hugged the phone to her chest. She had a date with Ted Bonner. A real date, not a date of desperation, like the dinner with his parents, or a please-help-me-decorate date, but a get-dressed-up-and-go-to-dinner date.

And only three long days to decide whether to risk giving in to her feelings or ignore them.

Chapter Nine

Over the next few days, anticipation of her dinner with Ted replaced Sara Beth's letdown over not being allowed into the vault. Strangely, however, since he'd extended the invitation, they'd lost their ability to talk easily to each other.

Did he regret inviting her?

He'd picked her up on Saturday morning right on time. They'd shopped for hours, buying almost everything left on their list, once again having it all delivered the same day. She'd brought her change of clothes with her, not wanting him to have to drive her home, find parking and wait for her while she got ready.

After they'd hauled empty boxes and bags down to the trash, and before she got ready for dinner, they both sat on the sofa, their feet propped on the new coffee table, an oversize ottoman covered in a fabric that complemented the brown leather sofa. They'd finished hanging all of his art, had decided he would need a few more pieces, but only when he found something he loved. She was especially happy with his bedroom, not just the art, but the luxurious bedspread, in a gorgeous black and chocolate brown fabric that suited him exactly.

"Did I say how good you look in jeans?" she said, toasting him with her soda. He was wearing jeans and a white dress shirt with the sleeves rolled up. Not completely casual, but very sexy.

"You may have mentioned it a few times. I think I got the point, Sara Beth." He returned the toast. "We did well."

"You should throw a party."

"Why'd you have to go ruin my good mood?"

She laughed. "Most people have a housewarming, you know. You'll get a few plants, which you need, some bottles of good wine—"

"Which I also need," he interrupted.

"Right, because you can't afford to buy your own."

He grinned.

"And you'll get other stuff you'll never find a place for," she went on. "Can't mess with tradition. Plus, you'll make your mother happy."

"True. I'd make her happier if I announced I was engaged."

Conversation came to a halt. Sara Beth didn't squirm, but only because she made herself sit still. Ted, on the other hand, put his feet on the floor and took a long sip of soda.

"Sorry," he said after a minute.

"No problem. I think that point had already been established at your parents' anniversary party. So, have you seen Tricia since then?" She hoped she sounded really casual, as if his answer wasn't crucial to her well-being.

"We're having dinner tomorrow."

If the previous silence had been loud, this one was deafening.

"I seem to be making room in my mouth for both feet today. Would you accept it as a compliment that I don't have my usual self-censors up?"

She had to think about that. She could be flattered—or not. A man who was romantically interested probably wouldn't talk about taking another woman out to dinner.

"I guess not," he said. "I do apologize."

"Forget it. She's an old friend, and I'm not your girlfriend. It doesn't matter." Her words came out more harshly than she'd intended. She *had* begun to feel proprietary toward him. She'd had a hard time keeping her hands off him in the lab, and he'd often made excuses for getting close to her, bending over her shoulder to look at something on her monitor, when he could've just sat next to her.

More important, he didn't go off into Ted-world as frequently, but was usually aware she was in the same room.

So, she'd begun to hope. Now she knew she shouldn't.

"She really is just an old friend," he said. "There's nothing there."

"You don't have to explain anything to me, Ted." She stood. "I'll go change."

Her excitement about the evening dimmed. She'd needed the reminder about their different worlds, his being one in which Tricia fit. Plus, they had a history. Histories mattered. Being able to trace your family tree to the dark ages mattered to some people, and half of Sara Beth's branches were missing.

She undressed, then looked at her image in the mirror. *Okay, so a future with Ted is out of the question, but what about now? This moment?*

Sleeping with him—provided he was even interested—would break personal rules, including those drummed into her head all her life by her mother.

But what about the adventure?

Even that was coming to an end. His loft was decorated. The investigation would wrap up soon. They wouldn't be thrown together anymore, but would have to make a conscious decision to see each other. Would he? Did she want to wait to find out?

She figured she had the next couple of hours at dinner to decide.

The longest two hours in recent memory.

Ted took a swig of his Coke, finishing it off, trying to ignore the fact that Sara Beth O'Connell was standing naked in his bathroom, right next to his shower, a place comfortably big enough for two. He kept the picture of both of them showering together in his mind for a while, savoring it.

Then, resting his arms along the back of his sofa, he inspected his decorated space, appreciating it, already forgetting how barren it used to look. Not to mention he'd actually taken off two Saturdays in a row—although his situation at the lab had allowed for it, too. He and Chance had put together a product that might increase sperm count and motility, their goal for years now.

Time and testing would tell.

In the meantime, they would continue the research. There was still much to accomplish. Plus there was the investigation to complete, to clear the institute's name.

After which Sara Beth would return to her former duties.

No, not immediately. She was supposed to help him put together a best-practices manual, which would take a little while longer.

He'd come to enjoy having her around, her presence oddly calming—oddly, because she also excited him. Even Chance had commented that Ted had seemed more relaxed than he could remember. Except that Chance hadn't caught him staring at her, enjoying the way her braid lay along her spine, swinging as she moved. Or the curve of her rear when she bent over. Or the eye-catching bit of cleavage or lace when she wore V-necked sweaters, as she had today. Black sweater, her bra trimmed with black lace.

Black underwear, too? He'd bet on it.

"All yours."

Her voice shot into his fantasy like a fire-tipped arrow. *All yours.* She meant the bathroom, of course, but he considered a different meaning for a few seconds before turning toward her.

She wore another basic black dress, but this one fit like a second skin. It dipped low, exposing the high curves of her breasts and more than a little cleavage, a gold oval locket brushing her flesh, dipping between her breasts. Her eyes didn't shine with her usual good humor but with intensity—or maybe anticipation.

"You look beautiful," he said, which was an understatement.

She gave a small, playful curtsy, then sniffed her arm. "I smell like you, or rather your hand soap."

He went to her and lifted her arm until the scent reached him. He remembered the moment a week ago when he'd hugged her, and her nipples had turned hard, which he could see happening now, too. He hooked a finger around her locket, lifting it free, the back of his finger sliding along her upper breast. She held her breath, yet still her flesh quivered.

"Are there pictures inside?" he asked.

"My mom and me."

"May I see?"

She nodded.

Gauging his welcome, he let his hands just barely rest against her as he undid the latch and opened the locket. "You must've been a teenager."

"Yes. Fifteen."

He snapped it shut then didn't let go, his fingers itching to dip below her neckline, wishing he could fill his hands with her. "You haven't asked me not to touch you," he said, lifting his gaze to hers.

"No."

The breathless sound gave him a broader answer, the answer he wanted. "Tell you what. I'll go change and give you time to think. If you've tested the idea in your hand, and it still comes up positive…"

"This isn't science, Ted," she said, a small, nervous smile forming on her kissable lips.

"We work together."

"Not for much longer."

He stared at her mouth and the pale pink lipstick staining her lips, which parted invitingly. He bent low, touched his mouth to hers. Heat zapped his midsection and rocketed through him, the after-burn scorching him everywhere. He grabbed tight, pulled her against him, deepened the kiss, wanting all of her, everything she had to give.

She drew a quick breath, flattened her hands against him, pressed her forehead to his chest.

"I'm sorry." He moved back slightly, having registered the surprise in her face—or fear. He didn't know which. "Too much. Too soon. I'll give you some time." He turned around.

"Ted, wait."

He felt like a teenager about to be reprimanded.

"It's okay," she said, laying a hand on his arm.

Not a reprimand, after all. "I lost control."

"So?"

He faced her. The shock or fear, whatever it was, was gone. "I would've hauled you down to the sofa without thinking twice about it."

"Then stop thinking." She smiled, slow and steamy,

a Sara Beth he never would have anticipated. She was so…girl next door. Or so he'd thought.

"I'd prefer my bed," he said, thinking that far ahead.

She looped her arms around his neck and moved against him. "Me, too."

He almost thanked her. Then he scooped her up and carried her to his bed, standing her beside it. He inched her zipper down, the sound crackling with anticipation. Her dress dropped to the floor, blanketing their feet. He'd guessed right. All black undergarments, including garter belt and stockings. Her body was about as perfect as a woman's could be. "Look what you keep hidden under your scrubs. Is this what you wear to work?"

"I like the feel of silk and lace against my skin." She unbuttoned his shirt, pulled it loose and pressed her lips to his chest. "Mmm. This feels nice, too."

He unhooked her bra, slipped it down her then tossed it aside. He filled his hands with her breasts, ran his thumbs over her nipples. His mouth watered.

"Um, Ted?"

Don't make me stop now. Please don't. "Yeah?"

"You know those pocket protectors you wear at work?"

"Seriously? You're going to get after me about that now? Now?"

"Um, no." She laid her palms against his chest. His muscles twitched. "I'm hoping you have a different kind of pocket protector here at home. I can't tolerate the pill."

Was that all? He nudged her hair aside with his nose, dragged his lips down her neck, tasting her fragrant skin. "I was an Eagle Scout. What do you think?" He reached into his nightstand, pulled out a condom and flipped it onto a pillow.

"Got more than one?"

He laughed, shoved the bedding out of the way, then finished undressing. Lifting her in his arms, he laid her on the bed, landing on top of her, kissing her until she moaned, her lips soft and yielding, her mouth welcoming. He unwrapped the rest of her, revealing the gift of her body, tasting and savoring her as he went until she was naked and shaking. He didn't let her touch him, afraid everything would happen too fast. This was his present to himself. He intended to enjoy it. So he spent a lot of time swirling her nipples with his tongue, sucking them into his mouth, her back arching, sounds of pleasure coming from her throat. He moved down her body, teased her with long strokes of his tongue until she grabbed his hair and pulled him up, groaning as they kissed, wet and openmouthed, desire flowing from her.

He drew her hand to him finally, wrapped it around his erection and closed his eyes at the erotic sensation as she moved her hand up, down and around, gently. Too gently. He needed a faster rhythm, stronger motion. Completion.

He ripped open the condom, rolled it down, pulled her under him and plunged. Then he didn't move a muscle, but felt, just felt…

Sara Beth waited for him to move, the pressure inside her growing by the second.

"You're perfect," he whispered, gruff and low, sliding __ds under her, lifting her impossibly closer, their bodies fused. He moved just a little, creating a tiny bit of friction at the most responsive spot. Her world spun, pleasure burst inside her. She threw back her head, sounds coming out of her that she'd never heard before.

Then just when she was coming down, he moved, rhythmically, powerfully, and she was sent soaring again, beyond the realm of the first time, taking her to a place she wanted to stay forever....

Because she was falling in love with him. Falling for the ethical, cause-devoted, brilliant man who tried to conform to expectation but was his own man, nonetheless. No one could tell him what to do or how to live his life. He just lived it.

Sara Beth dug her fingers into his back as the realization struck her. How could she love him? It was too soon, too fast. Unrealistic.

Idiotic.

Desire was one thing, but love? No. She was just reacting to the best sex she'd ever had. He'd paid complete attention to her, just like he worked, single-minded, but this time devoted to the cause of giving her pleasure. Twice.

Just then he rolled to his side, wrapped her close and held her. No words. No kisses. Just the beat of his heart thundering in her ear, gradually slowing into a strong, steady beat.

"You okay?" he asked finally.

Okay? No, she wasn't okay. She was shell-shocked. Satisfied. Sated.

"Never better," she said.

"Same here. Best birthday ever."

She tipped back her head to make eye contact. He didn't look relaxed, but serious and tense. "Birthday? Why didn't you say so?"

"Because it's not important."

"I think it is. I love birthdays. I would've gotten you something special. Or baked you a cake with thirty-three candles to blow out."

"You gave me a gift already. As for the cake, I don't need to be reminded that time is passing by that fast."

He tucked her close again, his chin resting against her head. He'd started thinking about other things, she could tell. She just wished she knew what.

"I've never known anyone like you," he said finally. "Never had a…friend like you."

Friend. The word sounded like a death knell on the heels of her realizing she wanted more from him. Friend? What marked the difference for him between friend and girlfriend?

And, really, what made her think she felt more? The heat of the moment, probably. Best sex of her life, too.

Friend. That probably was a much truer definition.

"Same here," she said, feeling him tense up as he waited for her to say something in return. "I can't think of anyone else I could work and play with without problems occurring in at least one of the situations."

"I'll be right back." He rolled out of bed, disappeared into the bathroom.

Sara Beth untangled the sheet to cover herself, was getting comfortable when he came walking back in all his naked glory. Yes, he was lean and lanky, but he didn't lack for muscles, either, and he had long, sturdy legs and a broad chest tapering to narrow hips. All that wonderful masculinity in one gorgeous package, one he knew how to use to bring unmatched pleasure.

He lifted the sheet and climbed in, settling on his side, resting his head on his hand, staring at her for so long she ran a hand over her mouth. "Do I have birthday cake on my face?"

He laughed. "You are a complete surprise, Sara Beth."

"In a good way?"

"In an exceptional way." He brushed her hair from her face. "I've been watching you for months. No, *admiring* you for months. I've listened to Chance praise your professionalism. I've seen you being competent yet kind. I know you have a depth of sympathy and empathy that make you a good nurse. When Lisa said you were going to be helping us, I was glad and relieved. Professional, competent, sympathetic and empathetic. That was good enough. But sexy, too? You're a fascinating woman."

Fascinating friend, you mean. And you have a date with an old girlfriend tomorrow night. "There's more to you than I first thought, too," she said, sidestepping the issue of Tricia. And parental wishes to procreate—with one of his own kind, Sara Beth was sure.

"So, size does matter?" His grin was wide, his eyes alight with humor.

"That falls into the category of bonus."

The phone rang. He ignored it, although he also

looked uncomfortable, since it would go to his answering machine, which she would also be able to hear.

"You can pick it up," she said, feeling sorry for him—until Tricia's voice came on the line, her nasally voice distinctive.

"Hey, Chip. Just wanted to send you birthday greetings on the actual day. I'm really looking forward to tomorrow. Your mom said you got your place decorated, so maybe I could meet you there and see it before we head out? We have lots of catching up to do—in more ways than one. Ciao."

Sara Beth pulled the sheet a little higher. Tricia's voice had a tantalizing edge to it, as if she had in mind an evening of unwrapping a special present of her own for him, too. It tarnished everything that had just happened with Ted.

She tried to keep her voice level. "Chip?"

"After the singing cartoon chipmunk, Theodore."

"Was that your nickname as a kid?" It sounded like a Boston royalty nickname—Chip, Muffy, Miffy, Trey.

Ted looked distinctly uncomfortable. "Not in general, no." He cupped her shoulder. "She's just a friend."

"Like me." She couldn't hold it in any longer. She didn't want to be just his friend, not if Tricia had the same significance. She started to climb out of bed, but he stopped her.

"You're more than that," he said.

"Am I? In what way?"

Confusion crossed his face. "I'm sleeping with you."

"...iends with benefits?" She hated that term. It

turned sex into something almost meaningless, just satisfying a physical need, nothing else.

"Works for me."

She'd gotten herself into this situation. He hadn't said
he felt more for her, so she only had herself to blame.

The problem was, she was jealous of Tricia Trahearn.
She'd never been jealous before—or had to share
before. She didn't want to start now.

She made herself sound light and unconcerned. "So.
Are we going to dinner? I'm starved." She didn't really
want to sit across a table from him right now, either, but
it was a better alternative to giving up more of herself
to him without getting enough in return.

He was quiet for several seconds. "You're upset."

"I'm hungry." She got out of bed, uncomfortable at
first, then deciding to let him see what he would be
missing in the future—because she wasn't going to
sleep with him again. No friends with benefits for her.

She had to dig through bedding to find all her clothes,
then she dressed as he watched, feeling her cheeks heat
up but ignoring it. She found the tote she'd brought,
pulled out her brush and went into the bathroom,
shutting the door. She leaned against the vanity, stared
into the mirror, seeing splotches of color in her usually
pale cheeks. Her lips were a little swollen from being
kissed thoroughly and well.

She soaked a washcloth with cold water, pressed it
to her face, her eyes stinging. *Idiot.* The word rang and
rang in her head as she brushed her hair and fixed her
makeup. Somehow she needed to find a way to smile,

not to let him know how it mattered that he only considered her a friend. It wasn't his fault that her expectations were higher than his ability to meet.

She wasn't a match for him, anyway, their places in the world too vastly different from each other.

He was waiting in the living room, standing at his window, watching the lights. He turned. He'd dressed in his more typical dark slacks and white shirt, but also a muted tie. He still hadn't gotten his hair cut, and it curled over his collar. Tall, dark and gorgeous indeed.

He walked toward her, stopped a foot away, close enough to touch but not doing so. His eyes were filled with concern. She smiled. He really was a good person, which was why she'd fallen for him. But she couldn't make him feel the same as she did, no matter how much she wished it.

"I'm sorry," she said, needing the discomfort between them to end. "I was being prickly for no good reason. It all happened so suddenly, you know? I needed a few minutes to figure it out."

"You regret what happened?"

"No."

He hesitated. "Are you still hungry?"

She wasn't sure how to take that. Hungry for food or him? "Yes," she said, since both possibilities were true. Let him figure it out.

"Do you have all your stuff?"

She pointed toward the elevator, where her tote bag sat. "Okay, then."

didn't know what they would talk about over

dinner, but they managed to spend the next couple of hours doing just that, talking, finding ease with each other again. Then when they arrived at her house, he didn't argue with her when she said she didn't need him to walk her to her door.

He kissed her cheek before she got out of the car. "Thank you."

She didn't want clarification of what for. "You're welcome. I'll see you at work on Monday."

"Yeah."

"Good night, Ted."

"Good night."

As soon as she made it into her apartment, she turned on lights. Lots of lights. She had no intention of wallowing. She only hated admitting her mother was right. Now she would have to see Ted every day at work, knowing how it felt having him make love to her. Knowing her emotions were wrapped up in him, but not his in her.

She would recover. Time was her friend. Distance, too. They would stop working together directly soon.

But deep down she knew the memory of this night would stay close to her heart.

Chapter Ten

The next night, Ted watched Tricia wander around his loft, offering her opinion about every piece, recommending changes here and there. He hadn't let her meet him here, but picked her up and drove her to dinner at a restaurant she'd chosen, one where they'd run into several old friends. She'd paid for the meal, her birthday present, she'd said.

Some things just felt wrong to him, and having a woman pay for his meal was one of them, no matter how successful she was.

This felt wrong, too, having Tricia here in his space. Sara Beth's space. Sara Beth was the one to ___commend the casual seating by the front window, ___ he was drawn to more and more, where he could enjoy the view as he relaxed, morning or evening. Yet Tricia thought there should be a larger table, and seating for four, that the scale was somehow off.

Maybe it was. He had no idea about such things. But he liked the coziness of the two chairs, and a table small enough to hold only a couple of small plates and mugs. Tricia hadn't thought much of the throw laid across the bottom of his bed, declaring the faux fur passé.

Perhaps she was also right about that, but it felt luxurious under his fingers. Sara Beth had noticed how he had fingered it at the store and said he just had to have it. So now he did, and he didn't care whether it was passé or not. He had plans for it in front of the fireplace with a certain sexy girl-next-door type head nurse.

His bedroom walls were painted a deep, rich brown now, too, which felt strong and masculine to him, something else Tricia questioned the wisdom of.

"Aren't you going to offer me a nightcap?" she asked. She wore a dress as low cut as Sara Beth's the night before, except Tricia's was look-at-me purple.

"What's your pleasure? Coffee? Brandy? Wine?"

"Brandy, thanks." She eased onto a bar stool as Ted went behind the kitchen counter. "I had a good time tonight."

"Me, too," he said, meaning it. They'd taken a trip down memory lane. He'd forgotten some events, wanted to forget others, and could never forget some, as well. As the top two brainiacs in their high school, they'd shared a unique bond.

He passed her a small snifter, poured one for himself, but leaned against the kitchen counter rather than suggesting they sit in the living room.

She raised her glass to his, touched it briefly. "To old friends."

"I'll drink to that." They both took sips, looking at each other over the rims.

She cupped her glass with both hands. "Speaking of old friends, what do you hear from Rourke Devlin?"

Ted shrugged. "Rourke's got the world on a string. From humble beginnings to self-made billionaire. He always had the drive and talent to pull it off, although I never would've guessed he would succeed to the degree he has."

"He lives in New York, still?"

"A huge Park Avenue penthouse with views of Central Park and the Manhattan skyline."

"Has he been seeing anyone since his divorce?"

"I would guess the answer to that would be *plenty*. But we haven't discussed it. Why? Are you interested?"

"Maybe. My first choice seems to be taken."

Ted didn't respond immediately. "How do you know that?"

"You didn't touch me once tonight. I never caught you looking south of my face, either."

Given the fact he was a healthy male, he'd looked. He just hadn't wanted to take it further than that.

"What do your parents think of her?" she added into ⌐ silence, swirling her brandy slowly.

⌐ not something I seek their opinion about."

"They've always had plans for you, you know. The only son, the golden boy."

"Did they say something to you?"

"About Sara Beth?" Tricia asked. "Not specifically. Just a general remark about how important roots are."

"I hear an echo from years gone by."

She laughed. "They mean well."

"No doubt. Shall I take you home?"

She made a point of looking at her watch, letting him know it was early still, only nine-thirty, then set her empty glass next to his barely touched one and picked up her evening bag. "I'd hoped for a different end to the evening."

"We had our day, Tricia."

"Yes, I suppose we did. So, how about sharing Rourke's phone number?"

He laughed as he walked her to the elevator. "He's not an Eagle Scout anymore."

"Meaning?"

"A man can't rise to the position he has without being…" The elevator door opened. He held it, letting her precede him.

"Ruthless?"

"That's part of it." He punched the garage button, giving *ruthless* a thought. "I just know he'd probably jeopardize your chances of rising to the Supreme Court."

"I'm not looking for matrimony, Chip. Just a little action. I have to be a lot more careful when I'm in my own town."

The elevator bounced to a stop. "Tell you what. I'll let him know you're interested."

"Never mind. I'm not sure my ego can take rejection from both of you."

He dropped her off at her parents' house a few minutes later. Without conscious thought he aimed his car toward Cambridge, making a deal with himself as he went. If he found a parking space within a block, he would call Sara Beth and ask if he could come up. If not, he would go back home. Leave it in the hands of fate.

As he neared her house he started looking, inching down the street, then beyond by one block, the parameters he'd set. No spaces anywhere.

He gripped the steering wheel. Okay. That was it, then. He made a right turn, then another, another, then one more, when he should've turned left, finding himself on the same route, and still no parking. He glanced at the dashboard clock. A little after ten. Too late to call, anyway.

Once again he made a right turn, another, one more. *Turn left. Go home....*

He turned right. A car pulled away from the curb in front of him. Fate, just a little delayed.

Ted nosed his car into the space and sat. And sat. He wasn't close enough to see if her lights were still on, but that alone wouldn't mean she didn't have company, either.

Or that she would welcome him. Things had ended on an iffy note last night.

At ten-fifteen Ted got out of his car and started walking. Her living room lights were out. He'd stalled too long.

Yet he kept on walking, not hesitating a step. He

rang the bell to her unit, waited what seemed like forever until the front door opened.

"Ted?"

She wore flannel pajamas with fire engines printed on the fabric, along with the words *hot stuff, sizzle* and *smokin'*. And teddy-bear slippers.

"Are you okay?" she asked, hugging herself against the cold.

"May I come in?"

"Why?"

"I'd like to clear the air."

She studied his face for what seemed like an hour then stepped back so that he could come inside. He signaled her to lead the way up the stairs. She smelled of toothpaste and soap.

"How was your date?" she asked as they crossed the threshold, her voice taut.

"On a scale of one to ten? A five." She didn't ask him to sit, which said a lot to him. "Are you wondering what I'd rate our date last night?" he asked.

"No."

He smiled. "Eleven."

"That's nice."

He would've laughed at how casually she said it, except she might not take what he had to say next seriously. "We left things up in the air last night, Sara Beth, and I wanted to be sure we're on the same page, so there's no confusion, no awkwardness at work tomorrow."

"About what?"

"We talked about being friends with benefits."

Her jaw clenched. "*You* talked about it."

"Yes, I realized later that you hadn't weighed in on it at all."

"Because I'm not interested."

"In the friends part, or the benefits part?"

She crossed her arms. "The combination."

He pondered that. "So, we could be friends. Or we could be lovers. Those are the choices?"

"I didn't mean it that way."

Because he couldn't resist, he swirled a lock of her soft hair with his finger, then tucked it behind her ear. "How did you mean it, Sara Beth?"

"I like both aspects. I just don't like the label, friends with benefits. It implies a freedom to have *other* friends with benefits. When I'm with someone, I'm exclusive."

"I didn't sleep with Tricia." He ran his finger around her ear, heard her breath catch. Encouraged, he rubbed the lobe with his fingers.

"Did she offer?" Sara Beth asked. When he didn't reply, she said, "She did. I knew it."

"What difference does it make? We didn't."

She pushed his hand away. "Why not? She's so right for you. You have all that history. You fit into each other's lives."

There were so many reasons, ones that were becoming clearer to him by the minute as she stood there in her pajamas and teddy-bear slippers looking once again like the girl next door. He knew when the pajamas were off, she was a fantasy come to life.

"She doesn't make me laugh, Sara Beth," he said. "I don't make her laugh."

Her big brown eyes opened wide. "That's important to you?"

"Isn't it to you?"

"Well, yes, but—"

"And I don't watch her walk away, wanting to put my hands on her."

"You do that? Watch me like that? Want me like that?" Her voice had gone softer, and a little breathless.

"For months. And since you started working in the same room? It's been hell."

"I never would've guessed."

"I'm surprised you didn't catch me eyeing you with lust a hundred times, even in your scrubs. I want you, Sara Beth. Only you." He reached for her. "Come to bed with me."

"The couch is closer," she said, diving for him. At first he tried to slow her down, then he caught up and took over, undressing both of them in a rush of unbuttoning, unzipping, tugging and tossing. His memories of last night were shoved aside, replaced by this incredibly passionate, sexy, demanding version of the endlessly complex Sara Beth.

He took the few steps to her sofa, pulling her down with him, letting her straddle him, lifting her hair over her shoulders so that he could see all of her.

"You're all I've thought about all day long," she said, kissing him.

"Same for me." Every minute. Relived every moment of the night before, the urge to have her again all consuming.

"Good. I wanted you to be as tortured as I was," she said against his mouth.

"Wish granted."

He filled his hands with her breasts, savored their taste and texture until she dropped her head onto his shoulder.

"Hurry. Please hurry," she said, demand and need melding in her voice.

He found home with her as she sank onto him, then arched back, holding that pose, agony and ecstasy on her face, driving him over the brink, as well. She made glorious sounds, moved in a rhythm he helped establish and maintain, and exploded with a climax that came fast and loud. His followed, held, lingered…then eased, but slowly, the sensation lasting, fulfilling.

She fell against him, panting, her face pressed to his shoulder. "That was phenomenal," she said, breathing hard.

"Yeah."

A few seconds later she went rigid.

"What's wrong?" he asked, sure that something was.

She sat up, her skin gone pale, her eyes deep and dark. "No pocket protector."

He swallowed. "What's the timing like?"

"I have to look on my calendar. Because I'm not on the pill, it's not regular. In fact, it's very irregular."

She started to move off him. He cupped her arms, keeping her there. "The chances are slim."

"I know."

He was a doctor. He felt he had to bring up a possibility. "There's the morning-after pill...."

She shook her head, adamantly. "I can't. Is that what you want?"

He held her hands tightly. "I have spent my career trying to find ways to help people have children. No, it's not what I want. We'll cross that bridge if we come to it, okay?"

"Yeah."

"In the meantime, we'll make sure we use condoms. No sense tempting fate."

Fate. He'd left it to fate earlier as to whether or not he would see her tonight. And fate had seemed to put them in a situation where they hadn't been careful. He was always careful. He was pretty sure she was, too.

She finger-combed his hair, then locked her hands behind his neck. "Would you like to stay the night?" she asked, not looking completely sure of herself, or his answer.

"Do you have pocket protectors?"

She smiled, slow and sexy. "I'm pretty sure I do," she said. "If not, we can get creative."

"What do you say we get creative, with or without?" He kissed her, was relieved when she relaxed into him. "How big is your bed?" he asked.

"We'll both fit, provided I sleep on top of you."

Her sense of humor had returned—or had it? "Are you serious?"

She laughed. "It's queen size. I realize you're a king-size man—in more ways than one—but I think we'll fit okay." She wiggled her brows suggestively.

"Let's go give it a try."

"Eat my dust, Teddy Bear."

He caught up with her at her bedroom door and scooped her into his arms. They landed on the bed together.

"That was a quick recovery," she said, her eyes sparkling.

"I aim to please."

"Yeah? Show me."

He brushed his lips against hers. "It'll be my pleasure."

Chapter Eleven

Sara Beth gripped the lab telephone a little tighter. "Dr. Bonner is in a meeting, Ms. Goodheart."

"I told his mother that, Ms. McConnell. As I said, she asked if you were available until he's free." The efficient, professional, fifty-something administrative assistant who acted as the receptionist for the Armstrong Fertility Institute, Wilma Goodheart, had worked there longer than anyone, now that Sara Beth's mother had retired. She never gossiped, never called people by their first name, nor did she wear anything other than white button-down shirts and a gray or navy blue skirt. And she was one of the warmest people Sara Beth knew.

"I have no idea how long Dr. Bonner will be tied up,"

Sara Beth said. *And I don't want to entertain his mother for an hour.*

"She says they're meeting for lunch."

Sara Beth glanced at her watch. Almost noon. She shouldn't have to be alone with Penny Bonner for long....

Provided Ted remembered his mother was coming.

"Okay. I'll be right out," Sara Beth said into the phone. She left the lab, smoothed her hair and headed to the reception area.

It was Friday. Six days ago she and Ted had become lovers, exclusively as of Sunday, when he'd spent the night. On Monday they decided to sleep at their own houses, because he had to get up very early to meet someone before work. But by nine o'clock he'd showed up on her doorstep, hauled her to bed, then stayed until dawn, leaving her still cozy under the covers, her body aching pleasantly. They hadn't spent a night apart since, although they arrived at work separately so that no one would know.

Sara Beth didn't have any illusions. *Exclusive* didn't mean forever. It just meant for the moment. Until they were done. Or, according to Ted, until he forgot about her often enough that she gave up on him. He didn't understand that she admired him, that his single-minded dedication to his work was an appealing trait to her, especially since when he got single-minded about making love with her, she reaped the benefits of being the sole focus of his attention.

She entered the lobby as someone pushed open the heavy front door—Dr. Armstrong's wife, Emily Stanton

Armstrong. Sara Beth had been close to Mrs. Armstrong for many years, but then something had changed when Sara Beth was a teenager. Now Emily seemed to merely tolerate Sara Beth because she was Lisa's best friend, but Sara Beth hadn't been to the Armstrong home since Lisa first went off to college ten years ago.

"Hello, Mrs. Armstrong," Sara Beth said. "It's nice to see you again."

"Sara Beth."

"Emily!" Penny Bonner got up from the sofa and headed toward Emily Armstrong, her arms extended.

Panic whipped through Sara Beth. What if Ted's mother said something about him dating Sara Beth? Even Lisa didn't know they were sleeping together.

"Why, Penny, how wonderful you look." They exchanged polite hugs.

"I could say the same of you. Very rested."

"Isn't it amazing what a vacation will do? We went to Greece. To Mykonos, actually. We got home last night."

"How wonderful! I do adore that island. And that must mean that Gerald is doing well."

"I traveled with my sister. Gerald couldn't manage a trip like that anymore. Too much walking. He's nearing his eightieth birthday, you know."

Sara Beth felt like a third wheel as the two women, obviously old acquaintances, chatted. She also didn't want to excuse herself, in case she needed to interrupt.

"Please excuse my rudeness, Sara Beth," Penny said finally. "I haven't seen Emily in ages."

"It's fine." As long as she could monitor it.

"I'm meeting my daughter for lunch, anyway," Emily said to Penny. "She hates it when I'm late. Give my regards to Brant, my dear."

"And mine to Gerald."

"Of course. Sara Beth," Emily said in farewell, not making eye contact before she swept out of the room.

"We've served together on several committees and boards through the years," Penny said.

"Her daughter Lisa is my best friend." Sara Beth wondered if that would give her credibility with Ted's mother, let her think Sara Beth wasn't untested in their stratosphere. She'd been to formal parties at the Armstrong house and knew what to expect—and what was expected of her.

Penny leaned close. "I guess Greece is the place to go for face-lifts now."

Sara Beth tried not to smile too much at the catty remark. She'd noticed the difference in Emily, too. However, she didn't dare make a comment that could come back to haunt her. "Did you want company while you wait for Ted?"

"I'd like that, yes, and the chance to get to know you a little better. Do you mind if we wait here? I know places like employee lounges are usually busy this time of day."

"The lobby's fine." Sara Beth let her lead the way to her choice of seating, a small sofa by the front window. "I'm sorry I can't tell you when Ted's meeting might be over." She wondered if she should have Ms. Goodheart get a message to Ted, to remind him of his lunch date.

Since he hadn't told Sara Beth about it, she wondered if he remembered it himself.

"My son has been elusive since Valentine's Day." Penny's gaze was direct and only slightly accusatory, but Sara Beth didn't feel responsible for Ted's lack of contact with his parents.

"He's doing such important work." She was uncomfortable calling the woman Penny, so she didn't call her anything. "He works long days. And in his little bit of free time, he's been furnishing his loft." *Which should make you happy.*

"How long does it take to call his mother? I had to catch him by e-mail to arrange this lunch today." She settled back. "So, he's well?"

"Yes, very well."

"And his loft looks presentable, finally?"

"It looks like him." Sara Beth smiled at the thought. "Masculine, stylish, contemporary."

"Stylish?" She looked doubtful.

"He has his own style. It's represented in what he chose as furnishings. And he has some truly amazing art pieces. He said he learned about art from you."

"Did he? Sometimes one wonders what one's children take away from childhood." She looked pleased. "I suppose I'll have to drop by sometime and see for myself, since he hasn't extended an invitation."

"I think you'll like it." Sara Beth didn't know if he was going to throw a housewarming party as she'd suggested, so she didn't bring it up. His relationship with his mother was his business.

"I suppose you stay in touch with your mother. Daughters tend to be better at that than sons."

"I'm close to my mom." In this case, it was the mother who was doing the avoiding instead of the child. Sara Beth hadn't heard from her since her text message a week ago saying she was staying for another week. She should be back tomorrow, unless she decided to stay even longer.

"What does she think of Ted?"

"Actually, they haven't met. Mom's been out of town. You know," Sara Beth said, lowering her voice, "Ted and I haven't gone public. Since we work for the same company, we want to keep it quiet. I'm sure you understand."

"That makes good sense. Why make things potentially uncomfortable for others? Ted has always been aware of propriety."

And how would you feel if your model-of-propriety son found himself about to be a father? Sara Beth tried to ignore the possibility, but it simmered in her mind at times.

The lobby door opened and a woman entered. Wilma Goodheart smiled and raced around her desk to hug the new arrival.

"It's Mother's Day at the institute," Sara Beth murmured, amazed. "That would be my mom," she said to Penny.

"Well, how nice. We get to meet." She stood, then waited for Sara Beth to do the same.

The way this was going, Ted would probably show up—

Yep. Right on schedule. He walked into the lobby, a pink message slip in his hand. Ms. Goodheart must have sent a note to say his mother was here.

Since Sara Beth was the common denominator of the group, she made the introductions, although she moved everyone away from the reception desk. She was grateful that no one suggested they all have lunch together. Small blessings.

Ted sent her a woe-is-me look as he left the building with his mother. Sara Beth tried not to laugh.

She finally hugged her mother, welcoming her home. "You look rested, Mom. And more tan than I can remember you letting yourself get. I guess I don't need to ask if you enjoyed yourself."

"I had a wonderful time. I'd go right back tomorrow."

"Let's have lunch. You can tell me all about it," Sara Beth offered.

"It'll have to wait. Wilma and I are going out. What's your schedule for the weekend?"

"Busy. Full." She and Ted planned a drive to the shore, were going to stay overnight, be out where they wouldn't run into people they knew. "Tuesday, as usual, then?"

"That's fine." She bent close to Sara Beth. "Are you and Ted an item now? You and his mother were huddled awfully close."

"I've seen him a few times. We're not being open about it, so don't talk to Ms. Goodheart about it, okay?"

Grace raised a hand as if swearing to it. "But remember this, Sara Beth. If you can't be public about a relationship, something's not right about it. It's an additional stress, and it can lead to arguments and hurt feelings. Be careful, okay? Please, sweetheart. Guard your heart."

Sara Beth hugged her mother, whose cautionary words rang true, unfortunately. Secrets weren't good, and eventually were exposed. "Thanks, Mom. I'll be careful."

Although it was hard to guard her heart when it was already being held captive, even if its captor didn't realize it…

Sara Beth went for a walk during her lunch hour, needing to be alone and away from the institute. It was nearly spring. Green was beginning to be a dominant color after the drab browns and grays of winter, and was always a welcome sight. Rebirth. New beginnings. Yes, spring had always appealed to her.

And now that'd she'd resigned herself to never seeing her mother's file, she could have an especially good new beginning this season, a truly fresh start. She would never know her father, but knew herself. Liked herself. That counted for a lot.

Ted was already in the lab working when Sara Beth returned. So was Chance. They acknowledged her but didn't stop their discussion, which was riddled with scientific lingo she couldn't hear well enough to make sense of. She finished the box of materials Ted had brought up the day before and needed more.

She waited for a good time to interrupt, then suddenly Ted left the room.

"Wait," she called out. "I need—" But the door shut, cutting off her words.

Chance met her gaze. "He'll be back. He's in one of

his zones and, frankly, I don't want to break into his thoughts. He's onto something. What is it you need?"

"Files. I'm not authorized to access the vault."

"I forgot. Why not, anyway?"

"I don't know. It wasn't something I'd ever had to do before, so it'd never concerned me."

Chance picked up the phone and dialed. "Lisa, it's Chance. Can I get authorization for Sara Beth to get files from the vault?… Right now…. Okay. How about temporary access?… Thanks." He hung up, then looked at his pager, which had gone off. "She'll meet you there. One time only, at least for now, so grab a couple of boxes while you're at it. I've got to get to the clinic."

It would be a special kind of torture, Sara Beth decided, being allowed in the vault while accompanied by a witness. Torture, and a test of her newfound sense of peace at having come to terms with never seeing her mother's file. Still, her legs were unsteady as she took the stairs down to the basement, carrying the box of files she'd just finished. She stumbled twice, her heart pounding so hard she couldn't hear anything but the thundering beat.

Lisa was right behind her.

"This place has always creeped me out," Lisa said.

"More lights would be a plus."

"Maybe. It's just old and scary." She slid her ID in the slot and pulled the steel door open. "Need some help?" Lisa asked.

Sara Beth's stomach churned as she went inside. She looked at the dates on the side of the box. "I need to refile these and fill up a couple more boxes from the next sequential dates."

Because the vault had previously been a panic room before the institute was rebuilt, it still contained a sofa and chair, as well as a bathroom. File storage was a room beyond the furnishings, out of direct sight. She and Lisa located where the folders belonged and returned them.

"Let's hurry. I hate being down here," Lisa said, shoving the empty box close to Sara Beth and grabbing another one.

A piece of her mourned the lost opportunity. She couldn't even manage a smile to soothe Lisa's fear of the dark. They filled the boxes without conversation between them, a rarity.

"Need some help?" Ted came into the room, making it seem half its size.

"Yes." Lisa headed out the door, calling back to Ted, "You can lock up. I'm outta here."

Her footsteps echoed as she ran up the stairs.

"Alone at last," he said, slipping his arms around Sara Beth, bending to kiss her. "I've been wanting to do this all day."

She couldn't kiss him. She couldn't even move. With Lisa gone, could she ask Ted for his help? Ask him to do something unethical? He'd found a six-dollar error on a furniture bill totaling thousands and had insisted on paying it. He'd reached the highest level of achievement the Boy Scouts had.

Everything he said and did advertised him as a highly

principled, ethical man. No, she couldn't ask him, couldn't back him into a corner like that. He would have to turn her down.

So she hugged him instead, then she did the only thing she could.

"Would you mind taking that box to the lab," she asked him, "while I finish packing this one?"

"I can carry two boxes, Sara Beth." He flexed his muscles and grinned.

She almost sighed. Apparently it just wasn't meant to be.

She gave it one last shot. "I think I'll pack four boxes. Then neither of us will have to come back down for a while."

"If ever," he said, sliding the last files into a box as she passed them to him. "I figure we'll have all the statistics we need by then." He hefted both boxes. "I'll be back."

A five-minute window of opportunity opened up for Sara Beth.

Not enough time to debate what to do. Only time enough for one thing—action.

Chapter Twelve

"Are you sure?" Lisa asked Ted in a closed-door meeting in Derek's office almost a week later. Chance leaned against a file cabinet. Paul paced. Lisa and Ted sat in visitor's chairs across from Derek's desk.

"Positive," Ted said.

"You have proof?"

"In the report I just handed you are statistics confirming that the institute has had a three-year run of above-average numbers of multiple births, enough to be suspicious that too many embryos were implanted. However, we also found similar statistics twice before in the institute's history, or at least in the past twenty years, which is as far back as we went for now. We believe in each case that it was purely happenstance. No one breached protocols."

"I told you," Derek said smugly. "We can use this information to our benefit right now. Let it be known that our in vitro procedures have a higher-than-average success rate. Business will boom."

Ted disliked Derek more each day, had come to resent the way he stopped by the lab almost daily, asking for a full accounting on the day's work, as if Ted and Chance were shirking their duties. They had decided not to tell Derek about their trial study until preliminary results were in.

"Just don't guarantee anything," Chance cautioned Derek. "As Ted said, it's happened before. Following that logic, it's likely to ease off, too."

Ted agreed. "What's important for the moment is that we found incomplete reporting of critical statistics. Sara Beth has done a thorough job of compiling the information and updating it into the new computer system. You'll be able to pull out any statistic you need, should anyone question the institute again."

"I can't tell you how grateful I am," Lisa said, then looked at her chief-of-staff brother, Paul. "It was hard having that shadow hanging over us."

"Yes, let me add my thanks," Paul said, something Derek hadn't bothered to do. "I think Lisa talked to you about writing a best-practices manual of lab protocols? It will be a required checklist that everyone will adhere to and enter into the computer. How long do you think that would take?"

"A week or so," Ted said. When they were finished with it, Sara Beth would return to her regular duties. He wouldn't get to turn his head and see her anytime he wanted. Couldn't watch her stretch out the kinks after an hour in front of the computer.

Or watch her stare into space now and then, unfocused. Was she pregnant and hadn't told him yet?

He thought back. She'd been distracted for almost a week—since the day they'd brought up the last boxes from the vault, actually. Their weekend at the shore hadn't been as relaxing as it should've been, even though they'd had all the privacy they'd sought.

"We need to bring Ramona in on this," Derek was saying. "Have her come up with a PR plan to let people know that the Armstrong Fertility Institute is seeing such great success. This is a good time for a push."

Paul nodded in agreement. Ted had met Paul's fiancée, Ramona, a few times and liked her. She had a good head on her shoulders and was an excellent strategist. Once a reporter, the institute had hired her as their public relations strategist.

"Let's talk to her together," Paul said finally, then glanced at his watch. "Thank you all again for your hard work to clear up this problem. I hope we can move forward now without distraction."

Ted and Chance walked down the hall to the lab.

"I don't suppose this means the end of Derek's visits to the lab," Chance muttered.

"I doubt it. He's always seemed more interested in our research than the disproportionate number of births.

I don't understand why he wasn't worried about that. The institute stood to lose a lot of money if, in fact, we had been implanting too many embryos, thus exaggerating results."

"I agree. The institute stands to pull in a hell of a lot of more money if our research yields results. And the sky's the limit if we can get beyond elevating sperm count and motility."

"He does seem interested more in dollars than reputation, doesn't he?" Ted mused. "I guess you don't become CFO without money being the main focus of your thinking."

"Speaking of the main focus of your thinking," Chase said. "You and nurse Sara Beth seem to have become…close."

Ted had promised Sara Beth he wouldn't talk to anyone about her, and he'd agreed. "I like her. It's been nice having her around. Breaks up the tedium when you're not there."

"Breaks up the tedium? Right." Chance laughed. "You're not fooling anyone."

Were they that obvious? Or had someone seen them together away from the office?

"You watch her with the same intensity as you conduct a tricky experiment. I think when you've finished writing the manual and she comes back to work with me, you should ask her out. I'm sure she would say yes."

Ted relaxed. "Maybe."

They went into the lab, finding it empty, except for a note from Sara Beth, telling him to call her when he wanted to start working on the manual, which he did right away.

He and Chance had barely gotten their computers up and running when the door opened, but Lisa came in, not Sara Beth.

"We have a problem," she said, handing them a sheet of paper bearing the Breyer Medical Center letterhead.

Before the door shut, Sara Beth arrived and said a happy good morning.

"Would you mind coming back in about fifteen minutes, please?" Lisa said to her.

"She can stay," Ted said as Chance grabbed the letter and swore.

"What's going on?" Sara Beth asked, coming closer, her gaze moving from person to person then staying on Ted.

"Our former employer is accusing us of unethical behavior regarding funding issues during our years there," Ted explained.

"No way," Sara Beth said. "No possible way."

"I appreciate your faith, but the burden of proof will be ours," Ted informed.

Sara Beth put a hand on Ted's. "You are the most ethical man on the planet. There's no way you've done anything wrong."

Guilt took a bite out of Ted. By not telling Derek or Paul that he and Chance had entered into a trial study with one subject, they weren't being forthcoming. And if a best-practices protocol manual had been in place a week ago, Ted couldn't have justified the secretive project.

"Are we ever going to be allowed to just do our jobs?" Chance asked, frustration in his voice. He threw the paper onto the lab counter and walked away to look out the window at the parking lot. "Ted and I came here to get away from the bureaucracy that Breyer burdened us with, constantly tying our hands. We've already made progress here that would've taken us years had we stayed there."

"What do they want?" Sara Beth asked.

"They say we recruited and used funds dishonestly," Ted answered. "That we promised impossible results."

"Can you think of anything they might have that they could use against you?" Lisa asked.

Ted shook his head as Chance almost shouted, "No. Nothing. We tried to do what we'd been hired to do. Even that was a daily uphill battle. We had to write our own grants, meet with potential investors, beat the drum. We were spending most of our time raising funds. It's no wonder we couldn't accomplish anything of value."

"Then it sounds like sour grapes to me," Lisa said. "When you left, their funds dried up."

"Did you keep copies of all the funding we got there?" Chance asked Ted.

"It's all on my home computer."

"I can't cancel my appointments today," Chance said. "But let's meet at your place tonight and go over it."

"Okay. If Lisa's right, and they're just trying to ruin our reputation, then we need to fight fire with fire. Let's ask Ramona to help, too. We could use a spin doctor's opinion."

Chance came back to the table. "If push comes to

shove, Ted and I know some things that Breyer wouldn't want made public."

Ted shifted uncomfortably. Yes, they knew secrets, which was one of the reasons why they'd left. They hadn't agreed with Breyer's methods all the time. "I hope it doesn't come to that," Ted said. "I don't want to be associated with dragging Breyer's name through the mud, either."

"The last thing we need is a loss of funding," Lisa said, her jaw tight. "I'll talk to Paul and Ramona. Um, I'd like to keep Derek out of the loop for a couple of days. See what we can come up with first." She looked at Chance, then Ted.

"No problem," Ted said.

Chance raised a hand in agreement.

"All right. Give me a call at home tonight after you've taken a look at your records." She walked out.

Chance swiped the accusatory letter from the counter, swearing as it drifted to the floor. "We left there to get away from chaos. Since then we've dealt with one problem after another. When will it end?"

He yanked open the door and left, angry and frustrated. Ted felt exactly the same. He just tended to internalize his emotions more.

"One scandal door closes and another one opens," he said to Sara Beth.

"You'll be cleared."

"It may not matter. Tarnished reputations are hard to polish." Like Chase, he was tired of the upheavals. "I've never been one to have secrets, Sara Beth."

Her sympathetic expression became guarded. "Are you still talking about your work?"

He shook his head.

"You want to go public about us," she said, not as a question, already knowing the answer.

"Not this second, but as soon as you stop working for me."

"Why?"

"Because right now I'd really like to hold you, and I can't do that. Anyone could walk by."

"There's always the supply closet."

Her response was so quick and unexpected, he laughed, then he hauled her to the closet, shut them inside and held her, just held her, until his anger dispersed, replaced with need for her, the incredible Sara Beth O'Connell, one of the kindest, most beautiful women he'd ever met.

He didn't want to keep her a secret anymore.

In the dark, he found her mouth with his, the taste of her familiar now, yet always arousing and exciting. They rarely spent a night apart, often talking into the late hours before falling asleep, her head on his shoulder, his arm around her, hers across his chest, then waking up in the morning with her wrapped in his arms.

One thing they'd avoided talking about was the possibility she could be pregnant. How long could they pretend not to notice?

"We'll go public," he said against her lips.

"We'll talk about it."

"Ted?" Derek's voice reached them inside the closet.

They went utterly still. Sara Beth pressed her face to

Ted's chest. Her shoulders shook. Laughing? Seriously? She was the one who was so worried about going public, and she was laughing?

"Where could he have gone?" Derek said, his voice fading, then silence.

After a few seconds, Ted turned the knob slowly and peeked out. The room was empty. "Hurry up," he said, patting Sara Beth on the backside.

She laughed and scurried out just as Derek looked through the window and frowned. "Uh-oh," she said when Derek opened the door.

"Where were you? I was just here."

"Restroom," Ted and Sara Beth said simultaneously. He didn't dare look at her.

She headed to the door, not making eye contact, either. "I'll arrange my schedule so that we can start on the manual tomorrow, Dr. Bonner," she said.

"That'd be great, Ms. O'Connell, thanks." He looked down for a second to smooth his expression, and spotted the letter from the Breyer Medical Center lying on the floor, face up. Had Derek seen it when he'd been in a few minutes earlier? Ted figured him for a good poker player. If he'd read it, he would probably wait to see how long Ted took to tell him.

He scooped it up, folded it and stuck it in his back pocket. "What can I do for you, Derek?"

He didn't answer immediately. "I realized I hadn't thanked you for the work you did on the stats. Good job."

Ted figured Derek called it a good job because it had turned out well. If it hadn't…

"All I did was compile and run the numbers. But I'm glad it's over." He grabbed his lab coat from the coat rack near Sara Beth's desk. The room seemed empty without her. "Anything else?" Ted asked, waiting for the ax to fall.

"Just wanted an update."

"Nothing's changed since yesterday. When there's something to report, I will."

"I know you think I'm pushing too hard. But just word of the possibility we're close to a treatment would sustain us for now."

"Sustain us for now?" Ted repeated. "Is there a problem with keeping the research going?"

Derek shifted a little. "The program is expensive. Setting up the lab to your specifications was costly. Your salaries. So far, there haven't been any returns."

"That's the burden of research." What was going on? Was Derek saying the institute was having financial problems?

"I realize that. We just have to hope there are no more rumors or scandals. We had some close calls."

Ted nodded. Lisa had asked him to keep quiet, so he would, for now—and because he didn't trust Derek himself.

After Derek left, Sara Beth quietly slipped in.

He smiled. "The coast is clear." *Except Derek may have read the letter.*

"So, everything is okay?"

"I wouldn't go that far. But we'll have to skip seeing each other tonight. Chance and I may pull an all-nighter trying to figure this out."

"I'll try to hook up with my mom, since she canceled on me last night."

"Call me when you're getting off the bus."

She cocked her head. "How will you explain that to Chance?"

"I'll figure out something. Have a nice time with your mom."

"Thanks. I'll miss you."

He didn't say anything in return. He probably should, because he would miss her, for sure, but his confusion over her unwillingness to let their relationship be public held him back. Maybe she saw what they had as temporary. "Talk to you later," he said.

A little light went out of her eyes. He was sorry for that, but it was the best he could do for now.

Chapter Thirteen

"You're different, Mom," Sara Beth said as they lingered that night over dessert, apple tarts with cinnamon ice cream. The restaurant was one of her favorites, a small café that offered comfort food with a twist. For dinner she'd had chicken and dumplings, prepared with a delicate touch and fresh herbs. "Are you sure you don't have a man in your life?"

"I'm sure." Grace sipped her coffee, eyeing Sara Beth over the rim. "I retired months ago, but I hadn't gotten the hang of it yet. Now I have."

"Shouldn't that mean you'd be more relaxed? Because you're not. In fact, you're edgier. And you're not being forthcoming about your trip."

"There's just so little to tell, sweetheart. I didn't do much but read, go for walks, eat and sleep."

"You didn't take any tours? Didn't see the Mayan ruins? And where are your photographs? You always took a ton of pictures wherever we went."

"I was recording your life, Sara Beth. Hence, the many scrapbooks of years gone by. And you haven't said a word about Dr. Bonner."

"There's just so little to tell." Sara Beth flashed a smile.

"Touché."

For almost a week Sara Beth had lived with what she'd done, taking advantage of the unexpected opportunity in the vault to look for her mother's file. And for almost a week she'd lived with the results, not telling anyone that she'd looked—and discovered it was missing. Ted had noticed there was something wrong. She'd denied it.

But she also knew she would never come to terms with it unless she talked to her mother.

Sara Beth's heart lodged in her throat at the thought of asking, but she had to know. "Why is your file not in the vault?" Sara Beth blurted out, the words almost choking her.

For a long time, Grace said nothing. Then, finally, "It took you a long time to look. You've worked there for twelve years, six years full-time."

Which was no answer. Sara Beth's anxiety about asking turned to frustration—again. "Because I wanted you to be the one to tell me."

"Tell you what?"

"Who my father is."

"I've told you all your life."

"An anonymous donor." Sara Beth shoved her dessert away, unfinished. "But there's no record of your procedure, not even someone using an alias that came close to matching you, either."

"Think about that for a moment. I worked there for over thirty years. A lot of people had access to patient files."

"Meaning you removed it so that no one would know?"

"Everyone knew I'd gotten pregnant with help from the institute. But the details weren't—and aren't—anyone else's business."

"I don't count?"

Grace sat back. "What would you do with that information, if you had it?"

"I don't know. I just have a need to know where I came from. I feel like half of me is missing. Or a third," she said, correcting herself. "I know you, and I know myself. I'd like to know the missing link. Do I have siblings? What about a health history?" *Would he have brought me a Valentine if he'd known about me?*

"Many of the donors all those years ago were college students, Sara Beth, who were in it for the money. They were able to walk away without feeling any attachment for a child who might come of that generous donation. Do you think it would matter now, after all this time?"

"It could, perhaps even more so. Maybe he never had other children. Or whatever the reasons might be. I could contact him through an intermediary. If he wants to be left alone, I would respect that."

Their server approached, a reminder that they were in public. They paid their bill then left the café, heading back to Grace's house and the bus stop nearby.

"Let me think about it, okay, sweetheart?"

It was the first time her mother had dangled any kind of carrot in front of her. What could she say? It wasn't the right time to keep pushing. "Thank you."

Rain began to fall, light but steady, putting an end to their conversation as they each opened an umbrella, creating distance between them. They reached the bus stop.

"You don't need to wait with me in the rain, Mom. Go on inside."

"I'm not made of sugar."

Sara Beth laughed. "No, you're not. Neither am I, in large part because you made me that way. Thanks for being such a good life coach."

"I would say you're welcome, except I haven't entirely succeeded."

"I think I turned out okay."

"Despite my many warnings, you've fallen in love with a doctor, and one you work with, at that."

"I haven't—"

"Oh, sweetheart. You have. Do you think I don't know your every expression? That it isn't always what you say but what you don't say that speaks the loudest? You haven't volunteered a word about him all night."

Sara Beth could feel herself closing up. "Because I know how you feel about him. It. The situation itself."

"For good reasons. I was a nurse for a long time. I've

seen it happen again and again. It's one of the oldest professional fantasies in the world—nurse falls for doctor. Do you know how seldom it works out?"

"I'm having fun, Mom."

"People will talk. Do you want that? Your coworkers will be whispering behind your back. It can cause irreparable harm to your ability to supervise if they don't respect you."

Sara Beth knew all that, had known it all along without saying the words out loud. "We won't go public with our relationship unless it becomes something more permanent."

"You mean, marriage?" Grace looked shocked, even horrified. She clamped a hand on Sara Beth's arm. "Sweetheart, please don't get your hopes up about such a thing. Ted Bonner is not only a doctor, he's from one of the oldest, wealthiest families in Boston. If you don't think his parents have plans for their only son, you've totally deluded yourself about him."

The bus pulled up, splashing an arc of water onto the sidewalk, making them jump back. Manipulating their umbrellas, they managed a quick, tense hug, then Sara Beth climbed onto the steamy vehicle, the windows too fogged up to see her mother as it pulled away from the curb.

Sara Beth drew a circle on the wet, foggy window, adding two dots for eyes, a short line for a nose, then a down-turned mouth. Her mother was right. Sara Beth *had* gotten her hopes up about Ted, maybe because he was willing to let it be known they were dating, where she'd been cautious because of lifelong warnings from her mother, which had gotten more intense now that Sara Beth was seeing Ted, making it real, not just hypothetical.

Which made Sara Beth also wonder if her mother had experienced what she so fiercely cautioned about. Had she loved a doctor? Been used and dumped? There had to be a reason why she never dated.

As soon as Sara Beth got off the bus, she dialed Ted's number. He picked up right away.

"How was your evening?" he asked.

"I had an incredible *meal*."

He laughed. "See why I don't make a habit of going out to dinner with my parents?"

She smiled. It was obvious that he liked his parents just fine. "How's it going with you? Are you finding anything?"

"It's been interesting. We may have found something. Mostly we think because we're not there anymore, the renewals on the grants probably didn't happen. We don't even know if they replaced us."

"They ran a lousy business," Chance shouted in the background, being much less circumspect than Ted. "Now they're paying for it."

"Except they want us to pay for it, too," Ted added. "At least with our reputation."

Sara Beth dodged a puddle. She picked up speed as the rain started battering her. "What's next?"

"Is it raining?" He went silent for a few seconds. "It's pouring. I hadn't noticed. How close are you to home?"

"I'm running up my walkway right now." She shoved

her key in the lock and rushed inside as a crack of lightning lit up the sky, followed by low, rumbling thunder. "Safe and sound," she said, then climbed the stairs. "So, again, what's next?"

"We're having lunch tomorrow with Ramona, away from the institute. She's doing some research on her own, as well as talking to a lawyer. We ended up telling Paul about the accusations. I didn't want to ask Ramona to keep it from her own fiancé."

"But you're still keeping Derek in the dark?"

"For now."

"I'll let you get back to work, then. My bed's going to be lonely tonight." She smiled at his silence, stuck as he was with Chance within earshot.

"Same here," he said, although not in a sexy way.

She tugged her raincoat off and hung it up outside her front door, toed off her boots, then went inside. "Remember my tiger-striped nightgown?"

"Down to the last detail."

"When you go to bed tonight, picture me wearing that."

"Do you remember the results of that particular experiment?" he asked.

She remembered every erotic detail—the fire in his eyes, the power of his erection, bold and flattering. How he'd looked at her as if she was the only woman in the world. She loved how he could focus like that, and not be distracted.

"I remember," she said, amazed at how aroused she'd become just from the memories. "If you want to call me after Chance leaves and you're in bed, we could talk about it. I've never had phone sex, but it might be an adventure. Not as good as the real thing, of course, but—"

"Experiments are only as effective as the results."

"Then we'll have to test the theory, won't we?" She was caught between pulse-pounding arousal and an image of him being frustrated at not being free to talk, which made her smile.

"It should prove to be an interesting discussion. I'll talk to you later, Sara Beth."

"For sure." She ended the call, shook herself into awareness again, then got ready for bed, keeping her phone close by.

When it rang finally, she drew a settling breath before she answered—to a dial tone. It rang again, then she realized it wasn't her phone but her doorbell. She slid her feet into her teddy-bear slippers and hurried down the stairs.

"Liar," he said, drenched with rain.

He seemed angry. "Ted—"

"I had to park three blocks away, and I ran all the way here, and you're not wearing the tiger. You've got your flannel fire engines on."

She smiled innocently. "It's cold without you."

He picked her up, carried her up the stairs, her pajamas getting wet where they touched him. He went directly into her bedroom, stood her by her bed and un-buttoned her top only enough to yank it over her head.

"I'm not complaining, Sara Beth. I have fond memories of these pajamas." He shoved her bottoms off, kneeling before her, teasing her by trailing his tongue along her skin as he exposed it. Then she helped him get rid of his wet clothes.

"No experiment, after all?" she asked, not at all unhappy about it.

"Did I say that? I think a little experimentation is definitely in order." He backed her up until she came against the bed, then fell onto it. "I think we should see how long it takes to make you beg."

She laughed, breathless and excited. He had her begging almost immediately, but he wouldn't give her the satisfaction of accommodating her, dragging it out until she couldn't think about anything but him, every aspect of him, so that when he finally plunged inside her, she was swept into a climax instantly and held suspended, so that she had no idea how much time passed, five seconds or five minutes. He started to pull out, and she wrapped her legs around him, knew the moment he gave in and let it happen for himself, too. Then he was draped over her, his weight on his arms enough that she could breathe, but his own breathing was heavy, his body adhered to hers.

Awareness crept in, like the sun coming up, first in pink then full light. He lifted his head and met her gaze.

"No protection," they said at the same time.

Then, "I got carried away," also simultaneously, which drew a shaky laugh from her and an even more serious look in his eyes.

"I have never been irresponsible, Sara Beth. I don't know…." He stopped and shook his head, then rolled with her to his side and gathered her close.

"Neither have I." She wanted to ask him what he thought that meant, that two such highly responsible people could be so irresponsible about sex, but she didn't ask, wasn't sure she wanted to know his answer. She only knew how she felt.

She also didn't want to trap him with a pregnancy.

He kissed her hair, tucked her closer, into their usual presleep configuration. "Sleep," he said.

Surprisingly, she did.

Chapter Fourteen

The Coach House Diner was within walking distance of the Armstrong Fertility Institute. Ted and Chance took a late lunch, hoping to avoid the possibility of running into anyone from the institute. Tall, blond Ramona Tate was already seated at a table in the fifties-style diner with its old-fashioned counter and leatherette booths. They hadn't even finished their greetings before Chance was pointing to a booth, tucked back in a corner.

"Let's sit over there. It's a better spot to see who comes in the door," he said. "Have you ordered, Ramona?"

"I was waiting for you."

"Thanks so much for your help," Ted said as they settled into the new booth.

"I get enormous satisfaction catching bad guys in the act."

"Hi, Jenny," Chance said to the waitress who approached with three glasses of ice water. "How are you this beautiful day?"

Because Chance had turned on the famous Demetrios charm, Ted took a closer look at the waitress, who was blond, like Ramona, but curvier.

"Have you looked outside, Dr. Demetrios?" Jenny asked.

"I like the rain. Don't you?"

"I guess that depends on whether I'm already at work or coming to work."

"Makes sense." He ignored the menu she'd set in front of him.

"Your usual?" she asked.

Ted and Ramona exchanged glances. It was as if they didn't exist.

"That'd be great," Chance said, then seemed to wake up to the fact he wasn't alone. "Have you decided?" he asked.

"We haven't had a chance to look at the menu yet." Ted bit back a smile and opened his menu. Ramona did the same, except she was grinning.

"I'll be back in a couple of minutes." Jenny left, without even asking for their drink orders.

"Come here often?" Ted asked Chance, studying the menu.

"Fairly. Why?" The belligerence in his voice made Ted look up.

"What do you recommend?" Ted asked.

Chance settled back, then toyed with his water glass. "I usually get the club sandwich and a cup of vegetable soup."

"Sounds good to me." Ted watched Jenny talk to some customers at the counter while occasionally glancing Chance's way—or maybe she was waiting for Ramona to set aside her menu, too, signaling she'd made her choice.

When their orders were taken and drinks served, they got down to business.

"Paul and I talked about your situation," Ramona said, twirling her engagement ring. "We agree that Breyer is probably being spiteful. If they move ahead with their threat, you'd have legal recourse, but for now, they haven't stated their intentions. So, we need to fight back before it gets to that point. Did you find anything new since we talked last night?"

"We're pretty sure the 'unethical funding' they're referring to is a grant that Breyer accepted from a company called McAdams Fertility Corp. They make a vitamin concoction they bill as a cure. Since we began our own research with a similar base, McAdams had a vested interest in our results."

"Meaning they expected our research to be tilted in their favor," Chance added. "But we didn't go after their money and, in fact, would have rejected the idea of writing a grant for it, had we known. We were forced to accept it, after the fact. That was ultimately what spurred us to move on."

"McAdams probably demanded their money back,"

Ted said. "And Breyer won't refund it, deciding to put the blame on us. We don't know that for sure, but it's the only scenario that makes sense."

"We could also nip this in the bud right now," Chance said with a sideways glance at Ted.

Ted had no doubt what Chance meant. "We're not going down that path. That would make us no better than them."

"Why? What?" Ramona asked.

Chance raised his water glass toward Ted. "We know something they don't think we know."

"And we're not using that knowledge," Ted said. "It doesn't affect patient care, but they *could* lose patients. They may not be cutting-edge in research anymore, but they still do good work with infertility issues."

"Well, if you won't stoop to their level…" Ramona smiled. "Actually, I admire that. It also makes me totally believe you when you say you're innocent. So, let's come up with a plan."

They ate lunch and talked, lingering until Chance was paged to return. He went up to the waitress, Jenny, handed her some money, said something to make her blush, then left.

"Smitten," Ramona said.

"Looks like it."

Ted and Ramona walked back to the institute later, then stood in the hall to finish their conversation.

"So, Ted, were you always this ethical?"

"It's always been important to me," he said, but his thoughts drifted to Sara Beth.

"Do you find it hard to live up to the standards?"

"What? No—Yes." He searched for the right thing to say when his head was filled with the fact he twice hadn't worn a condom with Sara Beth, breaking ethical standards, as Ramona called them. So much for being prepared.

Finally he said, "Doing the right thing matters to me. Always has, always will."

"I hope you're not a dying breed." Ramona opened the door to the employee lounge saying, "I'm going to grab some coffee to take to my office."

Sara Beth almost tumbled out.

Ted caught her before she fell right into Ramona.

"I'm so sorry!" Sara Beth said, straightening. "I'm glad I wasn't carrying a cup of hot coffee."

"Me, too." Ramona smiled. "How are you, Sara Beth?"

Her gaze flickered to Ted briefly then back to Ramona. "I'm very well, thanks. Have you and my favorite quasibrother set a date yet?"

Ramona laughed. "I forget that you and Paul know each other so well. No, not yet. Speaking of siblings, I may have found my half sister."

"Oh, how wonderful! Have you met her?"

"Not yet. We're trying to be sure of the connection. She's apparently an heiress living in New York City. Her name is Victoria Welsh."

"It's good that you're being careful of her feelings. I've heard a lot of stories about children who find out who their donor mother or father is, and have a hard time dealing with it."

"Exactly. We are using caution and care." She touched Ted's arm. "Maybe you don't know what I'm talking about?"

"I'm clueless."

"Sara Beth can fill you in. I don't mind sharing with certain people."

She said goodbye, then Ted and Sara Beth walked to the lab together.

"So, what's her story?" he asked.

"Her mother donated eggs here many years ago, and now she needs a bone-marrow transplant. Ramona isn't a match, so she's been trying to track down possible biological children. Looks like it may happen, after all. It's going to be complicated, no matter how careful they are with this Victoria."

She went quiet, not saying another word until they were inside the lab. They'd started writing the manual that morning, but he'd taken every opportunity to stall. She'd teased him about it.

But the elephant in the room was the fact they'd now slept together twice without protection, and neither of them wanted to talk about it. He guessed he should open the discussion....

"I'm a product of artificial insemination," she said out of the blue.

He just stared at her, at her hands tightly clenched, at how her cheekbones seemed sharp and her face pale.

"I don't know who my father is."

It was the sort of thing Ted wasn't good at—dealing with people's emotional issues, even someone he liked as much as Sara Beth, but he knew he had to say something. "Do you want to know?"

She gave him a sharp look. "Wouldn't you?"

Yes, he probably would. "Your mother won't tell you?"

"The donor was anonymous. My mother had been working here a few years when she decided to do it."

Ted guided Sara Beth to a chair, then sat beside her. "We hear all the time about children who track down donors," he said. "Ramona's a good example. Maybe you could talk to Paul and Lisa about letting you have the information, or letting one of them try to track down the donor, just like Ramona did."

"There's no file. It's gone."

"How do you know?"

"I hunted for it." She hadn't been looking him in the eye. Now she did. "While you were taking up boxes last week."

He wasn't sure what he was feeling about that, except that it didn't sit well. "Why didn't you tell me?"

"Because you're…you. I couldn't involve you." Her smile was small and tight. "And now you know I'm not as ethical as you."

"Under the same circumstances, I'm not sure I wouldn't have done the same thing." He wondered why he wasn't upset by her revelation. In fact, he was more upset that she'd kept it from him until now. No wonder she'd been different last weekend at the shore, less talkative, more distracted. He wished she'd confided in him earlier. That she'd trusted him enough.

"The end justifies the means?" she asked. "That's

generous, but I guess it doesn't matter. My mother said she couldn't leave her own information here for others to see. I understand that. Maybe I'll find it in her personal belongings years from now. Maybe she destroyed it."

Her eyes welled. Ted felt more helpless than he ever had. He rubbed her back. "I can't imagine what that would be like—not knowing."

She pressed the corners of her eyes. "It's gotten harder lately, and I don't even know why. On Valentine's Day—" She stopped, took a shaky breath.

"What happened?" Other than coming to his rescue that day…

"I was in a grocery store, and there was a dad buying a stuffed bear and some candy for his little girl. It about killed me, you know? I never had that, never was daddy's little girl. Sometimes I watch dads playing with kids in the park and my heart hurts. Not just aches, but hurts." She pushed her hand to her mouth. "I'm sorry for dumping this on you. I was excited for Ramona to find that connection—not only to help her mother, but because it also gives her a sister. It just hit me hard. I'll be fine. Really."

She got up. "I'll be back."

Ted didn't move for a minute, then he opened a desk drawer and took out an employee roster. It hadn't been updated since Sara Beth's mother had retired. He found Grace O'Connell's address, wrote it down, stuffed it in his pocket.

After all that Sara Beth had done for him, it was time he returned the favor.

And what if she *was* pregnant? He needed to step up to the plate *now.*

He left her a note, then for the first time in his life, played hooky from work.

He should have called first—etiquette demanded it— but he was afraid she wouldn't agree to see him. So, he surprised Grace O'Connell, ambushed her by showing up on her doorstep.

He hesitated when he saw her, because either she suffered from allergies or she'd been crying. Should he ask what was wrong? She probably wouldn't answer. Why would she, without knowing him? He was grateful, at least, that they'd met in the lobby at the institute, so she recognized him.

"This isn't a good time," she said.

"I wouldn't bother you if it wasn't extremely important, Ms. O'Connell. Please. Just a few minutes of your time."

"All right," she said with obvious reluctance.

Ted stepped inside, noticing that she and her daughter had similar styles in furnishings and art.

"Thank you for seeing me."

"You didn't give me a lot of choice, did you? Have a seat."

He saw Sara Beth in her, different hair and eye color, but similarities in their facial structure and body type.

She sat in a chair across from him. "What can I do for you?"

"I've been seeing your daughter."

"She told me."

Okay. That made it easier. He didn't have to break that particular ice. "Sara Beth talked with me today about how she was conceived."

Her mouth hardened. "I see."

"It weighs on her a lot that she doesn't know who fathered her."

"You're not telling me something I haven't known for most of her life." Her fingers curved into the chair arms. "Your point is?"

"She's in a great deal of pain because of it. I don't like to see her in pain."

"Do you think I do? You think it gives me pleasure to see her struggle with it?" Her voice kept rising as she defended herself. "What kind of mother do you think I am?"

"A loving one, according to Sara Beth. Except with regard to this particular issue, I gather."

She calmed a little. "My hands are tied by anonymity. You know how that works, right, *Dr.* Bonner?"

"Please call me Ted. Of course I do. Which is why I'm offering to track down the father and see if he's interested in meeting her—without involving her in the search, or getting her hopes up."

"My daughter suggested that very thing last night. So, you're the intermediary she chose?"

"We didn't discuss it. And she has no idea I've come to see you. It's just something I'd like to do for her."

"Why?"

"Why not? She means a lot to me." *She might be the mother of my child.*

She smiled tightly. "And you think this would make her happy?"

Ted didn't know what to make of the woman whom Sara Beth sang the praises of. He was finding her aloof and not very maternal. Why wouldn't she want Sara Beth to be happy?

"I know she's unhappy not knowing," Ted said.

"There's no guarantee that would change if she got the information she thinks she wants."

"True. But the curiosity she's lived with would be satisfied. She could move forward, one way or the other. She's long been an adult. It's time to stop treating her like a child."

It was the wrong thing to say. He saw that right away. Her expression closed up tight.

"She *is* a child, Dr. Bonner. *My* child. That will never change. And until you have a child of your own, you won't understand how strong that bond is, especially the need to protect your child from hurt. You think it will help her to find who fathered her? I don't."

"She's your daughter, Ms. O'Connell, and always will be. But she's no longer your child."

Grace stood. "It's time for you to go."

He'd already risen automatically because she had. Now he went to the door, guilt settling on his shoulders. He'd meant to help Sara Beth. Instead, he may have hurt her cause even more. "Thank you for your time."

"You haven't asked me not to tell Sara Beth about this," she said as he stepped outside.

"You won't have to. I plan to tell her myself."

"Ah. Honesty is the best policy?"

He smiled, more at himself than her, then recited his mantra. "I was an Eagle Scout."

"I guess that explains a lot," Grace said. "Maybe I should be just as direct with you."

"Please do."

"My daughter generally puts other people's needs before her own. It's part of what makes her a good nurse. But she's also gotten hurt because of it."

He considered that. *Don't mess with my daughter,* was what she meant. It was true that Sara Beth had often put his needs first. He'd been trying to pay her back some today, but without success.

"I hear you," Ted said. "Thank you for giving me a chance to speak. I hope you change your mind, sooner rather than later."

"Well, that day may, indeed, come. Who knows?"

He didn't know how to take that, but ultimately, it didn't matter.

The only thing that mattered now was how Sara Beth felt about what he'd done.

Sara Beth kept herself busy in the clinical wing. Ted had disappeared right after she'd shared her secret with him. He'd seemed okay with what she'd told him, but then he'd left the clinic for parts unknown, only leaving behind a note saying he'd let her know when he got back.

Chance's consultation room door opened and a couple came out, the Lombards, both of them smiling, the woman crying, Sara Beth recognized happy tears when she saw them.

"Did you hear, Sara Beth?" Mary Lombard said. "Twins. We're having twins. It's a miracle."

Sara Beth hugged her. "That is the best possible news. Congratulations to both of you."

They floated away, as delighted, expectant couples tended to do, one of the things that made her work fulfilling. She never tired of offering her congratulations, never tired of seeing their ecstatic faces when their children came into the world.

Sara Beth's pager went off. She figured Chance wanted her or Ted had returned, but it was Wilma Goodheart, asking her to come to reception. Sara Beth's footsteps slowed as she spotted Tricia Trahearn in the lobby, studying one of the paintings.

"I told her Dr. Bonner was out of the building, so she asked for you," Wilma said.

"Thank you, Ms. Goodheart." Sara Beth approached Tricia, who was wearing an expensive-looking black suit, probably Armani or some other designer.

"Hello, Tricia," Sara Beth said when she got within earshot. She thought she remembered the woman accurately, how voluptuous she was, as evidenced by her red dress on Valentine's Day, but this time she looked professional, more…judgelike.

"Hello, Sara Beth." She extended her hand. "My vacation has come to an end, and I'm heading home to Vermont. I wanted to say goodbye to Ted, but I understand he's not here."

"He'll be back, although I don't know when. It's already close to quitting time, so you probably wouldn't have long to wait. Do you want to do that or is there a message I can give him?"

She glanced at her watch. "I need to get on the road. If you would please tell him I enjoyed seeing him again, and that I hope we can stay in touch."

"I'll be happy to."

Tricia leaned close. "We went out to dinner once, but there was nothing else to it."

Sara Beth smiled. "He told me."

Tricia smiled back. "I reminded Ted that night and I'll caution you. His parents' expectations are high. They were friendly to you at dinner because their manners are impeccable, but if they thought for a minute that things were really serious between you and Ted? Who knows?"

"Why are you telling me?"

"For Ted's sake. Because I think you need to decide how important your relationship is. If you end up making him choose between you and his parents, and you're not serious about him, it might take a while for the rift to heal. In case you haven't figured it out already, Ted doesn't make waves. Doesn't like waves."

Yes, Sara Beth had noticed that. He avoided conflict, but so did she. Which was probably why they hadn't discussed the possibility she could be pregnant. They should. "I appreciate your directness," Sara Beth said.

The subject of their conversation paged her then, saying he was back. He'd probably come in the employee's entrance.

"He's returned," she said after barely a moment's hesitation. "I'll take you to him."

"Never mind. Just tell him goodbye, please. It's good enough."

On her way to the lab, Sara Beth stopped by the clinic to see if she was needed for anything, then continued on, hoping she was going to learn why Ted had disappeared.

"You're back," she said as she went inside the lab. "Just in time to go home."

"I'm going to work late tonight to make up for it."

"Of course you are." She smiled. "I can stay, too, if you want to work on the manual."

He put on his lab coat. "I have some other things to do."

He wasn't being cool, exactly, but he wasn't making eye contact, either.

"Tricia was just here. She's headed back to Vermont and wanted to say goodbye."

He nodded. She waited, wondering if he would say where he'd gone, but he turned on his computer and stared at the screen.

"I'll see you later, then," she said, wondering if she would, Tricia's caution still echoing in her head.

"Sara Beth."

"Yes?"

"I went to see your mother."

She took a couple of steps toward him. "Why?"

"To try to convince her to find out who your father is." He finally looked at her. "I wasn't successful in doing anything but irritating her."

She nodded, unable to speak.

"She wasn't happy to see me, although it also seemed she was upset about something before I got there." He took her hand. "I'm sorry."

"I appreciate that you tried."

"Do you? I know I should've asked you first, but my plan was to get the information then pass it along only if I was successful. I didn't want to get your hopes up."

She squeezed his hand, wishing she could just throw herself into his arms. Then suddenly she found she could smile. He'd done a wonderful thing, trying to help her. She appreciated that. Him.

"Thank you so much," she said.

"It's the thought that counts?"

"There was action involved, too. Will you come to my place after you're done here?"

"I'll even bring dinner."

"That's a deal." She went toward the door then turned around. "I like you a whole lot." It was the closest she could come to telling him she loved him, something she knew he wasn't ready to hear now, if ever.

He grinned. "Ditto."

The fact he'd remembered her saying that to him before kept her smiling—until nine o'clock came and he hadn't shown up or answered his cell phone.

She finally gave up at eleven-fifteen and went to bed, was almost asleep when her doorbell rang. She trudged downstairs and let him in, the cold air waking her up more than she wanted to be.

"Are you hungry?" she asked.

"Yeah. For you." He hauled her to him and kissed her, long and thoroughly. "I'm sorry I didn't call. I got lost in the work."

"It's fine. Truly it is." She cupped his face. "I admire your dedication, Ted. But..." She went up on tiptoe to kiss him.

"But?"

"Tomorrow I'm giving you your own key."

He went silent. "Are you sure?" he asked finally.

She nodded. She'd never been surer. "I don't want to go downstairs in the cold to let you in."

That was the least of it, and they both knew it. Giving him a key was a commitment.

"Okay?" she asked, holding her breath.

"Okay." Then he slipped his arm around her waist and walked upstairs with her, where he warmed her up in a hurry—and never mentioned giving her a key to his loft in return.

Chapter Fifteen

The following Monday morning, Sara Beth was working with Ted and Chance. The research protocols for the best-practices manual were complete. They'd started on the clinical protocols, which would take a few days more. They didn't have to work in the lab, but by unspoken agreement were doing just that.

A knock came on the door window. Ramona stood there, framed by the glass, smiling.

"She looks too happy," Chance said, letting her in.

"I would've brought champagne," Ramona said, "but I knew I couldn't bring it in here. Oh, how cute," she said, distracted momentarily as she picked up two small stuffed bears, one pink and one blue, from Sara Beth's desk.

"For the Johnson twins, born yesterday," Sara Beth

said as Ramona gave them back. She hugged them, loving the feel of their silky soft fur, the bears her traditional gift for every new baby at the clinic. She kept a scrapbook of photographs of the parents, babies and bears when the babies were dressed in their going-home outfits.

"Well, the Johnsons are celebrating and so can you," Ramona said to Ted and Chance. "You have been vindicated."

The sound that came from both men blended laughter and relief.

"How'd you manage that so fast?" Ted asked.

"Thanks to your meticulous records, which proved you didn't apply for the McAdams grant, *and* copies of your e-mails expressing your desire not to accept the grant, *plus* a pithily stated letter from the institute's attorney—" she stopped and drew a breath "—their claim has been declared null and void."

"Did you get it in writing?" Chance asked.

She passed them each a sheet of paper. "I don't think you'll hear from them again. Now, get back to the work you're supposed to be doing." She left, a bounce in her step.

Sara Beth whooped with joy. Ted and Chance grinned ear to ear, punching each other's shoulders. She knew how much the unjust claim had weighed on them.

"Let's try to avoid any more scandals, Chance," Ted said.

"You're directing that at me? I've been behaving myself. Have you?"

Sara Beth's cell phone rang before he could answer.

She saw it was her mother and handed the bears to Ted, laughing as he dangled them by the scuffs of their necks in front of him.

"Hi, Mom!"

A beat passed. "You sound chipper."

"That's a good word for it. What's up?"

"I need to talk to you."

"Oh. Okay. Hold on. I'll find an empty office—"

"Not on the phone. Please, Sara Beth. I need you to come here to the house. Right now."

"You want me to leave work?"

"Yes."

Since her mother was the original never-miss-a-day workaholic, Sara Beth knew it must be serious. "All right. I'll be there as soon as possible."

"Something wrong?" Ted asked as she took the bears from him and got her purse from the drawer.

"I don't know. My mom issued a command performance. I have to go." She could tell he wanted to ask more questions, but couldn't in front of Chance. "I'll be back as soon as I can."

Sara Beth fretted all the way to her mother's house. The only other time she could remember her mother sounding so upset was when *her* mother had died ten years ago. That mother-daughter relationship had been tense and tentative for as long as Sara Beth could remember, yet her mother had mourned deeply. Maybe because it hadn't been a good relationship? Sara Beth had wondered. Her mother told her once that she'd made a conscious decision to be a better mother than her own, a more loving one.

And except for the one big issue between them, Sara Beth agreed that her mother had succeeded. Their relationship was closer than most of her friends had with their mothers, although Sara Beth didn't want to disappoint her mother by having gotten pregnant. She wished she knew if she was.

Sara Beth jogged from the bus stop to her mother's house and went inside. Grace stood at the front window, her arms folded across her stomach, her face ashen.

"What's wrong?" Sara Beth rushed to her mother's side.

"I didn't want to tell you, sweetheart. Not ever. Now I'm being forced to. I'm sorry. I'm so sorry."

Sara Beth took her mother by the hand and led her to the sofa, sitting right next to her.

"This is how the rich and powerful operate, Sara Beth. I've told you for years. Now you'll know."

"Know what, Mom?"

"Emily Armstrong is gunning for your termination at the institute."

Sara Beth's first thought was that her and Ted's…relationship had been discovered. But the institute didn't have a nonfraternization rule, so what difference would that make? "Why?"

Grace put her face in her hands for a moment, her legs bouncing, then she looked her daughter in the eye. "Because she found out I spent two weeks with Gerald. He called me last week—the day Ted came to see me, in fact. Gerald warned me then that Emily knew. I've been waiting to see what would happen. Today I found out."

"Wait. Go back. Are you saying you went away with Dr. Armstrong? When?"

"When I said I was in Cancún. Emily went to Greece on vacation. She put Gerald in a private spa while she was gone to see if physical therapy could help him."

"Did it?"

"Not much. He's still using a wheelchair most of the time. I helped oversee his care, so I saw for myself how bad off he is. I hadn't seen him since he retired."

"I don't understand. Did you go there as his nurse?"

"I went as his friend. His longtime, caring friend. But Emily had forbidden contact between us outside of the institute, which I had respected—until Gerald called and asked if I'd join him."

"I've always known that Mrs. Armstrong didn't like you—and me, for years now—but to forbid contact? Why? Why is she so worried about your friendship with Dr. Armstrong? And what does it have to do with me?"

"Oh, sweetheart. Gerald Armstrong is your father."

The words landed hard on Sara Beth, a gut punch that drove her backward. "You…used—Mom, you used *his* sperm?"

Grace didn't answer, just looked at Sara Beth as if she could read her mother's mind. Then she did. Clearly. Vividly. Everything made sense now. Everything.

"You had an affair with him."

"Yes."

"You got pregnant with me."

"Yes."

Nausea, hot and sickening, rose in Sara Beth. She'd

thought she wanted to know. Thought it would complete her life. But not this. Not this.

She stood, her knees wobbling, and made her way to the front window, seeing nothing, feeling the pain of her mother's deception. "That means…Lisa is my sister. And Olivia."

"Yes."

She had brothers, too—Paul and Derek. "Lisa was born only a month after me."

Grace came up beside her. "Gerald and Emily had reconciled some major differences. We told everyone I'd gone through artificial insemination. Even Emily believed it. Then you were born, and as you got older, it was apparent you were an Armstrong."

"There is a painting on the staircase of Dr. Armstrong's mother." Sara Beth pressed the heels of her hands to her eyes, recalling a dim memory of the portrait. "Paul and Derek used to tease me about being a long, lost Armstrong. I looked so much like their grandmother."

"Emily confronted Gerald," Grace said. "He admitted to it."

"It was when I was fourteen. Wasn't it? Everything changed then."

"Yes."

"How long did your—" she could barely say the word "—affair last?"

"As I said, they'd been having marital problems. I had fallen in love with him years before, but had never acted on it, never said a word. Then he needed me, and

I gave in to my feelings. We were together for about a month, then he went back to her, and we never slept together again. We hugged each other once, just once. Right after you were born."

"He never came to see me?"

"He saw you, but at his house. Emily offered to keep you during the day, to share their nanny. You remember that, I'm sure. It saved me a lot of money, but, selfishly, I wanted you to know your siblings."

"Didn't he give you financial support?"

"He helped me to buy this house, but no monthly support, at my request. Then he made sure I was well taken care of in retirement. It was his way of assuring you an inheritance, through me."

Not ready to deal with it yet, Sara Beth ignored the revelation that Dr. Armstrong was her father. "How could you stand it, Mom? How could you work with him every day, side by side, loving him, not being with him? Why didn't you get a job somewhere else?"

"You say you're in love with Ted Bonner. If you are, you can answer that question yourself."

She shook her head. She could not do that, could not wait for a man to love her back, to be free to love her publicly.

"I have never admired or respected any man as I did Gerald, sweetheart."

"You denied me a father, even a stepfather, because you couldn't give up a fantasy, Mom. A fantasy!" She gestured wildly. "I thought you had your act together better than any woman I know. I've always admired you. Now I don't know what to think. What to believe. And that I could lose the job I love, too? What am I supposed to do about that?"

"I think we need to call Emily's bluff. She says she'll tell everyone that you're Gerald's daughter, making it too difficult for you to continue working there. She knows you're not only tenderhearted, but that you would never hurt Lisa."

"Why would she expose her husband's infidelity like that? Does she hate him so much?"

"I think she hates me more and therefore, you. But I truly believe she's bluffing. She's grasping at straws out of anger that I was with him for those two weeks, sharing his confidences."

"I don't blame her."

Grace assumed a defensive stance. "This is the first time it's happened. And obviously it wasn't physical."

"Mom, put yourself in her shoes. She must have forgiven him or at least accepted that your affair ended, even though I was a visible reminder ever since. But I don't think it's the physical infidelity she resents anymore. It's the emotional one. Two weeks with a former lover? The mother of your child? That would be hard for anyone to swallow."

Grace burst into tears. "I know, Sara Beth. I know. I'm so angry at myself. My instinct was to say no when Gerald asked me to come. I should've listened to my instincts. I should've respected Emily."

Sara Beth offered no comfort, wasn't ready to hug her mother as if nothing had happened.

"I'm glad you see that, Mom." But Sara Beth could see her own truth, too. That except for the fact that Ted wasn't married, Sara Beth could be in the same position as her mother had been, single and pregnant. She couldn't lose her job, too.

"I have to talk to her. Mrs. Armstrong. I have to get her to see that I won't tell anyone, that I'll take the secret to my grave."

"She won't see you."

"I have to try. And I have to see Dr. Armstrong, knowing he's my father, and that's he's known all this time and kept it to himself. I have to be able to understand how he could do that."

Sara Beth needed to think back through the years and try to remember any time he'd treated her daughterlike. She needed to get away from the one person she'd trusted most in her life, the one she'd never thought would break that trust, and yet who had lied to her all her life.

"*She* especially won't let you see him," Grace said, insistent. "He stays in bed. He wouldn't even know you were there, trying to see him. There's no way around it."

"If he knew that I knew the truth, would he? Would he talk to me?"

"If Emily weren't around? Yes, I think he would. He regrets keeping it—you—a secret. You know that Emily and Ted's mother are friends, right?"

The sudden shift in subject made Sara Beth frown. "Acquaintances, I think. Same-social-circle kind of thing."

"Which means that Emily has influence there, too. It would only take a sly comment."

Sara Beth clenched her fists, anger coiled inside her with no way to release it. She had to leave. That was the only thing she knew for sure.

"You know, Mom, it was only a couple of weeks ago that you said if I couldn't be public about a relationship, something wasn't right about it."

"And that was experience talking. Do what I say, you know, not what I do."

Sara Beth nodded, wishing that could be enough of an answer. She didn't want to talk anymore. "Give me some time, Mom. I'll be in touch when I can think more clearly."

"I love you, baby." Despair layered her barely uttered words.

"I know." Sara Beth closed her eyes against the pain. "I love you, too. I just don't like you very much right now."

She hurried out the front door. Where to go? What to do?

Ted kept an eye on the lab door, accomplishing so little he might as well just stop working altogether. He'd never experienced anything like it before.

Where was she? Why hadn't she returned? Why hadn't she at least called?

He'd never worried about someone like this. For her mother to demand her to leave work, it must be something huge. Sara Beth would need him....

Ted shoved his hands through his hair, much shorter now that he'd finally gotten a haircut. He stared at the employee parking lot, although he knew she would return by bus, and come in the front entrance.

He wandered away, tempted to go to the lobby and wait, tempted to call her, but resisting. He didn't want to add to the problem, whatever it was.

His gaze landed on the pink and blue teddy bears, which reminded him of her pain over not knowing a father, that special relationship between father and daughter.

A reminder, too, that she could be pregnant.

They hadn't talked about it. She hadn't brought it up, and he'd been wrapped up in worry about getting his name cleared. Now that was done. For good, he hoped.

The door swung open. Sara Beth came in, looking much like her mother had when he'd gone to see her, although more hollow-eyed than teary. She made an effort to smile.

He went toward her, needed to grab her tight and hold on, for his sake as much as hers. "Are you all right?"

She put out a hand, preventing him from getting closer. "I came to get the bears. It's my only chance to take the Johnsons' picture. They're on their way home to Quincy." She sidestepped around him, picked up the bears, clutched them.

She looked…lost. He wanted her to confide in him, to break down in his arms if that was what she needed. He wanted to be the only man with the right to do that.

He wanted to make babies with her. Maybe he already had. And he didn't want any child of his to grow up without both parents in a loving home.

"Marry me," he said.

She jerked back. Her expression was one either of shock or horror. "What?"

"Marry me. Please."

"Ted, please. I can't deal with this right now. Everything is too raw."

"Raw? In what way? You can't deal with a marriage proposal?"

"Not right now. I have to go. Please leave me alone for now. I have a lot to think about." She rushed out, leaving him standing and staring and bewildered.

Chance came in before the door had closed all the way. "What's going on with Sara Beth? It's like she didn't even see me."

"She's upset about something."

"That call from her mother?"

"I would assume, yes."

Chance laid a hand on Ted's shoulder. "And what's your excuse? You look like hell."

He spoke without thinking. "I proposed to her. She didn't seem to appreciate it." An understatement, he thought.

"Proposed? I didn't know you were dating."

"For a month or so. She could be pregnant, Chance."

Chance dropped into a chair. "You're the last person I ever would've thought might accidentally get a woman pregnant."

"I'm a little stunned myself." He sat down next to his friend. "I don't want anyone to think we had to get married. I want her to marry me so there's no question about it."

"So you want to marry her whether or not she's pregnant?"

"Yeah." It struck him like lightning then. He loved her. Forever-after loved her.

"So," Chance drawled. "Knowing you as I do, I'm going to guess that you proposed without the trappings."

"Trappings? I don't know what you mean."

"The traditional big deal, Ted. The roses and candle-light and perfect meal. The pledge of undying love. The special moment she'll want to paste in her mental scrap-book forever. Those trappings. The bare essentials."

He hadn't even come close. He hadn't even told her that he loved her. They'd been standing in the research lab. He should have told her. "I screwed it up. Big-time. No wonder she didn't appreciate it." Well, that and whatever her mother had said to her. His lack of sensi-tivity wasn't anything new, he supposed, but she was different. He'd noticed she was upset, but hadn't taken it into consideration, just forged ahead with his proposal as if her feelings hadn't mattered. He wasn't usually so egotistical.

"It's not too late," Chance said. "It'll just take some planning. If you're interested, I've got some ideas."

They came up with a plan, which was good, because Ted liked plans he could follow. Then he made phone calls to set the works in motion.

He was planning more than the bare essentials, but would it be enough?

Chapter Sixteen

The beautiful house where Sara Beth had spent a good deal of her childhood seemed cold now, and unwelcoming. She climbed the steps and rang the bell, her heart heavy, her legs feeling like she wore concrete shoes.

The door opened. Sara Beth thought she might get sick right there on the landing.

"What are you doing here?" Emily Armstrong asked, her tone haughtier than usual.

"I need to talk to you. Please."

"We have nothing to say." She started to shut the door.

"Don't make me create a scene. I will try, if I have to, to be loud enough that…Dr. Armstrong could hear me."

"Blackmail? How lovely." But she allowed Sara Beth

inside, took her to the dayroom that was Emily's personal space, a sunny, feminine room. "Make it fast."

Sara Beth hadn't been invited to sit, so she didn't. "My mother told me everything this morning."

"I thought she would." Emily took a seat in a flower-upholstered wingback chair that looked like a throne.

"I only want one thing, Mrs. Armstrong. A chance to talk to Dr.—my father. Just once. Then I'll leave you both alone. And in return you have my promise to keep the secret forever."

"And quit your job."

"I can't do that."

"Then, no deal."

"What do you expect to gain by telling everyone about me? About your husband's affair? How is that better than me simply keeping the secret?"

Her eyes turned icy. "He broke his promise to me. He said he would never see her alone again."

"So, it's revenge? What will it gain you?"

"Sympathy, I imagine."

"I understand he broke your trust. I would be furious and hurt, too. But telling the world will only hurt your children."

She picked a piece of lint off her sharply creased pants. "The casualties of war."

Sara Beth decided her mother was right. Emily was bluffing. She would not hurt her children that way.

"Until I was fourteen," Sara Beth said, "I loved you like a second mother. I thought you were so elegant, such a lady. And I always appreciated how you let me hang out here, and let Lisa spend the night with me, how you accepted me as part of your family. When that changed—when I was fourteen and you found out about me, I guess—I was devastated. I didn't know what I'd done. I cried about it a lot. Lisa's and my relationship faltered until we both started college, and she didn't have to account for her whereabouts anymore."

Sara Beth approached Emily, understanding how hurt she'd been that her husband had strayed—and with a woman whose child she'd accepted almost as her own, not knowing the connection. "Thank you for what you gave me. I appreciate it more than I can say. But I'm not leaving the institute. It's my home and my passion."

She walked out of the room, hoping Emily would follow her, to say it would be all right for her to see her father.

It didn't happen. She wasn't hailed back. And when she got home, there was no message on her answering machine saying she'd changed her mind, and to please return.

The silence was devastating.

Now what? It wasn't worth going back to work for the short time that remained of the workday, to try to pretend that her world hadn't just been turned upside down. She didn't want to see Ted, either—

Ted. He'd asked her to marry him.

Where had that come from? *Marry me,* he'd said. That was all.

She wasn't pregnant—well, she didn't know if she was pregnant—so why had he bothered? If he'd loved her, he would've said so. And then there was the issue with his parents, who had plans for their son. Plans that didn't include a woman who couldn't admit that the famous family tree she'd come from had to be kept secret—and who was also the result of an affair, anyway.

Not exactly parent-pleasing credentials.

She wanted to cry, to throw things, to stomp and wail and rend clothing. Instead she crawled into bed and pulled the quilt over her head. It didn't stop the thoughts from swirling. She needed to get out of the house, focus on something else for a while—

As if she could really be distracted. Right. Sure.

Sara Beth flopped the bedding away from her face, ready to take some kind of action. Ted loomed over her.

She gasped, her heart pounding. She couldn't scrape out a word.

"I want to take you someplace," he said quietly, gently, sitting beside her.

"Okay."

A beat passed. "That was easier than I expected."

He hadn't known her thoughts. He'd just come along at the right time, a lifeguard tossing a float to a drowning victim.

He held out a hand to her, helping her stand up. She saw him look her over, and take note that she was still wearing her shoes while in bed.

"Want to talk about it?" he asked.

"Not yet." Maybe not ever. She didn't know if she would ever tell another living soul what she'd learned today. "You proposed to me," she said, deciding to jump that hurdle before it blocked their way.

He smiled a little. "Let's just shelve that for now, okay? Let's just go have some fun."

Startled, worried that they *would* have to talk about it, she agreed instantly. "That's a deal."

She finally noticed he was wearing a suit—and a crisp white shirt and red tie. Red? It was so un-Ted-like, she ran her hand down it, then patted his stomach. He sucked it in.

"Where are we going?" she asked.

"It's a surprise."

She studied his face and the tender expression that she didn't dare try to interpret. "I'm guessing I should dress up?"

"That dress you wore on my birthday brings back fond memories, especially what you wore underneath."

"You mean my fabulous muscle tone?" The fact she could joke said a lot about how comfortable she felt with him. His expression changed, too, from concerned to relieved.

He slid his arms around her waist, moved his hands down her rear, bringing her hips to his. "Anytime you need to talk, I'm here, Sara Beth."

"I know that. For tonight, this girl just wants to have fun."

He kissed her before he let her go, the softest, most tender kiss he'd ever given her. Tears pricked her eyes. She hugged her hard, then she went to make herself look beautiful, figuring that at some point he would either repeat the proposal or apologize for it.

She wasn't sure which she wanted to hear, was ready to hear. It was all too much at once....

Which was a lie. She wanted him to repeat it.

"First a limo and now a private jet?" Sara Beth stared out the car window at the sleek jet with the stairs leading up to it. "How did you swing this? And why?"

"I wanted to wine and dine you in style. Something wrong with that? The plane belongs to an old friend, Rourke Devlin. A fellow Eagle Scout, by the way. It's how we met."

"I like him already." She smiled, took one last bite of a strawberry, then finished the sparkling cider in her flute. She hadn't commented on the lack of champagne, knowing he was just looking out for her in case she was pregnant, which meant he was as aware of the possibility as she was. She'd accepted the glass without a word.

The limo driver opened the door and helped her out. Ted followed, took her hand and led her up the stairs into the plane. "This is so much fun!" she said. "Thank you."

"The night has just begun."

She wouldn't have guessed he had a lot of romantic gestures in his arsenal, and maybe she was being hit by every one of them tonight, but it didn't matter if it was a one-time adventure. She wanted the memory.

Tomorrow she would have to face her future—whatever Emily Armstrong decided to do—but tonight she would enjoy herself.

"So are you going to tell me where we're going?" she asked, when she was buckled in.

"New York City." He presented her with another glass of sparkling cider and a tray of appetizers—prosciutto-wrapped asparagus, a variety of cheese and crackers, more strawberries. "To tide you over."

There was so much to talk about, yet neither of them did much talking. They looked out the window, tried to identify cities and landmarks, kept things light and simple, while beneath the surface, emotions bubbled, at least for her.

She caught him staring at her, his expression so serious that she cupped his face and kissed him before he said anything to change the happy mood.

Another limo awaited them. They were whisked away to Central Park, where a carriage took them for a long spin around the park, the night cold and clear. She couldn't remember them ever saying so little. Until now, they'd always had things to say.

By the time they reached the famous Boat House restaurant, tension had wrapped around them. They were seated at a table overlooking the lake.

She didn't think she could eat a thing, she'd gotten so worked up. Whatever had made her think she could just have an evening of fun with him? She'd learned today that her mother had had an affair with a man Sara Beth had known all her life, without knowing he was her father. That his wife was justifiably angry about it, but planning to take revenge on Sara Beth, the innocent victim in the whole affair.

And the man she loved had parents who would never accept her. Yet if she was pregnant, she wanted to marry him....

She wanted to marry him anyway, but she didn't want to burden him with the fact she was not just a child of artificial insemination, lacking the knowledge of her father's identity, but instead the child of an illicit affair, her father a wealthy, powerful man to rival Ted's own.

"You've stopped having fun," Ted said, after the waiter had taken their order for Caesar salad and grilled swordfish.

"I'm sorry to ruin the beautiful evening you planned. It's wonderful, truly. I'm just..." Her burdens came crashing down. She couldn't keep them at bay for much longer. She was ready to fall apart, ready to cry.

She'd put off reacting to everything she'd learned—had it just been today? Now she had to pay the consequences.

Ted gave her a long look then signaled the waiter and whispered something to him. He returned in a moment with a silver covered dish and presented it to Sara Beth, pulling off the lid, revealing a nosegay of white roses.

Ted reached for her hand. "I love you, Sara Beth."

She pressed her face into the fragrant bouquet, her eyes stinging, her throat burning, heart racing. When she lifted her head, Ted was beside her, on one knee, holding an open ring box with a gorgeous diamond and sapphire engagement ring.

"I love you. I want to spend my days and nights with you. Please marry me."

She looked into his hopeful eyes and saw true love there. More than anything she wanted to say yes, but what came out was, "I can't."

Chapter Seventeen

Stunned, Ted watched Sara Beth run off. Everyone was staring at the man on bended knee, the meaning of which couldn't have been lost on anyone. In that scenario, however, usually the woman smiled, misted up, said an enthusiastic yes and threw her arms around the man.

Chance had been wrong. Even the trappings hadn't mattered. She didn't love him—yet—in return. He should've waited for her to say it first. Now he'd embarrassed them both.

Ted canceled their dinner order, since he was sure she wouldn't want to sit there and have dinner as if nothing had happened. He dropped the ring box in his pocket. She'd taken the bouquet with her.

"Sir?" The waiter leaned close to him. "We think your companion needs you."

Ted sprang up. "Where is she?"

"The ladies' room, sir." He pointed. "Through there and to the right."

Ladies' room? How was he supposed to help her there? "Did she ask for me?"

"No, sir, but she is apparently having some difficulty—"

Ted took off running. He didn't hesitate when he got to the restroom but slammed the door open and rushed in. He found her on a small sofa, crying like he'd never seen anyone cry before. It broke his heart.

"Sara Beth," he said softly, soothingly.

She went silent for a moment. "Go away." She started crying again, trying so hard not to that her whole body shook.

"I'm not going away." He looked around for some tissue, found a box and passed her a few, then he sat beside her.

The door opened. A woman looked inside, saw them, then backed out.

"You're in the ladies' room," Sara Beth told him, wiping her eyes.

"There's a first time for everything."

"Dr. Armstrong is my father."

He almost didn't catch what she said. She had the tissues pressed to her nose and wasn't looking at him. After a moment the words sank in.

"Is that what your mother told you today?"

She nodded. "I said I wouldn't tell anyone, but you're a doctor. You have to keep secrets."

He didn't remind her that she wasn't his patient and this wasn't a medical issue, because it didn't make any difference. He would never share her secret.

"So, Dr. Armstrong was using his own sperm to help impregnate the women who came to the clinic?" he said. "That's happened before, unfortunately."

"No, Ted. They had an affair," she whispered.

Ted felt his jaw drop. Because she started to cry again, he wrapped his arms around her and didn't let go as she told him the whole story, including how she'd gone to see Emily Armstrong.

After a while, a knock came on the door, and the manager came in, saying that if they needed a private place, he could let them use his office.

They decided to return to where the limo waited for them. She clutched the bouquet, but barely made eye contact with Ted.

The driver took them to a building on Park Avenue.

"Where are we?" she asked.

"Rourke's penthouse. He's out of town. In Boston, actually. He said we were welcome to use it to-night…." Of course, Ted had thought they would be celebrating.

"I didn't bring anything with me to stay over."

He'd had fun buying something red and lacy, but now didn't seem to be the time to bring it up. "It doesn't matter. You must be tired."

She nodded, although her spirits seemed to be on

the mend. He took advantage of the moment, in case he was right.

"One question first, please, then I won't bring it up again." Tonight, anyway. He wrapped her hands in his. "Do you love me?"

She didn't say anything for a few seconds, then finally, as if she was in pain, "Yes. With all my heart."

Relief struck first, then he dug for patience, usually easy to find. "Then why can't you marry me?"

"If I'm pregnant, we'll talk about it again. Maybe I should take a test. It might give us an answer."

"I don't want to know. I don't care. It doesn't make a difference to me if you're pregnant or not. I want to marry you, no matter what. Right now."

She swallowed. He thought he'd finally gotten through to her, until she said, "Have you thought about your parents?"

"What? What about them?"

"They have big plans for you. They want you to marry a woman of your own kind."

He almost laughed. "My own kind?"

"You know what I mean. Not the daughter of—" She shook her head. "I'm so used to not knowing half of my parentage. Now, instead of thinking I was conceived scientifically, I have to remember I was conceived when my father cheated on his wife. What do you think your parents will think of that?"

"It's none of their business. That's what I think."

"Well, *I* think they love you and want you to marry the right person."

Her logic, or lack thereof, was starting to make its own kind of sense. "So, let me get this straight. You love me, but you won't marry me, even though I don't care whether you're pregnant or not, because you think my parents might disown me or something?" He waited for her to confirm it. When she didn't, he cupped her face, making her look into his eyes, willing her to see what was in his heart. "Marry me. Tonight. We'll take Rourke's jet and fly to Las Vegas. I want to have the right to show that I love you in public. And if you happen to be pregnant already, I'd rather no one know we jumped the gun. Not for me, Sara Beth, but for you, and our child, if there is one. Let me protect you from the gossip, please. Marry me tonight."

"Okay." Her voice was breathless and full of joy. "I love you, Ted."

He grinned and finally kissed her, said he loved her again, then dug into his pocket for the ring. He slipped it on her finger, pressed his lips to the soft skin above it, then tucked both of her hands in his lap.

"We'll need witnesses," he said.

"Lisa."

"Will you be able to handle that, knowing what you know now?"

"She's both my best friend and my sister. She's the only one I want to stand up with me. How about you? Chance?"

"Yeah."

She took a deep breath. "Our parents."

He shook his head.

"We can't not invite them, Ted. If I were a parent, I

would be so hurt not to be invited to my child's wedding. It'll be their choice. They can say no, but we can't leave them out. What kind of beginning to our marriage would that be? Your parents would blame me for denying them the chance to see their only child get married. My mom would blame you. It could take a long time to soothe those particular hurt feelings. At the very least we have to tell them before it happens, not after."

He thought it over, saw the hopeful look in her eyes. "My parents are in Toronto."

"I can't believe you're making excuses. That suggests to me that you do think they'll object to—"

"No. I don't, Sara Beth. I just want to get married without making a big production of it."

"I wouldn't call this wedding a big production."

She was right. "Okay, I do see your point. So, it looks like we have a lot of phone calls to make." He touched her hair. "Are you upset about not having the big, white wedding? Is it something you've dreamed about?"

"Maybe a little, but that was a girlhood fantasy. The reality is just fine."

"You are one incredible woman," he said.

She smiled and kissed him. "Don't you forget it."

It was the strangest, most wonderful whirlwind of Sara Beth's life, full of joy and surprises. First came the phone calls to Boston. Lisa whooped so loudly that Sara Beth had to pull the phone away from her ear. It was so hard not to blurt out that they were sisters, but Sara Beth had talked it over with Ted and decided to keep it to herself for now. Maybe the right time would come, but it wasn't today.

Chance came next but he'd been called in for a difficult delivery of triplets, plus he had no one to cover for him. He was disappointed that he couldn't attend, but promised to throw Ted a postwedding bachelor party.

Sara Beth called her mother next, inviting her to join them at the airport, to fly to the wedding, to be part of it. Sara Beth had held her breath, waiting for a question or an "Are you sure?" It never came. She said she'd be there with bells on.

Ted hadn't called his parents in front of her, and all he said was they'd try to make it. Sara Beth wanted to delay the event until they could, but Ted slowly shook his head.

Sara Beth refused to be hurt for herself, but she was sorry for Ted.

Ted's friend Rourke Devlin insisted on coming along and being the best man. When he climbed onto the plane, *his* plane, Sara Beth recognized him, remembered seeing him at Shots with Ted and Chance, solving that mystery. Then a new intrigue began as Rourke and Lisa made eye contact and went still for a few seconds. Lisa glanced away first, but Sara Beth caught them sneaking looks at each other the whole flight to Las Vegas.

It didn't matter that their flight landed in the middle of the night. The city was lit and teeming with tourists. They checked into the Bellagio, had something to eat, got a few hours of sleep, then Sara Beth, her mother and Lisa shopped for a wedding dress, finding a stunning white sheath scattered with a few beads to give it sparkle.

She felt beautiful.

At high noon, she linked her arm through her mother's and moved to the top of the aisle, ready to marry the man she loved, who looked at her with such love in return that it stopped her stomach from churning.

Then she saw his parents sitting in the front row, and joy filled her, warm and satisfying, completing her beautiful day. They stood, were smiling at her, as was Ted, who'd changed his tie to one she'd bought him covered with teddy bears. She carried the bouquet he'd given her in New York.

The processional music started. Lisa gave her a thumbs-up. Rourke cupped Ted's shoulder and said something that made him smile. Holding hands, Ted's parents eyed him as Sara Beth and her mother came down the aisle, Ted smiling at her. She beamed back.

He was right. Whether or not she was pregnant, this was good—perfect, in fact.

The ceremony was short but memorable, their I-dos followed by a kiss she would always remember. They didn't walk back up the aisle but greeted everyone where they stood. Got hugs from Lisa and Grace. Congratulations from Rourke.

Then Ted's parents approached.

Penny took Sara Beth's hand. "All his life, I've been wondering who he would choose, hoping he would find his soul mate, as I did mine. You make him happy. I've never heard him sound so carefree, and he's obviously so much in love. Thank you for bringing that to him." She kissed Sara Beth's cheek.

"Thank you," Sara Beth whispered, close to tears. "He's truly a gift in my life."

"Sara Beth," Brant Bonner said.

She waited, not expecting anything but kind words now. Still her pulse pounded in her ears as she waited for what he had to say.

"I know I didn't have the privilege of watching you grow up, like I did my son. I'll bet you were a beautiful, mischievous child." He smiled and looked to Grace for confirmation, receiving it in a nod and return smile.

"I know you didn't have a father around to make your life easier in ways that fathers can. But I want you to know that I'd be honored if you called me Dad."

Tears started to fall from Sara Beth's eyes, blurring her vision. "Thank you. Yes, I'd like to do that. Dad."

Everyone laughed a little shakily, then Brant pulled something from behind his back, a soft brown teddy bear with a red heart sewn on its chest. "Welcome to the family, daughter."

Sara Beth reached for it, this amazing symbol, such a small thing to bind people together. "You told him how much I ached for a father," she said to Ted, brushing at her tears. "About the teddy bear."

"Yes. And I won't apologize—" Ted emphasized.

She put a hand to his mouth, stopping the words. "No one's ever done what you've done—anything so kind, so thoughtful, *so loving* for me—and that's saying a lot, Ted, because I have a lot of great friends, and a wonderful mother."

Their guests had walked away, giving them a moment. "I am the luckiest woman alive. I love you so much." She went up on tiptoe to kiss him.

And the absentminded scientist gave her his single-minded attention, a silent promise that she would always come first.

* * * * *

THE TEXAS BILLIONAIRE'S BABY

BY
KAREN ROSE SMITH

First published in Great Britain 2011
Harlequin Mills & Boon Limited,
Eton House, 18-24 Paradise Road, Richmond, Surrey TW9 1SR

© Karen Rose Smith 2010

ISBN: 978 0 263 88869 0

23-0311

Harlequin Mills & Boon policy is to use papers that are natural, renewable and recyclable products and made from wood grown in sustainable forests. The logging and manufacturing processes conform to the legal environmental regulations of the country of origin.

Printed and bound in Spain
by Litografia Rosés S.A., Barcelona

Dear Reader,

"Firsts" are so important to parents. Most moms and dads remember a baby's first smile, first word, first step. I can remember our son toddling from sofa to chair in our small apartment before he managed his first step.

In *The Texas Billionaire's Baby*, my hero, Logan Barnes, is worried about his son Daniel because his first steps seem slow in coming. Only Gina Rigoletti can help Logan with Daniel. But Logan and Gina were each other's first love, and the hurt from their sudden parting so many years ago is a barrier to the bond they shared when they were young. Gina and Logan finally realize they have to take the first step by trusting each other so they can set aside what went before to reach what can happen ahead—true and everlasting love. Their romance is Book Four in my BABY EXPERTS series, and I hope you will look forward to Books Five and Six! Readers can learn more about THE BABY EXPERTS at www. karenrosesmith.com.

Have a wonderful spring,

Karen Rose Smith

Award-winning and best-selling author **Karen Rose Smith** has seen over sixty-five novels published since 1991. Living in Pennsylvania with her husband—who was her college sweetheart—and their two cats, she has been writing full-time since the start of her career. She enjoys researching and visiting America's west and southwest where this series of books is set. Readers can receive updates on Karen's latest releases and write to her through her website at www.karenrosesmith.com or at PO Box 1545, Hanover, PA 17331, USA.

For survivors

Acknowledgment:

Thanks to Stephanie Fowler for helping
with research sources.

Chapter One

Gina Rigoletti's heart pounded as she followed the sounds of deep male laughter and happy baby squeals to a child's playroom in the Barnes mansion. She'd been here before…years ago. Back then, this room had been a sitting area attached to Logan Barnes's bedroom. Fate had brought her here again.

On the threshold of the playroom, she shut down the memories before they paralyzed her altogether to focus on Logan Barnes. He was sitting on the floor in front of an easy chair. With ease, he lifted his fourteen-month-old son high in the air. Little Daniel giggled and his dad laughed again.

The love between father and son was palpable as Gina took a step toward them, swallowing her anxiety. She called softly, "Logan?"

The tall, muscled, tawny-haired Texan stilled. Then

he got to his feet and slowly turned—his son in his arms—and faced her.

"I should have called you after your pediatrician set up this appointment with me for Daniel. But I knew the conversation would be awkward. And Tessa gave you my name so if you'd wanted to cancel—"

"I did my homework on you after Dr. Rossi made the appointment," he cut in, stopping her.

Though he had been relaxed before she'd entered, now his shoulders were straight, his stance taut and determined as he went on, "You're the only expert near Sagebrush with your credentials—an M.A. in pediatric physical therapy and a Ph.D. in infant and toddler development. When did you move back here and open the Baby Grows practice?"

Yes, he *had* done his homework. She should have expected that.

She moved into the playroom, settling her bag of evaluation materials on the round coffee table, then nervously pushed her tangle of curly black hair behind one ear. "I returned to Sagebrush about six months ago."

When she'd learned the Family Tree Health Center in Lubbock—fifteen minutes from Sagebrush—was looking for a baby development practitioner, she'd impulsively submitted her résumé. It was the first impulsive decision she'd made in a very long time.

In the palpating silence, her heart beat hard and fast, and words seemed to jam in her throat. She had to act perfectly normal. She had to act as if years and distance and memories didn't make any difference.

"I'm living in the Victorian where Tessa used to live," she added, "sharing it with another doctor from Family Tree."

Logan's son, Daniel, was staring at her, just like his dad. Now the little boy tilted his head, laid it on Logan's shoulder and gave her a smile.

She'd take whatever she could get. "And *you* must be Daniel."

The toddler straightened again and babbled a combination of "Da da" and "Dan Dan" with a few other syllables thrown in. His hair was sandy-brown like his dad's, his eyes the same shade of green. He was adorable in his cargo pants and red T-shirt, much more casual than his father who was still wearing a white shirt and dress slacks.

"Do you do all your clients' evals?" Logan asked, patting his son's back. "You couldn't have sent someone else?"

"I do the evaluations. I have therapists who work with the children, but they follow my plan."

Although Logan had been confident and assured from the day she'd met him in the estate's barn when she was eighteen, now he seemed to be debating with himself.

Suddenly Daniel leaned forward as if to take a better look at her. She raised her hands automatically as she would with any child, and he practically jumped into her arms.

"Hello, there!" she said with a laugh, comfortably clasping him securely. After all, she was used to being around babies.

"You have him?" Logan looked worried, hovering close, his arms practically around her and his son.

Oh, how she remembered the strength of those arms. Oh, how she remembered Logan's six-foot-two height, his protective consideration that had made her feel like a princess. So near to him again, she could feel his body heat, could feel her own rise.

It had always been that way between them.

Daniel put his tiny hands on her cheeks, one on each side of her face, and looked into her eyes.

She was fascinated by this little boy who, if his records were correct, hadn't learned to walk yet at fourteen months. He'd been a preemie and she didn't know the whole story behind that.

Logan seemed to decide she was capable of holding Daniel and stepped away. He pointed to the flannel bag on the coffee table. "A bag of tricks instead of a briefcase?" he asked.

At one time, Logan's green eyes would have twinkled and there would have been a smile at the corners of his mouth. But now he was making conversation, trying to figure out what was going to come next.

"It's more interesting than a briefcase, don't you think?"

The blue flannel bag almost looked like something Santa Claus would carry, only it was the wrong color.

The housekeeper, who had introduced herself as Mrs. Mahoney, peeked in the door. In her late forties, she wore her brown hair in a gamine cut. After a smile at Gina, she asked Logan, "Is there anything you need?"

"No, Hannah." He glanced at Gina. "You two have met?"

"We introduced ourselves when I came in," Gina assured him.

Mrs. Mahoney made her way into the room and ruffled Daniel's hair. "I forgot to tell you Daniel had his supper early so he should be in a good mood until he starts getting sleepy. Logan, you have leftovers in the oven. I'll be watching TV if you need me."

Mrs. Mahoney bent and gave Daniel a kiss on the forehead. "I'll see you at bedtime, big boy." Then with a wave to them all, she headed out the door toward her quarters.

The silence of the big house surrounded the three of them.

The three of them.

Gina tightened her hold around the warm cuddly weight in her arms. This toddler could have been her life. This child could have been *hers*. If only she'd turned around and come home. If only she hadn't gone to that frat party and had her life changed forever.

Too late. Too late. Too late.

The window of opportunity with Logan had passed. Even if it hadn't, she wasn't the same woman now that she'd been then. Nothing had ever been the same after her freshman year at college. She'd had to rebuild her world...alone.

Gina shifted Daniel to get a better idea of his weight and balance. When she tickled his tummy, he giggled.

"Maybe we'd better get started." Logan's voice was low and husky.

Her gaze met his and what she saw there shocked her as much as what she didn't see. His eyes used to be expressive—caring, amused, warm, simmering to share what had begun with one chaste kiss. Now they were turbulent, and she couldn't hold eye contact. That one look had made her feel such guilt. How could he do that without saying a word?

Fortunately Daniel was getting restless, rocking back and forth in her arms, and she could focus on him. "Where does Daniel spend most of his playtime?"

"Here."

"Good. I want to evaluate him with his own things around him."

Daniel wriggled more vigorously and Logan reached for him. "Do you want me to take him?"

Her pulse sped up with Logan so close. She noticed the way his cheeks had gotten leaner over the years, though his shoulders had grown more muscled. His waist was still tapered, and she recalled exactly how taut those stomach muscles had been.

Apparently Daniel thought his dad was going to pull him away from her. The baby slid his fingers into her curls and held on tight.

For years Gina had straightened her curls into more manageable waves. But over the past few months, she'd decided to let it curl naturally again. Now her concern was more for Daniel and his desire to hold on to her than her hair. "It's okay, little one. I'm not going anywhere. We're going to play for a bit."

Instead of scolding his son, Logan settled his hands over Daniel's and loosened the boy's fingers. When his tall, hard body leaned into her, Gina was overwhelmed with emotion—and memories. Logan's fingers in her hair reminded her of the time he'd stroked her curls as they lay on the sofa in the poolhouse.

"God gave you too many curls to count so they'd drive me crazy."

"Crazy?"

"Silky and soft and I want to touch every one of them."

Now, however, Logan just tickled his son, letting his laughter spill around them. Then he lifted Daniel from Gina, high into the air, causing the little boy to give a cry of joy.

Watching them together, Gina's heart hurt and her

arms felt so empty. She wrapped them around herself, knowing her evaluation had to be objective.

She could do this…she really could.

Logan sat straight on the cranberry leather sofa watching his son. Daniel crawled to Gina gleefully as if he'd been doing it ever since he could.

Maybe he just wanted to reach those bright-colored pegs on the board she held on her lap.

Unclenching his fist, Logan attempted to relax his posture so he didn't look like a man on guard. Why should he be on guard? Gina was just evaluating his son.

His son. His and Amy's son…the son his wife had died to save.

He might as well admit it. He was angry Gina was in his house, reminding him of a time he'd shoved behind him, reminding him of her desertion, reminding him of his father's stroke and the fact she'd left and hadn't looked back.

As Daniel plopped beside her on the floor stretching his hand toward the pegs on her board, Logan had to ask, "Why did you come back to Sagebrush?"

She didn't answer right away, rather set the board aside, picked up the remote-controlled car she'd removed from her bag and set it on the floor in front of her.

"My mom heard about the opening at the Family Tree Health Center and called to tell me about it. She and my dad have always wanted me to move back here, or at least closer than New England."

She pressed the button on the remote and the car skittered across a patch of hardwood floor. Daniel crawled after it as fast as his little legs would go.

"You know he can crawl," Logan grumbled. "Why keep encouraging him to do it?"

"I'm not encouraging him to crawl," she answered quietly. "I'm watching how he problem-solves, what he reaches for first, what muscles he uses when he does. He's not even thinking about using the coffee table or any other piece of furniture to stand up, and I'm wondering why."

Logan wondered the same thing.

Tessa had given Logan exercises to do with Daniel since he was a few months old. But recently, with his son still not walking, Logan had worried. Was Daniel simply a premature baby, slow in development? Or was there another problem, perhaps more serious? Gina was here to assess that possibility.

She directed the car back to where she sat and Daniel followed it. Levering herself to her knees, she clasped the little boy at the waist and encouraged him to stand. He did…while she supported him. Slowly she let her arms take less and less of his weight until he was standing on his own.

"You're such a big boy! Can you take my hands and come over to me?" She offered them to him, but he ignored her and plopped back down onto the floor as if that was where he was safe.

Suddenly she asked Logan, "Do you and Mrs. Mahoney carry him wherever he wants to go?"

Logan tried to restrain his impatience. "The house is huge. Usually I just scoop him up and bring him along. I guess Hannah might do the same."

If Gina noticed his impatience, she didn't respond to it. Instead she asked, "What about when you're relaxing in here, watching cartoons, something like that? Do you go to Daniel if you want him? Or do you encourage him to come to you?"

Logan thought about it. "Now that you mention it, I probably go to him and take him what he needs."

"Like a puzzle, or crayons, or blocks." She saw all those on the colorful shelves to the side of the room.

"Are you saying this is my fault?" He knew he sounded defensive and, dammit, he was. After all he'd been through with Amy, as well as Daniel, he'd done the best he could.

Gina handed Daniel a plastic bowling pin and watched him turn it upside down. "I think you can call Mrs. Mahoney now. I'd like to talk to you about Daniel and I think it would be better if he's not in the room."

"He's not going to understand—"

Gina's concerned brown eyes locked to his and her voice held conviction. "Daniel will understand our tone of voice. He'll understand our expressions. He'll understand if we're happy, sad, angry or frustrated."

Gina Rigoletti *was* the baby expert and with reluctance Logan recognized that fact. He pressed a button on the console where the cordless phone sat on the end table.

Long minutes later, Hannah entered the room. "Is Daniel ready for bed?"

"If you could get him ready, that would be great," Logan said. "I'll be in as soon as Dr. Rigoletti leaves."

As soon as Hannah left with Daniel, Gina began gathering assessment sheets and toys she'd stacked on the coffee table and the floor around her. She slipped the papers onto her clipboard. The rest went back into that flannel bag.

She stood, seemed to debate with herself, and then joined Logan on the sofa. "I'll e-mail your copy of my formal evaluation tomorrow. For now, I'll give you the highlights." She looked down at the notes she'd taken. "First of all, Daniel was a preemie. He's within the normal range of walking, which is fifteen months. I think with encouragement—the right kind of encouragement—that can happen."

"What do you mean the *right* kind of encouragement? I'm always asking him to come to me."

"We'll get into that." She checked her notes again. Because she didn't want to look at him?

"I know you're doing exercises with Daniel now. We're going to expand those a little if you decide to put him under my care. I'd like you to do them with him daily in between sessions. In addition, you have to stop carrying him when he can get somewhere on his own. You need to be patient enough to wait for him, encourage him to stand and walk with you. I think he'll do it if you simply let him lag behind. He won't like that. He needs motivation to get up and walk. You have to help him develop that."

Logan let out a sigh and ran a hand through his hair. "I thought kids learned to roll over, sit up, crawl and walk instinctively. I never expected Daniel to have problems with those things."

"He might be slower talking, too—sometimes preemies are. But you can encourage him in that area, also. The more verbal he becomes, the sooner he'll talk. He already understands more than you think he does. If you bring him what he wants or needs without him asking, there won't be any reason for him to ask."

"So his *not* walking yet isn't a permanent problem?"

"In my opinion, I don't think it is. In a few weeks, we'll know better."

"In a few weeks, he'll be walking?"

"I didn't say that. Children have their own timetable. But I'll set up a program where we'll strengthen his muscles, encourage him and motivate him."

Logan made a sudden decision before he thought better of it. "You'll be able to come here to do it?"

Her eyes widened in surprise. "I thought just the evaluation would be here."

"I'll pay double. It will save me time running back and forth to your practice in Lubbock."

She thought about it. "I suppose one of my therapists—"

He cut in, "Aren't *you* the most qualified?"

"Yes, but…"

"Then I want *you* to handle his care." Logan couldn't believe he was inviting Gina back into his home. Judging by her silence, she was just as surprised. But he had to do what was best for Daniel. On the other hand, if he was honest with himself, he also had to admit he wanted to see the woman she'd become…if she felt regrets for leaving the way she had and turning her back on him.

Why did he even care?

He cared because when he looked at her…his body responded as it had when he was in his twenties. He resented that fact. He'd been happily married. He still missed the woman who had given her life for their son. Any reaction to Gina came from the past and he had to douse it. Daniel was his only focus now.

When Gina's gaze met his, he saw emotion flicker there. He thought he saw the corner of her lip quiver. That used to happen when she was upset or nervous. He was sure she was going to refuse his offer.

Instead, she straightened her back and didn't look away. "I can handle some of Daniel's treatment here, but I'll need him at Baby Grows for sessions, too. I can't start a program without you agreeing to that."

There was a bit of steel in her tone and an assertiveness she'd lacked as a teenager. She'd obviously grown into a strong woman.

Just as Amy was strong, an inner voice reminded him. Just as Amy had been unbending in her determination to keep Daniel safe.

"How often?"

"That depends on my schedule. I can commit to one evening a week."

"That's fine." He thought about his busy May schedule…watching Gina with Daniel even on a limited basis…and added, "When I can't be here, Hannah will be."

"Logan, you need to participate in the program I set up. That's important to Daniel."

Something about his name on her lips shook him a little. It cracked the vault of memories he'd carefully sealed and buried. "All right, I'll make sure I'm available. Is there anything else you need from me right now?"

She looked as if she was debating with herself but finally answered, "No."

"Daniel and I have a routine at bedtime. I don't want to disrupt that. Hannah will see you out."

The room had become stifling with them both in it. Memories seemed to dance between them, muddling the past with the present. He needed to hold his son and forget about what had happened so long ago.

He headed for the doorway.

"Logan?"

When he turned to face Gina again, she looked vulnerable. He almost crossed the room, almost gave in to the instinct to reassure her that everything would be all right, as he might have once done.

Now he kept silent.

Appearing flustered for a moment, she finally said, "Call me tomorrow to set up an appointment." She took a card from her pocket, covered the distance between them, and handed it to him. "All my numbers are on there. If you can't reach me at Baby Grows, you can reach me on my cell phone or at home."

His fingers grazed hers as he took the card, and he willed his body not to record the brief contact. His voice became rough as he responded, "Thanks."

Then he left Gina in Daniel's playroom and breathed a deep sigh of relief.

On Saturday morning, Gina sat in the small parlor off the living room in the old Victorian house in Sagebrush, tapping her foot, too edgy to admire the chintz material on the love seat, the dragonfly Tiffany lamp sitting on the corner of the library table she and her housemate, Raina, used as a desk. Her heart practically tripped over itself as she waited for Logan to answer his cell phone. She had to change the appointment the two of them had set up for Daniel a few days ago. It just couldn't be helped.

"Barnes," he answered in a clipped voice and she heard machinery in the background.

"Logan, it's Gina."

"Hold on a minute," he said to her. "I need to move into an area where I can hear you."

She guessed he was at the denim factory the Barnes family had owned and operated for decades.

Finally he said, "Okay, I'm in my office. What's up?"

Anyone listening in would think they knew each other…would think maybe they were friends again. Friends. Could they even come close to that?

"Logan, I need to change Daniel's appointment. Can we switch it from Monday night to Wednesday night?"

He was quiet for a few moments, then responded, "Gina, if you don't have time to do this, maybe I *should* find someone else."

They were going to have to clear the air at some point and bring everything out into the open…what had happened since she'd left. Not even her parents knew she'd been raped during her first year at college. But now just wasn't the right time to go into it with Logan.

"I'd like to help Daniel if I can, but Family Tree set up a meeting for all its practitioners on Monday evening. There are budget and billing concerns and the decision to have the meeting was made just last night. It's not something I can opt out of."

The only sound she heard was her pulse in her temples, then Logan's deep baritone, a little lower and huskier now. It affected her the way it always had, making her nerve endings come alive.

"I see. I shouldn't have jumped to the conclusion you didn't want to treat Daniel. But in our situation—"

"I don't run from clients who need me."

"No, but you might run from *me.*"

Because she had run once before. She couldn't get into that over the phone. "So will Wednesday at six work for you?" she asked, ignoring his comment.

After a pause, he agreed, "It will work. We'll see how Daniel responds at that time of evening. If you think the appointments need to be during the day, I'll take off work if I have to."

"You're there now?"

"Yes. A malfunction with one of the machines."

"Is it unusual for you to be there on a Saturday?"

"Not really. If we have orders, we cut the material. That's the only way to stay ahead these days. Fortunately, denim is as popular as it ever was, all different grades, old ways of making it and new."

They could talk about his business or…she could say what was in her heart.

"Logan, the other night…I wanted to tell you how sorry I am about your wife."

"Thank you." His voice was strained.

"Sometime maybe you can tell me about it. That might help me with Daniel."

"You have his medical records. You know he was premature. That's all you need."

She shouldn't have said anything because he wasn't going to give an inch with her…even after all these years. He wasn't going to tell her what his life was about, except for Daniel. Maybe she'd feel the same way if she'd lost her spouse.

"I didn't mean to pry. Really. But children are little sponges. Emotions play into their physical development."

She could hear Logan blow out a breath. "If there's anything that I think will help Daniel, I'll tell you. I'll see you at six on Wednesday."

"Six on Wednesday," she repeated. She thought she heard him murmur, "Goodbye, Gina," but she couldn't be sure.

When she said goodbye, he was no longer there.

Chapter Two

The following Tuesday evening, Gina stirred the pot of soup then tasted it. She wrinkled her nose. Why didn't her minestrone ever taste like her mother's?

She was replacing the lid when she heard the front door slam. Raina called, "I'm home. What smells so good?"

"Soup. And I stopped for a loaf of bread to go with it. Are you hungry?"

"For *your* soup? Yes."

Raina Greystone Gibson entered the kitchen. She was a beautiful woman with a Cheyenne heritage. Her hair was long, flowing past her shoulders. Usually she wore a headband or clipped it back in a low ponytail the way it was tonight. It appeared black until she stood in the sun and chestnut highlights gleamed. Gina had liked Raina, a pediatric ear, nose and throat doctor, immediately when she'd met her at Family Tree. She'd learned that Raina had returned to Sagebrush from New York City, where her husband, a firefighter, had been killed on September 11.

"Is Lily still joining us?" Gina asked, hoping the fertility specialist also practicing at Family Tree hadn't been held up.

"Yes, I told her she could drive over with me, but she had errands to run first. She'll be here in a little while. She was glad we invited her for dinner since Troy had a meeting. I'm not sure how she'll handle it when he's deployed to the Middle East."

This summer Lily's husband, Troy, a member of the Texas Army National Guard, would be deployed for pre-mission training. Lily couldn't even think about later in the summer when he'd be gone.

"The support group for military families will help her and so will we."

Raina went to the cupboard and began removing dishes she could use to set the table. "Speaking of support, I really enjoyed dinner with your family on Sunday."

Gina removed the lid from the soup once more and stirred. "My mom said you're invited again this week. Everyone liked you. Especially my nephew Evan. I think he has a crush on you."

Raina laughed. "Since he's twelve, give him a week and he'll have a crush on someone else."

Shortly after Raina had moved in with Gina, she'd admitted she didn't date. She'd also confided she intended never to marry again. She understood loving and losing better than most.

Maybe that was what prompted Gina to ask, "Do you know Logan Barnes?"

After closing the cupboard, Raina glanced at Gina. "*The* Logan Barnes? The CEO of Barnes Denim? The mover and shaker who dines with the governor and owns real estate from San Diego to Sydney…the man who set up a charitable foundation to fund cancer research?" She'd listed some of his accomplishments as if to say that *everyone,* especially in the state of Texas, had heard of him.

"That would be the one," Gina confirmed.

"We don't exactly move in the same circles," Raina said, flashing Gina a grin. "Why?"

"I met Logan the month I graduated from high school. His father hired me to work in the stables on the estate. Logan and I…well, we connected that summer."

Raina took the dishes to the table. "How seriously?"

Gina remembered Logan's mother's antique locket that he'd given her after they'd made love for the first time. She'd returned it when she'd said goodbye. "He wanted me to stay and marry him, but I left and went to college," Gina explained as simply as she could. "I ran into him this week and…it's obvious he's still angry with me."

Now Raina studied Gina. "Does it matter to you? That he's angry?"

If *that* wasn't a perceptive question. "Yes, I guess it does. After all these years, I thought maybe he'd think of me less harshly."

"Was college the only reason you broke up with him?"

One of the qualities Gina admired most about Raina was her ability to see deeply into any situation.

"Lots of reasons." She thought about Logan's father, his warning that he'd disinherit Logan if she got too serious about him. She recalled her parents' advice and her older sister Josie's practical admonition not to marry too young—because *she'd* had to. "I had a full scholarship," Gina explained to Raina. "No one in our family had graduated from college. But mainly Logan's father had his own ideas about who Logan should marry. I was too insecure to stay and fight for our love. I didn't think I had a chance. I thought about coming back and marrying him after I got to college, but then something happened that changed my life and I was on a different track."

"Changed your life?"

Even though Gina and Raina had only known each other a few months, Raina was fast becoming a trusted friend. Gina considered telling her about the date rape that had occurred two months into her first college semester.

The doorbell rang.

"That must be Lily," Raina said, halting their conversation with a concerned look.

"It's okay," Gina assured her. "We can talk about it another time."

Raina nodded. "Any time you want to."

When the doorbell rang again, Raina crossed the kitchen to the living room, unaware of what Gina had been about to disclose.

Moments later, Gina heard Lily's voice. As she entered the kitchen, Gina smiled broadly at the bubbly blonde who seemed to bring sunshine with her whenever she stepped into the room.

Lily held a bag in her arms and set it on the island counter.

"I told you you didn't have to bring anything," Gina protested.

"I didn't bring much. Just a couple of deli salads

and…" She produced half of a chocolate cake with peanut-butter icing. "I thought we needed a little decadence."

Gina didn't know when she'd last felt decadent.

"Thank you," she said, meaning it, glad she'd taken the time to get to know Lily at a practitioners' cocktail party at the Family Tree. Lily's specialty practice enabled women to conceive. She was upbeat, always ready with a smile and a hug.

Lily glanced around the kitchen to the patio beyond. "You two are lucky to have found this place. It's a great house."

"It's big, but it's cozy, too," Raina assured her. "It kind of wraps itself around you. When I first walked into the foyer to consider living here with Gina, it felt like home. It's hard to explain."

"You *have* heard the rumor about it, haven't you?" Lily asked.

"What rumor?" both women returned.

"Well, since Tessa Rossi, Emily Madison and Francesca Fitzgerald all lived here and have now gotten married, the rumor is that any woman who lives here will find true love."

"I like the rumor," Gina said. "But I think it's wishful thinking."

"Maybe for me," Raina decided. "But what about *you?*"

Lily looked from one woman to the other. "What don't I know…besides the obvious million things?"

Gina felt heat creep into her cheeks. "I…ran into someone I used to date before I left Sagebrush for college."

"There's a story there." Lily's blue eyes twinkled.

"There certainly is," Gina agreed. "But it will keep.

Bring over those soup dishes and we'll start our meal with minestrone."

"An old family recipe?" Lily asked hopefully, apparently aware Gina wanted to change the topic. "One that you can share?"

"Well, I can share it. Just don't ever tell my mother that I put canned tomatoes in the pot. She'd be horrified."

Gina focused on the soup recipe and the meal she was about to share with her two friends, sure she could prevent herself from thinking about Logan and Daniel.

Couldn't she?

Logan never expected to be in this position…in his house with Gina playing with his son in the family room. His and Amy's son.

On Wednesday evening, Gina encouraged Daniel to fall onto the ball that was just his size. She'd brought a mat along, too, so if he tumbled off, he wouldn't hurt himself.

"Come on, Daniel. Let's rock back and forth." She was holding his hands as he lay over the ball and pushed with his feet.

Logan knew they weren't actually playing. They were working. But Daniel would never suspect that, not from the way Gina interacted with him.

"We never use this room," Logan said to himself, but it must have been loud enough for Gina to hear.

"Why not? It's a beautiful room."

She was right. It was. The carpet was plush and an ocean-blue. The draperies were thick. The furniture was a mixture of tan and gray and blue-green, cushiony and comfortable. If he ever wanted to watch a game on the huge flat-screen TV, he'd feel as if he were in the middle of it.

Something Logan couldn't define urged him to be honest with Gina. "My wife redecorated this room. I thought we'd be playing on the floor with Daniel, watching kid videos with him on the TV."

After their gazes held for a long moment, Gina broke eye contact and let Daniel roll off the ball. She tussled with him a couple of minutes, making him laugh, then she let him sit with a few toys just to see what he would do.

"Would you rather I move Daniel into his playroom? I'd like him out of his comfort zone so he'll have to go a distance to get to wherever he wants."

"The room's here," Logan responded offhandedly. "We might as well use it."

Their gazes locked again, and he saw something on Gina's face that stabbed at his heart. Was it regret? Was it guilt?

He almost moved closer to her, anything to relieve the tension that had pulled between them from the moment she'd walked back into his life.

The tension was abruptly broken when Hannah came rushing into the room. "That reporter's here again, Logan. He wants to do a story on you for the Style section of the Sunday paper. What should I tell him?"

"I'll take care of it," Logan assured her and strode out of the room, glad for the interruption, glad to escape the web of emotion that seemed to surround him whenever Gina was within arm's reach.

After Logan left the family room, Hannah declared, "He doesn't like publicity, so that makes reporters want to come after him even more."

Before Gina could think better of it, she said, "If I

remember correctly, Logan's father didn't like publicity, either."

Hannah shot her a quizzical look. "You knew Elliot Barnes?"

"I can't say I *knew* him. He was my employer one summer."

Watching Daniel play with the toys Gina had given him, Hannah sat on the sofa. "Oh, I see. The two men are as different as night and day, though. Mr. Barnes, senior, didn't want publicity because he just didn't want to be bothered. After his stroke, he became quite a recluse. Little by little, he turned everything over to Logan. Now Logan, on the other hand, doesn't want publicity because he thinks it's foolish and should be saved for something important—like the charities he backs—not a dinner he's giving or an event he's attending. But reporters always want to know all about his life. That's when Logan clams up."

Gina hadn't known Elliot Barnes had suffered a stroke. Had it been severe? She was about to ask Hannah when Daniel crawled to the housekeeper and pleaded, "Up?"

She looked down at him with a fond smile. "Oh, no. I'm not picking you up. Those are the new rules."

Gina laughed. "I'll bet they are. That smile of his and those green eyes could melt any heart."

Daniel tugged on Hannah's slacks.

"I gave him quite a workout," Gina relented. "I think we're finished for today."

"We've gotten an official okay," Hannah said to Daniel as she stooped over and lifted him. "Time for your supper." She glanced at the balls, blocks and the push toy Gina had brought along. "Do you need help gathering all that?"

"Oh, no. You take care of Daniel. I'll be fine."

After Hannah left the room with the toddler, Gina began collecting what she'd brought. She'd been strung tight ever since she'd entered the house. Usually when she was working with a child, that baby was her main focus. Daniel *had* been her focus, but she'd also been aware of Logan watching her…aware of Logan. There was a vibrating energy connecting them, like a live wire. She didn't know how to break it, deflect it or let it burn out.

When Logan reentered the room, he'd rolled up his white shirtsleeves and opened the first few buttons of his shirt. He looked strong. Totally male. Absolutely sexy.

She swallowed hard, realizing how much she was still attracted to him. "Trouble?" she asked, just to say something.

"No. Just an eager journalism student wanting to make a name for himself."

Gina moved toward the corner of the mat she'd opened on the plush carpeting to give extra padding. As she folded it, Logan came to help her. They practically brushed shoulders. Both jerked away.

She knew she had to do something about the awkwardness between them. "Logan, I don't have to be the one who helps Daniel."

Logan rubbed his hand up and down the back of his neck. "No, I suppose you don't. But he obviously relates well to you. I don't want to mess with that. Hannah's been the only woman in his life since he was born."

"What happened?" Gina asked softly.

Logan's green gaze was penetrating as he studied her, trying to decipher why she wanted to know.

Finally he answered, "One day Amy and I were on

top of the world, the next an earthquake destroyed everything we thought we were building."

As if he knew he was being cryptic, he sat on the sofa, studied the carpet for a few moments, then met Gina's gaze. Something in his eyes drew her to him and she lowered herself beside him, though not too close.

When he started talking, Gina knew he didn't discuss this often because his voice was strained.

"Amy was ecstatic when she discovered she was pregnant," he began. "We'd been married a few years, and we both wanted kids. She'd been working hard at her career—she was a real estate agent and intended to keep selling properties after our baby was born. But soon after she learned she was pregnant, she had symptoms that sent us to a neurologist and then a neurosurgeon. She had a brain tumor."

Gina desperately wanted to reach out to Logan, to touch his arm. Yet she couldn't. She had no right. "I'm so sorry." She was. She'd never wanted anything but happiness for him. That was why she'd left.

Logan didn't seem to hear her. He stared across the room and explained, "Her doctor wanted to treat the cancer aggressively, but Amy wouldn't let him do surgery or put anything in her body that could damage Daniel. She decided if she survived the pregnancy, she'd have treatment after our baby was born. But that day never came. She had a stroke at thirty-two weeks. The doctors performed a C-section and she died shortly after."

One look at Logan's face and Gina knew he was reliving that time in his life. Did he want comfort? Did he want sympathy? Or did he just need to look forward?

Gina didn't want to trample over sacred ground so she asked, "How long was Daniel in the hospital?"

"Eight weeks…a terrifically *long* eight weeks."

"Who was his doctor?"

"Francesca Talbott. I think it's Fitzgerald now."

"Yes, it is. She shared the house with me until she got married," Gina said softly.

"It really *is* a small world, isn't it?" he asked, finally looking at her.

"It can be."

After a silence-filled pause, Logan asked, "Did you marry?"

His question surprised her. "No."

What would he say if she told him what had happened? It really made no difference to their relationship. She'd left him, no matter what had happened afterward. "I've been focused on my work all these years, trying to make a name in my field."

"So why come back to Sagebrush *now?*" He looked genuinely perplexed.

"I'm not exactly sure. I began missing my family more. I knew I needed something different—closer friends, bonds, actual fun."

The lines on Logan's face told her he hadn't had fun in a long time, not since before his wife died. Daniel might bring him joy, but Gina had the feeling it was fleeting.

"We really don't have to work in here, Logan. I understand how memories can suck the air out of the room."

Logan shrugged. "If I get used to seeing Daniel playing in here, crawling in here, maybe eventually walking in here, it will be fine."

She could only imagine what Logan had been through—his wife's diagnosis, losing her and at the same time dealing with Daniel's hospital stay. "It takes a while to recover from any trauma." She knew that all too well. Counseling sessions and talking and crying and just putting one foot in front of the other, even when you thought you couldn't, took energy, motivation and sometimes steel will. Logan had all of those. Still...

Logan stared at a picture of Daniel on a side table.

Gina assured him, "He's a wonderful little boy. Quick and learning more each day. When I arrived, I suggested to Hannah if you fill two of the bottom cupboards in the kitchen with pots and pans, colorful containers, anything Daniel might feel he'd like to get into, that might give him more motivation to explore his world."

Logan was quiet a moment, then he turned his focus to her. "I guess parents are always supposed to teach their kids to explore the world."

"That gets scarier for both the parents and kids as they get older. Learning to walk across the room suddenly becomes all-day kindergarten and then piano lessons, and then driving and dating!"

Logan remarked, "Your parents encouraged *you* to explore your world. Your education was as important to them as it was to you."

"It wasn't just my education," Gina said quietly, hoping she could break through the icy wall Logan had constructed between them.

"I know. There was your younger sister. Did she eventually go to school?"

"Yes, she did. Angie is a nurse and I'm proud of her." If only they could keep talking—

Suddenly Logan stood. "It's good you don't have any regrets."

She hadn't said she didn't have regrets.

Logan went on, "This is bath night and it's one of the things I enjoy doing most with my son, at least until he gets old enough to ride a horse. I'll help you gather this up and walk you out."

As he stuffed a toy elephant and lion into one of her drawstring bags, she asked him, "Are you still angry that I left?"

His answer was slow in coming as his gaze finally met hers. "I'll probably always be angry that you left. But…if you hadn't left, I wouldn't have Daniel. I love him more than anything in this world."

There was nothing she could say to that.

A few days later, when Gina stopped in at the Target that had recently opened in Sagebrush, she ran through the baby department. It was a habit, keeping her eye on the latest trends in toys and car seats, in strollers and play furniture. Tonight, she pushed her cart around the corner into the toy department. There, she stopped cold.

Logan stood in front of a shelf, holding a remote-control car in one arm, studying the RC truck directly in front of him.

For a nanosecond, Gina thought about turning around and going the other way. Logan didn't have to know she'd seen him. He didn't have to know she was here. But that was the coward's way out. She was no longer a coward. At least she hoped she wasn't.

Rolling her cart up beside him, she asked, "Looking for a new hobby?"

He went still, then he turned to face her. "No," he drawled in that Texas deep baritone that had always curled her toes. "I thought Hannah and I might take bets on who could run their car across the yard the fastest."

Gina laughed at his wry tone. "I bet Daniel would enjoy that. He might even chase one."

"That's the idea," Logan assured her.

At that moment, they both understood the motivation Daniel needed to learn to walk. It was the first tension-free moment she and Logan had shared.

He nodded to her cart filled with three pairs of shorts and a few knit tops. "New wardrobe for summer?" he joked.

Actually it was. She didn't owe him any explanations but she explained anyway. "I lost a few pounds so I needed something that fitted a little better than what was in my closet."

"Intentionally?"

"What?" she asked, lost in his eyes for the moment.

"Did you lose weight intentionally?"

He was looking at her in a way that made her nerve endings dance. She hadn't felt that way when a man looked at her for a very long time. "No, not intentionally. With the move, a new job, a new life really, it just happened."

"Are you glad you moved back here?"

Standing here face-to-face with Logan, she wasn't quite sure how to answer. Finally she responded, "I like the life I'm building. I like the new friends I've made. My practice is rewarding and it's good to be near family again."

"You stayed away a long time."

"Yes, I did, in part because I didn't want to face you."

For a moment, Logan's guard slipped and he looked astonished. Was he surprised she'd been so honest? Maybe that was what they needed between them, some old-fashioned honesty. Just how far was she willing to go with it?

"You didn't have to face me," he said evenly.

"We live in a small town, Logan. I knew eventually I'd run into you."

"Why didn't you send someone else from Baby Grows to evaluate Daniel?"

She expected this question had been bothering him since the night she'd appeared at his house. "As I told you, I do all the evaluations. I wasn't going to shirk my responsibility."

He seemed to mull that over. "You're an expert in your field."

"Some people would say that."

"And now that we *have* come face-to-face?" he asked, his voice challenging.

"I'd like you to forgive me," she blurted out, without considering the consequences.

There seemed to be a sudden hush all around them. Then Logan shifted, adjusting the toy under his arm. "I don't know what to say to that. When you left, the bottom dropped out of my world in more ways than one. I've never forgotten how that felt. I've never forgotten how you didn't even have time to have a conversation when I called you in Connecticut."

She couldn't deal with this here. What had she expected when she'd started this? That it would be easy? That he'd forgive her and they'd go on being friends?

"Logan, things had happened…"

He gave a short laugh. "Yes, I'm sure they had. You probably met someone at school and—"

"No, nothing like that."

He looked startled at her vehemence. "You're not the same Gina you were fourteen years ago."

"I certainly hope not." She tried to keep her tone

light. They hadn't spent enough time together to *know* how each other had changed.

Logan cocked his head, studying her with those penetrating eyes that had so often seen right through her. But not tonight. She held secrets he'd never know about unless they could find more common ground than this.

If she brought the conversation back to Daniel, maybe the tension between them would ease. "I was thinking…" she said slowly.

He waited for her to go on.

"Can you bring Daniel to Baby Grows on Saturday? I'd like to ask Tessa to stop in with her two children and I want to watch Daniel react with them, play with them. We have more equipment there, too."

"Tessa won't mind giving up her Saturday morning?"

"After rounds, she usually takes the kids to the library. She said she'd just bring them to Baby Grows instead."

"All right, I can do that. Do you have appointments before Daniel, or do you want me to pick you up?"

Logan had always been a gentleman, and thoroughly polite. He was being courteous now and she shouldn't read any more into his offer than that. "I do have other appointments, but thanks for offering." Before she saw more recriminations in his eyes, she pointed to the shelf. "So, which one are you going to buy?"

"You have a car when you work with him. I think I'll go with the truck."

"What about Hannah?"

He rewarded her with a small smile. "Maybe she'd like the motorcycle."

Gina laughed. "She probably would."

After he stacked the motorcycle on top of the truck, he asked her, "Are you finished shopping?"

"Yes."

"I'll walk you out."

More courtesy? Her heart was already in overdrive and now it sped up a little more.

Walking beside Logan, she was reminded just how tall he was, just how broad his shoulders were, just how slim his hips were in his black jeans. He kept enough distance between them that their arms wouldn't brush. She didn't glance at him, but she felt *him* looking at *her.* She pretended not to be affected either by his presence beside her or his gaze on her, but she was.

At the checkout line, they didn't speak as she used her credit card, then picked up her packages. He went through and paid in cash.

Then he took her bag from her. "I'll carry this to your car for you."

Being with Logan was a combination of bittersweet and exciting. She knew he'd be relieved if he went his way and she went hers, yet she didn't want to leave his company. Just like so many years ago.

At her car, she used the remote to unlock the doors and pop the trunk. They went around to the back and he dropped her purchases inside. There was a duffel bag there.

"Do you belong to a gym?" he asked as if he *was* curious about her life now.

"No, but I walk whenever I can. In Lubbock at lunchtime, sometimes I do a couple of laps around the center. In Sagebrush, I like to take the trail around the lake."

"You always did like the outdoors." He slammed the lid of her trunk.

"I still do. I hiked a lot in New England. Here, I'd like to take up riding again. Francesca and I have gone on a couple of trail rides at her ranch. I've ridden at Tessa's, too. I'd forgotten how wonderful it feels to be on horseback."

Logan walked to her car door and stood very close, so close she could reach up and touch his jawline, so close she could see that the lines around his eyes and his mouth weren't superficial. They'd been carved from pain. All she wanted to do was ease them away.

"You asked me about forgiving you..." His voice was low and husky.

She held her breath and waited.

"I can't give you an answer, Gina, and I don't know if time will help or not. That night after we split up, my father had a stroke."

That night. A rush of dread made her cold all over. "What happened?"

He looked away from her as if warring with himself over the answer. "We argued about you."

Her chest felt tight. "Why?"

"I went riding after you left, trying to figure out what to do. When I got back to the barn, Dad confronted me. He said I was better off without you. But I didn't believe that. I was going to talk to your parents...convince them they were interfering and they shouldn't be...convince you that we could make something work long-distance. Dad grabbed my arm. I tore away. And then—suddenly he couldn't speak and he collapsed."

Gina was stunned. A tiny shard of guilt pierced her heart at the realization that she hadn't been there for Logan.

"I called the paramedics and he was rushed to the hospital. We managed to keep all of it quiet. Dad

abhorred publicity and the hospital and medical personnel were cooperative. His recovery took about three
months. He was fortunate he regained his speech and
most of his mobility. But the whole process was—"
Logan halted as if he didn't want to admit how much
his father's collapse and recovery had affected him.

"I'm so sorry," she managed to say, feeling so
much sympathy for him that tears welled in her eyes.
"Three months," she murmured. "That's around when
you called—"

"I was hoping we could just talk. I was hoping—"
He shook his head. "But you didn't have time to talk.
You had to run off to take a test."

"You never called again," she said softly, remembering how numb she'd been for such a long time after the
rape. She *had* had a test that day. But more important,
she'd been too raw to talk to anyone. Should she tell
Logan that? Could he possibly understand?

No. This wasn't about her. The distance between them
was all about her letting down Logan in so many ways.
If she had fought for the love she'd felt for him, then
maybe more than one tragedy could have been avoided.

"Logan, I don't know what to say."

"You don't have to say anything."

She heard a car door slam…children laughing near
the store's exit.

So much had happened to both of them. She'd lost her
sense of safety, her trust in her judgment, her trust in men.
Logan had gone on to marry and lost a wife he'd obviously loved. He now had a son his wife had died to save.
How much more he must love her for that. How much
he must cherish Daniel as the gift his wife had given him.

The twelve-foot-high parking-lot light lit up the area

where Gina's car was parked. In the blink of an eye, she thought she saw a flash of tenderness in Logan's eyes. But then whatever emotion he'd felt disappeared.

They'd been standing as close as two people having an intimate conversation would be, but now he took a step back. "I'll see you Saturday morning at Baby Grows."

Her throat tightened and she wanted to reach out and hug him, hold on to him, cry with him. Instead, she simply nodded.

A few feet away, Logan waited until she slid into her car, closed the door and started the engine. Then he strode to his car as she drove away, swiping at the lone tear that rolled down her cheek.

Chapter Three

Logan could hardly hold on to Daniel Saturday morning. His son peered around at the colorful equipment in the therapeutic workroom at the Baby Grows practice, pointing to a big red ball. "Baw!"

As soon as Gina came toward them, Daniel reached for her and practically jumped into her arms.

"It's so good to see you again," she told the little boy, her face lighting up as it always did when she was around him.

In spite of common sense telling him to let it go, Logan couldn't help but wonder how she felt about seeing *him,* especially after their goodbye in the parking lot. Why couldn't he just tell her he forgave her?

Because it wouldn't be honest. It might smooth the waters, but it wasn't the truth. He didn't know what *was* the truth. Ever since Amy had died, his life had taken on a manage-each-day quality.

"I wasn't sure you'd come," she said to Logan.

He saw vulnerability in her brown eyes but didn't know what to do about it. "I've learned over the years avoidance only buys time. It doesn't solve the problem. So we're here to get Daniel walking."

"Logan, I just want to say again I'm sorry about everything that happened."

He could see she didn't want to let their conversation in the parking lot go, but he did. "Let's put the past behind us for now, okay?"

She seemed to tear her gaze reluctantly from his to focus on his son. "So what do you think we should try first?" Gina asked Daniel as if she had this kind of conversation with a fourteen-month-old every day.

"He's never tried a sliding board." Logan didn't know if that piece of information would be useful or not.

"The sliding board is a great idea. If he likes to ride down, he might try to climb up."

She took Daniel over to the three-foot-high sliding board and sat him on top. "No more carrying. Anywhere you want to go today, you have to get there on your own steam."

His green eyes sparkling, Daniel tilted his head and studied her face. Then he raised his legs up and down on the slide portion of the equipment and said, "Go…go…go."

"Great exercise," she encouraged him, watching his leg movement. "That will help strengthen those muscles." She crouched down at the bottom of the board. "Come on. Let's see if you can push yourself off."

After a few moments of squiggling and squirming,

gravity helped Daniel slide sideways down the short board. He careened onto the soft mat beneath it and grinned up at Gina.

Logan felt as if his heart was cracking into a few more pieces. Daniel should be looking up like that at his mother.

If Amy had lived—

Logan might not have Daniel.

If Gina had stayed—

Logan might not have Daniel.

How could he regret any part of his life when his son was the result of it?

Suddenly, from the reception area, Logan heard a woman's voice call, "Is anyone here?" He also heard the chatter of children.

Tessa Rossi entered the room in obvious mother mode. On her left side, she held the hand of nineteen-month-old Sean and on her right, that of little Natalie, who looked to be over two. Logan remembered hearing about the little boy and girl from Hannah, who knew Tessa's nanny and housekeeper. The children had been through a lot in their short lives, and now Tessa and her husband, Vince, were in the process of adopting them both.

Tessa headed straight for Logan. "Hi! Gina said Daniel could use some playmates."

"I never really thought about it," Logan admitted. "I was an only child and learned to occupy myself. I guess I thought Daniel would do the same."

"Oh, but they learn so much from each other—good *and* bad," she confided with a wise smile.

He laughed. "I suppose that's true."

Sean and Natalie both looked up at Tessa. When she gave a nod, they ran over to Gina and Daniel.

Logan watched as the kids both gave Gina hugs. "They seem to like her."

"Oh, they love her. She knows just what to say to them, just how to handle them, and it's all genuine."

"How long have you known Gina?"

"Since January. A mutual friend introduced us."

"Francesca Fitzgerald."

"That's right." Tessa's gaze asked how he knew.

"Gina mentioned Francesca and I told her she was Daniel's neonatologist."

"They're both women who are dedicated to helping babies."

Maybe so. But he was still curious about something. "I'm surprised Gina came back here."

"Why are you surprised?"

"According to everything I discovered when I searched her name on the Internet, she was headed up the career ladder. After undergraduate work, she earned her Ph.D. at a larger university. Then she moved on to become the dean of a teaching program in early development at a college in Massachusetts. All along she's published in well-respected journals. A couple of years ago she moved back to Connecticut to head up a new baby study at her alma mater. Lubbock just seems small potatoes compared to what she could be doing and where she could be going."

"Have you really *watched* her with the children, Logan?"

They stood about twenty feet away from Gina. He had to admit, up until now, he got distracted just looking at her. He always wanted to run his hands through the tumbled curls, to tap his finger on the little bump on her nose.

Now he really looked at her—the expert, the teacher,

the therapist. She was a combination of all three. As Natalie and Sean tumbled and pushed on a beanbag chair, Logan noticed Gina using more than the tools in her repertoire. Yes, she was competent, decisive and knowledgeable. But on top of all that, there was a pure love in her eyes for the children she was with.

"Gina just wants to work with babies who need help. When I met her, I wondered immediately why she hadn't married and didn't have a brood of her own," Tessa mused.

"Did she ever tell you why she hadn't married?"

"Not really. I think she was just too busy earning her degrees."

Too busy? Or some other reason? Gina herself had told him that something had happened after she left Sagebrush. Had she moved around so much for professional reasons? Or something else?

"Sean and Daniel seem to be getting along well," Tessa commented.

To Logan's surprise, Daniel crawled after Sean. Tessa's little boy found a stack of chunky blocks. While Logan held his breath, Daniel pushed himself to his knees and, using a small table for leverage, pulled himself up. But then his son sat again and stacked one block on top of another with Sean's help.

"He's teetering on the edge," Tessa said. "He could walk anytime."

"I think he might forget himself and just do it if he's playing with Sean."

"Kids help each other develop skills. It's wonderful to watch."

For the past couple of years, Logan's employees had been voicing their opinions about opening a day-care center at the factory. First he'd dismissed the idea because of the expense. But after doing feasibility research, he'd been much more open to it. Now he could see even more benefits, not just for the parents, but for the children themselves. He was glad the center was in the planning stages and he'd be meeting with the architect soon.

As he watched the children, Gina joined the boys, helping them decide what to build. Logan suddenly wondered if Gina would help with the project. He knew there were companies who sent representatives in essentially to take over and even staff the center. But he wanted to use a local contractor as well as someone from Lubbock to staff the facility. Maybe Gina could help with the preliminary stage.

Was he looking for an excuse to spend time with her?

Of course not. He didn't need one with her treating Daniel.

A half hour later, Tessa and her children waved goodbye. Daniel had obviously enjoyed their company, but he looked as if he'd had enough of these activities and was ready for something else.

Logan lifted his son into the air and wiggled him. "How about the Yellow Rose Diner and cheese fries?"

Daniel babbled, "Da da da. Fwies," and Logan laughed.

"I think that's a resounding 'yes.' Are you going back to Sagebrush?" he asked Gina.

"Yes, I am. Raina and I made a pact to clean the house this afternoon, then we're going to a movie as a reward later."

"Girls' night out?"

"You could say that."

"If you're going back to Sagebrush, how about stopping at the diner with us and having some lunch? There's something I'd like to discuss with you."

When Daniel fussed to be let down, Logan lowered him to a mat. "We could talk about it here, but I think Daniel needs a change of scene and something in his tummy. What do you say?"

He could tell Gina was giving his invitation major consideration. She asked, "Is this about Daniel?"

"No, it's not."

She seemed to think about the pros and cons but he knew what her answer would be. She wouldn't deny him this simple request because she still felt guilty about what had happened. He didn't want to push that button. She'd have to let go of the guilt and he'd have to let go of the bitterness. Maybe they could do that if they worked on the day-care center together.

Finally, she nodded. "Okay. I have to pick up some folders and lock up. I'll meet you at the diner."

Logan found himself looking forward to sitting across the booth from her and didn't examine his reasons why too closely.

Logan was settling Daniel into a high chair as Gina walked into the Yellow Rose and spotted them. She ruffled the little boy's hair as she settled into the booth and smiled at the dish of cheese fries on the table. "You must have called ahead."

Logan broke a cheese fry into pieces and set them on his son's tray. "I did. Experience is a great teacher."

Their gazes collided and the noise of the diner faded away. Damn, he was *still* attracted to her! Why couldn't he shut it down? Why couldn't he control the rush of adrenaline that wired him when she entered a room? At first he'd relegated that rush to tension, to regrets, to emotion packed away for a long time. But today, he knew better.

An auburn-haired waitress came over to take their orders and raised an eyebrow at Logan as if to say, "So when did this start?" Mindy kept her fingertip on the pulse point of anyone who came to the Yellow Rose Diner.

He ignored her curiosity. After a brief examination of the menu, he and Gina ordered and their waitress hurried away.

Fingering her knife, Gina moved it to the side of the placemat. "You surprised me when you said you were coming here. It wasn't a place I imagined you having lunch."

"No sterling silver or crystal goblets?"

"Hannah could make you anything you want at the estate and there are other restaurants that are a little more private."

"I'm not a hermit, Gina. I don't need electric gates around the house or a high wall to keep reporters out. There are much more interesting characters around than me. I know I can't live a normal life because I have more than most, but I don't have to live such a different life, either."

"Your father wanted—" She stopped abruptly. Picking up a cheese fry, she wiggled it into a scoop of ketchup.

"My father wanted what?" Logan asked.

"I think he wanted you to live the same life he did."

Logan hadn't realized that Gina and his father had had many conversations. His father had hired her to work in the stables and that was about it. But she *was* right. His father had wanted him to travel, to be invited to the governor's mansion, to have friends in even higher places. But his perspective on raising a son was much different from his father's, and that wasn't a subject he wanted to discuss.

"I read the articles you published online," he said, changing the subject as he poured water into Daniel's sippy cup.

That seemed to surprise her. "I see."

He doubted that she did. "I wanted to know what you had done with your life and the type of work you accomplished."

She took a sip of her water, then set down the glass. "Why?"

"I was curious whether the reasons you told me you left were honest."

Her cheeks took on some color. "They were honest, Logan. That full scholarship put me on the first rung of the ladder. I had a job when I was earning my master's and sent money home to help put Angie through school. I became the first college graduate in my family. When I earned my doctorate, even my dad had tears in his eyes."

She seemed to brace herself as if he might ask her something else. Like what? Was it all worth it? He couldn't go there. Not now. Not here.

"One of your articles concerned day-care centers. I'll be starting construction for one in June for my employees' kids, and I wondered if you'd give me some input, maybe give the architect I've chosen some input. You know what kids need. I would need it to be appropriate for ages two to five. What do you think? Would you be interested? I'll pay you a consultation fee."

She looked totally taken aback. "You've surprised me, Logan. Do you mind if I think about it?"

"No, I don't mind. I have a meeting with James Wolfe—he's the architect who designed the new elementary school in Sagebrush—on Wednesday. If you're interested, I'd like you to be there, too."

Their gazes locked. When she didn't look away and neither did he, he felt his chest tighten and other parts of his body come awake.

Had he just made a huge mistake?

On Wednesday evening, Gina sat in Logan's den at a long library table next to his architect, James Wolfe. She was studying the plans—and felt Logan studying *her*. He was sitting across the narrow table from them in a leather desk chair.

"So what do you think?" the architect asked her. His brown eyes sparkled with interest she didn't return. He was good-looking enough...but he wasn't Logan.

She concentrated on the plans. "The square footage looks about right for the number of children you're anticipating providing for. But—"

"But?"

Directly across from her, Logan's leg brushed hers as he leaned forward to take a closer look at the architect's drawing.

She swallowed and smiled. "I think you need to utilize the space better, maybe two rooms instead of one. That way the younger children can be taking a nap while the older ones are playing or working. You also need a common area where they can share snacks. But that's just my opinion."

James shrugged. "She makes sense."

In professional mode now, Gina tapped another line of the blueprint. "You might also want to consider a wall with an observation window. That way if a parent doesn't want to come in and get involved, they can just make sure their child is okay."

James grinned and patted her shoulder. "That's an excellent idea."

Reflexively, Gina leaned back and his hand fell away. Even after all these years, she didn't appreciate a man touching her without her giving the signal it was okay. But James didn't seem to notice that she was uncomfortable with his gesture.

Logan stood, signaling the meeting was over. "Work on those changes, Wolfe, and then bring the plans back to me."

Realizing the meeting had come to an end, James Wolfe stood, rolled up the plans and inserted them into the protective tube. "I'll take a few days with these then give you a call. When's the ground-breaking ceremony?"

"Mid-June," Logan responded. "As soon as I finalize the changes, we'll move forward."

James extended his hand to Gina.

She clasped it and shook it. "It was nice to meet you," she said politely.

"It was good meeting you, too. Take care now. Logan, I can see myself out."

Moments later, she and Logan were standing alone in his study. "I didn't mean to throw a wrench into what Mr. Wolfe had already designed."

"I invited you to this meeting for your input. I'm pleased you gave it. Your ideas are sound." Logan reached for the knot on his tie and pulled it loose.

"I know kids," she said softly. "And what they need."

After unfastening the shirt button at his neck, Logan came around the table and stood close to her. She didn't feel crowded by *him*. Oddly, she welcomed his nearness in the same way she'd shied away from James Wolfe's proximity, as well as his touch.

Logan's voice was low when he asked, "And what do *you* need, Gina?"

His green gaze was piercing and unsettled her. "I don't know what you mean."

"My architect is interested in you."

"He was just being friendly."

"But you weren't being friendly back."

"I…" She stopped, took a deep breath, then gave a nonchalant shrug. "I wasn't interested."

Logan came another step closer. Her temperature went up a few notches, especially when he said, "You're not stepping away from *me*."

What was he doing? Testing her? Trying to identify any attraction between them? Did he still feel attracted? Was that possible?

"I know you," she murmured, standing her ground.

"Not anymore, you don't. I'm not that kid who didn't know up from down or right from left, or much about what made women tick."

"You know what makes women tick now?" she teased, trying to lessen the intensity in the room.

He gave a short laugh. "Not by a long shot. But I *do* have a hint. After all, being married gives a man much-needed insight. If he doesn't learn fast, he'll go under without a lifeline."

Trying to take a step back from the sexual tension that had developed between them, she responded, "Basically, I guess men need to know women want to be respected, and listened to and that most care deeply about love and family."

Logan still held her gaze. "I learned family is important and children are the most important. Amy died so Daniel could live. I had trouble wrapping my mind around *that* one for a while. She gave up her life and *our* life for our little boy."

Immediately, Gina felt sympathy for Logan because he still seemed perplexed by the idea. Yet she knew a father's love could be as fierce as a mother's. "Logan, if you were in the middle of the ocean and Daniel fell overboard, you'd jump in after him without a second thought to try to save him." She'd seen him with Daniel. It was obvious that Logan cared about his son and wouldn't let anything hurt him if he could help it. Just as his wife had done, in her own way.

Shaking his head, Logan said almost to himself, "You're still that young, compassionate girl who could talk to a horse and understand the expression in its eyes, aren't you?"

"Why does that unsettle you?" she asked, feeling as if this conversation was quickly going down a dangerous road.

"Because I wanted you to have changed. To have become hard and ambitious and uncaring, because then I still wouldn't…be attracted to you."

She practically stopped breathing. His words made her feel as if she was eighteen again, and they were standing close, about to kiss.

She shook her head, anxious to get rid of the rush of emotion. "We're not who we were back then." She knew that more than anyone.

"Maybe not. But I feel something when we're in the

same room, just like I did back then. In fact, this close, I know exactly what I feel."

What should she do? She hadn't been involved seriously with a man since Logan. After the date rape, she couldn't think about "serious," though she'd tried over the years…tried without success. Counselors had told her she'd find a satisfying relationship when she found a man she could trust. But she never had.

Was Logan saying he wanted to kiss her? Should she let him?

He laid his hands on her shoulders, maybe just to see how that would feel. It was a contact that was almost chaste, a contact that could be comforting. Yet it wasn't chaste *or* comforting.

"Why did you ask me to work with you on the day-care center?" she asked, not sure if she wanted to hear the truth.

"I told you, you're an expert. I wanted your input."

"The *real* reason."

He cocked his head as if to say at one time she never would have questioned him. "I really did want your ideas. But I guess I also wanted to see what would happen if the two of us were together in the same room, without Daniel."

"Did you get your answer?"

"Oh, yeah."

His hands tightened slightly, but she felt no sense of panic.

"Why did you agree to work on the project?" he asked.

"I guess I wanted to see what type of man you'd become."

"You couldn't tell from our sessions with Daniel?"

"Daniel was a buffer. You could hide behind father-hood."

His eyebrows quirked up as if he definitely didn't like her conclusion.

She added, "You could concentrate on Daniel and not give me a second thought."

"Did you want a second thought?" he returned quickly.

"As impossible as it is, I already told you what I want." She had returned to Sagebrush hoping for his forgiveness. Now…since she knew about his father's stroke, it really seemed impossible. How could she tell him why she'd really left when it would change forever how he viewed his dad and their relationship?

Logan's gaze searched hers. He must have seen the corner of her mouth quiver because he focused there. "Dammit, Gina." He bent his head and before she had time to think, to protest or to back away, Logan Barnes was kissing her with more passion, more heat than he had when she was eighteen.

At first she stiffened, ready to run. Then she told herself to relax. This was Logan. To her surprise, she *wasn't* panicking. She wasn't imagining she was somewhere else. In fact, she was enjoying his kiss. It swept her back into the dream of romance that she'd given up.

Yet this wasn't a dream and she doubted if romance was on Logan's mind. When he put his arms around her to hold her tighter and his tongue slid into her mouth, she balked, put her hands on his chest and pushed away.

He released her. "I'm sorry. I know I shouldn't have done that but I wanted to see—" He swore.

She felt almost dizzy…breathless…and completely unnerved, too. "A kiss has to mean something, Logan. That one didn't. It was some kind of test. If we want to heal what happened between us, we have to do it with talking, not acting on a remnant of attraction that will only embarrass us both."

"Heal what happened between us?" Logan asked incredulously. "How would we *ever* do that? It was as if our breakup had a domino effect. How do I heal the fact that my father had a stroke and I was powerless to help him—and *you* weren't here for me when I needed you?"

"Are you saying you don't want to try to tear down this wall between us?"

Instead of answering her, he asked, "What do you know about walls?"

She realized he was merely taking a stab in the dark. "I know they protect us. Things happen, Logan. Things hurt us when we least expect. We want to keep ourselves safe. That's why we build walls."

He didn't respond, just ran his hand over his face then stuffed his hands into his front pockets. "I'll understand if you don't want to continue to work with Daniel."

Because he'd kissed her? Because there might be more left than that spark of attraction? She'd returned to Sagebrush to finish something with Logan. She had to see it through.

"I want to work with Daniel. He's making progress, and one of these days, he's going to grab on to a piece of furniture and take steps away from it without even realizing he did. I'd like to see that. And I'd also like to see your day-care center come together for the sake of the children."

Logan gazed out the window over the expertly manicured grounds and pool area. Then he swung around to face her. "Are you doing this to make up for leaving?"

There were so many reasons to help him and
Daniel…and not all of them had to do with guilt. "I do
feel I owe you something. But for now, I just want to
help Daniel walk."

Maybe by the time she did that, she'd figure out if
Logan could ever forgive her. Maybe she could tell
him at least one of the secrets she'd kept hidden for way
too long.

Chapter Four

The Rigoletti household was unusually quiet when Gina let herself in. Gina knew her mom was happiest when her kids were all under one roof, talking, laughing and eating.

"Anyone home?"

"In here," her mother called from the kitchen, as expected.

"In here," her dad called from the living room where he sat in his favorite easy chair watching golf. The ranch-style house wasn't big, but it had always held a lot of love.

Gina went to the living room first and kissed her dad on the cheek. "Who's winning?"

"Nobody you'd know," he returned with a smile that said it was okay if she didn't follow golf. "Go help your mom. She and Angie had some to-do and she's a little…frazzled."

Ever since Gina had returned, there had seemed to be more than the usual tension between her and her younger sister. They had been close once, but now that she was back in Sagebrush, Angie was keeping her distance. Gina knew that when her sister was ready to talk, she'd talk. But for now it made for uncomfortable Sunday dinners. Had her mother mentioned their rift to Angie?

Gina patted her dad on the shoulder. His face was weathered from all the hours he'd spent as a mail carrier walking his beat, so to speak. He always said his route kept him in shape and he didn't want to give it up. But last year, the heat and his new blood pressure medication hadn't mixed, and he'd decided to retire.

"I *do* want to know who wins," she told him with a wink, then she went to the kitchen.

Her mother's favorite room resembled a homey café with its bright yellow cupboards and blue-and-yellow gingham curtains. She took pride in everything about it, from the copper-bottom pan on the stove, to the hand-worked placemats on the table. The house didn't have a dining room, but the kitchen table was long enough for the whole family, grandkids included.

Gina hugged and kissed her mother and received a warm hug in return. "What can I help you with?"

The spaghetti sauce was already simmering on the stove, the smell of fresh garlic, tomatoes and onion wafted in the air. She also caught the scent of fresh-baked bread.

"I'm almost finished with everything for today. Are you bringing Raina to dinner tomorrow?"

"She said she'd love to come again." Gina hesitated a moment, then commented, "Dad said you and Angie had a disagreement?"

Gina's mother's black hair was straighter than her own and she wore it tucked behind her ears. As a little girl, Gina had thought her mom was the prettiest woman in the world and she still did. Mary Rigoletti was usually talkative, but now she kept silent.

"Mom?"

"You and Angie haven't talked much since you came back to Sagebrush."

"No, we haven't," Gina admitted. "She doesn't seem to want to talk...or to be around me. When I ask her what's wrong, she says nothing. But she seems uncomfortable and I wish she'd tell me why."

Mary sighed. "She feels beholden to you."

"Why?"

"You know why. You helped her through nursing school. Without your help, she would have been saddled with more loans than she has."

"We always planned that I would help her. That's why I accepted the scholarship." *And left Logan.* She didn't say it aloud, but she knew her mother could hear the words anyway.

"I think she wants to start paying you back."

"That's ridiculous!"

"Not where pride's concerned. If she comes to you with the idea, don't refuse her outright. Think about it."

After studying Gina, her mother asked, "How about a slice of fresh-baked bread?"

"That sounds great."

A few minutes later, the two women sat with glasses of iced tea, munching slices of buttered bread. "Why did you stop in today?" her mother asked.

"Can't I come over to visit?"

"Sure. But I think you have something on your mind."

Of course, she did. She might as well tell her mother what was happening before she found out from someone else. Gossip traveled the streets of Sagebrush with frustrating regularity.

"I saw Logan Barnes."

Her mother set her bread on her dish. "You *saw* him? What does that mean?"

Fourteen years ago, her parents had opposed her association with Logan on the grounds that she was too young, that she had a future ahead of her, and engagement and marriage were out of the question. After all, her older sister had opted for a young marriage and it had been hard going for her. Now Gina didn't know what her mother would think about her life colliding into Logan's again.

They'd never discussed him after she'd left Sagebrush for college. They hadn't discussed him throughout the years. But now she supposed they had to. However, as a professional, she could reveal nothing she knew from Daniel's records or her sessions with him.

"What do you know about him?" Gina asked, hoping to jump off from that.

"Only what's in the newspapers, and the rumors at the butcher shop. After his daddy died about five years ago, he took over the denim factory and everything else. He'd already expanded into other businesses in Dallas and Houston and even in foreign places. Rumor has it, the Barnes empire is three times the size it was when his father was living."

"I meant about his personal life," Gina murmured.

Her mother studied her daughter, then folded her hands in front of her on the table. "Actually the Barnes family wasn't in the news much for a couple of years after you left. Then, about five or six years ago, Logan married Amy Dunlap, who moved here from Dallas and made her mark in real estate. There was a splash about that in the paper. She was at the epitome of her career when she got pregnant. I'm not exactly sure what happened after that. I just know the baby was delivered early and she died and Logan now has a son. I think Angie knows the whole story but she's not talking. She just says that little boy fought for his life and won."

"Daniel is a cutie."

"You've met him?"

"Yes, I have. I can't say more about it than that."

Her mother didn't need Gina to spell it out. "And I can't ask any questions because you can't answer them. Just tell me this, are you and Logan interested in each other again?"

Gina was shaking her head before any words came out of her mouth. "That won't happen. He's still angry I left. In fact...his father had a stroke that same night. I know Logan believes it happened because they argued about me."

"Oh, Gina. The same night? I heard he was ailing but never heard the cause."

"I think Logan blames me for his father's stroke."

Gina and her mother had always been close. She'd confided in her about every teenage aspiration and dream, though they'd disagreed about her situation with Logan. Her mother had known exactly how she'd felt about everything. But that had changed after the rape. Gina hadn't told anyone about it except the counselor she'd seen. Even now, all these years later, she couldn't bear to see hurt in her parents' eyes. If she told them—

She didn't want to revisit the shame. She didn't want

to *feel* again as if some of it were her fault. On some level, she knew it wasn't. Her counselor's voice still echoed in her head every time she thought about it. *You did nothing wrong. His actions weren't your fault. You said no. He didn't listen.*

Still, Gina had gone to the party knowing full well there would be liquor there. She'd gone with the boy up to his friend's room. She'd been stupid and naive and had paid dearly for it. To admit all that to anyone close to her wouldn't have helped back then. There was no point in divulging it to her mother now.

"What's troubling you?" her mom asked.

Gina sighed. "At some point, Logan and I are going to have to talk about all of it."

"To make peace?"

"I don't know if we'll ever make peace. When someone hurts you as badly as I hurt him, peace is hard to come by."

"Not if the two of you want it."

She knew *she* did, but she wasn't sure about Logan. If he could forgive her—

That seemed to be an unreachable dream.

"I don't know how often you're seeing Logan…" Her mother hesitated then went on. "But we're planning a picnic and softball game at the pavilion at the lake next weekend. Why don't you ask him and his little boy to come?"

"Mom, you can't be serious."

"Didn't you say you want to make peace?"

"Yes, but I don't think he'd ever accept."

"You won't know until you ask, will you?"

"Why are you willing to get involved? Logan knows you disapproved of us being together."

"Time has passed. He's a grown man. You're a grown woman. I don't regret the choice we helped you make. Not only do you have your Ph.D. and the satisfaction of knowing you helped your sister through school, but your older brother and sister look up to you."

Yes, she had accomplished what her parents wanted. She was happy—wasn't she?

Then why did you return to Sagebrush? a little voice in her head asked.

To make peace with Logan? Is that why fate had brought him to her?

"I'll think about your suggestion, Mom, but don't get your hopes up."

"My hopes are always up," her mom reminded her with a grin.

Gina couldn't help but laugh as she stood, rounded the corner of the table, and hugged her mother. She was glad she'd come home.

Logan entered the kitchen on Monday evening from the garage, eager to see his son. Gathering Daniel into his arms was always the best part of his day. Yet tonight, he knew Gina was with Daniel. Her car was already in the driveway.

Suddenly he heard his little boy's cry. The sound of it made Logan shift his briefcase to the counter. He took off for the family room.

As he rushed into it, he found Gina holding Daniel, murmuring to him. But Daniel was crying and shaking his head and Logan couldn't tell if he was hurt or not.

Still, he tried to keep his voice calm as he took Daniel from Gina's arms. "Did he fall?"

"No," she answered without a reasonable explanation.

He leaned away from his crying toddler. "Are you okay? Did you get a bump or—"

"He didn't hurt himself," she said quietly.

Daniel was hiccupping, his cries softer now that he was in his dad's arms.

"Where's Hannah?"

"She said she had a batch of laundry to take out of the dryer."

Worried, Logan carried his son to the sofa and sat with him on his knee. "So why is he crying?"

In watching Gina with Daniel, he knew she was careful. He knew she didn't put his son in danger. Yet he hadn't been here to protect Daniel so *anything* could have happened. So much for returning that last call. Daniel was always his main priority. Just because his son was with Gina was no reason to let down his guard.

Snatching one of the small plastic animals from the floor, he handed it to Daniel. His son's cries subsided as he became interested in the toy.

Gina was studying them both as she explained, "He stood up by the chair. I wouldn't just hand over his toy, so he got stubborn, sat down and started crying. Mrs. Mahoney said he didn't have his nap today. He could just be tired, or…he could finally be realizing we're not going to give him everything he wants just because he hollers for it."

When Logan looked into Gina's eyes, his heart practically turned over in his chest. Damn, but she had the most beautiful brown eyes he'd ever seen. They were the color of brandy and had always melted him.

"Have you been here long?"

"About half an hour."

"I'm sorry I'm late."

"That's no problem, Logan. Sometimes it's better if you aren't watching."

"Excuse me?"

Her cheeks reddened a little. "I just mean Daniel responds differently when you're here than when you're not."

"How's he different?"

"He expects you to protect him, to make sure his world is right-side-up."

"That's a dad's job."

"Most of the time it is. But he's getting to the age where he's striking out, learning to do for himself. It's a long process. He needs the confidence to know he can."

"You're saying I'm still treating him like that preemie in the incubator who needed my every prayer to live."

With an understanding smile, Gina came over to the sofa and sank down beside him. "Your concern and worry for Daniel are normal. You almost lost him. But he's healthy and happy, and just trying to catch up to where he belongs." She held her hands out to the baby to see if he'd come to her.

Daniel looked up at his dad, then back at Gina. With a grin, he plopped down on his dad's legs and squiggled over to her.

She lifted him into her arms, held him up and laughed. "You're a charmer, but don't think that smile is going to get you everything you want."

Daniel smiled and babbled at her, and she laughed again.

Logan had noticed that Gina was different when she was with his son. She was the teenager he'd fallen in love with—lovely and sparkling and laughing. Since she'd reentered his life, he'd decided the tension between them had taken the sparkle from her eyes. Now he wasn't so sure. Maybe something else had. Something that had changed the girl he used to know. His years with Amy had changed him. What had changed Gina?

He told himself he didn't care, but a gnawing in his gut urged him to find out what had happened to her since they'd parted ways. Maybe she was struggling to let go of something in her past other than what had happened between the two of them.

He'd struggled to let go of Amy, but she was still there in Daniel's smile, the laughter in his eyes and the color of his hair. But he'd had no choice—he'd had to let go of her to concentrate on Daniel, to enable him to live and thrive.

Maybe he could let go of Gina, too, and be free— free to focus on his son and the life they'd built—if they were more honest with each other.

When Gina settled Daniel on her lap, he yawned a big, wide, baby yawn that told them both he'd had enough for today.

Logan had, too. He gathered his son up once more and stood. "I'm going to put him down for the night."

Gina looked uncomfortable, rubbed her hands on her jeans-clad knees and said, "I'll collect my paraphernalia and be going."

After he started for the doorway, he debated with himself. Turning back to her, he asked, "Would you like to go for a ride after I put him to bed? I don't think Hannah would mind sitting with him for a while."

Gina looked torn. "You need to clear the cobwebs from a long day?"

"I do. Silence isn't always the best way to do that, and the horses won't always make conversation with me."

She smiled, and this time the sparkle was there, even though they weren't talking about Daniel.

She pointed to her shoes. "I only have my sneakers."

"You know there are always spare boots in the barn. I'm sure there will be a pair there that will fit."

Her expression told him she did indeed remember the spare boots...and she remembered other things, too.

So did he.

He had the sudden urge to ask her to put Daniel to bed with him, but that was a bonding time with his son. He didn't want Gina that involved with his life. He nodded to the flat-screen TV and the magazines on the coffee table.

"Make yourself at home."

Although she nodded, she looked a bit lost. That was the way he felt now that he'd invited her for a ride. What did he really expect to come of it?

A half hour later, Gina walked beside Logan to the barn, well aware they'd taken this walk together before— almost fourteen years to the day. His silence told her he must have been conscious of it, too. Their romance had begun on a night like this—when the air was fragrant with damp grass, a three-quarter moon glowing in the twilight sky, begging their gazes to linger on it. His father had been away so often that summer they'd pretty much had the run of the place—swum in the pool, gone riding and made love in a vacant stall. She could still remember the scent of clean hay, the roughness of a wool blanket on her skin, Logan's passionate kisses and tender touches.

The scent of roses wafted to her on the breeze and she noticed the yellow roses alongside the barn were in full bloom.

Years ago the stable at the Barnes estate had been stone and wood. Now it had been modernized and weatherized and was relatively maintenance-free. The decades-old stone facing had been cleaned and preserved and the door Logan opened for her didn't squeak as the old one had.

As they passed the tack room, Logan stayed a few strides ahead of her, out of touching distance. No chance of elbows grazing as their steps slowed in unison, no conversation. Turning to look around, she saw that only four of the stalls were occupied now.

Logan suddenly stopped and faced Gina. "I'm going to give you Aquarius to ride. She's sure-footed and intuitive. Do you still remember how to saddle up?"

"That's something a rider never forgets. I saddle my own horse at Francesca and Grady's, and at Vince and Tessa's."

"Good. Then I don't have to worry about the saddle sliding around to the side after you're in the paddock."

His suddenly lighter tone gave her hope. "When I love to do something, I become an expert at it."

"That always was one of your qualities I admired."

Immediately a conversation vividly played in her mind. It had taken place in this barn…in a vacant stall. They'd made love for the second time, a week after the first. Logan's father had been home at the estate during that week. Gina's parents had disapproved of her dating Logan and had kept her at home with chores and babysitting most days. But on Friday night, Logan's dad had gone out of town and her parents hadn't found another excuse to keep her at home. After all, she *was* eighteen.

Eighteen, in love and confused about what her future could be. Eighteen and uncertain about everything from her looks to her intelligence to her capabilities. Logan had lain beside her on the blanket in that stall, stroking the curls around her face. She'd been bolder with him that night, touching him more, reacting to every one of his caresses.

Holding her chin in his hand, he leaned forward and took another deep, wet kiss. She surprised him by wrapping her arms around his neck, pulling him down to her, returning each stroke of his tongue.

When he broke away, he laughed. "You catch on fast."

They were still naked and she took advantage of that, running her hands down his chest, over his stomach...and lower. "You're a wonderful teacher. When I'm really interested in a subject, I can become an expert in no time."

"An expert, huh? In the art of loving me?"

She panicked when he'd asked her that. After all, her love for Logan was new and frightening—because it had the power to change her life. She'd already committed herself to a future her parents approved of, to helping her younger sister through college, then working in a field where she could make a difference.

Still, she couldn't ignore her heart. "I'd like to become an expert in the art of loving you."

She'd been living in the moment, wanting to feel Logan's arms around her again, needing his approval, too. And she had loved him. She just hadn't realized how much until it was too late.

Now she saw him looking at her and knew he was remembering that night, too. What could she say? "I meant it, but I was so young and naive"? "I didn't know what love meant until your father warned me away from you"? "Until my heart broke when I left"? "Because I felt unworthy of you and unable to tell you what had happened"?

Logan stepped toward her, his hand raised as if to reach for her. But then he abruptly turned and unlocked Aquarius's stall door.

Gina felt shaken, wanting to get close to Logan again at least in friendship—but not knowing how. She placed her hand on his arm. "Logan."

He acted as if she wasn't touching him. "She'll read your slightest signal," he said. "The easiest touch on the reins is all she needs."

"Logan," she repeated. "Maybe we should talk about—"

"I don't want to talk, Gina. Not now. Let's just saddle up and get out on the trail. That's the only place I seem to find peace these days."

She dropped her hand from his arm, not wanting to stir the cauldron of emotions that wouldn't help either of them.

A few minutes later, they'd left the safety of the paddock and were headed along the marked trail by the white fence line. Thought and planning had gone into the trails that wound through the trees as if they were a natural route rather than a groomed one. The canopy of live oaks made their ride quiet and intimate, the last lingering light spilling through the leaves, dappling their path.

"Do you have time to ride as far as the lake?" he asked.

The Barnes property held a natural lake of its own. It was surrounded by cottonwoods and willows and was one of Gina's favorite places, day or night.

She answered softly, "I have time."

They rode side by side and Gina felt a companionship in that, as if they were gaining some footing, finding that common ground from so many years ago. But Logan must have been thinking of *other* things.

As they drew up to the cottonwoods on the shore of the lake, he said, "Amy and I didn't come here much."

Gina went still, then she asked conversationally, "Did your wife like to ride?"

"No, she didn't. I mean, she would ride because *I* liked to. It was a pleasant way to spend a Sunday afternoon when she wasn't showing properties. But she didn't have a real yearning for it. It was a pastime, like golf." He looked over his shoulder at Gina. "And I think she preferred golf."

Their legs almost brushed as Gina drew up beside him. "Did *you* learn to prefer golf?" She'd seen her friends' lives change with marriage and maybe Logan's had, too.

"Actually, I hate golf. I'm not bad at it. I learned the game for business reasons as well as social ones after I met Amy. The idea of chasing a ball from hole to hole doesn't hold much interest for me. I'd rather be on a horse, learning his nature, learning his habits, learning how we can communicate. Do you know what I mean?"

"You're talking to a believer. I know exactly what you mean. I enjoyed skiing in New England. It's challenging in its own way. But it's not part of me like riding is, like horses are. Are you going to buy Daniel a pony?"

"Maybe. Do you think it's a good idea?"

"Sure. Under the right supervision, horseback riding can teach children balance in a way not much else can. In fact, I've often thought about organizing a horseback

riding camp for developmentally challenged children."
She shrugged, a bit embarrassed by sharing that with
him. "It's just one of my dreams."

"Do you have a lot of them?"

She laughed. "An assortment. I've considered volun-
teering in Appalachia, too. The children and families
there need so much help. I've also considered writing a
book for parents, and I would love to tour Alaska
someday."

"You have a lot of dreams left."

"Don't you?" She hated to think his dreams had died
with his wife.

"My dreams now are for Daniel. Will he want to
become a world leader, an economist, a soccer player?
Should I let him take piano lessons as well as try out
for a football team? How soon should he learn Spanish,
climb a tree, have a pet other than a horse? Small
dreams and big ones."

"You still need your own dreams, too."

"No," he said quickly. "Not anymore. Raising a child
and running a business can keep a man busy for a lifetime."

She could hear what he wasn't saying. That his
dreams had gotten crushed and he wasn't going to invest
in them again.

"Do you believe in fate?" she asked.

"Fate or coincidence?" he asked with a sideways
glance.

"I think fate brought Daniel's chart to my desk."

"Or coincidence."

"Maybe I was meant to work with Daniel so that I
could make up for the hurt I caused you."

He brought his horse closer to hers so the animals'
noses were almost touching. He leaned forward and

looked into her eyes. His were shaded by the brim of his Stetson and she couldn't see them clearly.

But she definitely heard the vehemence in his voice. "The past can't be fixed. You can just try to move it aside and go on. After you left, I got over it. Amy died, and I'm trying to get over that. Fate has *nothing* to do with Daniel's chart landing on your desk. This really *is* a small world, Gina," he returned. "You know Tessa. She's Daniel's pediatrician. We all link together, one way or another."

He made the coincidence sound so reasonable. But she felt she'd come back here, not only to be with her family, but to mend fences with Logan. Fate had made that a little easier.

That was what she believed but she also knew she was the one who had to choose the next step. She wasn't sure what that step was going to be.

"Enough of the lake?" Logan asked.

She could never get enough of the lake—or enough of him. But his the-past-can't-be-fixed attitude proved that he didn't forget or forgive easily.

And she didn't know how she was going to change that.

Chapter Five

Gina glanced at the sky with its thousand tiny twinkles of light, the moon softly brilliant and illuminating their return path. This could be a romantic ride if only—

If only what? As far as she could tell, Logan didn't even want to be friends. Why would he? Telling him what had happened to her wouldn't change the fact that he'd felt deserted by her.

When they reached the paddock, Logan dismounted to unhitch the gate. In jeans, boots, snap-button shirt and a Stetson, he was every inch a Texan, every inch a strong, compelling, virile man. He had more confidence now than he'd had at twenty-two. He was quieter and more introspective, but then so was she.

He walked and she rode until they reached the exterior doors to the barn. There she stopped Aquarius, intending to dismount.

But distracted by memories of the past and the tension of the present, she caught her foot in the stirrup and almost landed on the ground.

Logan was quick and caught her around the waist, holding her snugly until she pulled her boot free. She felt tossed back into a time when being in his arms like this had been right. Now she felt awkward and embarrassed, afraid to face him and see nothing in his expression. But she had to do it.

The brim of his Stetson might have hidden his eyes but as he set her back on her feet, the barn light lit the angles of his face. They were standing close, much closer than they should. She held her breath, not knowing what he might say, not knowing what to expect. The night air drifted across them, but she wasn't chilled, not when she was standing this near to Logan, feeling the heat of his body. He reached out and slid his hand under the hair at the back of her neck. She couldn't breathe, couldn't speak. She just stared into his eyes, hoping to see a glimmer of the gentleness she once knew.

"Gina?" His voice was rough.

The desire she saw in his gaze made her tremble. He wanted her. That was obvious in the tension in his fingers, the tightening of his jaw, the tautness of his stance.

The anticipation of another kiss brewed and ripened between them. Yet she knew what she had to do…until they could find an emotional bond once more.

She stepped away from him before anything could happen, before the desire in his eyes became another kiss they couldn't undo.

His expression changed, becoming remote, guarded.

"Logan—"

"I'm sorry. I don't know what I was thinking, or I guess I wasn't. For a minute old memories made things seem different than they are."

"So many things have changed," she murmured.

"For both of us," he agreed.

She could tell him now. She could just open her mouth and let it all come pouring out. But the timing seemed off. They didn't even have a friendship to lead them to share.

Yet if she wasn't honest with him, they'd never be able to share anything substantial. "Logan, I didn't back away because I didn't want you to kiss me again. I backed away because I thought it was the right thing to do."

At her words, he studied her with deepening determination, looking behind them and underneath them. "Right for you, or right for me?"

"For both of us. We have enough regrets between us. I didn't want to add to them."

"You have regrets? You did what you had to do."

"It isn't that simple."

"Nothing in life is simple, not even what seems right. I found that out when you left. I found that out when Amy died."

He stiffly handed her the reins and led his horse into the barn, saying, "We'd better groom them."

Grooming horses together felt familiar, too, yet she knew familiar wouldn't be comfortable. Nothing was comfortable between her and Logan now. She'd been right to back away from another kiss.

Yet she knew she'd dream about it tonight.

After keeping his distance for a couple of days, Logan called Gina and asked her to his office on Thursday to examine the revised day-care plans.

This wasn't complicated, he told himself as he ushered her in to his office. But the perfume she wore, some kind of fruity floral scent, had already distracted him.

Gina had never dressed provocatively—she'd dressed practically. In summer she'd worn mostly jeans and T-shirts, or a pair of shorts when they weren't going riding. She'd never needed clothes to enhance her beauty. Now, however, it was as if she chose clothes that would hide her womanly curves.

This evening, she wore a shapeless navy pantsuit— a boxy jacket, slacks with wide legs— and navy ballet flats. As always, though, his attention went directly to her face, to her huge dark eyes, to the full mouth that he'd almost made the mistake of kissing again. He was still attracted to her, damn it, whether they were on a night ride, or in his office. So he'd better be careful.

"Hi," she said brightly, as if the other night hadn't happened at all.

Just wipe it off the slate? he wondered. The same way she'd wiped him out of her life for the past fourteen years?

How could he be angry with her when he'd done the same? No point asking, really—he still was. Even though he'd met, fallen in love with and married Amy, he'd never forgotten Gina's betrayal because she'd been the first woman he'd really cared about.

He pulled one of the burgundy leather captain's chairs from in front of his desk around the corner, next to his own. "I think you're going to like these. James took all of your suggestions seriously."

Setting her purse on his desk, she came around the corner. Instead of sitting, she studied him. "You didn't need me to look at these plans. If this is about the other night—"

"This is about the day-care center, Gina. I asked for your ideas because I thought they'd be valuable. If you don't want to see what the architect has done, just say so."

After another long look at him, she turned the chair slightly toward his and slid into it. "Okay, show me."

Those words—*show me*—thrust him into the past, into the pool house after an evening swim. *"Show me how you want me to touch you,"* she'd requested. *"Show me how to make you satisfied, too. Show me what passion is all about."*

He could hear her voice in his head now, as he sometimes did in his dreams.

"Logan?"

He had to get a grip. After all, this was a business meeting of sorts. Blueprints carried a serious message—Job in Progress. They were going to focus on that job.

They had to sit close together or they couldn't see the plans. His arm brushed against hers as he leaned forward. The tension between them was already ratcheting up and he knew talking about it would only make it worse. So he acted as if sitting with her like this was the most common occurrence in his world.

He pointed to the blueprint of the day-care center. "That's a small kitchenette. Great idea so the personnel can deal with snacks. We'll be feeding the kids from the cafeteria. Those meals can be wheeled in on individual trays or we can keep the food hot with warmers. We have either option. And James divided the larger space into two with observation windows in both."

Gina pointed to the outside space. "I like the shape of the area with the jungle gym and the swing sets."

"The equipment and ground covers are made of the latest materials. Safety is a major issue."

"This really looks perfect, Logan," she said enthusiastically. "If your personnel are as great as the facilities, I wouldn't hesitate to send my child there."

"Are you as good at furnishing day-care centers as you are at planning them? I also need a list of equipment that might be useful."

She glanced down at the plans and then back at him, and he knew what was coming.

"Are you sure you want me to help you with this? Wouldn't you be more comfortable with a professional?"

"You *are* a professional."

"Logan, you know what I mean. Whether we want to admit it or not, everything is still awkward between us. Do you want that interfering with planning the day-care center?"

She was so damn honest. She always had been. It was one of the qualities he'd liked about her. Amy had always softened her opinion when she knew he might disagree, but Gina had never done that. But he shouldn't be comparing his wife with Gina.

"We're adults. Working together doesn't have to be awkward."

"The other night was awkward."

Moving his hand through his hair, he thought about what his reply should be, then decided to be as honest as she was. "I don't know what got into me. Probably memories. We spent a lot of time in that barn and outside it. I almost felt as if I were twenty-two again."

She ducked her head for a minute, then returned her gaze to his. "I know what you mean. Wouldn't it be nice if we could escape that easily?"

What did Gina have to escape from? Was she running from something in New England? Or was she trying to escape into the past instead of looking for a future? He knew all about that.

They were still sitting very close, almost leaning into each other. He knew he should move his chair, get up and walk around the room, anything to be away from her perfume, her softness, the understanding in her eyes. That understanding twisted a knife in his gut.

"More than anything else, Logan, I want to be friends again."

Friends. Could he do that? Could he relegate Gina to that category? Even in friendship, there had to be loyalty. His rational mind told him she'd been young. She'd had a future ahead of her. She'd been afraid to risk believing in them. Yet another part of him wondered about that loyalty and if she'd break it again.

However, risking friendship was a hell of a lot easier than risking more.

He had no intention of risking more ever again.

"I don't know, Gina. It can't be forced."

Sadness clouded her eyes as if she knew the trust she'd broken with him was going to affect them for the rest of their lives. Still, she forced the clouds away and smiled. "I won't force anything. That would make us both uncomfortable, but—"

She looked pensive and uncertain for a few moments. Finally she said, "My family is having a picnic by the lake on Sunday. We'll probably play softball, eat hamburgers. Would you and Daniel like to come? There will be children for him to play with." She stopped. "You probably already have plans."

He imagined extending this invitation hadn't been

easy for her. They still weren't from the same side of
the tracks. Their lifestyles were very different. That
didn't matter to him—but did she feel the same way?

"What about your parents? They weren't fans of mine."

"My dad respects what you've done with your
father's company. And my mother knows we're not
young and naive anymore."

He couldn't keep from touching Gina. He just
couldn't. He held her chin gently and asked, "When did
you stop being naive?"

Something flickered in Gina's eyes that almost made
his breath hitch. For that moment, he thought he
glimpsed excruciating pain. But from what? Another
breakup? Was that her MO? Love 'em and leave 'em?

She recovered quickly, all expression dropping
from her face.

She responded, "College was a learning experience
for me. I lost my naïveté there."

Partial truth? Complete truth? Just when in college
had she lost that naïveté? He had the feeling it had to
do with a boy and it had to do with sex. That was an old
story. But he didn't press her for more.

Suddenly emotion flickered in her eyes and he could
see she was worried that asking him to the picnic had
crossed a line. Maybe it had. Long ago he'd told himself
that if she ever came back to Sagebrush, he'd avoid her.
So why had he asked her to become involved in the day-
care center? Why continue Daniel's care with her?

Why continue thinking about her night and day?

Because Gina was a puzzle to him now, one he
wanted to unlock, to understand. Maybe he never would
but he had to try. Maybe if he tried and succeeded,
some of his own shadows would finally vanish.

"All right," he decided. "I'll come to your picnic. I'm sure Daniel will find it a lot more fun than crawling around his playroom with me. Hannah will be gone for the weekend and it will be just the two of us."

"Gone?"

"She does have a life," he said with a smile. "She's made us her family, but she has a son in college as well as a sister and nieces and nephews in the area."

"You trust her, don't you?"

"Implicitly. She was our housekeeper before everything turned...serious. She was wonderful with Amy and when Daniel came home, she mothered him when he needed it most."

Gina's eyes grew shiny.

"What are you thinking?" he asked, leaning closer, reaching out and twirling one of her curls around his finger. "Everything's in your eyes, no matter how you try to hide it."

"You've had a tough road," she murmured, her voice catching.

She was obviously feeling compassion for what he'd gone through and that touched him in a way a woman hadn't in a long time. Maybe that was why he revealed, "When Amy died, I wanted to—" He halted, then went on. "There's that old saying, *Fake it until you make it.* So I did, for my sake and Daniel's. About six months ago, I stepped outside one morning, took a deep breath of fresh Texas air, stared up at that blue, blue sky, and realized I was glad I was still here."

"And how do you feel about Daniel?"

He withdrew his hand, wondering why she could possibly be questioning his feelings for his son. "I love Daniel."

"I don't doubt that, Logan, but after Daniel was born, how did you feel then?"

"I told you, I faked it. I put one foot in front of the other and got through each day. I spent most of my hours at the hospital, watching over him."

"But how did you *feel?*"

His jaw tightened. He could feel the muscle in his cheek jump. Finally he gave in to her question. "I felt nothing. Amy died so he could survive. I couldn't absorb it. All I knew was that she was gone and I had a son who might not live, either. How do you *think* I felt?"

She studied him with huge, dark, sympathetic eyes. "Have you ever talked about this with anyone?"

Now he shrugged and ran his hand through his hair. "Talk about it? Gina, get real. Why would I want to talk about it? Talking only brings up everything I want to forget." He sighed then blew out a breath. "I'm not clueless. I know what you're getting at. You think I didn't bond with Daniel."

"I didn't say that."

"You didn't have to. And the truth is, I didn't the first month. He was so frail... I could touch him, but couldn't hold him. He was hooked up to machines in a plastic bubble. But eventually...he grabbed my heart. Luckily I have a good team at the factory because I took a lot of time off. And when he came home, I was there, along with Hannah."

"I can see you and Daniel have a wonderful relationship."

"But..." he said warily.

She laughed. "Nothing. Except maybe..." She smiled. "You indulge him a little too much. But that's a parent's prerogative, right?"

"Except when it gets in the way of Daniel functioning as well as he should."

"You're doing all the right things, Logan. Just give him some time. If you come to the picnic, he'll have kids to play with and sights to see and new foods to try."

"So you're inviting me to this picnic for *his* sake?"

"No, I'm inviting you both so you can relax. My family can be fun."

He knew what she was thinking. He'd never had a chance to know them because they hadn't approved of him. Maybe now that would all change. Did he really care if it did?

Logan couldn't stop the collision.

Rounding the bases during the Rigolettis' softball game, he and Gina reached home plate at the same time. Her shoulder slammed into his. Somehow their feet tangled and they both went down.

The end-of-May sun shone brightly on them as his arms went to protect *her* rather than the ball in his glove. He didn't know why, but holding on to her at that moment was more important than winning the game.

They landed with a jolt, his worse than hers because he was on the bottom. That was good and that was bad. He could feel the hard ground under him—his shoulders pressed into it. But *Gina* was soft. Her T-shirt had ridden up and his hands were on soft skin. Her body was everything a woman's body should be as he registered the imprint of her breasts and her pelvis, her thighs stretched along his. Memories flooded back of another time in this position and he knew that she knew he was aroused.

"Damn it, this was supposed to be a safe game of

softball." He didn't realize he'd said it aloud until she'd scrambled off him as fast as she could.

He reached for her and snagged her arm. "Gina, I just meant—"

She was kneeling beside him, her face red. "It just meant you came today for a beer and playtime for Daniel. Don't worry, Logan, I understand that."

He didn't let go of her arm. "Are you okay? I mean, did you get hurt in the fall?"

"No. Did you?"

Other players were gathering around now and they were close enough to hear what he and Gina were saying. He levered himself to his feet and held a hand out to her. "I'm fine. I think we both just had the air knocked out of us."

Gina's brother, John, who'd pitched the ball to Logan, shook his head at his sister. "Sorry, kiddo. He caught it about a second before you slid in. You're out."

"Only for this inning," she said with a smile Logan knew was forced. Then she walked away without a backward glance and headed for the cooler of water.

Logan was still staring after her when he felt a presence close beside him and turned to see Angie, Gina's younger sister, rolling Daniel toward him in his stroller. The little boy was grinning from ear to ear, kicking his feet and babbling his enjoyment of the day and the company. Gina's mother and sister had convinced Logan to go play the game while they took care of Daniel. He'd seemed perfectly comfortable with them, so Logan had agreed.

Now he took his little boy from the stroller. "Are you having fun?"

Daniel babbled and leaned forward to put his little arms around Logan's neck.

Angie laughed. "He likes us, but he likes *you* better."

Logan knew Angie was twenty-seven now. She was a beauty with dark brown wavy hair and golden-brown eyes. She was a little shorter than Gina, but slender like her sister. Now she tilted her head at Logan and asked, "So I guess you and Gina are…friends again?"

He shifted Daniel to a comfortable position in his arms, much more comfortable than answering that question. "We're not friends, exactly. She's working with Daniel so we're getting to know each other…again."

"You mean you can't go back to what you once had." Angie was frowning and looking troubled.

"You can't relive the past, Angie, no matter how hard you try." They were both watching Gina, and Logan found himself saying, "She's different now."

"Different how?" Angie asked warily.

"She's quieter, more introspective, even around all of you. She sort of sits back and watches, rather than entering the fray. Do you know what I mean?"

"Yeah, I do. She changed after her first year of college, but we all just thought—"

"What did you think?"

"We thought it was because she really missed you."

Had the decision to leave him been much more difficult than he'd imagined? She'd never looked back. She'd been too busy to take his call when he tried to reach her at school. In fact, he could remember the conversation even today. Three months into his father's rehabilitation, he'd been worn-out and overwhelmed. Gina had been the one person who could understand that. He'd thought—hoped—that she might have changed her mind…that they could work out some way to stay connected…to eventually be together.

"Logan, I can't talk right now," she told him. "I have a class and a test."

"Can we talk later? Just because you're in Connecticut doesn't mean we can't keep in touch."

She paused for a long few moments. "You and I both know a long-distance relationship won't work. And, Logan, I can't see me ever coming back to Sagebrush. Not for more than a visit. So I don't think there's any point...to talking."

Had her voice caught? Did she wish she hadn't chosen the path she was on?

It had taken him three months to set aside his anger and his pride and call her. But during that painful conversation, his pride had reared its head again. Her life had been going on, his would, too. Next semester if his dad continued to make progress in his recovery, he'd be working on his MBA. There had been more than one woman who'd shown an interest in him. Gina had chosen her path and her rejection had only made him more sure of his.

Or so he'd thought—

"You *could* become friends again," Angie said, intervening in the past, as if she was hopeful about the future.

The sensation of Gina's body on top of his, his fingertips on her skin, the fresh scent of her hair, taunted him. "We could. But I don't know if we will," he commented and slipped Daniel back into his stroller.

After a nod to Angie, he pushed his little boy over to the bench where he would wait until his turn at bat.

Chapter Six

"So tell me, Logan," Gina's mother said. "What does it feel like to be CEO of your father's company?"

Gina looked at her parents, who were sitting next to each other across the picnic table from her. Daniel was happily kicking his legs in a high chair at the end of the table. He grinned at them as he poked little round cereal Os into his mouth.

Gina wished *she* felt like grinning. What was her mother up to?

Suddenly conscious of Logan beside her, his elbow lodged next to hers now and then, she wasn't sure inviting him here today had been a good idea. He and Daniel seemed to be having fun but her stomach was tied up in knots and she wasn't even sure why.

Logan didn't seem to be bothered by her mother's

question. "It's an honor to run an enterprise he built from scratch."

"I heard you're running it better than he ever did," Angie said, looking Logan in the eye.

Logan just shrugged. "New styles for denim as well as advancing technologies have made it easier for me to expand markets. I see change as opportunity."

"That's a good way to look at it," Gina's mother decided. "I hope Gina sees her return to Sagebrush as a new opportunity. I don't want to believe she did it just for us."

Feeling Logan's gaze on her, Gina shrugged. "Everyone's life needs a change at some point. Now seemed to be a good time." She stood and picked up the empty dessert plates. They'd all eaten every bit of her mother's homemade pies.

At the next table, her brother, John, called, "Hey, Gina. If you want to clean up our table, too, I'll leave you a tip."

She wrinkled her nose at her brother. "Be careful. The next time you want me to babysit, I might not wash off their sticky fingers before they point to their favorite characters on your new fifty-two-inch TV."

Everyone laughed, but Gina still felt the heat of Logan's gaze. That made her excited and nervous all at the same time. She dumped the plates into the trash can and heard her mother say, "Gina waited tables when she was in college for extra money. I think she was even a short-order cook at one point, weren't you, honey?"

"I was," she answered, turning from the trash can with a bright smile. "Eggs overeasy, burgers medium well. They were my specialty."

"She suddenly decided she didn't like waitressing, that

she'd rather be back in the kitchen. I didn't get that because as a cook, she didn't get tips," her brother explained.

"I worked more hours that way because nobody else wanted to do the short order."

Logan suddenly stood and climbed out from the picnic bench. Approaching his son, he unfastened the tray from his high chair.

Angie asked, "You're not leaving, are you?"

Gina wondered what that was all about. She told her sister, "Daniel has a regular routine at bedtime. Logan probably doesn't want to disrupt that."

Logan's eyes settled on her once more and she felt hot from head to toe, even though the day had simply been pleasantly warm.

"Gina's right. In a little while, he'll be good and cranky. I find I can get him to sleep easier if I do it on his timetable."

"The world revolves around our children," Gina's mom said, nodding. "Most men don't get that."

"I had to get it," Logan said seriously.

Gina's mother stood now, too, and went to Logan and Daniel. "I just want to tell you how glad we are you could come today."

"Yes, we are," Angie said quickly. "You'll have to come to one of our family dinners. Mom makes the best ravioli."

Gina didn't understand what her sister was doing. Why was she pushing Logan's continued connection to her family? Gina had to have a talk with her and soon. There were times when Gina had wanted to start a serious conversation with her sister, but Angie always found an excuse not to. They *were* both busy women. Angie didn't always work the same shift. She was also signed up for the hospital's disaster relief team and flew out unexpectedly when they were needed. Besides Angie's commitments, Gina often stayed late at Baby Grows. That didn't make getting together easy.

"Maybe sometime," Logan answered diplomatically, already gathering Daniel from his chair.

"Would you like me to take him while you pack up?" Gina asked.

Already leaning toward her, Daniel wanted her to hold him. But she didn't want to overstep any boundaries.

"That would be a help," Logan said. "Before I round up his diaper bag, toys, food and chair, not to mention his stroller, he could be asleep."

Gina laughed.

Suddenly Logan leaned close to her and murmured near her ear, "If you want to stay with your family, I'm sure one of them will take you home. You don't have to leave now."

Logan had insisted on picking her up this afternoon and she didn't know now if he was offering simply because he thought she might want to stay, or because he didn't want to be in close quarters with her again. He hadn't indicated at all how he felt about being around her.

What about that kiss?

That kiss had been on her mind way too much. But she couldn't help wondering if Logan thought about it, too.

"I'm ready if you are. I have an early appointment in the morning," she assured him.

Her mother heard that. "Do you? I was hoping you'd come back to the house for a while."

"Not tonight, Mom. I promise, I'll come visit soon."

While Logan loaded up his vehicle, she and Daniel made the rounds of her family, giving hugs and saying goodbye. Angie, her sister-in-law, Kristi, and her older sister, Josie, were standing together so she really couldn't ask her younger sister why she'd almost invited Logan to dinner. But she'd find out. After she gave Angie a squeeze, her sister hugged her back.

Angie readjusted one of the shoulder straps on Daniel's overalls. "You are one of the cutest little boys I've ever seen."

Daniel laid his head on Gina's shoulder, cuddling in close to her neck.

"He's getting attached to you," Angie said.

"No, he's just a friendly little guy. He'd cuddle with anyone like this."

Angie adamantly shook her head. "I doubt that. You know—" she lowered her voice "—he could probably use a mom."

Gina didn't have a chance to respond as Logan returned from his trek to the Range Rover and held out his hands to his son. Daniel didn't fuss but went to his dad, poking his thumb into his mouth, closing his eyes as he laid his head on his dad's shoulder.

"Aha," Logan said. "I thought so. Fresh air and sun will do it every time."

After a final round of goodbyes, he and Gina started down the path to the parking lot.

Gina was still thinking about Angie's last remark, and what might have caused her to voice it.

"Are you tired?" Logan asked her.

"Not really." Then she added, "It was fun just to be outside and get some real exercise."

"As opposed to…"

"As opposed to the treadmill Francesca left behind. I'm beginning to hate that thing, even though it's great to have when I'm up too early to walk outside or I return home late at night. I thought about joining that new gym in town, but I don't know when I'd find time to go."

They walked in silence in the growing dusk until they reached the Range Rover. Gina helped buckle in Daniel and took her place in the passenger seat.

After Logan climbed inside, he started the ignition. "Your family made me feel welcome today. I wasn't exactly sure what would happen."

"My mother wouldn't have invited you if she didn't want you there. I think today was meant to make up in part for their attitude toward you."

"I suppose."

Logan put his hand on the gearshift and Gina thought they'd back out of the parking place and be on their way. But he didn't put the vehicle into Reverse; rather he glanced to the backseat and saw that Daniel's eyes were closed already.

He shifted as well as he could with his seat belt on and faced her. "You're different than you were when you were eighteen."

"Aren't we all?" she joked, hoping to deflect his perceptive observation.

"Something's different, Gina, that I can't put my finger on. I knew you well, very well. You were irrepressible, joy-filled, ready for any new adventure. Now—"

"Now I'm mature, and I like my world a little more organized."

He shook his head. "No. The old Gina comes out with kids. You played tag, you told jokes, you even swung Daniel on the swing like that girl of eighteen. But the rest of the time, you're quieter, more…withdrawn.

So I guess I'm asking, what had the greatest impact on who you are today?"

"It must have been that short-order cooking," she teased.

"Gina."

The gentle expression in his voice was hard to miss. But did she really want to tell him what had happened, here with his son sleeping in the backseat? She really believed what she'd told him early on when working with Daniel—children were little sponges, no matter what the age. She didn't want to go into something as serious as date rape with Daniel around.

She took a deep breath. "When I was in college, something happened to change the way I looked at the world."

"Some*thing,* or some*one?*"

"A mixture of the two, but I don't talk about it. There's no point. I'm sure there are things that happened that gave you your view of life today. You said you see change as opportunity. Your father didn't. I remember how he fought against bringing in the newest types of machinery. He liked the old ways of doing things."

"I swore I'd never be like him."

"I'm sure his stroke and passing affected you."

"They did. I was pressed into responsibility in a way I'd never experienced after his stroke. We became closer than I ever thought we could. But we weren't talking about *me,* and I'm not so self-absorbed that I didn't notice you changed the subject."

"You have to get home and put Daniel to bed."

He looked frustrated but then gave her a wry smile. "You know how to escape a sticky conversation."

"I do my best."

He put his hand on the gearshift again and shifted into Reverse. "We'll have to finish this soon."

He wasn't going to let it drop, and she supposed she didn't want him to. The time would be right soon.

And then what?

That was the problem. The traumatic event in her life had nothing to do with them and with what Logan felt about her. She had to regain his trust if she wanted even friendship between them. But even then, could she tell him about the threat his father had made? How could she ruin Logan's image of his dad? Somehow she had to rebuild her relationship with Logan without hurting him. But she knew regaining trust would be as difficult as rewriting history.

Gina's emotions had held a tug-of-war with her logic since the picnic. Maybe she should have told Logan about the rape. On the other hand, was he ready to hear? After she told him, she couldn't take it back. After she told him, he'd look at her differently.

On Monday evening Gina decided to tell Logan the truth—about everything. She had an excuse for stopping by. She'd brought lists of requirements for staff for the day-care center and catalogs for furnishings. But as she pulled into the circular driveway in front of the house, she noticed the black stretch limousine.

Logan had company...apparently important company. She pulled up behind the limo, thought about her timing then switched on the ignition again ready to pull away.

However, before she could, Logan came to the door. Seeing her, he beckoned her inside.

She would simply hand him the information. The rest would have to wait.

Parking quickly, she ran up the walk and handed him the manila envelope. "Just some catalogs with things I thought you might need for the day-care center. You'll have an idea of cost estimates when you go through them. Staffing requirements, too."

Logan was dressed in a Western-cut suit, white shirt and bolo tie and looked as if he'd stepped out of the pages of *Country Gentlemen* magazine. In her jeans and sandals she felt as she had fourteen years ago on the evening his father had told her he would never let his son marry a nobody.

"I didn't mean to interrupt your evening. I wasn't thinking. I should have called."

He took the envelope from her. "You're not interrupting, believe me. I'm just having dinner with an oil man and his wife who are interested in donating to the foundation."

"Foundation?"

"After Amy died, I set up a foundation for donations to help with research for women who are pregnant and have cancer. That seemed to be one of the most positive things I could do to try to get over feeling powerless."

Logan admitting to that feeling surprised her. Maybe she really *didn't* know him. Maybe she hadn't known him all those years ago, but had just been caught up in romantic dreams, without the maturity to realize what was real and what wasn't.

"That's a wonderful cause. I wish you luck tonight. What will it take for your guests to write a huge check?"

"Lots of conversation, martinis and a look at my horses. Chad's thinking about purchasing a couple of new ones and would like some tips."

"You should do okay then."

After a long moment, when they couldn't seem to look away from each other, Logan broke into a smile. "Why don't you stay and have dinner with us? I'm sure Chad's wife would like to talk about something other than baseball scores and the price of crude."

But Gina was already shaking her head. She knew where she belonged and where she didn't, and if she wanted to help Logan make an impression, she certainly couldn't do it dressed like this. "I think I'll pass, but thank you for asking."

"You didn't even give it a minute of thought." He sounded more puzzled than annoyed and she saw now that he had meant that invitation seriously.

"I didn't have to, Logan. I might have professional credentials, but I'm not prepared for an evening of suits, upswept hair and jewels."

His mouth turned down in a frown and now he *did* look annoyed. "So you're a reverse snob?"

The word *snob* made her stumble for an answer. She wasn't one and never would be. But maybe she needed to give Logan some understanding of why she'd left. To heal past hurts they needed honesty between them. "Your father hired me to work in the barn. Whenever I enter this estate in any capacity, I think of myself as a hired hand. Your dad never thought I was good enough for you and he told me so. So no, Logan, but on a night like this, dressed as I am, I wouldn't feel comfortable joining you. Think about it—how would you feel coming to one of *my* department meetings?"

"My father told you you weren't good enough for me?" He'd heard what she'd said and understood what it had meant.

Should she say more? They couldn't get beyond the past if she didn't, could they? "You and I were…becoming more involved. Your dad came home early from a trip and found us together in a chaise by the pool. When you went inside the pool house to change, he told me I shouldn't even consider a relationship with you because I was a nobody, and he had plans for you to marry someone in your same social stratum."

"Gina! Why didn't you ever tell me?" His voice showed his shock and he looked troubled.

"At the time, I thought it was best not to, and then…it didn't matter." She heard laughter float from an interior room. "I shouldn't have told you now. I just wanted you to understand why I didn't feel comfortable staying tonight. But I do appreciate the invitation."

When she turned to leave, he caught her arm. "You can't just go like this."

"Yes, I can. Have a good night, Logan. I'll see you Wednesday for Daniel's session."

"You always run away before we're finished," she heard him mutter. But she didn't linger and listen to anything else he had to say. His reaction to her revelations had indicated to her that he might have stood up for her. The fact that he'd wanted her to stay tonight said he didn't care about appearances.

All those years ago, Gina had thought she'd left Logan for all the right reasons. But now she realized she'd simply been too insecure to stay and fight.

Logan rang the doorbell of the Victorian, not sure what he was doing there. He just knew he and Gina had to talk. For almost twenty-four hours, he'd mulled over what

Gina had said about his father. Long dusky shadows were beginning to fill corners as he pressed the bell again.

Suddenly the door opened and Gina was there, looking breathless and beautiful in jeans and a lime-colored blouse. "I was out back," she explained. "The evening was just too nice to stay indoors."

"Are you home alone?" Logan asked, thinking they could go for a drive if she wasn't.

"Yes, Raina is at her brother's. Come in," she said, motioning him inside.

She switched on the Tiffany light in the foyer and its jewel tones dispelled the shadows. When she led him into the living room, he noticed the kitchen beyond, then the hall that led to other rooms. It was an intriguing house, definitely large enough for two or three women to share.

"Would you like something to drink?" she asked. "I have…a local wine, soda, juice, beer."

Did she think he'd turn down anything but the finest champagne? Did she have the beer for men friends she might invite over?

"I'm fine."

She nodded as if she didn't know what to do next.

"I thought we should talk," he said bluntly, motioning to the sofa to indicate this wouldn't be a quick conversation.

They rounded opposite sides of the coffee table and met in the middle.

He waited for her to be seated, and then he lowered himself a good six inches away. "I want to know more about the conversation you had with my father."

She took one of the fringed throw pillows into her lap and held it as if she needed something to hold on to. "I'm not sure there's any point."

"I believe there is."

Staring across the room rather than at him, she pulled the pillow into her chest. "The truth is—I wasn't mature enough or assertive enough to stand up for myself, but I think that's because I believed he was right."

"That you were a nobody?" She'd been intelligent and bright and sweet.

"*You* made me feel like somebody, but I knew that wasn't enough. I felt I had to be your equal. Your father didn't think I was, didn't see that I was, so I was sure I wasn't."

"You really believed that?"

She nodded and swung her gaze toward him. "I didn't have the latest clothes. I wore Josie's hand-me-downs. I wasn't a cheerleader or even a debater because I always had to get home to take care of Angie. I never resented that because I found satisfaction in taking care of her and fulfilling my role in my family. It was important to me, and it helped my mom bring home a paycheck, too. But that role also kept me isolated from my classmates. When I met you, you didn't know that I wasn't the most popular girl in school. You didn't care that I wasn't a cheerleader. You were somehow beyond all that. At least, that's what I thought."

"But my dad made you feel differently."

She hesitated, then seemed to choose her words carefully. "Your dad made me see who I truly was. That wasn't going to change unless *I* changed it. I could do that by going to college. I could not only change who *I* was, but who Angie could become. Oh, Logan, I wanted to stay. But there were so many pressures that pushed me to leave. Once I was in college, I still had regrets, but I—"

The look on her face forewarned him that he

wouldn't like what was coming. For a moment, just a moment, he glimpsed that something soul-shaking had happened to her.

"So when I called, why didn't you talk to me? Did you really have a test?"

She looked down at her hands folded across the pillow. Her dark lashes were so feminine on her cheeks, but he sensed her calm exterior was hiding a wealth of turmoil underneath.

"I had a test that day, but…I couldn't call you back."

More than anything, he wanted to reach out and take her hand. He wanted to reach out and touch her face. When they touched, all heaven broke loose and he could use a little of that now. But this wasn't about him and his feelings. It was about *her.* He'd never put himself into her shoes because he hadn't wanted to, because her reasons for leaving weren't as important as the reasons she should have stayed.

"Tell me what happened."

It was a request more than a command, but the intensity behind it made her hold the pillow tighter.

"You'll never look at me the same again if I tell you," she said, so reasonably he almost believed her. But then he saw she wasn't being reasonable at all. She was afraid…afraid of his reaction.

"What happened?" he asked again, gently so she'd know she had nothing to fear.

He saw the pulse at her neck was beating fast.

She took a deep breath, held it, then let it out. "I was date-raped."

She uttered the words very softly, but they slammed into him like a body blow. Their impact took his breath away. If they did that to *him,* he could only imagine what they did to her. Should he gather her into his arms? Let her explain? Tell her she didn't have to say anything else?

He was at a total loss. He felt frozen.

She must have seen how absolutely he'd been affected by what she'd told him because she said, "You don't have to say anything. I just wanted you to know why I didn't come back, why I didn't call, why I felt even more insecure about the differences between us."

"My God, Gina, insecure? You were raped! Insecurity has to be the least of it. Who in the hell did this? Did you press charges?"

Agitated now, she tossed down the pillow and walked over to the bay window looking out into the front yard. "I didn't bring this up to rehash it. I got counseling. It's over."

He couldn't stay away from her now. Crossing to her, he gently laid his hands on her shoulders. "If you don't want to talk about it, that's okay, but please turn around and look at me."

She did then, and he could tell it took an effort for her to keep her chin lifted. He could feel the tension in her body, see the lines on her brow, and abruptly he realized what facing him like this cost her. Without a second thought, he wrapped his arms around her and brought her into his chest. They stood that way for what seemed to be a very long time.

Seconds passed. Minutes passed. He didn't know how many.

When Logan finally leaned back to look at her, he thought he might see tears in her eyes, but he didn't. That surprised him.

"You say you're over it, but can you really be over something like that?"

A long sigh escaped her lips. "For the most part. I still have some trust issues with men, trust issues in general, really. I didn't tell anyone what happened. It would have been a 'he said, she said' situation. He didn't even go to the college I attended. He was a friend of one of the frat guys and just happened to be at the party that night. I was lonely and had drunk punch that was spiked. I don't know how much liquor was in it. But that was no excuse. I never should have gone with him to that room. I thought we were going to talk." She let out a humorless laugh.

That laugh was like a lance to Logan's heart. Gina had been trusting and innocent, shy and vulnerable. How much of that had been taken away from her? He was filled with righteous anger.

She pushed away from Logan. "I can see what you're wondering. I said *no,* Logan. After a few kisses, I said *no.* But he wouldn't listen, and he was stronger and bigger than I was."

"Don't, Gina. I'm not doubting you."

"Aren't you? The counselor warned me about any responses a man in my life might have. That's why I never told my parents. Can you imagine what my father's response would be?"

"And your mother doesn't know, either?"

"No, no one does. It happened in Connecticut. I dealt with it there. I didn't want it intruding on my family or on any time we spent together."

"Don't you think they had a right to know so they could help you?"

"They *couldn't* help me, Logan. I had to handle it on my own. I had to take my power back. I had to work through the anger, and then I had to go on."

"But did you go on? Or is this the reason you never married and had a family?"

"I don't know. I do know I got caught up in my studies and my work and that's what became all-important to me."

As he studied Gina, he saw there were no external remnants of what she'd been through. But he suspected on the inside, she'd been changed in an elemental way. As he thought about everything she'd told him, he found his fists clenched by his sides.

She glanced at him warily. "You're going to be different now, aren't you? Please, Logan, don't be. I just told you all this so you'd understand why I couldn't…stay in touch."

"Essentially, you didn't trust me to understand. You thought I'd blame you."

"Trust? I don't think that even entered into it. It took me a long while to recover—months, a year, probably even longer than that. I just put one foot in front of the other and took a step each day. My counselor and group therapy were a large part of my college years. I made excuses not to come home until I had put myself back together."

He instinctively wanted to touch her again, but didn't know if he should. "Does it bother you to be…close to a man?"

"Strangers. Sometimes if they get close, I pull away. But with you, I'm…fine."

Was that longing he saw in her eyes? Longing for what? What they might have had? For his kiss? For his forgiveness? He'd come here to settle something between them. Instead, everything had gotten more complicated. He was at a loss as to what to say or do, and he wondered just how he would have reacted if she'd told him right after the rape had happened.

"So the guy who did this—"

"I didn't even know where he was visiting from, or who his friend was. I only knew he was charming and complimentary and seemed like a genuinely nice guy until after we went into that room. Could I have found out who he was? Maybe. But I wasn't in any position to play detective. Shouldn't I have discovered who he was and outed him? Yes. As soon as it happened, I should have gone into the hall and screamed bloody murder. But I didn't. What I did do was rebuild my life. I made my parents proud. And I helped put Angie through school."

She walked away from him, over to the sofa, agitated, as if telling him had brought everything out of the dark of the basement, and she didn't want to see it in the light. He couldn't blame her. He shouldn't have asked her questions. He should have just listened.

Logan went to her, caught her hand, and tugged her around to face him. "Do you have plans this evening?"

She looked flustered. "No."

"Then come home with me. We can spend some time with Daniel and take him to that carnival that's in town. He's never seen Ferris wheels or merry-go-rounds. I'd like to take some pictures when he sees all of it for the first time."

"Why are you inviting me?" she asked, her huge brown eyes direct. "I don't want you to feel sorry for me. I put the past behind me and I have a life I'm proud of."

No matter how courageous, forward-looking or optimistic anyone was, trauma colored their future. He remembered the weeks by Amy's side as she was dying, Daniel's birth, not knowing whether his son would live or die. He'd pushed all of that to the back of his mind and to the back of his heart, but it never really went away.

"I'm asking you along because Daniel and I want to enjoy his first carnival with someone, and you're the someone I'm choosing. There's nothing complicated about it, Gina. Just cotton candy, a merry-go-round and an escape from everyday reality for a little while."

When she didn't respond immediately, he prodded her. "So what do you say? Will you ride on the merry-go-round with us?"

Chapter Seven

What are you doing here? Gina asked herself later.

Beside her, Logan pushed Daniel's stroller over the ruts and bumps of the unpaved walkway in the field where the carnival had been set up, heading toward the cotton-candy vendor.

She knew Logan had only asked her along because he felt sorry for her. That had been the problem with telling him about what had happened. She didn't want his pity and knowing he felt sorry for her might put even more walls between them.

Or maybe he thought she was a coward for not trying to prosecute her attacker. He might also believe she'd invited what had happened. She'd analyzed her behavior over and over again until her counselor *had* told her she had to let it go. But that was difficult to do.

Every time Logan glanced at her now, she thought

he looked at her a little more kindly. But she didn't want that, either.

What *did* she want?

Wasn't that the most mind-boggling question she'd ever encountered? She'd said she wanted Logan's forgiveness, but maybe what she really wanted was to find the missing piece of herself she'd left behind in Sagebrush fourteen years ago.

Logan had wheeled Daniel up to the cotton-candy cart that sat next to a corn-dog stand and a funnel-cake maker. "Can you watch him while I get the cotton candy?" he asked her.

He trusted her more and more with Daniel and that made her feel better than she should.

She gave Logan a smile and crouched down with Daniel to talk to him in his language for a few minutes, to play with the small toys on the tray on his stroller. It was a state-of-the-art stroller with all the bells and whistles, sturdy and solid with a canopy that would protect a child against almost any element. She could only imagine what it had cost. In the future, how would Logan keep from spoiling his son and buying him the best and the finest? How would he teach Daniel he had to earn what he wanted most? Would Logan even make him do that? She remembered how Josie had married right out of high school—secondhand supplies were all her older sister had ever known for her kids. It had broken Gina's mother's heart and she'd helped provide what she could, but the rest of the family had been on a thin budget, too.

When Logan returned, his smile was bittersweet.

Gina had been at a carnival with Logan that summer she was eighteen in another small town an hour away.

They'd wanted just to be themselves, go someplace they weren't known and where people wouldn't talk. They'd shared a stick of cotton candy and gotten it all over their mouths, their fingers, their hands. They'd kissed it from each other. When Logan turned her way, she could see that he was remembering that night, too. Those sparks of desire in his eyes were easy to decipher.

Now, however, he merely offered her a pink wisp of the candy. She took it, feeling her fingers get sticky. When she touched it to her lips, she remembered Logan feeding it to her that summer night when they hadn't had a care in the world. At least that was how it had seemed until Logan's father had warned her away from his son…until her parents had talked to her about the future and her dreams…until her older sister described being saddled with a baby when she was practically still a child herself. If she had followed her own heart back then and fought for the love she and Logan shared, there might not be this distance between her and Logan now. There would have been no trauma to explain.

Daniel reached out to her swath of pink fluff, filling one little hand with it and squeezing it into his fist. It turned into pink goo. Daniel chortled and touched her cheek with his messy hand, leaving sugary fingerprints. Gina heard Logan's camera beep.

Laughing, she took Daniel's hand and kissed it, then wiped it and her face as best she could with her napkin.

Logan's voice was husky when he said, "I have a jar of baby food in the backpack of the stroller. There's a canopied dining area over there. If you want to head that way, I'll grab some food and drinks. Root beer, right?"

He'd remembered. Tears formed in her eyes. She didn't know why that little thing unlocked the door where feelings waited to rush out, but it did. Still…it took until she found them a table in the cordoned-off area, until she took Daniel from his seat and held him on her lap, for the tears to stop. She'd had an unexpectedly emotional evening. That was all.

A few minutes later, Logan came toward them managing to balance two boxes—one with food, another with drinks. She helped him unload the corn dogs, burgers and chili, then the sodas.

While Logan held Daniel, Gina fed him the baby food.

"It must be awful to be down there sitting in that stroller all the time, unable to see what's going on up here."

"Do you think he minds?" Logan asked, as if he hadn't considered the idea before.

"I just think he'll like it better up here."

Daniel seemed content to stare at all the sights while they ate. Lights were beginning to come on now, transforming the carnival into a magical place.

"I forgot to ask if you got donations for your charity from the oil man," Gina said, finished with her cup of chili, needing to make normal conversation so emotion wouldn't get the best of her again.

Logan's eyebrows lifted. "I wish you had come in for dinner."

She kept silent.

"You're going to have to deal with your insecurities, Gina," he said, a little sternly. "You have a Ph.D. and a successful practice. You have nothing to be insecure about."

She glanced around, seeing that nobody sat at the tables close to theirs, and anyway, everyone else was involved in their own conversations.

They were being so honest with each other. Should

she tell him what his father had threatened to do? She'd always wondered what Logan would have chosen. Would he have chosen a life with her, without riches? Or would he have turned his back on her for the life his father had planned for him?

"What are you thinking about?"

She shook her head. "Nothing."

He frowned. "Nothing you want to talk about, you mean."

"You think you can still read my mind?" she joked.

"Obviously I can't."

Daniel squirmed to be let down, ready to explore something else. "Why don't we take Daniel on a pony ride?" Logan suggested. "After that, maybe we can listen to the bluegrass concert. I have a blanket in the car we can spread out. He might fall asleep on it if we're lucky."

"And if we're not?"

He shrugged. "We can take him home."

Logan seemed more relaxed with Daniel's schedule tonight than he'd been the evening of the picnic with her family. Maybe he'd been uncomfortable with them, but tonight he was at ease with her. Or maybe he sensed what was best for Daniel and just followed his instincts.

Gazing into his eyes now, she knew that was the case. "You really understand putting kids first, don't you?" she asked softly.

"I do," he said.

A bond of understanding tied them together. A hot tingle skipped up her back as she gazed into his green eyes and remembered all the things she'd felt as a teenager. Now she was feeling more…excited? More wishful? More intoxicated by his mere presence?

Why *was* she here?

Maybe by the end of the night, she'd find out.

Logan's gaze fell on Gina for the umpteenth time as they sat on a blanket listening to guitars strumming along with a banjo and fiddle. He couldn't get her revelations out of his mind. The rage he felt for her was similar to the fury he'd felt against Amy's cancer. His wife had been a beautiful, vibrant woman, cut down by an evil disease. There had been no good answers for her, not where she and Daniel had been concerned. So she'd lived with the decisions she'd made, and she'd died because of them...without regrets.

Admitting he had regrets was difficult. He regretted that they hadn't laughed more and traveled more and tried to have a baby sooner. He wished he'd been more attentive. Then he might have caught her symptoms sooner, maybe even before *she* had. Those feelings still weighed him down in the middle of the night. He was always digging through it all, coming to terms with the pain, learning to live with it.

And Gina...she sat here tonight, years removed from what had happened to *her*. But he knew trauma like hers couldn't be left behind so easily. He'd already noticed the ways it had affected her personality, making her quieter and more self-conscious where men were concerned. He'd seen that with James Wolfe.

Yet she'd kissed *him* without hesitation. Because he'd surprised her? He'd surprised himself. That kiss hadn't been the kind of intimacy they'd once known. How would she handle *that* kind of involvement?

Why was he even asking?

There were many sleepless nights when still he tossed and turned because of the decisions he'd let Amy make…because of the way he hadn't bonded with his son the first month, because he'd been afraid Daniel would die. After Amy's memorial service, he'd vowed loving a woman hurt too much. When he was ready, he'd have no-strings sex. It would be about having a physical need fulfilled, no more. But he hadn't even contemplated it. He hadn't gone out on dates, or asked a woman to any of the dinners he attended, the cocktail parties, the charity functions. He went alone. Because?

Because it was safer. Because he only had the energy for Daniel and work. Because getting involved in any fashion just hadn't been in the cards he'd been dealt.

He did *not* want to get involved with Gina now. Yet sitting on this blanket across from her made his insides jump, made him feel heat under the collar of his shirt, made him resurrect the past when that was the last thing he should do.

"You're frowning," she noticed, her voice soft in the growing darkness as the band took a break. "Is it getting too late for Daniel? We can leave anytime."

Daniel was sitting on the blanket between Logan's legs, chewing on a plastic giraffe he liked to carry with him. Suddenly the giraffe held no more interest and he tossed it at Gina. As she grabbed for it, her T-shirt sneaked up her midriff and Logan caught sight of skin. She was as slim as she'd ever been, her breasts still as pert.

Unnerved by desire that had no place here tonight, he picked Daniel up from a sitting position and balanced him on his feet. His little sneakers rocked on the blanket but he kept hold of Logan's hands.

Gina turned to face Logan squarely, and touched her

feet to his, making a channel between them. She lifted
Daniel's giraffe and waved it at him. "Look here,
Daniel, see what I've got. Do you want him?"

Logan turned Daniel around so he was facing Gina.
He knew what she was trying to do and he held his breath
to see if it would work. But at that moment, Daniel
decided to plop down onto the blanket and knee-walk
toward her.

She gave him a bright smile. "Well, *that's* new."

He took the giraffe from her and began to gnaw on it.
A drum roll startled all of them and, for a moment, Logan
thought Daniel was going to cry. He was ready to go to
him and comfort him, but Gina already had her arms
around his son. She stood him up, supported his hips and
pointed to where the band started to play again. She
looked like any mother would, her face close to Daniel's,
her lips at his cheek, telling him about something new.

But *Amy* was Daniel's mother. Logan could never
forget that. He could never let Daniel forget it, either.

So why *had* he invited Gina tonight? Because he felt
sorrow for what she'd gone through? Because he
wanted to know more? Because the old attraction was
tickling his libido in a way he couldn't scratch?

He crossed one ankle over the other, kept his gaze
on his son and concentrated on the music.

"He's still asleep," Gina murmured as Logan pulled
into the driveway at the Victorian, feeling as if the
ground beneath her feet had shifted again.

Ever since she'd told Logan about the rape, he'd been
different. During the concert, he'd distanced himself
from her. Yet that shouldn't be a surprise. He'd been
doing it ever since fate had brought them together again.

"If I'm lucky, I can get him into bed before he wakes up too much. I think he had a good time tonight."

"Did *you?*" She probably couldn't eliminate the distance between them if Logan was determined to keep it there, but she could chop at it.

"Yes, I did," he responded, but Gina knew it was a reflexive, polite response.

"I shouldn't have told you."

Logan put the Range Rover into Park, but let the engine idle. "What do you want me to say, Gina?"

"I want to know what you're feeling. You're thinking I deserved it for leaving? Do you—"

"No, Gina. For God's sake, don't you know me better than that?"

"I don't know. Everything between us is so complicated. One minute I think we're becoming friends again, then I feel this wall between us. Tonight, we were having a good time and then suddenly, you were a thousand miles from me. I felt as if I'd done something wrong."

Logan cut her a sideways glance. "You and Daniel have bonded."

"Isn't that a good thing? If he and I have a connection, when I work with him, we'll make better progress."

Logan kept his gaze straight ahead at the detached garage twenty yards away. "You don't understand what's happening, do you?"

She wished she did. Maybe he'd explain the turmoil she felt in him when they were together. "Tell me."

The engine of the Range Rover hummed in the background. The only other sound was the pounding of her heart as she waited, giving Logan time to put his thoughts together.

Finally he wrapped his hands around the steering wheel, still not looking at her. "Hannah and I have cared for Daniel since he came home from the hospital. I trust her to care for him the same way I do. I'm used to seeing them together."

In a jolt of insight suddenly Gina knew where this was going, and her heart hurt for this man she'd left.

"You together with Daniel," he went on, "that's different. When he looks up at you and laughs, when he puts his little hands on your face, whenever you hold him, I think about Amy and the way this should have been."

"Logan, I can bow out of your life. I can have one of my therapists work with Daniel and you won't ever have to see me."

Already Logan was shaking his head. "That's the thing, Gina. If we do that, nothing's resolved. Do you understand?"

Oh, she understood. She'd returned to Sagebrush to resolve something in her life, something that had to do with Logan. "Maybe what happened between us and what happened afterward will never be resolved."

She touched his arm, her fingertips aware of the strong sinew of his muscles, strength in Logan that he also used as a defense mechanism. "You miss Daniel's mother. I do understand that. You not only miss her, but you miss the life you would have had together…you *should* have had together. Nothing I can say will change that."

In the silence, Gina could hear Daniel's little sighing noises as he slept. He was becoming dear to her, maybe too dear. Maybe in trying to reconcile the past with Logan, she was setting herself up for another world of hurt.

Releasing Logan's arm, she wasn't sure what to do. She sensed he'd said everything he was going to say.

Maybe they'd had enough of talking and they were both better off if they kept a lid on the emotions they considered private and too painful to share.

She unfastened her seat belt. "I'd better go in. You have to get home and put Daniel to bed."

He didn't protest or argue, and she knew she was right. Daniel's next appointment was scheduled for tomorrow evening. "If you want me to find another therapist for him, just let me know."

"I'd walk you to the door, but I don't want to leave Daniel alone in the car."

"I know. I don't have far to go," she said lightly, hoping Logan would at least look at her.

"I'll wait until you're inside." He did glance at her then. It was only a glance. She understood why he didn't make eye contact. If he looked at her, they'd both feel more than they already did—more regret, more sadness, more uncertainty about the future.

She opened the car door and climbed out. When she closed it, she felt as if she were shutting the door on a chapter in her life. She looked over her shoulder, wishing she could give Daniel a kiss, wishing she and Logan could wipe the slate clean.

With her heart hurting, she hurried up the walk to the Victorian, unlocked the door and stepped inside. As the door clicked shut, she heard Logan backing out of the driveway.

Raina called, "How was the carnival?"

Gina had left a note on the refrigerator so her housemate would know where she was. When she walked into the living room, Raina took one look at her and from the easy chair used the remote to turn off the TV. "What's wrong?"

Gina shook her head and dropped down onto the sofa. "It can't be so obvious."

"You sat in the driveway for a long time, so either you were making out or having an intense discussion."

"We could have just been talking about the weather," Gina tried to joke.

"When I was married, Gina, my husband and I had a few of those in-the-driveway talks and make-out sessions. Young love was wonderful—all highs and lows and not much room for anything in between."

"I remember," Gina said solemnly. "I made the biggest mistake of my life when I left and turned my back on Logan."

"Why didn't you return to Sagebrush sooner?" Raina asked, reaching for a hair band on the end table, sliding it into her hair.

Gina knew it was time that she started letting go of the past, too. A part of her letting-go process had to be talking about it.

"When I left Logan, I told myself I was doing the best thing for both of us. I tried to forget about him and throw myself into my studies and into college life in general. About two months into the semester—"

She revealed to Raina what had happened to her at that frat party.

As soon as she was finished talking, Raina came over to her and gave her a hug. Sitting beside her on the sofa, she said, "I'm so sorry that happened to you."

"I told Logan about it today. I wanted him to know why when he called, I couldn't talk to him, why I couldn't make contact afterward. I've never talked to anyone about it but my counselor. Now you and Logan in the same night."

"I'm glad you confided in me."

"We haven't known each other long, but I feel I can trust you."

"I feel the same way," Raina agreed. "I couldn't have moved in with just anyone." She patted Gina's hand. "How did you and Logan leave it tonight? What was the discussion about?"

"It was about everything, although a lot went unsaid. Do you know what I mean?"

"Oh, yeah. I know exactly what you mean."

"I think Logan believed he was ready to move on with his life. But when he sees me with Daniel, he misses his wife."

"I don't doubt that. But there's got to be a reason he also wants to spend some time with you. If everything he felt for you was in the past, he wouldn't feel the need to be with you now."

Gina could only hope that was true, because she was falling for Logan all over again. This time, the fall could be even more devastating than the last time.

The knock on Logan's home-office door was a welcome intrusion. He'd been distracted for the past week and not very productive in whatever he'd tried to accomplish.

"Come in."

Hannah did and asked, "Got a few minutes?"

Logan checked his watch and the video monitor on his desk where he could see Daniel sleeping. "Shouldn't you be hand-deep into a bowl of popcorn, watching your favorite detective show?"

Hannah smiled broadly. "I will be in about ten minutes. I just wondered if you're going to make an appointment with Gina this week."

Logan's back stiffened and he told himself not to be defensive. Yet he was. He'd canceled this week's appointment, knowing it *wasn't* the best thing to do. But he'd needed some time to think. "I'm not sure yet, why?"

"Because he misses her and because I think he's right on the verge of walking. She might be the motivation he needs."

"*We* aren't enough?"

"Apparently not, or he'd be walking by now, don't you think? Logan, I don't know what happened between you and Gina, but don't let Daniel suffer for it."

"It's one session," he muttered.

"One session right now could make a difference. Besides that, he needs another woman in his life, one who cares about him as much as Gina does."

"And just how do you know she does?"

"Don't play games with me. I can see it whenever she's with him, and she cares about *you,* too."

"Hannah—"

"I know. I should stay out of your personal life." She glared at him. "Not that you really have one. Don't you think Amy would be glad if you found someone to look after you and Daniel?"

"*You* do that."

Hannah just rolled her eyes and shook her head. "You need more than work and you need more than Daniel, whether you'll admit it or not."

Logan leaned back in his chair and studied his housekeeper/nanny. "So your reason for interrupting me tonight is…"

"Make an appointment for Daniel and keep it. Or better yet, make a date with Gina and keep it."

"You're overstepping," he grumbled.

"No, I'm not. I've been with you long enough to express my opinion."

When he didn't respond, she came toward his desk, put her hands on it and leaned forward toward him. "You need to start living your life again, Logan. There's no point being here if you're just going through the motions." Then she straightened, smiled, said, "You know where I'll be if you need me," and left his office.

Logan stood and paced across the room. He went to the back window and stared at the outside floodlights illuminating the pool area. So much...and so little.

After a few moments, he shifted his gaze again to the monitor on his desk where he could see Daniel. His son appeared to be so peaceful, so caught up in baby dreams.

Dreams. Logan had told Gina he didn't have them anymore. Should he dream, or should he just take what came, day by day?

Gina had dropped into his life on one of those days and she'd shaken up his universe. Denying his attraction to her was absolutely useless, especially when it seemed to be mutual.

What could come of it?

Didn't they both deserve the chance to find out?

He checked his watch again. Ten-thirty. Too late or not too late?

Again he studied his sleeping son, then he picked up the phone on his desk. It rang three times and he was almost ready to hang up when Gina answered. "Hello?"

"It's Logan."

"I know. Caller ID."

"Right." There was an awkward pause and he knew

he had to be the one to fill it. "I shouldn't have canceled Daniel's appointment."

"I see," she said slowly. "You want to schedule another one now?"

He had to smile. "Yes…and no."

"I have my appointment book downstairs." Her voice was still filled with puzzlement.

"Gina, I called because I'd like you to spend some time with me on Saturday. I thought Hannah could pack a picnic lunch and we could take it to the lake. I still have a rowboat and…" He felt at a total loss for words. "And there's a family of baby ducklings you might want to watch."

She laughed. "Baby ducklings."

He swore. "I'm not doing this very well. I'd like to spend some time with you, just you and me. What do you think?"

Her answer seemed forever in coming, but finally she answered him. "I'd like that. What time should I come over?"

"Around noon."

"I'll see you then."

When Logan hung up the phone, he wasn't sure if he'd done the right thing. He'd find out on Saturday.

Chapter Eight

Logan balanced on his feet in the rowboat beside the cooler, holding his hand out to Gina, who was standing on the dock.

Gina thought he looked too tall for the rowboat. Too muscled, too broad-shouldered, too ruggedly ready for rowing. This was a different boat from the one they'd taken out on the lake fourteen years ago. Thank goodness. As it was, a memory of the night they'd kissed under a full moon while floating in the middle of the water slid before her eyes as if it had happened yesterday. Was Logan remembering, too?

Since she'd arrived, his expression had been unreadable. She wasn't sure exactly how to act or what to think. Was this a *date?*

When she stepped down into the boat, Logan held her hand a little longer than he had to. The warmth around her fingers made her feel safe, though the boat teetered a little.

"Do you want to have lunch on the lake, or should we just row for a while?"

"Let's just row. We have the cooler. If we get hungry, we can eat." She didn't know whether to sit beside Logan or across from him. Across from him, she could see his eyes and look at his face. Maybe at that vantage point, she could interpret glimmers of what he felt.

Logan settled himself with the oars and began rowing.

"Do you want me to help?"

"I'm good. I've been coming out and rowing around the lake for exercise. It helps work off frustration." As soon as the words came out, he looked sorry he'd said them.

"Frustration from work? Or frustration from having me back in your life?"

He grinned ruefully. "You always did see too much."

"I don't think I saw enough. I'm only four years younger than you, but back then, those four years meant a lot. I hadn't broken my ties with my parents yet, definitely not with my family."

"I didn't know about the kind of ties you had with your parents," he said. "After my mother died, my father really started earning his fortune. He was never home. We lost a lot of years until he was interested in me because I was growing up and could be groomed to take over the business."

She heard his father's voice echo again. *If he marries you, I'll disinherit him.*

"Did you *want* to take over the business?"

"I don't think I ever thought about it. To me it was expected. On the other hand, it did interest me. I knew the business here could lead to a wider range of opportunities. I've invested in condos in Sydney, a winery in the Loire Valley, and I even have an interest in a high-rise in Hong Kong. Not that I'm trying to impress you," he said with a grimace. "I'm just saying my father didn't have the curiosity I do for the world at large."

Would Logan have developed those interests if she hadn't left? Did she want to tackle that subject, too? Maybe in a roundabout way. "How do you feel about the rest now that you have Daniel?"

He continued rowing slowly, his Stetson shading his face so she really couldn't see his eyes.

"Now my world revolves around Daniel," Logan responded. "That means when I'm working, I think about leaving him a legacy like my father left me. It means I make time away from work to be with him. It means nothing is more important than *his* welfare."

"You can't give him a perfect world," she warned.

"No, but I can do my best to make sure it is in every way possible."

Suddenly Logan stopped rowing. He was looking over her shoulder and he patted the seat next to him. "Come here."

She wasn't sure what he wanted her to see, but she gingerly managed to step over the cooler to sit beside him on his seat.

He pointed to the edge of the lake under the willows and she had to smile.

"Ducklings!" There were five of them all swimming after their mama. "You weren't kidding," she said, laughing again.

"No, I wasn't." The gravel in his voice turned her head toward him and their gazes locked.

In that moment, everything he'd been through and

everything she'd been through fell into the background of their lives. She was close enough to him that she could feel the restrained desire in his body, the kiss that was brewing in his thoughts. If he kissed her again, what would it mean? More than the fact that he was still attracted to her?

"The last time I kissed you, afterward you said a kiss has to mean something. I understand that better now. So I have to ask how you feel…about being close to a man. Being intimate."

She took a deep breath, stared at the diamond sparkles on the water and considered his question carefully.

"Gina?"

When she looked at him, she wanted to tell him desire was a good thing. It was healthy. She'd felt it once more when he'd kissed her. But it was a complicated issue. "I can't give you a simple answer to that. I had counseling, Logan. Yet, faced with a man's desire, that's a different thing than talking about it, analyzing it or even wishing for it. I've dated since the rape. I've been kissed and I didn't panick. But I don't know how much I was there for it, either. I didn't respond very well and I guess that's why the relationships didn't go any further. Maybe I just wouldn't let them."

He was studying her, trying to figure out what was behind the quiver in her voice, the emotions she still kept in check. "What do you mean, you weren't *there?*"

"Do you know what dissociation is?"

"I've heard the term, but tell me what it means for you."

"When he started violating me, I went away in my mind. He was strong and big and I couldn't escape, at least not physically. But I disappeared mentally and emotionally. I closed down because I didn't want to feel anything that was happening."

"Gina," Logan murmured, his voice filled with tenderness as he took her hands.

"It took a couple of years to let myself feel in the moment because afterward I filtered everything, everybody. I just wanted to be alone and study and focus on the print in a textbook because there wasn't any danger there. I kept my apartment door dead-bolted and chain-locked. I had a can of mace in my purse and kept it under my pillow. When the counseling began to have some effect, I became more proactive. I took several self-defense courses and then finally I started getting 'me' back. I found my people-radar was darn good and I had absolutely nothing to fear from children. They were honest and innocent and responded to love. I could totally be there for them. They didn't question motives or agenda. I just wanted to help them develop into healthy adults."

She felt unsettled by everything that had poured out. "That's more information than you wanted to know, I guess."

He squeezed her hands and his thumbs moved over her palms in soothing circles. "It's hard to hear. But I want to know, Gina."

"I think that's enough for now," she said with a small laugh, wanting to cut the tension that had coiled around them.

"You were *here* during our kiss, unless I'm totally off the mark."

"Yes, I was. I don't know if it was because the kiss was a surprise or because of what we once had, or because I'm not afraid of you."

"I hope that's the reason," he said with heartfelt sincerity.

"I haven't talked about this with anyone because I don't want them to walk on eggshells around me. I don't want *you* to walk on eggshells."

"I suppose all we can do is be honest with each other." He brushed a tendril of hair from her cheek and she wanted to curl into him, lie against his chest, feel his strong arms around her. But that might never happen for lots of reasons. Today, the most she could hope for, was that they would finally begin to reestablish a real friendship again.

Beside Logan now, she helped him row to the other side of the lake. There was no dock there so they paddled as fast as they could into the shore and pushed with the oars to find a secure mooring. As they climbed out, mud squished around their feet. Gina's foot slipped and Logan caught her. His arm held her securely around the waist, and she reached to his shoulder for support. The willow branches seemed to stop swaying, the birdcalls faded, the sun's heat mingled with theirs.

"I don't know how to treat you," Logan said huskily.

"How do you want to treat me?"

He shook his head. "I'm not sure."

"Then we shouldn't do anything we'll regret," she decided reasonably, not feeling reasonable at all.

His gaze lingered on her lips, then his hands released her as he mumbled, "Right."

After he fetched the cooler, he carried it through some brush and over grass laced with tiny blue and white wildflowers. The quilt Logan had brought for the occasion looked brand-new.

"We'll get it dirty," Gina protested as he spread it over the grass near a cottonwood.

"Hannah says it will wash. I use it on the ground for Daniel when I take him outside."

"Do you do that much?"

"Not enough. I've had too many conference calls lately. This week I've been discussing foundation work with the governor."

"You're trying to find more funding?"

"That and we're planning activities that go state-wide—coordinated walk-a-thons, bike races, that kind of thing."

As they lowered themselves to the quilt, she and Logan settled their backs against the same tree trunk.

"I've been thinking about the day-care center," Gina said.

Logan seemed to be relieved at that subject. "What about it?"

When she didn't respond quickly, he opened the cooler and took out two wrapped sandwiches.

"Do you have a name yet?"

He shrugged. "I hadn't thought beyond getting it built. What's your suggestion?"

"How about the Amy Barnes Day-Care Center?"

His hand with the sandwiches stopped in midair.

"It's just a suggestion, Logan. I wasn't sure if it would be a good one or a bad one. How do you feel about it?" She knew "how do you feel" was a very different question than "what do you think?" Would she get either answer?

"I didn't consider that. Naming the center after her would be a tribute to her, wouldn't it...a tribute for what she did for Daniel."

"And you."

"Right. And me."

He laid one of the thick roast-turkey sandwiches in front of her on the quilt. "As Daniel grows older, he'd understand better what his mother did for him." Logan seemed to be warming to the thought. "Thank you, Gina, it really is a wonderful idea. I don't know why I didn't think of it."

Gina knew suggesting his wife's name had been the right thing to do. She also knew that the day-care center would be a huge reminder of the life Logan had shared with Amy.

She picked up her sandwich, unwrapped it and began to eat. But she had no appetite.

Later, as Logan drove back to the house, Gina sat quietly, staring out into the cotton fields.

"Are you up to a game of tennis?" he asked.

Her attention veered from the rows of green leaves to his profile as he drove.

"You don't have to entertain me, Logan. If you'd like to look in on Daniel, we can do that."

She'd always had the damnable habit of reading him too well. Amy had never even attempted to read his thoughts. She expected him just to tell her if he had something important to say.

Don't compare, he told himself sternly.

"I'd like to look in on Daniel," he said. "But tennis might be good afterward. I haven't had anyone challenge me in a while. Have you kept your game?"

He'd taught her how to play and she'd been good.

"I still play now and then, but I doubt if I'm as good as you are."

A recognizable tune played somewhere in Gina's

vicinity. She said, "Sorry," and dug in her purse. She brought out her cell phone and checked the caller ID. "It's my mom. I'd better take this."

Logan knew Gina's family came first. She'd proven that. When he glanced at her, their gazes held, and he suspected she knew what he was thinking once again.

Her cheeks became a little brighter as she answered. "Hi, Mom. What's up?" There was a pause. "Sure I'll be there tomorrow. I wouldn't miss Josie's birthday… I can pick up the balloons. Okay, I'll see you tomorrow."

Gina closed her phone.

"A birthday party?" he asked.

"My older sister's. My mom wanted to make sure I'd be there."

"You're not as close to your family as you once were."

"It was hard to stay connected when I was so far away."

"But now you're back." After a pause, he added, "Maybe you should tell them what happened."

"I can't do that!" The idea really seemed to horrify her.

"Why?"

She sighed. "I think my parents are still fairly naive. They were sending me to a good college where I'd study hard and find a brilliant future. They would never even imagine something like that could happen there."

"But it did. Don't you think your mom and dad have worried about the changes they see in you?"

"I always acted perfectly normal when I called, and it was almost a year afterward until I came home for a visit. They didn't suspect anything."

"Oh, I'm sure they *did*. They just couldn't put their finger on what it was. Even my father, as remote as he was sometimes, could read me better than I liked."

"Tell me what happened after he recovered."

He knew what Gina was doing—switching the focus from her to him. "I'd taken a semester off to help with his rehabilitation. At the start of the new year, he insisted I go back and get my MBA. He had a valet who was with him twenty-four hours a day. He also had a physical therapist and a nurse when necessary. I knew he was well taken care of so I got my MBA at Texas Tech instead of going back to Texas A&M. I was around as much as he wanted me to be around. Since I'd taken over most of his business dealings during those first few months, I kept my hand in. After I earned my degree, I started some ventures of my own. He didn't approve of condos in Sydney or even of the golf courses in Arizona. But I wanted to build, and I felt I had the foundation to do it. After a while, he stopped protesting. He had some memory problems after the stroke. Because of the weakness on his left side, he'd stopped riding and hated that. He hated having someone help him do anything."

"He died five years ago?"

"Yes. A year after I married Amy."

"Did he like your wife?"

"He adored Amy. He'd known her father and—" As soon as Logan said it, he knew he shouldn't have. "Gina, I didn't mean—"

"It's okay, Logan. Your father knew the kind of woman he wanted you to marry."

"I didn't ask Amy to marry me because of my father."

"I wasn't insinuating you did."

"You were insinuating I chose from the right crowd."

"Logan, I was not. You chose the woman you loved. Your father happened to approve. That was good."

Logan knew he shouldn't have sounded so touchy

about it, and why was he? He had married the woman he wanted. But deep down, he'd known his dad had disapproved of his involvement with Gina. Had he suspected that was one of the reasons she'd broken off her relationship with him?

The stifling silence was only broken by the sound of the tires on the gravel lane as Logan wended his way toward the house.

Ten minutes later, Logan found Hannah and his son playing in the sunroom.

"I thought he could use some fresh air," his nanny explained, motioning to the sliding doors that pushed open to reveal long screens. The windows were all open, too, giving the feeling of being outdoors.

As soon as Daniel saw Logan, he waved, and said, "Da da da da," then jumped up and down in his play saucer. Logan felt deep abiding happiness make his chest swell. He picked up Daniel, kissed him on the cheek, and tucked him into the crook of his arm.

"Did you miss me, buddy?"

Daniel babbled something Logan took as a definite yes. "I missed you, too. Gina wanted to come say hello. We came to play with you for a while. What would you like to do?"

Daniel pointed to the big exercise ball that Gina often used with him. "Baw," he said.

"Good choice." Gina captured the ball and sat on the floor with it as Logan brought Daniel to her.

Instead of going for the ball, Daniel crawled straight to her, saying, "Gee, gee, gee," and climbed into her lap.

When Gina hugged him close, Logan's heart ached. How could he feel so many things at once—Amy's absence, regrets about Gina, worry that Daniel had bonded with Gina, the intensity of his attraction to her?

He took off his Stetson and tossed it onto a side table. Then he lowered himself to the floor to enjoy playtime with his son.

Gina knew Daniel's attention span and switched from one activity to the next before he got cranky. They were playing with blocks on top of a step stool when Hannah brought in a snack for Daniel, bites of banana on a dish. "Look what I have for you," Hannah said, setting the dish on the wicker table.

Daniel didn't seem interested. He was too busy watching Gina build a tower.

Logan was engaged in building a bridge, hoping his son would help him. His hip was lodged against Gina's. Once in a while, their arms brushed. Leaning this close to her felt unsettling as well as exciting. Sitting like this, playing with Daniel, felt simply…nice.

Gina added a blue block to Logan's all-orange structure. "You need some variety," she teased.

He stared at her tower. "This from a woman whose building wobbles with every new floor."

They both laughed.

Daniel, suddenly interested in the dish of fruit, crawled over to it on his knees. Unable to quite reach the top of the table, he pulled himself up to stand and snacked on a bite of banana.

"The blocks will stay together now," Logan warned her. "They'll have sticky fruit between them."

"Oh, look." Gina pointed to a prairie dog who had just run between the bushes near the side of the room.

"Daniel, look there," Logan directed.

The little boy turned, saw the animal, planted his legs

wide apart and took three toddling steps away from the table toward it.

Logan's gaze went to Gina's, both of them realizing what had just happened.

Gina quickly held out her hands to Daniel.

"Come here, honey. Let's go over to the window and see if we can find him."

His toes pointed out, Daniel shakily walked the three steps it took to put his hand in Gina's. When he did, she squeezed him tight. "Oh, you wonderful little boy! Do you know what you just did?"

Logan clapped, then hugged his son.

"You walked six whole steps, six whole steps. That was terrific! Can you do it again?"

Propping himself at the chair next to Gina, Daniel looked uncertain for a long while. Logan just waited with his hands held out. "Come on, buddy. I know you can do this. I'll catch you. Come on."

After a look at Gina, a glance at where the prairie dog had vanished, then a look at his father, Daniel grinned and took three lurching steps toward his dad, who caught him and swung him up, laughing, so grateful his son was walking.

"What's all the commotion?" Hannah asked, coming in.

"Daniel *walked*. About nine whole steps."

Hannah clapped and made a fuss for a while. Finally she said, "You know what? Those first steps deserve a scoop of ice cream. Want to come with me to get it?"

Apparently Daniel knew those words because he bobbed his head and held his arms out to Hannah. She scooped him up and said, "We won't be long."

When Hannah left, Logan grinned at Gina and pulled her into his arms for a hug. "Thank you."

She leaned away from him. "I didn't do much. I just encouraged his natural tendencies."

Logan felt more elated than he had since Daniel had come home from the hospital, and *his* natural tendencies were telling him exactly what he wanted to do. He lowered his head to Gina's and began what was supposed to be a quick, simple, thank-you kiss. But as his lips settled on hers and the warmth of their compression burst into heat, the kiss became more than a simple thank-you. He didn't want to go too fast. He knew he couldn't push too hard. Would she even react or respond?

That question was a moot point as her arms wrapped around his neck. When she pressed closer to him, she proved to him she definitely *wanted* to respond. He remembered what she'd said, and he wanted her to be *here* for him, *here* for them. He gave her time to think about what they were doing by nibbling at the corner of her mouth, tantalizingly licking her lower lip, pressing both of his lips to hers again. She laced her fingers in his hair and her fingertips started moving. He knew what that meant. She was becoming as excited as he was.

He knew that at any time he'd have to stop. He knew that at any time he might have to put the brakes on, forget about his need and acknowledge whatever she was feeling. Yet she didn't seem to want to stop. She opened her mouth to him and he accepted the invitation. When his tongue slid over hers, he heard her moan. When hers dashed around his, he groaned. They were in sync as they'd always been, giving and taking, reacting and responding, participating in a dance that had so many places to go.

Yet, when he reluctantly broke away, her lips clung to his. She gazed at him with undisguised passion—and more than a hint of confusion. After she took a deep breath, she caressed his face. "Well…where do we go from here? What did that mean, Logan?"

His stomach sank as his elation met reality. Because despite the desire he could no longer deny, he didn't have the faintest idea where they were headed.

Chapter Nine

Gina held her breath, hoping for the answer she wanted. Had the kiss meant forgiveness? Or something more?

Logan frowned. "What did it mean? Don't analyze everything to death, Gina. We were both happy about Daniel walking. It was an expression of gratitude. You helped him."

She couldn't let this go, not that easily. "So you would kiss anyone who helped him?"

"Don't be ridiculous." He was scowling and his stance was defensive.

"Then I don't think my question was so out of line. Why does it bother you? Because you don't want to think about what you're feeling?"

"You might have had lots of counseling, but I don't need it," he snapped. "Don't analyze me."

She took a step back from him, her fears confirmed. *That's what happens when you share your worst experience with someone. They could use it against you.*

Immediately he saw that he had hurt her and he reached out.

But she moved away. "Logan, I'm confused enough. I don't want you holding me and patting my head, or holding me and denying you feel anything."

"I'm not denying what I'm feeling. I'm attracted to you…and you're attracted to me."

"But does the attraction come from the past…or now? Is that confusing you as much as it's confusing me?"

"That kiss didn't seem confused, did it?" he asked in an I-don't-want-to-admit-this voice.

"No, it didn't. But it had little to do with Daniel walking."

Now he closed the distance between them and looked down at her with tenderness and maybe more. "I had a really good day today. How about you?"

It had had highs and lows, but at the end of it, they *were* still connected. "Yes, it was a good day and I especially liked the ducklings."

He chuckled. "I thought you might." He took her hand, drew it to his mouth and softly kissed her knuckles. His lips were warm and firm and seductively erotic.

Tingles streaked down her spine and she wanted to be in his arms again, longed to kiss him again. But neither of them knew what would happen if they went further. Logan didn't want to feel more. She was afraid she'd feel too much. They'd both be thinking about her last experience. How could they ever get over that hurdle?

They could if they loved each other.

Gina suddenly realized her love for Logan had never truly faded. When she'd left, she'd had to deny the depth of her pain. That pain had to be less important than what her parents wanted for her, what her sister needed and what she herself wanted to accomplish. It couldn't compare to the pain Logan would have felt had he known his father could disinherit him.

Nevertheless, her love for him had always been there. What would have happened if she'd run back to him after the rape? Would he have supported her, stood up against his dad or backed away? It simply didn't matter. But she knew now, she still loved him. She'd returned to Sagebrush to find out if she had to bury that love for good. What she was finding was that it was more alive than it had ever been.

He still held her hands as he said, "I want to issue a special invitation to you for the groundbreaking of the day-care center. Can you take an hour off on Monday when we dig the first shovelful? The ceremony is at four o'clock."

"I'll see if I can rearrange appointments and let you know."

He gently tugged her toward him and placed a kiss on top of her head. They stood that way a few seconds and then she pulled away.

"I really did have a good day," she assured him.

"Me, too. It was the first really good day in a long time. Thank you."

He looked as if he wanted to kiss her again. "I'd better go."

"You *could* spend the evening. We could play tennis and later watch a DVD with Daniel."

"Enough is enough for today," she said, not wanting

to go but deciding leaving was best for now. "I don't want to spoil the day by expecting too much."

He studied her face…brushed his thumb over her lips. "You're right. We should take this slowly whether it's friendship or attraction or whatever, not only for our sakes but for Daniel's."

His finger on her lips brought back the sensations from their kiss. Yet the mention of Daniel's name brought all of her focus to his little boy. She already loved Daniel. But if she told Logan that, she'd be moving way too fast.

He dropped his arm around her shoulders. "I'll walk you to the door."

He didn't stop at the door but went outside with her. The evening air was cool and Logan kept his arm around her the whole way to her car.

At her door, he tipped her chin up and kissed her again. It was a light kiss and carried feeling as well as that indefinable taste that Logan wanted more. That taste wouldn't go away until she saw him again. It wouldn't go away until it became hotter, bolder—until it became desire they were both ready for.

White, puffy clouds skittered across the blue sky as Gina stood in the group of onlookers at Barnes Denim, ready for the first shovel of dirt to be cast. The workers had come outside for the ceremony. Logan stood in a place of honor at the open field. Beside him, a pretty blonde talked animatedly to him.

Gina had heard one of the women in the crowd say, "That's Amy's sister. She came from Amarillo."

Logan settled a hand on the blonde's shoulder and gave it a squeeze, then he faced the crowd. Gina stood in the front row and he smiled at her. Then his focus shifted away.

He said to the group gathered, "As you know, I'm going to name our day-care center the Amy Barnes Day-Care Center in memory of my wife. I'd like her sister Maggie to say a few words."

Amy's sister stepped forward and smiled at everyone. "I just want to tell you how honored I am that Logan is doing this for Amy."

As Maggie spoke, Gina watched Logan's face. There was pain there, and an element of the grief he wouldn't express. The lines across his forehead, the tight set of his jaw, the tension in his stance told Gina this was difficult for him. She wished she could be beside him, but that was impossible. Especially today.

The late afternoon sun was hot, and Gina could feel prickles of perspiration wending their way down her back. She thought about Daniel and how Logan would shape the memory of his mother for him. Did Maggie visit often? Was she involved in Daniel's life?

After Maggie finished speaking, someone handed Logan a shovel and he dug a few heapfuls of ground from the earth. Then he thanked everyone for coming and guided Maggie toward Gina.

As they approached, Gina pasted on her I-can-handle-anything smile.

Logan introduced the two women and then said, "Gina helped Daniel learn to walk. She's a developmental specialist. I'm also using her as a consultant on the day-care center."

Daniel's specialist. A consultant. Gina wondered what other words he could use to describe her.

"I spent the evening with Daniel last night," Maggie

mentioned. "He's growing so fast. I wish I could come to Sagebrush more, but my work is so...sporadic."

"What do you do?" Gina asked.

"I write scripts for children's videos and TV shows. I'm usually on deadline and work late most nights when I'm in the middle of a project."

"That sounds like a great job, though," Gina said, meaning it.

"Oh, it is. I just wish my schedule weren't so crazy. It's either feast or famine. I drove in yesterday morning. I have to leave tomorrow morning. It's a short visit."

"We'll pack as much into it as we can," Logan assured her.

Maggie nodded. "Tonight I want to collect those videos of Amy you were talking about. I'll take them along and have everything digitized. It will be an important memento for Daniel when it's finished."

Gina could see this was going to be an evening for the two of them to remember Amy Barnes and everything she'd meant to both of them.

Logan said to Maggie, "Why don't you go over to the building and get out of the sun. I'll be there in a minute."

After a wave and a goodbye to Gina, Maggie walked away. Logan turned to Gina. "Thank you for coming today."

"I know this must be difficult for you."

"It's bittersweet. I'm glad you suggested naming the day-care center after my wife. It's a solid reminder of what she meant to me and Daniel. Are you going to come in to the social? Punch and cookies for everyone."

"No, I think I'll go now. I brought enough work home to last me all night."

"New clients?"

"Some. And financial projections for Baby Grows, too. I'm not keen on that, but it's part of the job."

Logan looked torn for a moment. "I'd ask you back to the house, but—"

"I understand, Logan. Really I do." She wanted to give him a hug, but didn't know if that would be appropriate here and now. Instead, she said, "Call me if you want to talk. If I don't hear from you, I'll see you at your place Friday at five for Daniel's appointment."

He studied her for a few moments and then nodded. "I'll talk to you later."

As Logan headed back to the factory and Gina went to find her car in the parking lot, she knew he wouldn't be calling.

On Wednesday evening, Gina was still in her office at Baby Grows when her cell phone rang. She picked it up automatically, not even looking at the caller ID. "Yes," she said absently, her mind on the file she was studying.

"Gina?"

Her attention snapped into focus. "Yes, Logan, it's me. Sorry, I was in the middle of something."

The silence between them vibrated with emotion and tension. She could still remember the pain on his face as Maggie had spoken of her sister.

He began, "I want to thank you again for coming to the groundbreaking."

"I wasn't so sure it was a good idea that I attended."

There was a long pause before he asked, "Because the ceremony was about Amy?"

"Because you didn't need your attention divided that day."

"It wasn't divided. Lots of people who were helping with the center were there. You were one of them."

"One of the crowd."

She could hear him swear under his breath. "That didn't come out right, Gina. I have a habit of making a muddle of things with you."

"You called to tell me that?" she teased kindly, wondering why he needed to talk to her. She'd be seeing him Friday night. Unless he was canceling.

"I thought we could do something different Friday night."

"With Daniel? Do you want to bring him to Baby Grows?"

"No, I'd like to take him swimming. I thought maybe you'd have some exercises in your repertoire we could do in the pool. Then afterward, maybe you and I could just swim."

Swimming with Logan. Sitting by the pool. Talking for hours. History repeating itself?

"I have to ask you something, Logan."

"I'm not going to like this question very much, am I?"

"Probably not. Do you want a diversion so you can stop thinking about Amy?"

The complete silence told her exactly what he thought of her question. But then she heard him blow out a breath. Finally, he admitted, "Maggie stirred up all kinds of memories when she was here, especially when we went through the videos. But at the end of all that, by the time I said goodbye to her, I realized naming the day-care center in Amy's honor was the end of something. She's gone. She's never coming back. The center will be the tangible proof of that. I need to see more for my future than what might have been. So, to answer your question, I don't want a diversion. I just want to go on and live my life."

"That's honest," she assured him, thinking he was taking a big step in moving on.

"I'm glad you think so because I don't know how to be anything else but honest with you."

She hadn't been completely honest with him—not where his father was concerned. What good would it do to reveal now what his father had threatened her with?

"So how about swimming?" he asked.

"Does Daniel like the water?"

"He's not particularly fond of getting his face wet."

"I know a few adults who have the same problem," she said with a laugh. "I'll bring a life vest along. I think I'd like to do a land routine with him first, then we'll just do a few exercises in the water."

"Sounds good. Do you think you might be in the mood for steaks on the grill? I can tell Hannah we'll handle our own supper."

"Steak sounds fine. Have you had much experience being a chef?"

"I'm better on the grill than I am in the kitchen. Remember my attempt to make beef stroganoff for you?"

"I remember that very well. You ended up with overdone beef tips, lumpy sauce, sticky noddles. But it tasted wonderful."

"I thought you just said that to be kind."

"No, it *did* taste good. It just wasn't four-star-restaurant presentable."

He chuckled. "I promise I'll do a better job with the steaks tomorrow night."

When Gina closed her phone a few minutes later, she

was smiling. Maybe she and Logan could become friends again…maybe so much more.

"I think we've tired him out."

Logan lifted Daniel from the water and went up the steps to the deck around the pool. He unfastened the Velcro of Daniel's life vest and Gina held a towel ready to wrap the toddler in. Daniel did love the water as long as it wasn't splashing his face. At her encouragement, he'd kicked his legs and arms and had fun with her and his dad.

Now, as she held him and patted him with the fluffy towel, he wrapped his arms around her neck and snuggled his cheek against her shoulder. A lump crowded her throat and for a few moments she dreamt of being his mother.

Then reality struck. He *had* a mother, and Logan wasn't going to forget her. And he shouldn't. But denying the longings in her own heart was impossible. They weren't going to go away.

As she sneaked a peek at Logan—he was toweling his hair—she knew she was falling deeper in love with him. She held Daniel a little tighter, rested her cheek against his wet hair, and wished for everything she'd wished for when she was eighteen…everything that hadn't had to do with college and a career and her family.

Hannah opened the sliding screen of the sunroom, walked across the patio and opened the gate that led into the pool. She brought a tray of hors d'oeuvres with her and set it on the table where Gina's and Logan's bottles of water sat with Daniel's sippy cup.

"Why don't I take this little guy inside, get him a bath and something to eat. You two can swim some more if

you want. I'll bet you didn't get much of a chance while
you were entertaining *him*."

"That's a good idea," Logan said with a thankful
smile to his housekeeper. "Do you want to do some real
swimming?" he asked Gina.

Now his gaze was on her bathing suit and her legs.
Glad she'd bought a new one—a blue and green flow-
ered maillot—she stood perfectly still, accepting his
male appreciation, though she felt a little unsettled by
it. For years she'd gone out of her way *not* to be noticed.
But today, she liked Logan noticing. She liked the sparkle of hunger she saw in his eyes and his interest in her
that she believed was more than friendly.

"Logan to Gina," he teased as he once might have
during their summer together.

She quickly smiled. "I'm here."

"I can tell when you're thinking. Smoke puffs out of
your ears."

She smacked his arm with a towel.

He caught the edge of it and pulled her toward him.

By this time, Hannah had taken Daniel inside and
they were alone. Their gazes held.

Gina was amazingly aware of Logan's bare
chest…the tawny hair arrowing down under the waist-
band of his wet swim trunks. Her heart beat even faster
at the thought of being here with him.

"You look terrific in that suit. With your creamy white
skin, you look like a princess who's never seen the sun."

"I never consider myself a princess."

"Even *I* remember Cinderella's story. She worked
and slaved and then Prince Charming swept her away.
The problem was you didn't want to be swept away."

Over the years, she'd had to learn how to express many

emotions that she'd kept hidden. She'd had to learn not to take the backseat, to realize her opinion was important.

She returned, "Modern-day Prince Charmings don't sweep women off their feet. They stand beside them and support them and whisper in their ear at night that they can do anything."

"That's the fairy tale now?" Logan asked with arched brows. "That's not nearly as romantic or life-changing."

"I'll bet it's more life-changing for the man than being swept off her feet ever was for a woman."

Leaning back to study her more thoroughly, he asked, "Are we going to have an argument about this?"

"Not if you agree."

Logan laughed out loud. He put his arm around her, towel and all, and led her to the edge of the pool.

With Logan's arm circling her, she felt protected and not at all afraid. She thought about the security system she'd had installed in every apartment she'd lived in. She hadn't even thought of having one installed at the Victorian.

She knew safety was an illusion. Alarms and locks and self-defense courses couldn't always keep a woman safe. Since her experience in college, she'd been hyper-vigilant, waking up several times during the night just to make sure everything was quiet, and no one was trying to break in. Relaxation exercises helped her fall asleep, but staying asleep—

Yet here with Logan, she felt as if she could let that vigilance slip. She could relax. How crazy was that?

Because you're still in love with him, that tiny voice in her head told her.

And all of a sudden, his arm around her changed from comforting to exciting. As she turned into his chest—

But before the thought could become action, he started down the pool steps and took her towel from around her shoulders, tossing it onto the terra-cotta pavers. The look he gave her now was long and appreciative, and she felt her cheeks getting hot.

"Sorry," he apologized. "I didn't mean to make you feel uncomfortable. But you do look beautiful."

She tried to treat his compliment lightly. Running her fingers through her damp hair, she asked, "Even all wet?"

"Especially all wet."

Her mouth went dry and it was hard to swallow.

"Do compliments like that bother you?"

Now she said something that seemed bold to her. "Not coming from you."

The expression in his eyes changed in the evening light and she realized those green depths were reflecting the passion in her own gaze.

How would she react if he gave in to it? Was she ready for that step? Was *he?*

He took her hand and drew her into the water. "Thoughts are going through your mind at the speed of light."

"More smoke coming out of my ears?" she joked.

"No." He reached out and brushed a finger over her forehead. "But there's a crease here." He touched each corner of her mouth. "And little lines here. I know those lines. They mean you're analyzing. What are you debating so vigorously?"

The water was above their waists now, and she realized she had nothing to lose by being honest. "I'm trying to decide if you're afraid to let an attraction between us go anywhere."

"I don't think *afraid* is the word. Besides a history, we both have baggage. I'm concerned."

"I won't tell you not to be concerned. But that concern won't go away if we act like best friends rather than—"

"Rather than lovers?" he finished, looking at her with an intensity that made every nerve ending tingle. He circled her waist and brought her closer. "Does being close to me like this, without much between us, make you nervous?"

"No," she assured him with all the certainty in her heart, believing all the tingling in her body had to do with arousal, not anxiety.

As he bent his head, she lifted her chin. His lips met hers without hesitation and she was glad of that. Her fingers went to the back of his head and she relished the feel of his hair, the crisp strands, thick and damp under her fingertips. He groaned and his tongue slid into her mouth. She was ready for the intimate play, the chase and retreat, the exploration. She welcomed it and responded to it. Her body sought Logan's like a ship searching for its harbor. Pressed together as they were, she felt his arousal, had one flutter of panic that went up in flames as their passion turned hotter.

Logan's hands caressed her back, slid to her backside, and then gently urged her to wrap her legs around him. When she did, he pushed against her at just the right spot. He kept up the rocking motion until she exploded in his arms. Their lips clung together and the sounds in her throat told Logan of her pleasure. He held her even tighter.

When her body stopped trembling, she whispered into his neck, "Why did you do that? Why did you stop before—"

"I wanted to give you a gift. I wanted to give you

pleasure that had no price tag, no reason to be other than to make you feel good."

She leaned back so she could gaze into his eyes. "What about you?"

"This wasn't about me, Gina. It was about us finding a new direction, searching through the rubble of years ago to find something good."

"Do you think we found it?"

He shook his head and she saw the doubts in his eyes when he said, "I'm not sure. I have to ask you something."

"What?"

She ran through at least ten questions before he asked, "Are you going to stay in Sagebrush?"

That wasn't one she expected. When she didn't answer right away, he let her legs slip down and took a step back from her. "The fact that you can't give me an unqualified 'yes' means you might leave again. You've been hopping around from one place to the next, moving every three or four years. Why?"

She'd faced that question herself before she'd returned to her hometown. "Because I didn't feel safe… because I didn't feel settled. Because I wasn't exactly sure what I should be doing to feel…fulfilled."

"You were always searching for something better." The fact that she'd wanted "better" didn't sound like a compliment.

"Even all those years ago, I was searching for where I belonged. I was hoping when I came home to Sagebrush, I'd feel at home. But life isn't that simple."

"So you're going to move again?"

"I didn't say that."

He sighed and ran his hand over his jaw. "Gina, let's

just say we decided to become involved again. I'm an adult. I know fate strikes blows. I know irreconcilable differences happen and relationships break apart. But Daniel is just a little boy who knows he likes you. He's attaching to you. I don't want him to get hurt. If you decide someplace else will make you more ful-filled...where will that leave him?"

How could she tell him this was all about the two of them and what they worked at and built together? *That* was what would keep her in Sagebrush. *That* was what would make the difference. But Logan wasn't ready to commit to anything. She knew he wasn't just using Daniel as an excuse. His adorable little boy was part of this equation, too. Yet Gina wondered—

She put her thought into words. "Do you want an excuse to hold back...not to try this at all?"

"I don't know," he responded hoarsely. "Maybe I *am* looking for a reason not to get in too deep. Do you blame me?"

No, she couldn't blame him because she had left once before. They should have had this conversation before she'd felt the wonder of intimacy with him again.

He must have seen the regret on her face because he said, "I was going to ask you to help me put Daniel to bed tonight. But maybe it's better if you don't."

"Maybe it's better if I don't," she agreed, heading for the steps and her towel and a life in Sagebrush that possibly didn't include Logan.

Chapter Ten

Gina's heart went out to Lily two weeks later as they sat in the living room of the Victorian. "I'm surprised you came over tonight."

Lily was obviously attempting to keep her spirits up, though it seemed to be tough. "Troy's deployment ceremony is Tuesday. He'll be gone for training, and then he'll be in Afghanistan for a year." She sighed. "I can't think about it. I'm simply going to concentrate on this weekend."

Thunder grumbled outside as a storm moved across Sagebrush. Gina and her friends were waiting until it passed to enjoy their movie night.

In response to Gina's original comment, Lily said, "He had some furniture he wanted to finish in his workshop tonight. But I think he needed a few hours for himself."

Gina knew Troy was a general contractor and did

woodworking as a hobby. The couple had only been married a year and were still settling into married life.

Raina moved from the easy chair to join Lily and Gina on the sofa. "I have a feeling you're going to be celebrating the Fourth of July weekend with fireworks of your own," she teased Lily.

Lily blushed and was about to retort when the phone rang. Raina plucked it up from the side table. "It could be my mother—her regular Saturday night check-in."

Lily remarked wistfully, "It must be nice to have family."

Lily had no family except for Troy. Gina felt compelled to say, "You can call me or Raina whenever you need somebody to talk to."

Raina handed the phone to Gina, her brows drawing together. "It's Hannah Mahoney."

Gina's panic button screamed a warning as she took the phone and put it to her ear. "Hannah?"

"Gina, I know this is Fourth of July weekend and you're probably busy, but Logan's away and Daniel's scared of the thunder. He's calling your name."

"He's saying my name?" He'd started saying "Gee, gee, gee, gee" whenever she was around.

"It seems like it to me. He misses his dad. He's calling for him, too."

"Logan's away?"

"Since Thursday night. He's in Seattle on business, but that's hard to explain to a fifteen-month-old. It's even harder to explain why he hasn't seen *you* for two weeks."

It sounded as if Hannah wanted an explanation, too. "Daniel is doing well on his own now. Dr. Rossi can give him regular assessments and can also recommend a parent group to Logan if he feels like attending."

"Uh-oh. You two had a fight."

Gina remained silent. Sometimes she felt as if Hannah was trying in subtle ways to play matchmaker. She could hear Hannah sigh as Daniel's crying rose in volume. His nanny must have taken the phone over to his crib.

"Well?" Hannah asked when she came back on. "Are you going to come over here and give me a hand? I don't want him to make himself sick."

Gina didn't want that, either. "All right. I'll be there in ten minutes." She settled the phone back on its console and found Raina and Lily watching her expectantly.

"Daniel's crying. Hannah said he's calling for me. Logan's away and she thinks I can help."

"Sounds reasonable to me," Lily said with a shrug. "Kids want what they want when they want it. Maybe all you have to do is hold him for a little while and he'll fall asleep."

Raina's response was a little more tempered. "Daniel will have to get used to not seeing you if you're stopping his sessions."

"I know, but—"

She didn't have to say more because Raina finished for her. "But you've grown attached to him. So go save the day."

Lily assured her, "I'll leave the DVD and you can watch it tomorrow if you'd like."

"I might be back before you're gone."

Shaking her head, Raina said, "I wouldn't count on it. With kids, the unexpected always happens."

Knowing that was true, Gina grabbed a light jacket from the living-room closet to wear over her navy shorts and navy-and-white striped knit top in case she got caught in the rain. After she waved to her friends, she grabbed her purse from the foyer table. "See you later."

"Later," Raina and Lily called in unison.

Gina liked the fact that she had friends who cared about where she was going, where she'd be and when she'd return. She hadn't let anyone get as close as Raina and Lily in many years. Maybe one day soon, she'd confide in Lily the way she'd confided in Raina.

The windshield wipers struggled to keep up with the sudden downpour. Thunder rolled ominously in the distance. She wasn't surprised that it had spooked Daniel. Most kids were afraid of loud bangs, especially at night. She wondered how many business trips Logan took in a year. Maybe as Daniel grew older, he'd take more. Yet Logan was the type of parent who'd want to stay close to his son. A child needed a committed parent, even when they were older. And even then, with a parent's guidance, a son or daughter could make the wrong decisions.

Like your wrong decision? her conscience asked her.

Precisely like that, Gina thought. A teenager might not yet be able to sort out what would make her happy, to sort out her inner voice from all of the voices outside of herself. But Gina wasn't that teenager anymore. She knew what her heart needed.

At the estate, Gina parked at the top of the circle near the front walk. She was going to get wet. She dashed up the stairs to the house and didn't even have to ring the bell. Hannah was there waiting to let her in, holding Daniel, who was red-faced and still crying.

She shook her head as Gina stepped over the threshold. "I know he's heard thunder before, but it never affected him like this."

"Has Logan ever been gone during a storm?"

"That's a good question. This is his first trip in a while, so I suppose not."

Daniel was already leaning over Hannah's arm toward Gina, reaching for her.

"See, I told you he wants you."

As if on cue, Daniel said, "Gee…gee, gee, gee."

Smiling, feeling her heart warm, Gina held the baby close, running her hand over his sweat-dampened hair. His little body was hot from all the pent-up emotion, all the words he couldn't yet say, all the feelings he tried to express with tears and gurgles and the kick of his legs.

She rocked him back and forth and murmured, "You're fine, big boy, just fine. You're safe here and no one's going to hurt you." His tears slowed as he cuddled close to her and expressed a baby sigh of ease.

"Well, look at that," Hannah said, hands on hips. "You'd think I hadn't been taking care of him since before he was born."

"You know it's not you, don't you? He just needed something different tonight, I guess."

"He missed you, and no matter what Logan says, I know it's so."

No matter what Logan says. Apparently they'd discussed it. "Do you think it would be all right if I take him to his room, change him into another set of pj's and wash him up a little?"

"I think you could do anything you want with him," Hannah joked. "While you're doing that, I'll fetch him some milk, then maybe you can rock him to sleep. I'm sorry I called you out like this, but he was just so unhappy."

"This reaction of his worries me, although I imagine if Logan were here this wouldn't have happened."

"Maybe," Hannah said, not sounding sure about that at all. "Pretty soon he'll be able to get your whole name out and Logan will see for sure he wants *you*."

A half hour later, Gina had washed and freshly dressed Daniel for bed. She was sitting in the rocker in his room, holding him and his bottle. He'd fallen asleep while drinking and she couldn't bear to put him down in his crib.

"What are you doing here?"

Gina jumped, startled when she heard Logan's voice. The reflexive action wakened Daniel and he started to cry. She cooed to him, and when he looked into her eyes, his tears stopped. He reached for her, winding his little arms around her neck. She wasn't going to pull away from him because Logan was watching. She was going to give this baby the comfort he needed.

Patting his back, she murmured, "It's okay. There's no more thunder."

Logan crossed to her and crouched down, eager to take his son from her arms. He'd left his tie somewhere and the top buttons of his shirt were open. It was wrinkled and he looked tired...even more tired when Daniel turned away from him, holding on more tightly to Gina.

Daniel mumbled, "Gee," and wouldn't let go.

"What's going on, Gina? Where's Hannah?"

Suddenly Gina was annoyed with his attitude. It wasn't as if she'd planned this. It wasn't as if— "Hannah's in her room. I told her I'd buzz her after Daniel fell asleep. I didn't come here to steal the silver, Logan. She called me because Daniel was crying, and she couldn't get him quieted. Apparently the thunder scared him. She insisted he was calling my name."

Logan raked his hand through his hair. "I don't get why he'd call your name. It's not as if you—"

"It's not as if I take care of him every day, feed him, bathe him, put him to bed. No, I don't do those things. But over the past weeks, he and I have developed a rapport. He knows he can trust me, even though he doesn't like some of the things I ask him to do. He knows I…I love him."

Their gazes locked and neither of them could turn away. Gina wished she hadn't divulged what she had, but it was the truth. Logan was very big on the truth. What would he say if she said she still loved *him?*

She wasn't going to go there. She couldn't.

Finally, he tore his gaze away and stood, still studying his son as if he didn't understand what had happened.

"I don't think Hannah expected you home tonight, did she?" Gina asked.

"No. I told her I'd be home tomorrow or the next day. I kept thinking about Daniel, this being my first trip away from him for a while. When I called, Hannah said everything was fine."

"It was, until the storm hit."

"Do you want me to take him? I mean, I know you have to get home."

"I'm my own person now, Logan. Raina knows where I am. But if you don't want me here, I can leave."

He looked torn between what was best for his son and what was best for him. Finally he suggested, "When he falls asleep, lay him in his crib. I'll take over from there. I have to take a shower. I've been in meetings for the past forty-eight hours, then storms delayed us in Chicago."

Again he studied her with Daniel, but his gaze lingered on her face. She saw those sparks in his eyes, the same sparks that had been there when she was eighteen.

Daniel stirred and her attention shifted to him.

When she looked up again, Logan had left the room.

Logan stood in the shower, letting the stinging cold water hit his body. He willed it to chase away the desire for Gina, the need he struggled to hide. Damn it, but he wanted her and there were so many reasons why he shouldn't, not the least of which was Daniel.

He switched the water from cold to hot but the warmth did nothing to ease the tension in his neck and shoulders from too many meetings and too much negotiation. He'd packed a week's worth of work into two days so he could return to his son.

And his son had turned away from him—toward Gina.

Was it simply the fact that he was a man and Daniel needed a woman's touch? Apparently Hannah's hadn't worked.

He soaped with a vigor that was almost abrasive and he toweled off with the same vehemence. He'd never in a thousand years expected Gina to be here when he got home. What had Hannah been thinking?

She'd been thinking about Daniel.

With a sigh, Logan admitted he couldn't be upset with Hannah. She always did what was best for his son. He wished he knew exactly what that was at this point.

Maybe Gina would be gone by the time he returned to Daniel's room.

Avoidance? That's your strategy? his common sense asked him.

He thought that avoidance might be a good thing right about now as he slid into a pair of gray jogging shorts, still aroused. The air-conditioning in the house sent drafts across his wet back, but he hardly noticed as he pulled on a T-shirt, forgot about shoes, ran his fingers through his still-wet hair, and with some reluctance went to Daniel's bedroom.

Gina had switched off all the lamps except for the Winnie the Pooh nightlight that glowed like a beacon in the corner of the room. She stood at the crib, patting his son on the back. Her profile was backlit, limned in the golden light. Her soft curls lay along her cheek, down her neck to her shoulder. Her nose was straight except for that tiny little bump. Her small chin was defined and the outline of her lips—

She apparently sensed him watching her because she dropped her hands to her sides and turned his way. "He's asleep. He's tuckered out from all that crying."

As she walked toward him, Logan stood perfectly still.

She stopped in front of him. "I'll be on my way now." She didn't even take a breath before she walked into the hall.

Swiftly, he went after her and caught her hand. "Gina, wait."

She looked up at him with those big brown eyes that had captivated him when he was twenty-two. "This is difficult for both of us, Logan. I didn't know whether to come or not. I didn't mean to overstep—"

Before he could even think about what he was doing, he swore, brought her close, then held on to her as if she were a vision who might disappear. She didn't push away. Not wanting to scare her or panic her or let any demon from her past raise its head, he gently pushed her hair back from her ears and kissed her. It was a soft tender kiss that told her he remembered everything they'd once had.

She wrapped her arms around him tighter and buried her head in his chest. "Logan."

He didn't know what she was trying to tell him. He was aroused and he knew she could feel it.

"Gina," he murmured. "There's a connection between us that's been there from the moment I met you. And it's still there."

After she pushed away from him, she gazed up at him and took his face between her hands. "I know."

"Do you want to come to my bedroom with me?" He nodded to the door down the hall.

"Is that where you and your wife slept?"

He shook his head. "No. We took a suite upstairs. This one was a guest room. I had it and Daniel's room redone before he came home from the hospital."

Gina's voice was soft, as if she was afraid to say the words out loud. "I want to come to your bedroom with you."

Unable to help himself, Logan swept her up into his arms. His bare feet made no sound on the carpeted hallway and when he pushed open the door to the bedroom, it creaked. The hall light spilled inside, but Gina wasn't looking around at the decor. She was looking at him.

After he set her by the side of the bed, he tossed back the covers, then hesitated. He'd heard of rape victims having flashbacks. He didn't want to trigger anything that would cause her panic.

"Logan, don't look so worried. Try to forget about my past, please."

"I want you to understand something, Gina. I haven't been with a woman since before Amy died. I'll try my best to hold back with you, to do whatever you need. I *will* stop if you ask me to. I want to make that clear. But I want you with a need that's been building for weeks. You have to understand that, too."

"Undress me, Logan," she said shakily. "Let's just start with that."

He was heading into troubled waters. Once they started getting swept away, how difficult would it be to turn back?

When he looked into her eyes, he didn't care. When he let himself feel the heat between them, nothing else mattered. That was what concerned him most.

Still he went ahead, slid his fingers under her top, and slowly pulled it up and over her head. Standing before him in her bra, she smiled at him, a sweet, encouraging smile that told him she definitely wanted to go ahead with this.

As she reached for his T-shirt, she said, "Maybe we can do this at the same time." She lifted his T-shirt up, stood on tiptoe to drag it up over his chin and his head.

He mumbled, "Maybe we can."

When she slid her hand over his chest, his breath hitched.

"Your skin is still damp."

To talk, he *had* to breathe. "It was still wet when I dragged on my T-shirt."

"Do you often dress without drying off?"

He laughed. "Only when I'm in a hurry."

"No hurry now," she said, leaning forward, kissing his chest.

He slid his hands into her hair and gently tugged her

away from him. "This is about *you,* too. You don't have
to prove anything to me. I know it's probably easier for
you to focus on my pleasure than yours, but I want you
to be *here,* Gina, really *here* while we do this."

He saw her chest rise and fall as she closed her
eyes for a few seconds and then opened them again.
"I'm here."

Her vulnerability awed him. She trusted him completely. That was the responsibility he had to handle like
a treasure.

Bending forward, he kissed her while his hands caressed her back and unhooked her bra. His mouth told
her in a hundred ways how much he desired her. She
didn't hesitate to stroke his tongue with hers, to put her
hands on his body, to rub down his spine until all he
wanted was to bury himself deep inside her. When he
broke off the kiss, her fingers went to the drawstring at
his waist and his went to the button on her shorts. They
stripped each other quickly and crawled into bed together, eager and short of breath.

They lay face-to-face for a while, touching and kissing. Logan wanted to make sure Gina was ready for
him…wanted to make sure she didn't doubt what they
were doing…wanted to make sure he didn't do anything
to make her afraid.

Finally, when he didn't think he could hold back any
longer, he asked, "Are you on birth control?"

She shook her head. "No, I didn't even think about
it. I never thought we'd—"

"I have condoms in the drawer."

Her eyes asked him what her lips wouldn't.

"The box has never been opened," he said with a wry
chuckle. "I was saving them for the day I was ready."

"Are you ready?"

He nodded. "All I know is that at this moment, I want you, and I need you."

As Gina caressed him, he groaned, wondering at the same time what was going through her head.

But she didn't say. She just whispered, "Get the box and I'll put one on you."

He slid over to the nightstand, searched in the drawer and found the box in the back. Quickly he took out a packet and handed it to her. He was a man who usually took control of any situation he was in, but he knew tonight he couldn't. He had to let Gina take the lead.

He lay back and watched Gina tear open the packet. She was beautiful as she sat up and slid out the condom.

He'd turned on the bedside lamp and now he asked, "Do you want me to turn that off?"

"No. I want to see you, and I want you to see me."

He knew exactly what she meant. She didn't want him to get confused and imagine his wife's face in his mind.

"Gina—" He had to keep her focused on him, in the now, right here.

She didn't roll the condom on right away, she teased him first with her fingers. His jaw locked. His hands clenched into fists. He had to last for her. He had to do whatever was necessary to make this good for her.

After she'd finished, he exhaled and reached for her. "On top of me, Gina. You set the pace."

Now she looked a little rattled, as if the extent of what they were going to do had hit her.

"We can stop," he forced out when it was the last thing he wanted to say.

Instead of answering directly, she stretched out on top of him and requested, "Kiss me again."

Logan gladly fulfilled her request, alert for any nuance of change. Soon, however, he was absorbed in their passion, aroused to a limit he'd never experienced...using willpower in a way he never thought possible.

She must have realized he was at the end of his control. As she broke the kiss, she sat up and straddled him.

Logan's aim was to give her mindless pleasure. He stroked her breasts and thumbed her nipples until she moaned and murmured his name.

The next thing he knew, she was allowing him to slowly enter her. He gazed into her eyes and saw only pleasure as she began to move. He held her hips as they both began to glisten with passion, as her soft cries mingled with his groans. When she moved faster, he rocked with her. Seconds later she cried out, calling his name.

He knew everything was all right. He knew she'd stayed *here* and had allowed herself to fly with him. She kept moving, her body tightening around him until his climax hit, too, and his need was satisfied in a shuddering release.

It was a long time until they could both catch their breaths. After they had, he gathered her into his arms.

"Are you okay?" He leaned away slightly to study her face.

She smiled at him. "I'm more than okay. How about you?"

"More than okay."

The problem was he didn't know where they should go from here.

* * *

Gina was still floating in a sensually induced haze when Logan returned from the bathroom. Everything about tonight had been unplanned and surprising. She didn't know what was going to happen next.

Is that so bad? she asked herself, knowing organizing and compartmentalizing and planning had become defense mechanisms over the years. If she knew what was in a room before she walked into it, she could stay safe. If she dotted every *i* and crossed every *t,* nothing would surprise her. If she ate the right foods, exercised enough and took self-defense courses, she could defend herself no matter who came after her. She'd lived her life without any deviation from her carefully chosen path.

Until she'd impulsively decided to return to Sagebrush. Until destiny or serendipity had put Daniel's chart on her desk. Maybe fate wasn't that mysterious. She'd moved into the Victorian with Francesca, become friends with Tessa—

The Victorian. The rumor. Any woman who resided there would find true love. She'd found true love once with Logan and turned her back on it. But now…

When he climbed into bed beside her, she didn't know what to expect. Did he have regrets? Had tonight been physical rather than emotional for him? What would he want now? What would he do next?

"Do you want something to drink?" he asked.

She shook her head. She didn't need something to drink. She needed to know what was in Logan's head.

"That really was good for you?"

She knew he meant their lovemaking. He couldn't bring himself to use the words, she supposed. She knew tonight might not have been possible with anyone but Logan. She'd known he'd never hurt her. With each kiss and each touch, he'd respect who she was and what she'd been through. She trusted him implicitly, at least where a physical intimate connection was concerned. She wasn't sure about their emotional one. Was he really ready to move on? Had he truly forgiven her? Would he trust her to put a commitment to him and Daniel first above all else?

"Logan, I'm more than okay. Tonight was wonderful. This couldn't have happened with anyone but you."

"I didn't intend for anything to happen."

"I know."

They both looked toward the monitor and Daniel sleeping soundly in his crib. "We're getting to know each other all over again," he murmured.

"Is that something you want?"

"I thought I didn't. I thought Daniel and I would be better off going it alone. But tonight, when I came home and saw you with him, I began to doubt that decision."

"For your sake or his?"

"For *both* our sakes." Now he brushed his thumb across her check and laced his fingers in her curls. "Maybe we should try being friends, try being lovers, and see where it goes. We won't rush headlong into anything."

So he could hang on to his wife's memory? Or was he protecting himself in case she turned her back again? She wouldn't do that. She couldn't.

"I'm not sure I understand what you want," she admitted. "A weekend together, now and then? Should I stay in or out of Daniel's life? Do you want me here to help put Daniel to bed? Do you want to go riding together, be seen in public, have dinner at my mom's house?" She hadn't intended for all the questions to spill out, but they just had.

"I don't have the answers, Gina, but I do have a suggestion."

"What?" She liked the sense of anticipation in his voice.

"Next weekend, I have to go to Houston. How would you like to come with me?"

She didn't hesitate. "I'd love to go with you."

"I'm having a full day of meetings with the people who run my foundation," he explained. "They're going to catch me up on the research, explore ways to help pregnant women with cancer. If you'd like, you can sit in on the sessions with me. There's a dinner and dance Saturday evening to raise money. We'd have Friday night together and Saturday night after the dance. I'm thinking about asking Hannah to go along with Daniel. I don't want to leave him again after what happened tonight. That way I can spend time with him on and off while we're there. What do you think?"

From the sounds of it, he would be incorporating her into his life. And not just his life, but Daniel's, too. "I think it's a terrific idea. I can help with Daniel."

Logan slipped his arms around her and brought her close to him. "I'm not asking you to go along for that reason."

"I know."

"Do you think he'll handle a plane ride okay?" Logan wondered.

"We'll make it okay. With you, me and Hannah, he won't be bored."

Logan laughed, an honest-to-goodness, genuine laugh. "You're right about that." He lifted her chin and kissed her deeply. Afterward, he said, "I guess we should get some sleep."

She'd like nothing better than to sleep all night in his arms.

She suddenly realized that wasn't exactly true. She'd like nothing better than to spend *every* night in his arms.

Chapter Eleven

Gina sat quietly beside Logan at the dinner-dance Saturday evening, taking in the conversations swirling around her at the long table.

"The guide who led the white-water rafting trip was exceptional," Logan commented as he continued his discussion with the fundraising guru on Saturday evening.

Then Logan glanced at Gina, their gazes lingered and she felt anticipation building between them.

Last evening hadn't gone as planned. After they'd landed in Houston in the late afternoon, Daniel had to be acclimated and settled in. Logan had reserved a suite for Daniel and Hannah and an adjoining room for Gina and himself…to enjoy more privacy. But last night Daniel hadn't wanted to go to sleep, so they'd ended up playing with him and watching TV until it was time to turn in. Even then, however, he'd wanted his father. So Logan had wheeled the crib into his room and he and Gina had just snuggled while his son slept.

Now happy excitement danced in her stomach as she looked forward to her time with Logan tonight... dancing...and making love later.

Dr. Katz, the guru, targeted Gina now. "Have you ever been white-water rafting on the Colorado River?"

"I've never been white-water rafting," she had to admit, considering the fact that being with Logan now was so different from when they were teenagers and she'd worried about fitting in with his crowd.

"Gina has skied in Vermont, though," Logan interjected, giving her arm a squeeze.

"What part of Vermont?" Katz questioned her.

"Killington."

"Did you enjoy it?"

He was in his fifties and his heavy brows almost came together in the middle of his forehead. She was beginning to realize his gruffness was just part of who he was and didn't reflect on her. "I did enjoy it, but I like horseback riding more."

The gentleman across from Gina, Dr. Silverstein, pushed his silver-rimmed glasses higher on his nose and addressed her. "Logan mentioned you worked with his son."

Meetings all day had involved PowerPoint presentations on the effectiveness of certain treatments and the difficulty of treating a pregnant woman. Introductions had been made, but Gina had listened more than she'd interacted with anyone there. But Logan had been involved in several private conversations.

It pleased her that Logan had spoken about her time

with Daniel. "I work with babies who have developmental issues," she explained.

"You have a degree in child development?" Dr. Silverstein asked with interest.

"I have a master's in pediatric physical therapy as well as a Ph.D. in infant and toddler development."

"Who do you work for?" Silverstein wanted to know.

"I work for myself. I have a practice called Baby Grows in Lubbock."

"That's very interesting." The doctor looked thoughtful. "There's such a need for that kind of practice with all kinds of children—children with Downs, with epilepsy. Children who have been in accidents."

"She's published articles," Logan said proudly. "If you search the Internet, you'll find them." He folded his napkin, laid it on the table and pushed his chair back. Standing, he said, "I think I'm going to ask my beautiful companion to dance with me before the band stops playing."

Logan's gaze lingered on her as if he'd been waiting for this dance all night. Whenever he looked at her like that, she felt so special…so pretty. She'd worn a black dress with a white bow on her left shoulder, no sleeve on the right. Sterling jewelry sparkled at her ears and around her neck. She'd never felt more self-confident…or appreciated.

Logan helped her with her chair and then swept her away to the dance floor. There he pulled her close.

"I'm not ready to sacrifice any more time for mingling and conversation. Last night should have been different. We should have had some time to ourselves."

"Logan, when a child is involved every situation is in flux."

His green eyes were gentle as he studied her face. "You can understand that with your head, but do you understand it with your heart?"

"I do," she assured him, her lips almost touching his jaw. "I loved you holding me last night. That was enough."

"Tonight will be different. Hannah took Daniel down to the kids' area before supper. I looked in on him while you were getting dressed. His eyes were almost closing over his dinner."

"We're good as long as we don't get any storms," she teased.

"No storms tonight. I checked the weather report."

The weather outside might be perfectly calm, but she could see the hunger building inside Logan. The simmering intensity in his eyes told her he wanted to give way to it. She wished he would. She wished he wouldn't continue to hold back with her. But she sensed he wasn't just holding back his passion, he was holding back part of his soul, too. Tonight she wanted to give herself to Logan completely. She wanted him to realize that he could depend on her and trust her, that she wouldn't turn her back on him again.

The music was smooth and dreamy. They gazed into each other's eyes, searching for answers that maybe they could find tonight.

Logan moved his hand to the small of her back. When he did, her breasts pressed into his chest. As she laid her face against the lapel of his suit jacket, she inhaled his cologne, anticipated what was to come and felt the excitement heat her whole body.

Logan's lips were close to her ear. "Do you feel it, too?"

"The music?" she teased, looking up at him.

"Gina," he murmured in part exasperation and part amusement.

She knew she had to be the one to say it because he wasn't going to push her into feelings or into physical pleasure if she didn't want to go there. "Yes, I feel it. I feel you. I'm ready to get naked if you are."

He laughed.

She realized she could be provocative with him as well as share pleasure with him. She could be the girl she'd been at eighteen.

Bending to her, he kissed the shell of her ear and she felt his tongue on her earlobe. Shivers danced up and down her arms. She wanted to kiss him long and hard, but not in the middle of the dance floor, not with these people who respected and admired him and expected propriety.

She leaned back and warned with mock sternness, "If you don't want me to undress you right here, you'd better stop teasing."

"No, what I'd better do is take you up to our room." With that he stopped the pretense of dancing, wrapped his arm around her and guided her back to their table. Fortunately everyone was mingling, talking or dancing, so they didn't have to make excuses. They just slipped out of the room and headed for the elevator.

The sounds of the hotel lobby were background noise as they stood at the bank of elevators glancing at each other. Gina's heart was racing and she wondered if Logan's was, too. But it was impossible to read him. He was so good now at hiding what he was feeling.

She just wished he'd talk to her about what was ahead of them...about the future. They hadn't had much

time together this past week. Both had had full sched-
ules. Logan had called her mid-week before bed, but it
had been a short call and she'd wondered if he wanted
to avoid talking about the future.

When the elevator doors opened, they stepped inside.
Alone now, Logan enfolded her into his arms. She
forgot about the future, caught up in right now. Logan
kissed her. His mouth was more demanding, more pos-
sessive than it had been before. He broke off the kiss to
look at her, checking if she was okay.

"Don't treat me as if I'm going to break," she
pleaded. "I want you, Logan. I want *us*."

His expression was tender as he said, "I'm afraid I'll
trigger something."

She knew what he meant and she didn't know how
to reassure him except to say, "*You* are not that man. My
mind, my heart, my body and my soul know that.
Please, don't hold back with me tonight." She hoped he
understood she wanted to give herself to him completely, and she wanted him to do the same in return.

At their floor he curled his arm around her as if he
didn't want to let her go. After he opened the room
door with his key card, he brushed his hand down her
cheek and said, "I'll be right back. I'm going to check
on Daniel."

Gina had barely had enough time to undress when he
returned from the adjoining suite. "He's sound asleep."

Logan shed his suit jacket and tie and began unbuttoning the buttons on his shirt, his gaze focused on her.

She'd donned a satiny nightgown in swirls of pink
and yellow. As she moved toward the bed, she could feel
the spaghetti straps slipping slightly, the material mold-
ing to her.

His hands stilled on the placket of his shirt and he watched her as if she were a mirage which might disappear in the blink of the eye. "You're beautiful," he said hoarsely. "I want you so much my hands are shaking."

Crossing to him, she took his hands in hers, opened one and kissed his palm.

When her lips touched his skin, tension rippled from him to her. Their gazes locked. Not hesitating, she pulled his shirt from his trousers. Logan tugged her close for a impetuously erotic kiss that told her exactly how much he wanted her. Excited, thrilled to be with him again, she kissed him back, needing him to know how much she wanted him, how much she *loved* him.

The feelings welling up in her heart were no surprise. Logan had been there all these years. He was the man she'd always envisioned spending her life with. He was the man who could put the past truly in the past.

When he broke off the kiss, he ran lighter kisses down her neck to the pulse at her throat. His hands caressed her back and he began to lift her nightgown in handfuls. After he slid it over her head and tossed it aside, a ruddy flush darkened his cheekbones.

He mumbled, "I've got to get out of these clothes."

Moments later they were lying in bed. Logan stroked her face, gently kissed her lips and lingered on her breasts. His tongue teased her nipples until she was pulling at his shoulders, almost begging him to enter her. But he didn't. His hand gently reached between her thighs, his fingers sliding in and out of her, doing wonderful fluttery things that made her feel as if she were going to fly apart.

"Do you want to be on top?" he asked when she was practically senseless with desire.

"No. I want *you* on top, all over me, inside me." She closed her eyes.

But his deep voice coaxed them open again. "Look at me, Gina. Look at me and know I only want to give you pleasure."

Tears came to her eyes—because she was so sure of that, so absolutely sure Logan would never hurt her.

He rose above her, his gaze locked to hers. When he entered her, all the pleasure in the world seemed to be theirs. It filled her heart. It filled her body. And it filled the room. Logan and the sensual sensations rippling through her burned away the past and healed any part of her that still held pain. She felt whole again. She let go of herself and flew to the stars with Logan.

His release came as the tremors of her orgasm still washed through her, as she held on to him and murmured his name.

Stretched out on top of her, he dropped his head to her shoulder. When he rolled them onto their sides, still joined, she snuggled into his chest as he kissed her temple. They fell asleep holding on to each other.

A few hours later, still tucked into Logan's arms, Gina awakened. She relived making love with Logan—every detail, every wonderful sensation. Suddenly, however, her breath caught. She realized something she hadn't given any consideration to a few hours before. They hadn't used birth control! They'd been so caught up in each other and the moment that it hadn't even entered their minds.

The hush of night was veiled by the hum of the air conditioner. Logan's chest hair brushed her cheek, his scent surrounded her and she felt as if she'd been born to be held in his arms. What if they'd made a baby last night?

What if she was carrying his child?

Gina closed her eyes again, embracing the idea, perhaps even hoping for it.

But would Logan feel the same?

The sun was just peeking through the draperies when Gina opened her eyes the following morning. Logan had moved away from her during the night. She reached out a hand before she turned and felt his muscled arm. Then she shifted to her side to look at him.

He was lying on his back, one arm tucked under his head as he stared at the ceiling. Something was different and she suspected what it was. After all, Logan was as pragmatic as he was passionate.

"Good morning," she said lightly, hoping he'd come to the same conclusion she had about a pregnancy.

"I'm not sure about that," he said, sitting up, pushing pillows behind him and hiking himself up against the headboard.

He was out of reach now and she felt the distance emotionally as well as physically.

"My condoms are still in the suitcase," he said wryly.

"I know."

"You mean you thought of them and you didn't say anything?"

Now she quickly sat up, too. "No, of course not. I woke up in the middle of the night and that's when I realized it. Logan, why would you think I wouldn't say anything?"

"I shouldn't have said that," he muttered. "Of course you wouldn't. You wouldn't want to be pregnant any more than I'd want you to be pregnant. You've got a career, a practice."

"Yes, I do. But I wouldn't look on a baby as an awful thing happening. I mean, a child would be something wonderful, wouldn't it?"

His silence wasn't the answer she wanted, and she realized that last night might have been something different to her than to him.

Finally he said, "You really sound as if you might want a baby."

Not any baby. Your baby. But she decided to keep that comment to herself.

Looking troubled, he assured her, "If you were to get pregnant, you don't have to worry. I'll support you."

He would support her. She was afraid to ask what that meant. Did he mean monetarily? Did he mean emotionally?

She simply said, "I appreciate that," and slid out of the bed. Without another glance at him, she hurried into the bathroom. She needed to take a few deep breaths before she said something she couldn't take back…before she said something she'd regret almost as much as she regretted leaving him when she was eighteen.

She was brushing her teeth when Logan rapped on the door. "I'm going to check on Daniel."

"Okay," she murmured around her toothbrush.

"Will you be ready to go down to breakfast in about half an hour?"

She took the toothbrush out of her mouth and swallowed. Wiping her mouth with a towel, she said clearly, "I think I'm going to skip breakfast and pack. I'll order something from room service, then we'll meet back here in time to leave for the airport."

He opened the door, then stepped inside.

She'd put on the white, fluffy robe the hotel provided, and right now she was grateful for it.

"Gina, about the birth control—the possibility of you being pregnant just threw me for a loop."

His green eyes were turbulent with emotions she didn't understand or know anything about. "Why?"

He seemed to debate with himself then said, "When Amy told me she was pregnant, I thought it was the happiest moment of my life. But then a few months later everything went to hell. Just thinking about the idea brought it all back."

"I can see how it would," she said softly, grateful he was sharing this with her, thankful he wasn't closing himself off to her.

Logan had pulled on jeans and a snap-button shirt. His tall, hard body seemed to fill the bathroom. She remembered how his body had covered hers, how he'd kissed her, how he'd touched her. And she wanted last night back. She hated this tension between them. She wished he'd hold her.

But he didn't. He just asked again, "Are you sure you don't want breakfast?"

"Positive," she said with a smile she didn't feel.

"All right. I'll meet you back here in a little while."

She stood perfectly still, unable to go to him. He seemed unable to move toward her.

He left the bathroom and closed the door behind him.

Gina gripped the sink, took a couple of deep breaths, then shed the robe and stepped into the shower. The hot water was soothing and she let it wash over her, trying not to think...trying to deny the

fact that Logan might not be ready for a new relationship. He might not be ready for her to be an integral
part of his life.

Fifteen minutes later, she'd toweled off and dressed
when the phone in her room rang. She picked it up,
thinking it might be Logan.

"Dr. Rigoletti?" a male voice asked.

"Yes, this is she."

"Good morning. It's Dr. Silverstein. We spoke briefly
at dinner last night."

She remembered the man. He had kind eyes and
silver wire-rimmed spectacles. "Yes, Dr. Silverstein, I
remember. Do you want to speak to Logan?"

"No, actually I'd like to meet with you for a few
minutes. Is this a good time?"

She checked her watch. "I have a few minutes."

"My room is down the hall from yours. There's a
sitting area at the end of the hall. Shall we meet there?"

Gina's radar had told her she'd have nothing to fear
from Dr. Silverstein, so she didn't hesitate to say, "Sure.
I'll meet you there in five minutes."

Gina had dressed in white jeans and a navy knit top.
Now she quickly slipped into sandals and stopped long
enough to dab some gloss on her lips. After picking up
her purse, she let the hotel-room door close behind her
and went down the hall.

Dr. Silverstein was standing at the windows that
looked out over the city. "I'm grateful that you could
give me a few minutes."

"What's this about?" she asked, puzzled, as they
both took a seat.

"I searched your credentials and work history on the
Internet last night. They're very impressive."

"I feel as if I'm interviewing for something," she said, joking.

"Not interviewing exactly, but I did wonder if you do any consultation work…if you do any outside training."

"I did in Connecticut and Massachusetts. But when I set up the Baby Grows practice in Lubbock, I concentrated on that."

"Would you consider doing it again?"

"Where?

"My company has facilities in Houston, Dallas and Tyler."

The way Logan had acted this morning, she didn't know what the future held for them. Still, she thought about Dr. Silverstein's offer and said, "I'm really flattered by your offer and thank you so much for considering me. But for now I want to concentrate on my practice in Lubbock."

"You won't even discuss a consultation fee?"

She smiled at him. "Not at the present time."

Thoughtfully, he studied her. "Logan told me a little about your sessions with Daniel. You know, don't you, that there's a need for DVDs for parents and more centers like yours? I'd really like you to consider that."

She thought of a business plan she'd developed after she wrote her dissertation. The plan was similar to what Dr. Silverstein was suggesting.

"You *have* considered it, haven't you?" he asked perceptively. "More than one center? In more than one city?"

"Years ago after I worked on my Ph.D., I wrote up a business plan."

"Would you consider letting me see it?"

Something about that idea was exciting. After all, what if Logan decided she had no place in his life? The idea of having a baby with her had definitely unnerved him. For the past hour she'd been thinking about the repercussions of that. She did understand the pain he'd gone through with his wife. But if he really wanted a future with Gina, would he be in as much turmoil as she sensed he was in?

She thought about the future and dreams and she knew she couldn't count on a life with Logan in it. "I'd have to think about it."

"Well...I'd like to see your concept. Our hospital system is large enough to invest in a project like that." Dr. Silverstein slipped his hand into his suit-coat pocket and brought out a card. He handed it to her. "That's my contact information—e-mail, home phone, fax and cell phone."

She slipped the card into a pocket in her purse and stood. "I'll keep it in a safe place."

"On your refrigerator under a magnet would be good. Then it will be front and center and you won't forget about the idea."

She laughed. "I won't forget."

After they shook hands, Dr. Silverstein headed toward the elevator and she hurried toward her room. She had to finish packing for her trip home with Logan.

Home. Maybe soon he would see that the three of them *could* have a home together.

Logan had gone from paradise to hell almost as fast as he could say his name.

As he drove home from the airport Sunday afternoon, he glanced over at Gina in the passenger seat. She went from staring distractingly out the side window to checking on Daniel in the back where he sat in his car seat beside Hannah. His son was oblivious to the tension between him and Gina, but Logan was sure Hannah could feel it.

Last night with Gina had been world-splitting. The first time they'd made love he'd been so concerned about her and her reactions he hadn't gotten lost in the immensity of it. But last night, not using birth control—

The idea of Gina being pregnant unnerved him. Because he wasn't ready for another commitment? Because Amy had died for Daniel? Because Logan had thought sex with Gina would stay in the realm of satisfying physical needs?

If he accepted the fact that Gina had a place in his life, everything would change. Absolutely everything.

He did not want another commitment that could tear his heart out. He'd been through the wringer twice and the bottom line was, Gina had left once before. She could leave again.

Logan's cell phone rang. He checked the readout on his hands-free apparatus and pressed a button, aware that both Gina and Hannah would be able to hear the conversation. "Hi, Maggie. What's up?"

"Hey, Logan. Do you have a minute?"

"Sure. I'm on the way back to Sagebrush from the airport."

"How was the trip? Are the clinical trials from the new cancer drug proceeding on schedule?"

He summed up what he'd learned in his meetings on Saturday. Then he asked, "Is that why you called?"

"Not exactly. I finished digitizing the videos. I have a break between scripts. I had this bright idea that I could drive down this afternoon, spend the week with

KAREN ROSE SMITH 189

you and Daniel, and you could see what I've done with the DVD. I think you'll like it."

By *like it* she meant he'd *remember.* He could watch Amy float across the screen, hear her words and think he could go back in time. His chest tightened at the thought. But then he understood this was something he had to do for Daniel. He was sure Maggie had put her best effort into producing the DVD. "Sure, drive on down. It doesn't matter how late it is when you get here."

He had a feeling sleep wasn't going to come easily tonight.

"See you in a few hours," Maggie said and clicked off.

Gina looked over at him and their eyes caught and held for a second—a very intense second. Had she expected him to invite her to stay over at the house tonight? What had *he* expected? That they'd go their separate ways? Entwine their bodies together again?

They entered the outskirts of Sagebrush. "Do you want to come home with us for a while?" he asked Gina, not at all sure what he wanted her to say.

"Just drop me off at my place," she said. "I have cases to look over before tomorrow."

Logan couldn't blame the hollowness in his heart on fate this time. But he had some heavy thinking to do and it would be easier to do without Gina laughing and playing with his son.

On Sunday evening, Gina's heart ached. She thought about Logan, Maggie and Daniel together at the estate. Maggie had most likely re-created the past for Logan with her DVD. Would he even want to think about the future?

Gina understood why he might not want her there during Maggie's visit. But another part of her just didn't understand—not after what she and Logan had shared.

When she climbed the steps to the attic of the Victorian, she hoped to find her business plan right away. She headed toward the seven boxes stacked in one corner, a bit set apart from two trunks, an old wardrobe and a few more cartons. Tessa had told her the wardrobe and trunks had been there when she moved in. They belonged to the landlady.

In spite of herself, Gina flashed back to the expression on Logan's face in bed that morning as they'd talked about the possibility of her being pregnant. *I'll support you,* he'd said and she'd heard the duty in his voice.

If she was pregnant, she'd have to think about her child's future. She would *not* depend on Logan for monetary support, especially if he didn't want to be their child's father.

By the time she'd sorted through box number three, she was almost ready to give up. But at the bottom of the box, she saw the blue folder. She paged through the plan inside the folder, remembering how ardently she'd worked on it. In the pocket in front, she found the disk.

There would be no harm in e-mailing the files to Dr. Silverstein. Would there?

Chapter Twelve

A week and a half later, Logan stood at the day-care center site and swiped the sweat from his brow. He didn't know what he was doing out here in the afternoon sun in a dress shirt and suit slacks, but he couldn't seem to work, couldn't concentrate, needed to be outside. He might as well go home. But he wasn't that kind of CEO. He wasn't that kind of boss...unless Daniel needed him.

Last week Maggie had convinced him to go clothes shopping with her. Daniel was outgrowing everything. Logan had gone, but the whole time all he could think about was that he'd rather be doing it with Gina.

Was she pregnant? Just how soon would she use a pregnancy test?

He should call her, but—

His cell phone beeped and he checked the caller ID,

knowing he had to call Gina but not sure of what he was going to say when he did. It had been ten days since they'd talked. Would she call him if she was pregnant? If she wasn't? He recognized the name on the screen. "Dr. Silverstein. What can I do for you?"

"This time it's much simpler than asking you to raise a million dollars for the foundation."

Logan chuckled. "Well, I'm glad to hear that. What kind of help do you need?"

"I wanted to talk to you about Dr. Rigoletti."

"I see," Logan said, hoping to prompt more information.

"She sent me the business plan for Baby Grows. It's comprehensive and timely. She's going to fly to Houston the first week in August to discuss giving seminars here for our pediatric physical therapists. She'd be a great asset and your endorsement might help her make up her mind—about the seminars *and* the business plan."

"Tell me about the business plan," Logan requested, in turmoil about where this was going.

"Essentially, it proposes setting up Baby Grows practices all over the country. There would be a central headquarters for training personnel who would then be sent to other locations."

Logan considered how Gina had moved around from Connecticut to Massachusetts then back to Connecticut again. He thought she'd returned to Sagebrush to settle in and stay. But maybe that hadn't been her plan. Maybe she wanted to travel all over the country. If she did, what would that mean to him and Daniel? What if *she* was pregnant?

At Logan's silence, Silverstein continued, "Logan, I

think this is a profitable idea in the making for investors and for her. She could make money hand over fist and never have to worry about her future again."

After Logan got off the phone with Silverstein, he had to ask himself if Gina really *did* want to be CEO of her own corporation. Just how would a baby figure into that? He had to talk to her. He had to know.

Logan left work early after all. But instead of going home he headed into Lubbock—to Baby Grows. He needed to have this conversation with Gina *now*.

The drive to Lubbock intensified his concerns. In spite of himself, he found he remembered too well the day Gina had left…the evening she'd returned his mother's locket and rejected his proposal. The old resentment grabbed on to him and held tight. He'd been here before—with Gina putting her future ahead of anything they might have together. How could they spend time together if she was running around the country? What if she decided to move her practice to somewhere more inviting? What if she decided to leave this practice under other management and set up headquarters somewhere else? He knew how that worked. Businesses did it all the time.

One thought after another ran rampant in his head. Daniel would miss her. Maybe she'd never meant to stay.

When the sliding-glass doors opened to give him entrance to the Baby Grows practice, he spotted a therapist working with a group of three babies and their moms. The moms were sitting on the floor and the babies were lying on their tummies.

He knew those exercises. He'd done them with Daniel at Tessa's encouragement.

The door to Gina's office was closed, but the blind

in the door was open. She was working at the computer to the side of her desk.

He rapped on the door.

As she glanced up, she spotted him through the open blind. Rising from her chair, she came around the desk to the open door. She was wearing her smock with babies and rattles printed all over it. She must have been working with infants earlier.

"Logan, this is a surprise! Is Daniel okay?"

"Daniel's fine. I need to talk to you in private."

At the tone of his voice, her forehead creased with concern and she seemed to pale. Then she straightened her spine and looked him straight in the eye. "Come in. We'll talk."

Once he was inside, she closed the door as well as the blind. He'd wanted privacy and they had it. She motioned to the two chairs in front of her desk. "We can sit and—"

"I don't need to sit. I have a question for you. When were you going to tell me your plans for Baby Grows? Silverstein says you're flying to Houston again to talk about consulting…that you'd like to open developmental centers across the country. Was this in your plans when you came to Sagebrush?"

To her credit, she didn't become defensive. "I shared with Dr. Silverstein a business plan I had developed a few years ago. It's a dream, Logan. It's a dream to set up programs where parents can learn how to strengthen their babies and help them grow."

"I thought you returned here to be with your family and settle down."

"And to make peace with you."

He was silent.

"It's never going to happen, is it, Logan? Peace between us? Forgiveness from you?"

"I forgive you," he said tersely, as if that was all she needed to hear. "Last Saturday night I proved that, didn't I? I couldn't have—"

"Made love with me the way you did if you hadn't forgiven me? Can't you say the words, Logan?"

He felt his face flush.

She went on. "Or maybe love didn't enter into it for you. Maybe it was all about physical release and nothing else." She waited, as if she wanted him to deny it.

"All I know, Gina, is that you left once before. How can I trust that you won't leave again?"

She looked upset…in as much turmoil as he was. The corner of her lip quivered. "I want to make sure I understand you. Are you saying you won't give me your love until you're sure I'll make you and Daniel the focus of my life?"

"How can we have a relationship if you don't?"

"*Do* we have a relationship, Logan? I haven't heard from you for over a week."

"Maggie was here and…I've been busy."

She let his words stand between them until she said, "I know Daniel has to be the focus of your life. And you have an empire to run. Do I fit in at all?"

He knew she did; maybe he just didn't want to admit it. "Did you use a pregnancy test?"

She sighed. "Yesterday, I had an appointment with my gynecologist. I'm *not* pregnant. I was going to call you."

He felt relief, yet another part of him was sad at the news, too. "So now you have nothing standing in your way if you want Silverstein to buy into your plan."

She shook her head. "You're using that as an excuse."

"An excuse for what?"

Hesitating for a few moments, she looked down at her hands then back up at him. The emotion in her eyes spilled over into her voice. "An excuse not to love at all, ever again. You're still angry I left when you proposed. You're still angry because Amy chose Daniel over her life with you."

Her words struck him like a physical blow. "How *dare* you say that. I could *never* be angry with Amy for wanting to save our child."

"You wanted her to fight."

"Of course, I wanted her to fight! I wanted it all. I wanted my wife *and* my baby."

"But she didn't see it your way."

No, she hadn't. But he wasn't going to get into that with Gina now. He'd wrestled with all of it when Amy had been diagnosed with cancer and made her decision. He wasn't going to wrestle with it again.

So he tossed a question at Gina. "What about *you?* Can you really love? Sure you were young when you left, but you knew what you wanted. You wanted that Ph.D. You wanted to *be* somebody. Apparently being my wife wouldn't have been enough. That's *why* you left. All the talk about not wanting to let down your parents, putting Angie through college. Those were side issues that coincided with your ambition. You had it then and you have it now."

"My ambition?" Now Gina's cheeks were red, her eyes were wide, dark with something he hadn't figured out yet.

"You think ambition was my main reason for leaving? Let me tell you, Logan, there were a lot of reasons why I left. One you don't even know about."

"And that was?" he prodded.

"That reason was your father telling me he'd disin-herit you if I married you."

In the ensuing silence, everything inside Logan went stone-cold. "I don't believe you."

"I have *never* lied to you, Logan, and I won't start now. At first I thought he was bluffing. I thought he'd never do that to you. So I kept seeing you. I kept falling deeper in love with you. Then at the end of the summer, when my mom and dad talked with me about it, about how young we both were—about how we both had futures we shouldn't limit—I kept wondering, what if your father *wasn't* bluffing? You were going to take over the company. You were going to be his protégé. You'd told me how remote your father could be. But the family business was your connection. You'd looked forward all your life to working with him, making him proud, becoming the one in charge someday. I couldn't let him take that away from you. *I* couldn't take that away from you."

Logan felt sweat break out on his brow. When he'd set eyes on Gina again two-and-a-half months ago, the numbness that had been inside of him since Amy died had begun melting. But now it was back. It kept him from feeling too much, from seeing too much, from analyzing too much.

But he still didn't want to believe what Gina had said. "Why didn't you tell me before you left?"

Sinking down on the desk, she took a deep breath. "As you said, I was eighteen and not very sure of myself, especially not with you. Why would Logan Barnes want *me?* I had so many insecurities. Why would I think you'd choose me over the life you'd been born for?"

Yes, he would have had to make a choice—Gina or the legacy his father had promised him.

"Tell me something, Logan. At twenty-two, what *would* you have chosen? A life with me without all the trimmings? Or a future with your father—the man you'd worked your whole life to get to notice you?"

Logan had been hopelessly in love with Gina at twenty-two. If he'd had to choose, he would have chosen his love for her. But then he thought about his father's stroke, his father teaching him everything he knew, his father approving of some of his decisions, disapproving of others, How long had that taken? One year? Two? Three? Would he have stood up to his father if the stroke hadn't happened? He'd never know.

Gina's eyes were shiny with unshed tears. "At least—" Her voice broke. "Fourteen years ago, you told me you loved me and wanted to marry me. I was foolish to walk away. I should have stayed and fought for you, and believed you would fight for me. But now I don't think you're willing to fight for anyone but Daniel. After we made love without protection, you withdrew."

"Gina—"

"Please, let me finish. The idea of a baby with me totally rattled you. I've been sorting through all the reasons why. Because you don't love me and we're together again for old times' sake? Because you felt sorry for me and wanted to make up for the fact you weren't there for me? Why *didn't* you come after me, Logan? I know now your dad had his stroke. But after our conversation, couldn't you tell by my voice that something was wrong? Why didn't you ask? Why didn't you call again? Why didn't you come and see me? If you had…"

A tear rolled down her cheek and her voice caught.

"If you had, maybe we could have held each other. Maybe we would have had each other. I've taken the blame for our breakup all these years, but I'm not sure I should have. Some of that blame was *yours,* too."

"You left," he said almost stubbornly.

"Yes. And I came back."

"So why are you flying to Houston in August?" His tone was still accusatory. He didn't want to see what she was trying to show him. He *did* want all the blame to be on her.

She sighed, a deep, sad sound. "Because I realize deep in my heart that you're going to pull away. When we were in the car and Maggie called, I sensed you didn't want me anywhere near you and her and Daniel. I understand that you want to cherish Amy's memory. But if I were truly going to be part of your life, if you were really going to let me in, wouldn't you want me there, too? And if not, if you thought Maggie might not understand, wouldn't you explain that to me so that I didn't feel as if you were pushing me away? You pushed me away hard, Logan. The dream of my business plan coming to fruition, and the idea of doing consultations was a way for me to pick up myself by my bootstraps, stay in Sagebrush near my family for now, and figure out what comes next. When I learned coping mechanisms, one of them was planning for every possibility. After all, loving you all those years ago brought *me* pain, too."

Looking at Gina's beautiful face, seeing her tears run down her cheek into the black curls there, noticing the way she was holding on to the desk for support, he realized he never should have come here to have this conversation. Her office wasn't private. He should have shown her more respect than to do this at her professional home base.

"You'd better leave, Logan." She swiped the tears from her cheek. "I have a session with a new client in fifteen minutes and I need to pull myself together."

She'd given him a lot to think about. He felt barraged by emotions and feelings and knowledge that he had somehow to shake into place, sort the good from the bad and figure out what he was left with.

Were he and Gina finished? He just didn't know. And because he didn't know, he turned and left her office. After he closed the door behind him, she left the blinds shut.

That about said it all.

Angie gave Gina a ferocious hug the following evening. Both of them were crying. Gina had stopped by Angie's apartment to tell her *everything*. She should have done it a long time ago.

Now she leaned back to study her sister's face. "I shouldn't have waited this long to tell you."

Angie backhanded the tears running down her cheek. "I thought you blamed *me* for your breakup with Logan. I thought that's why you wouldn't talk to me for so long. I thought that's why you didn't come home for Christmas that year."

Gina felt terrible that she had let her sister down. "I had to get myself together. I couldn't let any of you see what had happened."

"So you told Logan everything? How did he take it?"

"He was wonderful. He went really slow with me. But I knew I never had anything to fear from Logan and being with him was wonderful."

"Then why do you look as if you haven't slept for a while?"

"Because he's not ready to love again. I can't just be friends with him. Not when I love him and Daniel so much. He doubted I'd stay in Sagebrush. He was afraid I'd leave again."

"Why?"

She told Angie about the offer Silverstein had made.

"You could be rich and famous!"

"I don't want to be rich and famous. I want to be successful, but I just want to love my work. And I do."

"And what about you and Logan?"

"He'll never forgive me for telling him about his father. I never should have done that. But I was so frustrated and hurt. Oh, Ange, you should have seen the hurt in his eyes. I had no right to cause him that pain."

"You were just defending yourself."

"Maybe, but at what cost?"

"Don't you think he deserved to know the truth?"

Gina shook her head. "I'm not so sure."

"Sis, the truth doesn't hurt us. It might make us re-examine what we think, maybe even who we are. But you can't tuck it away and pretend it doesn't exist. It's like this secret of yours. If we'd known, we could have supported you. We wouldn't have thought *we* had done something wrong."

Gina felt her throat close again and she and her sister shared a heartfelt glance.

"You *are* going to tell Mom and Dad now, aren't you?"

"I don't want to hurt them. I know what I'll see in Mom's eyes—pain for me and what happened. And with Dad, I know I'll see rage—rage that someone could hurt his little girl."

"You're going to have to let them deal with it, just as I have to. In time, maybe we can all put it in the past."

"We *will* put it in the past," Gina said with an assurance she truly felt. Telling Angie, just like telling Logan and Raina, had been freeing. Her parents were a different matter, but she was hoping they'd become even closer than they were now.

"So what are you going to do about Logan?"

"There's nothing I can do." As she said the words her heart felt broken.

"Maybe when you go to Houston you should think seriously about expanding Baby Grows."

"That seems to be the logical thing to do—to throw myself into a new project and let that change my life. But I think I just need to be me for a while. I have plenty of clients, plenty of work to do here. Logan and I certainly don't run in the same circles. With a little luck I won't see him for a very long time."

Just saying the words practically stopped her heart. When she thought about him…when she thought about Daniel…

She rose from the sofa in Angie's living room and nodded toward the kitchen. "Let's get a glass of iced tea. Now I want to know everything about *your* life. I want us to really be sisters again."

Angie rose, too, and gave Gina another hug. "Afterward, do you want me to go with you to Mom and Dad's?"

Gina shook her head. "No. I have to do that alone."

She was used to being alone, but at least now she had her family and Raina and Lily. She'd face each new sunrise and create a life for herself. Without Logan.

* * *

Logan pulled up to the gas pump at a station on the outskirts of Sagebrush Friday night, intending to fill the tank quickly before he headed home. Daniel would be waiting for him.

Gina wouldn't be, though.

With a frustrated sigh Logan took off his Stetson, ran his hand through his hair, then plopped his hat back on his head. The empty feeling in his heart, in his chest, in his stomach hadn't left, not for an instant over the past two days. He wasn't sleeping, he was eating only when he had to, and he was rowing or riding when he wasn't working or playing with Daniel. Being with Daniel was almost painful when he called, "Gee, gee," and Logan's conflicted emotions about Gina seemed more confused than ever.

He filled his gas tank, then went inside the small convenience store to pay. He spotted Raina Gibson right away. Back when he was a teenager and had come home from boarding school in the summers, he'd often admired Raina's beauty as she waitressed at the Yellow Rose. But he'd never tried to date her. Her older brother, Ryder—now a cop on the Lubbock police force—had been more than a little protective. Logan had respected him for it.

Knowing Raina might rebuff him now because of her friendship with Gina, he approached her anyway. After she paid her bill, he tapped her shoulder. When she turned and saw him, she froze.

"I have to pay for my gas," he said. "But I'd like to talk to you for a few minutes after I do. Would that be all right?"

She looked torn between loyalty and—maybe—curiosity. Tucking her wallet into her purse, she nodded to the back of the store near the cold-beverage cases. "I'll wait for you there."

As soon as he paid, he joined her. "How is Gina?"

Raina met his gaze squarely. "Why?"

"Because I care about her. Because—"

Raina didn't make him finish. She tucked her purse under her arm. "She's doing about as well as you from the looks of it. She's not sleeping. She doesn't have an appetite. She works late. Does that about sum up *your* life, too?"

"I shouldn't have stopped you," he muttered. "There's no point." He turned to go.

But Raina called his name. "Logan."

He paused and turned to face her. This friend of Gina's, who probably knew the whole story, would be one hundred percent on her friend's side.

So she surprised him when she said, "I know where you are, Logan. I lost my husband. Going on and fighting for a new life is like climbing Everest without the proper tools, without preparations for the blizzard you know you're going to run into. The difference between you and me is that I didn't have a child to remind me even more deeply every day of what I'd lost."

She really *did* seem to understand, and, more important, she didn't seem to be judging him. "I believe I *am* ready to move on. I think Amy would want me to. But Gina and I— For years I believed one thing. I thought she'd betrayed me. I had doubts. But then Wednesday she dropped a bombshell about my father and I didn't know how to handle it."

"Gina told you the truth."

He nodded. "We always think we want to know the truth, but then when we hear it, we change our minds."

Raina didn't disagree. "Your father attempted to interfere with your relationship with Gina all those years ago. Are you going to let him do it again now?"

That was a punch Logan hadn't been expecting. "You don't beat around the bush, do you?"

"Not usually. And I won't lie to Gina about running into you today. But I probably won't say anything unless she asks, either."

When Raina didn't move away, he realized she wanted to tell him something else but didn't know if she should.

"What?" he asked.

"Putting the past behind is never easy. Gina has struggled with that, too. But maybe you should know… She told her family everything, too. It was time."

"No more secrets. Nothing else kept in the dark."

"Exactly," Raina agreed.

Logan saw a wisdom in Raina's dark eyes that he wished he possessed himself at this moment. "Thanks," he said, meaning it.

"No thanks necessary," she said with a shake of her head, her long black hair falling over her shoulder. "I just wish you and Gina could get on the same page before it's too late."

The words *too late* echoed in his mind as he drove home. The sound of their hum was somewhat muted as he had supper with Daniel, played with him and then put him to bed.

In his crib Daniel's expression when he looked up at Logan and asked, "Gee, gee? Gee, gee?" made Logan's heart feel like a lead weight. The words *too late* rever-berated like a clanging bell as he settled in his office.

Raina's words became louder than the bell. *Your father tried to interfere in your relationship with Gina all those years ago. Are you going to let him do it again?*

Why *hadn't* he gone after Gina after she'd left? Sure, his father's stroke was the easy answer. But there was another answer, deeper and more unsettling. His pride had been hurt. Oh, he'd known it all these years, but he just hadn't admitted it. Until Gina, he could have had any woman he wanted. After all, his father was wealthy and Logan knew he could attract pretty women. But when he'd met Gina, she honestly hadn't seemed to care about his money. All she'd wanted to do was take care of the horses. They'd been a priority for him, too, and the two of them had bonded over the birth of a foal. They'd looked into each other's eyes and known…they were soul mates.

They'd talked for hours on end before they'd gotten physical. And once that had happened, every moment with Gina had been one to be cherished and savored. When he'd asked her to marry him, he hadn't expected her to hesitate. Not for an instant. But she'd not only hesitated, she'd said no. She'd left him. He'd been dumped. That feeling had been new and raw and tearing. So when he'd finally called her and she'd rebuffed him, he'd decided he didn't need that humilia-tion. He was Logan Barnes. He could find another woman easily.

But he hadn't. Not until Amy. Because Gina had never left his mind and he'd compared every woman he'd met to her.

Now she'd turned his world upside down again. The

father he'd thought had loved him had been as cold as everyone had said he was. He had no doubt that Elliot Barnes *would* have disinherited him if Logan had insisted on marrying Gina. Why hadn't he seen his father's hand in everything back then? How could he have believed that the love that he and Gina shared hadn't really been there but had been a figment of his imagination?

And now? Oh, yeah, he still had his pride. Small comfort *that* was. Maybe he'd have to learn how to toss it away.

No—there was no *maybe* about it. If he wanted Gina back—and he now knew down to the soles of his boots that he did—he'd have to trade pride for happiness.

If it wasn't too late.

Chapter Thirteen

On Saturday evening, Gina didn't know what to make of Raina. Or Lily, who had arrived at the house with several containers of Chinese food, as if she and Raina had planned it.

Raina forked lo mein onto a dish. "We thought you'd enjoy something different for a change."

Lily waved at the tallest container. "The lemon chicken's wonderful. You've really got to try it."

Neither of them said anything about her lack of appetite but she knew this dinner was all about that.

"Rice, too," Raina prompted. Then she added, "Lily's going to teach us how to crochet. That way you'll have something to concentrate on instead of staring into space."

"Do you really think I need something else to concentrate on? I picked up three new clients this past week."

"Just think, you can get an early start on Christmas," Lily advised her. "You can make a sweater for everybody in your family. They'll love it."

Gina supposed that was true, but she didn't see crocheting as a real outlet or hobby. She'd still be able to think while she was doing it.

"There's another reason for me to crochet." Lily's cheeks took on more color.

Gina studied her and began to smile—a genuine smile she felt straight from her heart. "Are you—?"

"Pregnant!" The word erupted from Lily in a burst of joy. "Can you believe it? I e-mailed Troy yesterday. He's through-the-roof happy. I can't wait until—"

The doorbell rang.

"Are you two expecting someone?" Gina asked.

A knowing smile crossed Raina's lips. "No, but you are. Why don't you go answer it?"

What had they done? Sent her balloons and a singing clown to cheer her up?

"If this is something that's going to embarrass me," she called over her shoulder as she hurried to the door, "I'll make sure that on your birthdays—"

She never finished the sentence because as she entered the foyer she saw a shadow through the side glass. A tall, very broad-shouldered shadow.

She felt like running back to the kitchen, but she knew she couldn't do that. Not and face life as she should. So she opened the door. Although she'd suspected who that shadow belonged to, she was still shocked to see Logan there.

"You look like you've seen a ghost." His voice was deep and husky and she wondered if she saw a bit of uncertainty in his eyes.

"I never expected to see you at this door again."

"Would you come with me?"

She took a step back. "Where?"

Lily and Raina had appeared now. Raina had brought Gina's purse. Lily was carrying the light shawl Gina used for cooler nights. "What's this?" she asked them.

"We think you should go."

Gina felt a little angry now. "So you know what's going on? Would you please tell me?"

"Logan will tell you if you give him a chance," Raina advised her.

If she'd give him a chance. A chance to do what?

"Go with the flow," Lily whispered in her ear in a fairy-godmother type of way.

Just why was she hesitating? What did she have to lose?

More pieces of her heart. She remembered what Logan had said. *How could I ever trust you'd stay?*

"Don't think, Gina, please." He stretched out his hand for hers. "Just come with me."

She looked down at the sundress she'd put on, simply because it was light and cool. "I'm not dressed for—"

"You're dressed just right." He was still holding out his hand and she was truly afraid to think about what this could mean.

Raina gave her a little nudge and Gina took Logan's hand.

He smiled at the two women behind her. "Thanks. I owe you."

"Count on it," Lily said with a smile.

Then he was leading Gina out the door to his Range Rover. When he helped her inside, she was aware of his face close to hers. But then he stepped away and shut her door.

After he climbed into the driver's seat, he said, "I have something to show you, so just be patient. Okay?"

She sighed and looked out the window. Even though night had fallen, she realized quickly they were headed toward the Barnes estate. "Does Daniel want to see me?"

"He calls for you often."

"That wasn't exactly an answer."

After they drove between the entrance pillars, Logan didn't veer toward the parking circle, but rather to the unpaved side road that led to the lake.

"Where are we going?"

"Trust me, Gina." He glanced over at her.

Could she trust him now? The better question was, did he trust *her?*

She said nothing as they bumped along the potholes and over the ruts. Logan parked and helped her out of the SUV, a large flashlight in his hand. He shone it ahead of them as they walked through a crop of trees to the small dock.

Once they'd cleared the foliage, everything changed. There were candles everywhere...surrounding the dock, along the rim of the lake, even in the rowboat.

"What is this?" she asked, her breath hitching, her voice small with wonder.

He led her to the dock and stood with her surrounded by candles. "It's light in the darkness, Gina. It's you lighting up my life. Will you row out into the middle of the lake with me?"

Hope began to take root in Gina's heart, so much hope her throat closed. She finally murmured, "Yes," and let him lead her to the boat.

He climbed in first and then held up his hands for her. She didn't hesitate to take them after she tossed her purse and shawl to one of the seats.

Once they were positioned in the middle of the lake, sitting next to each other directly under the almost-full moon, they settled their oars in the boat. Logan shifted slightly to face her, and held her hand, his thumb rubbing along her knuckles.

When a tremor went through her, he asked, "Are you cold?"

She shook her head. She was as warm as warm could be, not knowing what to expect, a wash of sensual current running through her.

"Nothing has been easy for us, and that's mostly been my fault," he admitted.

She began shaking her head, but he kept going. "You know it's true. If I'd come after you when you went to college, you would have told me the truth and we could have confronted it together. We could have confronted my father together."

"That's what you would have done? You would have given up your inheritance?"

"I would have given up anything for you. The problem was, I didn't give up what I needed to give up most—my pride. If I hadn't been so damned stubborn and self-absorbed, I would have recognized the change in your voice when I called you. I would have realized something was wrong."

"You were worried about your dad. There was so much on your mind. And I was still in shock."

"You should have told me why you left sooner." There was gentle rebuke in his voice.

"I didn't want to hurt you. Not just as far as the inheritance went, but I knew what your father said would put a wall between you. You were finally beginning to believe he wanted you in his business...that he wanted to be the father he'd never been."

"You shouldn't have to protect me. *I'm* supposed to protect *you.*"

"It goes both ways."

"About Houston—"

"We don't have to talk about that," she said, concerned it would tip the happiness she was beginning to believe they'd find together.

"Yes, we do. No more half truths, no more misunderstandings. I want you to succeed, Gina. I want you to go after whatever you feel is going to fulfill you. But that day when Silverstein called me, all I could see was your interest in travel growing, your interest in setting up the centers growing. All I could see was you leaving me and Daniel someday when we weren't enough to hold you in Sagebrush."

She didn't know where this was leading, but she did know she loved Logan. She squeezed his hand. "I would never do that. Not if you want me to stay."

At that, he draped his arm around her, pulled her close and lifted her chin. His mouth was tenderly passionate claiming her, making promises he wanted to keep. "I'm sorry, Gina, that I had so many doubts. I'm sorry that I didn't know how to let go of Amy to concentrate on us."

She wrapped her arms around his chest and held him tight. "She's part of your life, part of your past, and she'll always be Daniel's mother."

"She'll be his mother, but not the one he remembers. *You're* going to be the mother he remembers."

She gazed into Logan's eyes, searching for sadness. But she didn't see any. Suddenly, what he'd said dawned on her. "You want me to be Daniel's mother?"

Instead of answering her, he slipped something from his shirt pocket and held it in the palm of his hand. The gold locket glowed under the moonlight.

"It's your mother's locket—the one I returned to you!"

"Yes, it is. I've kept it in the back of my dresser drawer all these years." He opened it, showing her the picture of the two of them when they were much younger. "I couldn't give it to Amy because it belonged to you."

As she lifted her hair, her heart so full she couldn't speak, he clasped it around her neck. Taking Gina's hand, he asked, "Will you marry me, Gina Rigoletti?"

Somehow she found words, happiness a tangible essence flowing through every fiber of her being. She wrapped her arms around his neck. "Yes, I'll marry you, Logan Barnes. And I'll love you always." Her love for Logan had begun so long ago, and she knew it would live forever.

"For always," he repeated and kissed her under the light of the Texas moon.

* * * * *

ABBY AND THE BACHELOR COP *by Marion Lennox*

Abigail had her life mapped out. Good job, wealthy fiancé—it was perfect...*too* perfect. Then gorgeous bad-boy-turned-cop Raff re-entered Abby's life.

MISTY AND THE SINGLE DAD *by Marion Lennox*

When Nicholas strolls into her classroom, with his son Bailey and an injured spaniel in tow, Misty falls for all three. But is she ready to follow her heart?

DAYCARE MUM TO WIFE *by Jennie Adams*

Businessman and single dad Dan's got his hands full. Jess couldn't have stepped in at a better time. She works magic...on Dan's heart, as well as the kids!

ACCIDENTAL FATHER *by Nancy Robards Thompson*

All Julianne knew about Alex was that he'd rejected her sister and never claimed their son. Yet the moment she sees Alex's tenderness with baby Liam, her heart melts.

MATCH MADE IN COURT *by Janice Kay Johnson*

Matt will do anything to get custody of his precious niece Hanna. Even if it means going up against Linnea—a woman far more enticing than he remembers!

CINDERELLA AND THE PLAYBOY
by Lois Faye Dyer

Jenny knows she shouldn't be attending a posh ball with a scandal-plagued playboy. But as the clock strikes twelve she's *still* wrapped in Chance's big strong arms...

THE TEXAN'S HAPPILY-EVER-AFTER
by Karen Rose Smith

Rancher Shep's mad about Rania, so when she discovers she's pregnant a convenient marriage is the perfect solution. Until their real feelings begin to bloom...

IN THE AUSTRALIAN BILLIONAIRE'S ARMS
by Margaret Way

Stunningly sexy billionaire David vows to stop Sonya taking advantage of his uncle. Until he discovers her real intentions...and his undeniable attraction to her.

Cherish

0311/023b

2 FREE BOOKS
AND A SURPRISE GIFT

We would like to take this opportunity to thank you for reading this Mills & Boon® book by offering you the chance to take TWO more specially selected books from the Cherish™ series absolutely FREE! We're also making this offer to introduce you to the benefits of the Mills & Boon® Book Club™—

- **FREE home delivery**
- **FREE gifts and competitions**
- **FREE monthly Newsletter**
- **Exclusive Mills & Boon Book Club offers**
- **Books available before they're in the shops**

Accepting these FREE books and gift places you under no obligation to buy, you may cancel at any time, even after receiving your free books. Simply complete your details below and return the entire page to the address below. You don't even need a stamp!

YES Please send me 2 free Cherish books and a surprise gift. I understand that unless you hear from me, I will receive 5 superb new stories every month, including two 2-in-1 books priced at £5.30 each, and a single book priced at £3.30, postage and packing free. I am under no obligation to purchase any books and may cancel my subscription at any time. The free books and gift will be mine to keep in any case.

Ms/Mrs/Miss/Mr _____ Initials _____

Surname _____

Address _____

_____ Postcode _____

E-mail _____

Send this whole page to: Mills & Boon Book Club, Free Book Offer, FREEPOST NAT 10298, Richmond, TW9 1BR